P9-DMR-033

"Wonderful...Award-winning novelist Freveletti lends her imaginative talents to the Covert-One series with a book that is nearly impossible to put down and moves at the speed of light without pause...[It] races forward with the energy of a super-charged Bourne film."
—BookReporter.com

"A fast-moving, well-written thriller."
—*Oklahoman*

"Freveletti turbocharges tension to nonstop levels in this Covert-One thriller."
—*Kirkus Reviews*

"Masterful...The action is quite cinematic, the characters well-drawn, and the plot as tight as they come."
—CriminalElement.com

"Exciting...Great read, really well-done, and a great finish."
—BestsellersWorld.com

THE ARES DECISION

"The action never flags...Mills nicely integrates relevant military and scientific details into the story line, while his skill at characterization will leave many hoping he'll become a permanent posthumous collaborator with Ludlum."
—*Publishers Weekly*

"A tight and tense page-turner...Mills does the large-scale thriller better than anyone else working the genre today."
—*Booklist*

"Fast-paced and action-filled, with iconic characters and

contemporary themes, the story is a stand-alone-worthy entry in the Covert-One series...Fans of Ludlum and Mills thrillers will find *The Ares Decision* right on target."
—*Fredericksburg Free Lance-Star* (VA)

"Plenty of comfort food for those with an appetite for the thriller genre."
—*Kirkus Reviews*

"It should have the dual effect of sustaining interest in the series and moving Mills onto the must-read list of many. If your boat is floated by thriller novels that are set in the real world and have the ability to scare the pants off you, you will absolutely love this one...I can think of no greater compliment than to tell you that portions of the novel made my skin crawl. And I loved every minute of it."
—BookReporter.com

"The pacing and the premise are pure Ludlum."
—WomanAroundTown.com

"Filled with action, intrigue, and a plot that puts the team in a tight spot and their lives in constant danger. The end result is an exciting read."
—TheSunDaily.my

ROBERT LUDLUM'S™

THE
GENEVA STRATEGY

A COVERT-ONE NOVEL

SERIES CREATED BY ROBERT LUDLUM

WRITTEN BY JAMIE FREVELETTI

GRAND CENTRAL
PUBLISHING

NEW YORK   BOSTON

Copyright © 2015 by Myn Pyn, LLC
Preview of *Robert Ludlum's The Patriot Attack* copyright © 2015 by Myn Pyn, LLC

Grand Central Publishing
Hachette Book Group
1290 Avenue of the Americas
New York, NY 10104
www.HachetteBookGroup.com

Grand Central Publishing is a division of Hachette Book Group, Inc. The Grand Central Publishing name and logo is a trademark of Hachette Book Group, Inc.

The Hachette Speakers Bureau provides a wide range of authors for speaking events. To find out more, go to www.hachettespeakersbureau.com or call (866) 376-6591.

The publisher is not responsible for websites (or their content) that are not owned by the publisher.

Printed in the United States of America

Originally published in hardcover by Hachette Book Group

First mass market edition: August 2015
10 9 8 7 6 5 4 3 2 1
OPM

For Barbara Poelle, my agent and friend,
who started this adventure with me.

THE GENEVA STRATEGY

1

Lieutenant Colonel Jon Smith, MD, picked up on the man tailing him five minutes into his stroll. A second stood on a corner three-quarters of a block ahead of him, lighting a cigarette. The match flame revealed that he was Asian. Between the two lay a shadowed street lined with tall trees, houses set back from the curb, and Smith.

He'd left the cocktail party in the tony area of Georgetown in Washington, DC, after attending a reception for Chang Ying Peng, a world-renowned micro-biologist who had just been smuggled out of a Chinese prison. That one of the men tracking Smith was Asian made Smith think the two facts were related. Most of the attendees had held positions of power and pres-tige, and Smith suspected some were undercover CIA and FBI operatives, there to glean any intelligence they could from the man. In this last endeavor they were thwarted, because he'd arrived with the activist attor-ney hired to defend him by one of the human rights organizations, and she had hovered nearby and run in-terference whenever anyone attempted to probe too deeply.

Smith slowed and analyzed his options. Perhaps the trackers were simply more FBI agents keeping tabs on all the attendees of a party for a controversial figure. Maybe the Department of Homeland Security? He was six steps closer to the smoking man when his speculation came to an abrupt halt. The man flicked the match away and reached with his right hand into the side of his jacket for what Smith presumed was a gun in a holster.

Smith spun left and ran down into a front yard on a path that led between two houses. He heard rather than saw the smoking man running behind him. Smith was six feet tall and was obliged to duck his head to avoid a jutting bay window that narrowed the small path even more. As he approached the backyard, a motion-activated spotlight flared to life, bathing him in a glaring white glow and sending a ray of panic through Smith. The attacker would have to be the worst shot in DC if he missed at that distance. Smith reached a chain-link gate about four feet high, lifted the latch, and stumbled into the yard. A quick glance revealed that a garage blocked the exit on the yard's far end, forcing him to continue in a straight line. He sprinted along the lawn's edge and past the garage, breathing a sigh of relief as he came out the other side into the backyard of another home.

He crossed the lawn, past the building and onto another street, only to see a third man step out from a tree at the block's far end. Smith turned right and kept moving along the sidewalk, walking, but at a brisk pace. He glanced behind him and saw that the smoking man had cleared the house and was heading Smith's way.

It's a pincer movement, Smith thought.

The three men began closing in, but unlike Smith, they walked toward him in a leisurely manner, sure that they had the upper hand.

Smith cut into another narrow walkway between houses, breaking into a run the second he determined that the two buildings blocked the attackers' view of him. His wing tip shoes echoed in the space as he ran down the narrow walkway. He reached into the inner breast pocket of his suit jacket to remove his stainless-steel pen. As a member of the military, Smith would have had a gun at his disposal, but security at the cocktail reception had been tight and he didn't think it wise to carry concealed and risk the questions that might have been asked. Without a gun, he could still hold his own in hand-to-hand combat if it was required, but he would have liked to have had a better weapon. The pen would have to do.

This time he ran past the garage and entered a narrow alleyway. To his left a large metal Dumpster offered the only cover. He rolled it from its position against a brick wall and slipped behind it, waiting.

The man stepped into the alley, a knife in his hand and his attention aimed high and focused upward. To Smith it seemed as though he was looking for something in the sky. Smith slipped from behind the Dumpster, rose in one fluid movement, placed both hands on the attacker's back, and shoved. Caught by surprise, the man pitched forward and Smith stayed with him, following his trajectory downward, until the man was face-first on the asphalt. Smith hammered a knee into the man's back as he knelt, grabbed him by the hair, lifted his head, and slammed his face downward. Blood poured from the man's nose as Smith held his cheek hard against the ground while he shoved the pen tip into the small divot behind the man's earlobe, where the jaw hinged. He pressed it deep. The man groaned from the ground.

"You move that knife out from under you nice and slow. Try anything and I'll dislocate your jaw and sever your carotid artery."

The man slid his right arm out from under him, and Smith dropped the pen and grabbed the knife, jamming it back into place.

"Why are you following me?" Smith asked.

From the corner of his eye Smith saw movement, and he heard a buzzing sound. In the alley's dull light he saw the flash of either a large insect or small bird. It hovered twenty feet away and lowered from fifteen feet in a precise, vertical line. The man gasped and Smith looked back at him. Only one of the man's eyes was visible, but

Smith could see that he was panicked at the sight of the insect.

"What is it?" he asked.

The man began to struggle. Smith pressed the knife deeper, and blood began to ooze from the puncture wound and slide down the man's neck. The buzzing insect flew closer, and the man struggled harder. Smith focused all his weight onto the one knee that was shoved into the man's back.

The second attacker stepped into the far end of the alley to Smith's right, blocking the entrance to it. He started forward but caught sight of the insect and stopped. Smith watched, fascinated, as the man's gaze locked on the bug. He took several careful steps backward, all the while keeping his eyes on the insect.

The third attacker stepped into view next to the second. He began to move forward, but the other put a hand on his sleeve and pointed to the insect. This attacker, too, stepped back. Both remained at the edge of the alley and stared. The only sound was a police siren in the distance and the buzzing of the insect. It finished lowering and began to fly toward Smith, once again in a remarkably straight, unwavering line.

"Get him, not me!" the man on the ground yelled. He heaved upward, trying to dislodge Smith without success.

Now Smith could see that it wasn't an insect, but some sort of radio-controlled device designed to look like a massive cicada. Two curved and serrated stingers protruded from its mandible, and its LED eyes glowed red.

Whatever the hell that is I don't want it near me, Smith thought.

When the buzzing thing was five feet away, Smith pulled on the struggling man's hair and hauled him to his knees, jamming the knife deeper into his neck to keep the man's face and body in the buzzing thing's line of trajectory.

"Tell it to stop," he said to the man.

"Be sure you hit him, not me!" the man yelled. The insect began to bob and weave, circling them both in an obvious attempt to gain access to Smith. Smith pulled the man to his feet, using him as a human shield. Smith dug the knife in deeper still, and the man groaned in pain. The blood pouring down the man's neck was quickly soaking the top of his jacket.

"I said tell it to stop," Smith said.

"Stop!" the man yelled. The insect feinted closer and bobbed back again when Smith pushed the man's face in its direction.

"Say it again. I'm not letting go, and I'll be sure it hits you as well," Smith said.

"I can't control it. You can see that. My job was to isolate you so it could get a clear shot." The panic in his voice drove Smith's own adrenaline higher.

"Then get ready to run," Smith said. He dragged the man backward as he spoke, twisting and turning to avoid giving the device a clear shot at him.

"Forget it," the man said. "You can't outrun it. Once it hits you, it will poison you. Like a spider with a fresh catch." He turned to look at the other two men, who still waited at the alley's end. "Get over here and help me!" he shouted.

Both stayed put. It was clear to Smith that neither wanted to get anywhere near the device. It swooped closer in a curving arc. Smith jerked the man's body toward it just as the insect made a popping sound and a stream of smoke shot from the center of its mandible directly into the man's face.

Smith let go and stumbled backward, keeping his nose pressed into the crook of his elbow. At the edge of the alley, the second and third attackers were backpedaling even farther away, keeping an eye not on Smith but on the cloud of smoke.

Smith turned and started running, holding his breath as he shot down the alley. He swerved in and out between the occasional garbage can and activated a series of garage-mounted lights as he did, creating a kaleido-scope of blinding white flashes. His eyes watered at the glare and his lungs ached from sprinting while holding his breath, but he kept going, unwilling to provide the insect a clear shot or the men at the end of the alley with an easy target.

He took one look behind him as he reached the alley's end. The man who had chased him had fallen to his knees, his back straight and his body upright. He was still, frozen, and the insect hovered in front of his face. To Smith he looked catatonic. The strange device rose up into the air, adjusted its position, and flew straight toward Smith.

2

Smith heard the buzzing behind him and kicked up his pace, his arms and legs pumping as he emerged from the alley and raced down the shadowed sidewalk, looking for a place to hide. He needed to get into a house, building, or car—anything that would allow him to get behind closed doors and windows. His own car was parked several streets away, and he doubted he'd be able to outrun the device long enough to reach it. He turned a corner and hit pay dirt. Katherine Arden, the activist attorney, was striding down the sidewalk while sorting through a keychain in her hand. Smith fell in step with her, ran his arm through hers, and dragged her forward, increasing both their paces.

"Ms. Arden, how nice to see you. Did you enjoy the party? Are you heading home?"

Arden gave him a surprised look, shook out of his hold, and stopped walking to face him. Wishing that she would keep moving, he cast a quick look behind her. The device wasn't in sight, nor were the two other men, and so he returned his attention to her.

She frowned. "Aren't you one of the scientists from Mayo Clinic?" she asked.

He shook his head. "Not Mayo." He glanced behind her again.

"Is something wrong?" She turned to look in that direction as well.

"I think I'm being followed. Have been since the party," he said.

"Ah," Arden said. "I'm not surprised, given the number of undercover FBI, CIA, NSA, and God knows who else at that party. If it makes you feel any better, I get followed all the time."

Now he focused on her. "By who?"

"Tonight, probably by all of them, but the alphabet soup of my trackers changes depending on whatever client I'm currently representing. I've come to see eluding them as a game." She beeped open a new-model hybrid car parked only six feet away. At that moment Smith saw the device reappear high up and over a stand of trees. Its buzzing sound was faint but still audible. It hovered in place and began to rotate slowly. To Smith it looked like it was sweeping the area to find him. At street level the second attacker stepped out from beside a house about a block away. They were back in control and once again closing in.

Arden turned and spotted the man as well. "That him?"

"Yes. I see you have your car here—would you mind giving me a ride? Quickly?" he asked. The device was now facing Smith, and he watched as it began to lower.

"Let's go," she said. "We'll see if I win this round."

Smith swung open the passenger door, slid into the car, and was relieved when Arden jogged around and fell into the driver's seat. She slammed the car door shut, hit the lock button, and punched the starter just as the device came into sight at the top edge of the passenger window. Smith got a close look at it. The LED eyes still glowed, but a small light at its belly displayed an icon of a battery that was blinking red. The device wobbled, as if it was losing power, and flew into the window glass. Smith jerked his head away, even though he knew the window was between them. The bug bounced off the glass and rose higher, above the car's roof, and hung there, six inches away.

Arden glanced to the side.

"An insect hit the glass," Smith said. Get this car moving, he thought.

The second attacker came into view in the passenger-side mirror. The man craned his neck to see who was driving, but it was clear that he had no intention of getting closer while the insect hovered. To Smith's great relief, Arden hit the gas and pulled away from the curb. Smith heard a yell as the car took off.

They accelerated smoothly into the street, took a right at the next corner too fast, and with a squealing of tires sped down the straightaway. Smith watched in the side-view mirror as the second attacker hit the corner and began to run but soon slowed and then stopped. At the next block Arden turned left, and the man disappeared from view. Smith sat back with a sigh of relief.

Arden gave him a glance. "Don't worry. It can be alarming at first, but they generally don't create a problem. At least, they haven't in my case."

For a moment Smith thought she was talking about the device, but he swallowed and forced himself to calm down. As he did he realized that she was discussing being followed by government agents. He took several slow breaths and considered his options. The device's blinking lights told him that it wouldn't function much longer. Arden was racing down the street, punching the gas and taking corners with calm efficiency, so she was putting quite a bit of distance between them and the insect.

"Thank you," he said. "I have no idea who that was, but I got the definite impression that it was best not to wait to find out."

She nodded as she took another corner with a slight squeal of tires.

"You're pretty sanguine about it," he said.

"As I said, they follow me a lot. In addition to Mr. Chang, I'm defending two clients in Guantanamo and one that's currently in hiding from an African strongman who's vowed to kill him. And there's been a fatwa calling for my death placed on my head by an extremist organization. That was a few years ago." She shrugged. "Anyway, I've gotten used to it. But I can see how it would be frightening. I know how it is when the industrial governmental complex guns for you."

Smith wasn't sure how to reply. He looked at her profile as he pondered a response. She was about thirty-five years old, her hair bleached white and cut short like a man's, which emphasized the fine features of her face. Her skin held a translucent pale color that Smith associated with some vegans or with people who rarely ventured outside. She was slender, bordering on too skinny. She wore a diamond stud, cuff, and hoop in the ear that he could see. She was tall for a woman, and her navy suit with narrow pant legs and jacket over a white V-neck shirt was tailored and well fitting. On her wrist was a large man's watch with an analog face and a tan leather band that overwhelmed her narrow bones.

"I don't know what you mean," Smith said.

She gave him a knowing glance before returning her gaze to the road.

"I mean that the attendees of tonight's party are going to be added to the NSA's hit list. Better toss your cell phone and get a burner." Her voice held a trace of amusement.

"I've done nothing that would raise their interest. I assume you're joking," Smith said.

"Not at all. No one is safe from our government anymore."

Smith refrained from rolling his eyes at the statement. Instead, he strove for a polite reply.

"I'm not sure we've met formally. I'm Lieutenant Colonel Jon Smith, a microbiologist stationed at the U.S. Army Medical Research Institute for Infectious Diseases in Fort Detrick, Maryland, which I presume makes me a card-carrying member of the industrial governmental complex to which you refer."

She gave him an amused glance. "A fact that won't protect you. They'll spy on their own."

"Oh, no—you're a conspiracy theorist," he said.

She shrugged. "I'm a realist. And I'm not the one being chased down a dark street by a guy in a suit. Do you want me to drive to the nearest police station?"

Smith exhaled and looked out the window. While her views were extreme, she had a point. The men *had* looked like undercover agents for the FBI or CIA, even perhaps intelligence officers for the DHS, and the device that had chased him seemed to have been loaded with some sort of paralyzing drug that would have disabled him long enough for the three to hustle him away. Perhaps he was being targeted to be debriefed. He'd reach out to his contacts before filing a report at the local level.

"No, thanks. I'll handle it through other channels. Maybe you should let me out at the nearest train station. I'll head home from there."

"No car?"

He shook his head. "I had parked it in the neighborhood and was headed to it when I discovered I was being followed. Best I not go back to get it."

"USAMRIID. Wasn't it one of your colleagues that the FBI claimed laced the letters with anthrax that killed some people several years ago?" She slowed to a stop at a red light and turned to look at him.

Smith felt a bit of irritation rise, but he tamped it down.

"Two scientists were investigated and one was presumed to be involved, yes. A definite link was never proven."

"Maybe they're looking to hang you for it."

Smith had had enough. He opened the door. "Thanks for the ride," he said, and he stepped out of the car. The light turned green, but the car didn't move. The passenger window lowered and she leaned over to look at him through it.

"I didn't mean to upset you. This isn't even close to a train station."

The car behind her honked, and Smith backed up

onto the curb as she moved her car over and switched on the hazard lights. The vehicle behind her pulled alongside and honked again. She flipped the driver the bird, which made Smith smile despite his irritation. The car sped away. She looked back at him.

"'As a child, I was taught what was right, but I was not taught to correct my temper,'" she said.

"So it would seem. Where have I heard that before?"

"Jane Austen's *Pride and Prejudice*. Darcy says it. Get in the car, Lieutenant Colonel, and I promise not to offend your pride again."

Smith relented and resumed his seat. "*Pride and Prejudice*? Given your reputation, I would expect a quote from *The Art of War*."

She smiled as she drove. "'He who exercises no forethought but makes light of his opponents is sure to be captured by them.' Sun Tzu knew what he was talking about. I never make light of opponents. Especially when they're as powerful as the government."

"Are you always so blunt?" he asked.

She nodded. "Always. I find that it saves time in the long run. Anyone who can't take the truth doesn't belong in my world. It's too exhausting to keep up a front for them, and I find that most people who require handholding are just too weak to stomach the issues that I deal with on a daily basis in the human rights field. Wouldn't work for either of us."

"You have a lot of tough cases, then?"

She nodded. "Beyond tough. Take Mr. Chang. He was tortured in that Chinese prison."

"The Chinese deny it."

"I know they do, but I believe him. So why do you think that man was chasing you?"

Smith shook his head. "I honestly have no idea."

"That's a shame, because there's a car tailing us and coming on fast."

3

A quick glance in the side mirror confirmed that she was right—they were being followed.

"Keep turning as often as possible," Smith said. He pulled out his phone and dialed a private number that he knew would be answered, day or night. In addition to his duties at Fort Detrick, Smith was a member of Covert-One, a highly secretive organization run by the president and not overseen by any congressional authority. As a covert operative, Smith often worked with a small, select team of other operatives from various walks of life. The one he was calling was a high-ranking CIA officer.

"Make it fast—I just woke up and haven't had my coffee yet." Randi Russell's voice was pitched low and held a note of humor. Smith heard the clink of a glass in the background.

"I'm in a car with a famous human rights activist lawyer and being chased by men in suits. Any idea who they might be?" Smith said.

"Who's the lawyer?"

"Katherine Arden."

"Whoever they are, let them have her. She's a pain in the agency's ass."

"She's a bystander. They're chasing me."

"Not good. How did the two of you end up in the same car? That's like fraternizing with the enemy."

"I was at a cocktail party for Chang Ying Peng—as were, I suspect, many of your CIA colleagues. And while you're at it, can you have someone swing by this location?" He gave her directions to the alley.

"Okay. What's there?"

He glanced at Arden while he thought about how to answer Russell.

"I may have tripped one of the men and he may have hurt himself."

He saw Arden smirk.

"Hmm. How bad is he? Are they going to have to contain a situation?"

"Perhaps. I'm not sure. There's more, but I'll have to fill you in on that later."

"Okay. Hold tight. I'll call you right back."

Arden turned twice and then maneuvered through a stale yellow light. The trailing car was forced to stop when it turned red and the cross traffic began moving.

"I couldn't help overhearing; did you just call a CIA officer?"

Smith pointed to a narrow street on his right. "Turn here. This street feeds into a larger one that is often empty at this time of night. You might be able to get some speed going."

She did as he asked and gave him a questioning look.

"May I hire you as my attorney?" he said.

She raised an eyebrow. "Of course. But doesn't the military have its own lawyers?"

"Here." He reached into his wallet and placed a twenty-dollar bill on the console between them. "Now you're my attorney and the attorney-client privilege applies. So what you just heard you can't repeat, correct? Besides, it was a slip of the tongue." His phone rang, the screen displaying "RR."

"Good news?" he asked Russell.

"I'm afraid not. The local FBI office is denying any interest in you. They routinely keep an eye on Arden but didn't bother tonight because they had three agents attending the Chang cocktail party. Likewise, the CIA also attended the party and they said they have no one on the street following attendees. Looks like your guys are private contractors. And one of the officers from the party was still in the neighborhood and drove down the alley. There was nothing there. Seems like they cleaned up their own mess. The FBI offered to help. Want me to send an official escort? Back everyone off?"

He checked the side-view mirror. "They're not behind me now, so we may have successfully lost them, but they could have another team ready at my house. I'd appreciate it if you could have that checked for me. And I left my car near the party. Would love another to use tonight."

"I'll make a call. If you see an unfamiliar number on your phone, answer it. It'll be your bodyguard with the information about your house and the location of a car you can use. Either way, I don't suggest that you go home right away."

"Understood. I'll head over to the lab for a couple of hours, finish up some paperwork." He gave her the Metro stop that he would be taking.

"I'll be sure to tell them to arrange for a car somewhere along the line," Russell said. "Is that all?"

Smith paused. He wanted to tell her about the device and the drugged man in the alley, but he didn't want Arden to overhear.

"I'll contact..." Smith paused. He was going to say that he'd call Nathaniel "Fred" Klein, the head of Covert-One, but he didn't need Arden overhearing. "...Our mutual friend. The rest I'll handle on my own," he said.

"Well, *that* certainly sounds cryptic. When you get a chance, I'd love to hear it."

"Oh, you will. But in the meantime, thanks. I owe you one."

"Anytime," Russell said.

He turned to Arden. "Looks like we lost him, but for safety's sake, turn left here again." She turned. After a few minutes, she sighed in relief.

"Nothing behind us that I can see." She handed the

twenty back to him. "I hate to inform you, but I require a much bigger retainer. Don't worry—your slip is safe with me."

Smith believed her. He pocketed the bill. "I'll take that Metro stop." He pointed to a sign half a block ahead on their right.

She pulled the car over to the curb. "Well, Mr. Smith, it's been an interesting and enlightening ride. Should you ever need an attorney, please feel free to give me a call."

"Thanks—I'll remember that," he said. And he meant it. His phone buzzed with a text from an unknown number that instructed him to take a train to a particular Metro stop where a car would be available for his use. Once out of the car, he jogged down the steps and was relieved to see a train pulling into the station. Within twenty seconds, he was on his way.

4

The kidnappers came at midnight. Carter Warner, the undersecretary of defense, had just stepped inside his house outside Washington, DC, when a hood was thrown over his head and a rope around his neck. A baton swept his legs out from under him. After the first few seconds of shock, Warner's former military training kicked in, and he began to fight. He'd served in Vietnam and though forty years of civilian life had dulled his reflexes and aged his body, they hadn't dimmed his will to live.

He was flat on his back and blinded by the hood, so he used his feet, kicking in a frenzy of hard blows and rage. He connected twice, as was evidenced by the grunts of pain that he heard after a lucky strike from his hard wing tip shoe. One of the attackers began kicking him in the ribs. Warner gasped in pain when the steel-toed boot sank deep into his side. Another attacker flipped him over and yanked his arms behind his back. He felt the clamp of handcuffs; the rope around his neck tightened to cut off his airway, and in that moment he knew the physical aspect of his fight was over. He went still.

Warner had climbed the political ladder in DC by virtue of a formidable intelligence coupled with a practical, clear-eyed manner. Tapping into his typical self-control, he did his best to keep the overwhelming fear at bay and think. As they worked around him, tying his ankles together and wrapping a strip of cloth over the hood and around his face in a gag, he tried to rein in his unruly mind and focus. They lifted him, hands under his arms and clutching his feet, and moved him along the hall to the back of the house, where they laid him on the floor. He heard a series of beeps as one of them fired up his computer in the home office he maintained in the rear of the narrow town house. The PC played the usual tones as it allowed access to the main drive.

How did they get my password? he wondered.

As undersecretary, he had high-level clearance, a government-issued PC system, and a cell phone with extraordinary threat protection provided by the best minds in the cyber counterterrorism unit of the Department of Homeland Security as well as the se-cret military communications unit located at Fort Meade, Maryland. What he didn't have was Secret Service protection, a perk given to cabinet-level per-sonnel only.

He never worked with confidential material on the home computer—it wasn't allowed, a fact for which he was now grateful as he listened to the clicking sound of rapid typing. While they would access routine emails between him and his secretary, nothing of national im-portance would be linked to the home unit. He lay on the floor, listening to the harsh breathing, his own and that of the attacker near his feet, as the other kidnapper worked on the PC. The clicking stopped, and Warner felt someone at his shoulder.

"We just sent your secretary an email from your com-puter telling her that you're ill and won't be at the office. Now, I'm going to dial your secretary's number and place a phone to your ear. I expect you to leave a voicemail telling her that you're sick with the flu. Ask not to be disturbed. Tell her to forward on the email that explains this. If you say anything else, I'll slit your throat immedi-ately. Nod once if you understand."

Warner nodded. He heard some rustling, felt the cloth gag being removed, and he jerked as a hand slid under the hood and placed the receiver to his ear. When he heard the beep, he did as he was told. When the call was finished, the attacker put his hands under Warner's arms, the other took his feet, and they carried him out the back door.

He wasn't one to avoid the hard truths of life; he knew that whoever was currently stuffing his bound body into a waiting vehicle wasn't going to treat him with any human dignity. When the torture came—and he had no doubt it would—he needed to be mentally prepared. He heard the engine turn over and felt the vibration as the vehicle started to move. He lay in the darkness and prayed.

Richard Meccean, the head of Health and Human Services, was walking his dog for the last time that evening when he heard running footsteps behind him and spun around in time to see a pair of men, their faces covered with hoods, racing toward him. His dog, a Weimaraner and Doberman mix, reacted. The dog planted her four legs, hunched her back, and began barking with such force that her entire body shook with the effort. One of the men shot the dog with a gun equipped with a silencer, and the other man made an irritated, hissing sound before placing his own gun against the small of Meccean's back. A van slid to a halt on the road beside them, and Meccean was hustled into it. As they trussed Meccean, the image of his pet lying on the ground rose in his mind. He tried but failed to stop a tear escaping down his cheek.

Nick Rendel was sitting in front of a computer screen in his home office, his fingers tapping out a staccato beat as he waited for a page to load, when the security alarm in his house began to blare. A small monitor placed in the wall near the door showed two men, dressed in black, approaching at a jog down the main hall from the house's backyard entrance.

Rendel, a slender man in his late twenties, used his mouse to turn on several internal closed-circuit televisions, slid open a nearby drawer, and removed a gun. He held the Beretta in one hand as he worked on the keyboard with the other. The computer page loaded, and he accessed two passwords before the men stepped into the home office.

"What do you want?" Rendel asked.

"Put the weapon down on the carpet. Slowly," one of the men said. His heavily accented English was laced with an Eastern European pronunciation. Rendel lowered the gun and shot a glance at the alarm keypad on the far wall.

They successfully killed the system, Rendel thought.

As if reading his mind, the man nodded. "It's disconnected. Won't call the authorities, and that button in your humidor won't work either. Now move. Down the hall to the backyard."

Rendel padded toward the man, who stepped aside for him to pass, and he continued into the hall. The door at the far end was open and guarded by another man with a balaclava covering his face. When he reached the door, Rendel looked back at his kidnapper.

"May I put on my shoes?" He indicated a pair of shoes resting next to the door. The kidnapper shook his head.

"Where you're going you won't need them. The slippers will do." He gave an order in a foreign language to the man holding the door and pushed the gun's muzzle into Rendel's back. "Around the side and to the van."

Rendel gave a quick look to the CCTV camera the size of a pack of cigarettes set high in a corner at the hall's end. The LED light glowed red. Moments later, as they tied him up in the back of the van, Rendel wondered when the blowback that would follow his kidnapping would begin. He figured forty-eight hours for someone to notice that he hadn't appeared at work, and then another twenty-four before the Metro police would start a serious investigation. If by some dumb luck they found him, Rendel didn't think they'd survive a rescue attempt. The crew driving this van was professional, cool, and deadly.

5

Smith found the rental car at the stop exactly where he'd been told he would. He retrieved the keys from under the mat and drove toward the office, mulling over his options. His biggest issue was what to do about the tail and the drone, for that is what he decided the device had been. After a moment's thought he dialed the cell number for Mark Brand, a man he'd worked with on a Covert-One matter in New York and whose regular job was with the FBI. He was relieved when a sleepy-sounding voice answered the phone.

"Brand? It's Jon Smith. Sorry to wake you, but I recall you telling me to call you anytime if I had a problem, and I have one now." Smith heard static on the other line and a pause that made Smith think that Brand was not going to speak to him. "You there?" he asked.

"Yes. I'm here. It's been a long time and I was just catching up. When I told you to call me I meant it. What's the problem?"

Smith told him about the attack and drone. "One of your guys already canvassed the alley, but both the man and the drone were gone."

"Didn't this Chang guy work for the Chinese in their defense department?" Brand asked.

"Yes. He's actually the Chinese equivalent to me: a microbiologist working in cutting-edge biochemical warfare research. The Chinese imprisoned him after he blew the whistle on some illegal testing they were conducting on the general population. They accused him of treason, saying that even if they were wrong Chang had a duty not to reveal confidential defense secrets."

"Think they wanted to get you and debrief you on what you might have learned from Chang?"

Smith rubbed his face. The night had been long, and just the idea of the Chinese thinking he knew more than he did made it seem even longer.

"I guess it's possible, but you have to be incredibly paranoid to think that two microbiologists would discuss confidential defense research in the middle of a cocktail party."

"Take it from me, the Chinese *are* incredibly paranoid when it comes to their defense secrets. Just like us. What bothers me the most is the drone and the drug. What the hell could cause paralysis like that?"

"I've been thinking about it. Lots of drugs can cause that. Common ones, like marijuana or LSD. Crystal meth when it's first administered will as well. But why use a drone? It's not an efficient way to go about drugging me. It would have been a lot easier just to spike my drink."

"Do you know what it was that Chang claimed the Chinese had been testing? Think they're testing it here?"

"It's an angle definitely worth following up on."

He heard Brand groan over the phone. "This one's for the counterterrorism unit. I'll start waking everyone up right now. And I'll be sure to check with the guys at the party and ask them what they know about Chang's allegations. You want me to send someone to watch your house?"

"No. Russell's already offered."

"Good enough. I'll be in touch if I learn anything. Watch your back." Brand rang off.

Smith pulled up to the USAMRIID entrance, waved at the guard, parked his car, and used his keycard to enter the secure lab facility. He removed his tie and shoved it into his pocket as he headed to his office at the end of the hall. As he did he rolled his shoulders to release some tension and inhaled. He wasn't too keen on going home just yet. He'd wait a bit to give everyone he'd called some time to get their calls out. He had several pressing matters that required immediate attention and he decided that as long as he was at the office he may as well dig into them.

As a senior researcher, he had a larger office than most, but it was decorated in a spare, utilitarian manner that Smith thought of as army basic. The majority of the work done at USAMRIID was conducted in the new high-security Biosafety Level 3 and 4 labs. Researchers simply uploaded their results from laptops situated in a large room partitioned by cubicles with walls on wheels that could be moved and repositioned. The laptops were protected by encoded passwords stored on an encrypted server. Only senior researchers had private offices.

Smith's rectangular desk sat in the middle, with two chairs facing it. To the right and against the wall stood a tall cabinet; a low credenza to his left held books and a couple of framed commendations that he'd received over the years. There were no pictures of family; Smith had none, girlfriend likewise, nor even a dog. If Smith dropped off the face of the earth tomorrow a new researcher could occupy the office with a minimum of effort. A window on the far wall looked onto a parking lot. Smith kept the blinds closed against the harsh glare of the lot's many light posts.

He dropped his keycard on his desk, draped his suit jacket over the back of the chair, grabbed his favorite coffee mug, and went down the hall to the break room, where he punched the button on the coffeemaker that promised a double-shot espresso. He topped that off with regular coffee, added some cream, and headed back to his office.

When he reached the door he glanced at the desk and paused. His keycard was gone; in its place was a manila envelope and what appeared to be one of his own reports. He took a slow step closer and glanced around.

When he was sure no one was there he went to the desk, set his coffee down, and checked his suit pocket for his wallet. Whoever had taken his card had left the wallet alone. While he was concerned about his identification and cash there, he was even more concerned about his second keycard, which was necessary to access the secure labs. He breathed a sigh of relief when he saw that both the second keycard and all his identification and cash were undisturbed.

He slid open the side drawer. The gun that he kept there also had not been taken. He was relieved because guns weren't generally allowed in federal facilities, but after the last mass shooting on an army base, he'd asked for and received an exception to the rule. Next to the gun he kept a box of medical gloves. He pulled two out, slipped them over his hands, and picked up the envelope. It was sealed, and the name "Lt. Col. Jon Smith" and a series of numbers that looked like a date were scrawled across the front in blue crayon. Next to it was a copy of his own final draft of a report that gave his findings on the viability of an aerosolized version of the Ebola virus.

He sat down, opened the flap on the envelope, and slid out what appeared to be a research paper by one of his colleagues, Dr. Laura Taylor, titled *The Effects of Protein Synthesis Blockage on Long-Term Potentiation and Post-Traumatic Stress Disorder*. Smith hadn't seen Taylor in quite some time, since long before her transfer to a mental health facility. Only thirty-five years old, she'd been hailed as one of the leading scientists in neuroscience and memory research. Her future had been bright until almost a year ago, when she began to have moments of increasing paranoia.

He flipped through the paper, scanning pages that were filled with graphs and charts that documented her findings. It appeared as though she was working on a drug but was having trouble minimizing a long list of side effects that it created.

A door slammed somewhere out of sight and Smith heard the sound of men talking in soft voices. He slid open the desk drawer and tossed the envelope inside before stripping off the gloves. USAMRIID served as the Department of Defense's lead laboratory for medical and biological defense research. The vials of anthrax used in the anthrax attacks in 2001 had indeed been developed and stored here, as were several types of virulent and deadly bacteria and viruses, Ebola being only one example. An entire department was attempting to aerosolize several pathogens and viruses, and the new building had been constructed with a specialized ventilation system that would scrub any errant pathogen before it reached the outside. The population around USAMRIID had protested the construction of the new BSL-3 and -4 labs, but work was allowed to continue once assurances were given that the catastrophic pathogens housed in the facility would be locked down tight. Access to the facility was restricted to prescreened personnel with high-level security clearances only. That someone made it deep enough into the interior to be able to steal his keycard was strange. If the men in the hall were responsible for the theft, he wanted to be prepared. He removed the gun while he reached for the phone to call security. As he did, two men stepped into the open doorway.

Both wore dark pants and windbreakers. One was bald, with a thick neck, small ears, and a solid body of average height. The other sported a full head of black hair and was thin and wiry. Both carried with them an air of menace. Every survival instinct that Smith had screamed to life.

6

They had temporary security passes stuck to their jackets. The bald one spread his arms wide and smiled a crocodile smile filled with uneven teeth at Smith.

"I'm Dr. Westcore and this is Dr. Denon. You must be Dr. Smith." He indicated the nameplate on the desk.

Smith nodded. "I am." He didn't rise to acknowledge the offer of a handshake. If Westcore noted the rude behavior, he didn't give any indication.

"You always point a gun at people while you're working?" Westcore said.

"I just discovered that someone's been in my office without my permission. I thought it best to be prepared for whatever may occur. Who are you?" Smith asked.

"We're from the mental health facility nearby. One of our patients has gone missing. Dr. Laura Taylor. She's a colleague of yours. Have you seen her recently?"

"I have not," Smith said. He'd kept the phone in his hand, prepared to punch the speed dial to the security desk, but the temporary passes allayed some of his concerns about the men and he hung it back up.

Denon leveled a glare at Smith. "We think she ran onto this floor not ten minutes ago. You sure you didn't see her?" Denon's voice was filled with suspicion. The accusatory tone irritated Smith.

"Before I answer that, why don't you show me some identification," he said.

"Of course." Westcore reached his hand into the

windbreaker and for the second time that evening Smith's instincts told him that something wasn't right.

"Stop," he said.

Westcore looked at the weapon and raised an eyebrow. "You said you wanted our credentials. They're in my pocket."

"Remove them slowly, please."

Westcore slowed his motion and Smith could see from the shape that the nylon took on that he was removing a square item, not a gun. He relaxed a bit. After five seconds his hand reappeared holding a black wallet. Through it all his companion remained silent.

Smith stood and reached out. "Toss it to me."

"Of course," Westcore said. He lobbed the wallet at Smith, who caught it and flipped it open. "The hospital identification is in the first card slot."

One side of the wallet consisted of a windowed section with a driver's license and Westcore's photo stamped on it. The other side held several cards in slots. Smith removed the card in the first one. On it was the same name as the license, another photo, and the words "U.S. Department of Veterans Affairs."

"Since when do doctors track down errant patients? Don't you have security to handle that?"

Westcore nodded. "We are security, but hold PhDs as well. We're from Stanton Reese, which I'm sure you know provides contract personnel for government positions."

"Hired by the Department of Defense," Smith said.

"Exactly. Then you know us."

Not only did Smith know of them, but he was aware that they were under congressional investigation for some of their actions worldwide. Smith handed the wallet back without comment.

"You sticking with the story that you didn't see her?" Westcore asked again.

Smith nodded. "I am, because it's true."

Denon took one step closer. "You'd better tell us the truth..." he began. Westcore waved him to silence.

"If she is here, she knows this facility well, so I don't think you'll find her."

"It's really important that we do. Our jobs are on the line. She climbed out a window and it looks bad for us. We'll just take a look around."

Smith stepped closer to the two. "No, you won't." He noted the flash of irritation that ran across Westcore's face. "USAMRIID is a high-security lab. Lots of viruses and bacteria that are outside the norm and quite dangerous. Some weapons-grade. I'm not sure what you told security to obtain those temporary passes, but they don't grant you access to the secure labs and I'm sure that security never meant for you both to get this deep. You'll have to leave out of the door that you entered."

"They gave us clearance to find her. That's all we need," Westcore said.

Smith shook his head. "Not enough. I'll arrange for a guard to come escort you both." He picked the phone back up.

Denon shot Westcore an alarmed look, confirming what Smith had assumed. They both knew that they were beyond their clearance. He waited, and moved his finger back to the gun's trigger, more to intimidate them than use it. The last thing he wanted to do was fire on a DOD employee with a security pass, albeit limited and temporary, attached to his jacket. But despite all their outward credentials he still felt there was something off about the two. Westcore glanced down, noted the small movement, and took a step back.

"If you see her you'll inform us immediately?"

Not a chance, Smith thought. "If I see her I'll follow protocol and inform security," he said.

Westcore threw a final glance around the room, then turned and left. Denon trailed behind and both disappeared from sight. Smith put the phone and gun down and went around the desk to follow them.

They stood fifteen feet down the hall at a lab door. Westcore placed a hand on the knob and tried to turn it; nothing happened.

"Read the sign," Smith said. "That's not the door you came through. That's a BSL-3 lab. It's locked." Westcore and Denon exchanged glances. Westcore reached into his pocket, removed a white keycard, and placed it on the reader. Nothing happened.

"You don't have access," Smith said.

"Maybe we use your card." Denon's voice was harsh.

Smith shook his head. "Can't."

"Why not?" Westcore shot back.

"You'll need all kinds of prescreening to go in there. Screening that you don't have. I would never give you my lab pass, and my general pass is missing."

"Since when?" Westcore said.

"Since ten minutes ago."

Westcore looked outraged. "I'm standing here asking you about Taylor and you don't tell me that your keycard's been missing? What the hell is this? Deliberate obstruction?"

"I was calling security when you appeared. USAMRIID security, which is the proper channel to handle any possible breaches in this facility, and a protocol that I'm bound to follow."

"If it's determined that you've deliberately helped her then that's a criminal act. You know that, right?"

"The only people that I've seen on this floor are you two. I haven't seen her."

"She could have taken your card and collected some bacteria to take with her. If it's found on the outside, then the consequences will fall on you."

Smith shook his head. "The card only allows access to the entrance and general hallways. It won't allow access to the storage equipment or the higher-security labs. The pathogens are locked."

"I suggest you find another card and open this door immediately."

Smith shook his head. "Absolutely not. You'll need personal protective equipment and clearance to get in there. Clearly you don't have either."

"You let her through," Denon said. "And we were only minutes behind her, so she didn't have time to put on a suit."

"Like I said, I never saw her and I suggest that you quit claiming that I did."

Westcore stormed up to Smith and stopped only inches from him. Smith could see five o'clock stubble forming on his chin.

"Quit dicking around and let us in."

Smith held his ground. "No."

Westcore vibrated with anger and from the corner of his eye Smith saw Denon moving at a forty-five-degree angle to Smith. The thought flicked through Smith's mind that if Denon had a gun he was in a perfect position to get a clear shot. Smith wondered how far the two would go. He wished he'd brought the gun from the desk with him.

He decided to let the two know that they were being watched on closed-circuit television. He gave Denon a pointed I-see-what-you're-up-to glance and then looked at the corner where the CCTV LED light glowed. Westcore caught the movement and turned to look behind him. The lens swiveled a bit as if to follow Westcore's movement. Smith knew that the device wasn't actively tracking them, it swiveled in a timed sequence, but neither Westcore nor Denon would realize that. Westcore took a step back.

"I'm watching you. Next time you won't be so lucky." He stepped around Smith and marched down the hall. Denon followed at a more leisurely pace and walked straight toward Smith to play a ridiculous game of chicken. Smith stayed put and Denon's shoulder bumped into him, knocking him back one step.

Smith held his tongue as Denon and Westcore disappeared through the main hall doors.

7

Smith's cell phone began ringing and he ducked back into his office. He retrieved it from his suit pocket.

"What the heck is going on now?" Russell's voice streamed through the phone. "I just had enough time to take a shower and get a cup of coffee and I learn that you're in trouble again."

"I don't know what you mean," Smith said. "And where are you?"

"I'm in central Europe. The guys tell me you picked up the car that we sent you."

Smith held the phone against his shoulder as he angled one arm into his suit coat. "I did, thanks. It's here at USAMRIID."

"I know it is. It's a company car and has a tracking device on it. It also has an onboard hidden camera that's activated by movement and it just sent a silent alarm to the central office. They said two guys in suits jimmied the door and they're ripping through every nook and cranny in the vehicle."

Smith bolted to the window, with half his suit coat hanging down, and opened the blinds. The car sat at the far end of the parking lot under a tree. The doors hung open and from inside came the shadow of someone working through the vehicle. One of the men pulled back and out of the car's front seat. It was Denon.

"I see them," Smith said. "They're from the Department of Veterans Affairs. Well, actually they're Stanton Reese guys hired by the VA. They're chasing down a scientist from the facility that skipped out of the psych ward and came here."

"So why are they breaking into your car?"

"They claim that the scientist came to my office. I guess they think they'll find something to help them locate her."

"Are these the same guys who followed you from the party?"

"No. Can you back them off? Does the car have a defense system?"

"What, like its own weapon? It's a Toyota Camry, not a Bond car."

Smith smiled and shifted the phone to his other shoulder while he finished putting on his jacket.

"You know what I mean. Disable it."

"That's been done already. How did they find the one car that's yours in a lot full of cars?"

"My parking space is designated with my name."

"A reserved parking spot. I'm impressed."

"As well you should be," Smith said. He heard Russell's soft laugh over the phone. He reached to the desk, picked up the Ebola report to refile it, and pulled the manila envelope out of the drawer. "The scientist they're chasing gave me something. Hold tight and I'll snap a picture." Smith focused his phone's camera on the envelope, snapped a shot, and sent it.

"Got it," Russell said. "Is that scrawl in crayon?"

"Blue crayon to be exact. If they're right and Taylor was in here, I presume that she left it for me. I suppose they don't hand out pens or pencils in the psych ward. Too easily used as a weapon."

"What's inside?"

He opened the envelope and slid out Taylor's report, snapped a picture of the title, and sent it to Russell.

"Looks like a research paper that she was working on before her breakdown," he said.

"Now I can see why the VA is involved. PTSD is a huge issue in the military right now, isn't it?"

"Yes. The suicide rate for returning vets is exploding. But that doesn't explain why they're chasing Taylor or why she thought I should see this report."

Smith shoved the report back into the envelope and returned to the window to check on the car. He was relieved to see Denon and Westcore deep in conversation with the soldier in charge of the security station at the entrance. The soldier was shaking his head and motioning the two back toward the exit.

"Looks like security has taken over the situation. USAMRIID security, not contract mercenaries. Should I go back to the car?"

"No. I'll have one of the guys retrieve it. We've already sent out a driver to pick you up and take you home. Even though we did a sweep on your residence and it was clean, that was before these two showed up. Now I've ordered a surveillance watch on your house for the next twenty-four hours. You can go home. And I'm sorry to say it, but if you get into any more trouble I won't be able to help. I'm going dark until later this evening."

"I don't expect to do anything except sleep for the next eight hours."

"Perfect," Russell said.

8

Kimball Canelo marched his troop along the edge of a small ridge overlooking the ocean in Djibouti. It was six in the morning and warming up with each step. Soon the heat would make marching impossible. They walked in a straight line behind Canelo, accompanied by the soothing sound of the ocean. The breeze blowing in over the water smelled tangy and clean and Canelo was relieved to be out of the dingy, smelly, litter-filled streets of Djibouti, if only for a few hours. His men seemed equally at peace. None complained and none spoke. They marched in silence, with only the rhythmic crunching of boots on gravel to mar the quiet of the morning.

They reached the top of the cliff and Canelo turned to walk along the rim. The path wound only ten feet from the edge and the hundred-yard drop to the stony beach below, where waves crashed over scattered boulders and an outcropping of stones. The only thing between them and the drop was a narrow ledge. A bee the size of a small hummingbird buzzed at Canelo's ear and he swatted it away without taking his eyes off the trail.

Behind him he heard a gasp and he looked on in horror as his first lieutenant hurtled downward, his arms pinwheeling and his face a study in fear. His body hit the rocks below and lay there as the waves washed over him.

"Johnson, what the hell happened?" Canelo yelled at the man walking right behind the lieutenant. Johnson, a fresh-faced new recruit from the Watts neighborhood in Los Angeles, didn't respond, but instead stepped toward the cliff edge and continued until the path fell away and he was hurtling downward.

"Halt!" Canelo said to the troops, all of whom continued forward, still in lockstep and not slowing. The third man followed Johnson, and Canelo lunged to grab at his arm, missing it. "Washington, stop!" he yelled, nearly in Washington's ear, but the man simply looked over at him, smiled, continued forward, and plummeted over the edge to his death.

Canelo grabbed the next man, holding him by both arms. "I said, *Halt!*"

The man smiled into his eyes but continued forward, leaning against Canelo's opposing pressure. This solider, named Wilmington, was a foot taller and forty pounds heavier than Canelo and he pushed the lighter man backward with little effort. Canelo glanced down, saw that they were only inches from the edge. He released the man and flung himself sideways. Wilmington stepped off and hurtled downward.

Canelo regained his balance and planted himself firmly in front of the next man. "Halt!" He roared the word, infusing it with as much authority as he could muster. The next man smiled, ignored the command, and walked into Canelo, knocking him back. Canelo wrapped his arms around the other man's torso, dug in his heels, and hauled the man off balance. The soldier staggered away from the ledge, but started to struggle to release himself. Canelo propelled off his back foot, forcing the soldier away from the ledge. The man leaned against Canelo, but this time Canelo was ready for the resistance, however crazy it was, and he swept the man's feet out from under him in a throw Canelo had learned in judo almost five years before. They fell together to the hard ground.

Canelo lay in the dirt, sweating, and he watched three more men walk over the ledge. The soldier he'd thrown sprang to his feet, took two steps, and on the third encountered nothing but air.

"No!" Canelo screamed.

Monroe was next, a man from Baltimore who was one of the best new airmen Canelo had ever had the pleasure to command. Monroe was three steps away from the edge. Canelo swallowed, pulled his sidearm, and shot him in the fleshy part of his thigh. Monroe staggered and fell, landing on the trail and moaning. The troops behind him walked around him without looking down. Monroe began crawling to the edge and disappeared from sight as he fell over it. Canelo shot at the next man, but missed.

The last remaining member of Canelo's troop walked off the ledge.

9

S mith entered a conference room at Fort Meade and took stock of the attendees. There were three people present: his commanding officer and the man in charge of USAMRIID, Colonel John Siboran; an anxious-looking man in a standard military prison uniform with "Canelo" on the name tape; and Katherine Arden. Colonel Siboran rose and Smith saluted him.

"It's good to see you, Colonel Smith. This is Major Kimball Canelo and his attorney Katherine Arden."

"Mr. Smith and I have met before," Ms. Arden said.

Siboran looked surprised at this information, but waved Smith into a conference chair.

"I've brought you here at Ms. Arden's express request. As you know, a soldier can hire private counsel in his defense at court-martial and Major Canelo has done so. It appears as though Ms. Arden believes USAMRIID can assist her client in his defense and she has petitioned the court to allow her access to USAMRIID's research files."

Smith raised an eyebrow. USAMRIID engaged in biochemical and biological warfare detection and defense and conducted heavy research on multiple angles involving pathogens known and unknown. While it often partnered with the civilian Centers for Disease Control and the World Health Organization, as well as many civilian governmental contractors from the Department of Defense, there were still a whole host of research topics that required confidential clearance to access. Smith had no doubt that many of the more sensitive research protocols would be protected from the normal channels of discovery in a court process.

Siboran regained his seat and nodded at Arden. "I'll let Ms. Arden explain the situation."

"Major Canelo was in charge of a troop stationed at Camp Lemonnier in the capital of Djibouti that plunged to its death. If you've been watching the media at all in these past few days I'm sure you've seen the reports."

Smith nodded. "I'm familiar with the story. As you say, it's been all over the news."

Arden grimaced. "What the news media hasn't seen fit to report was that Major Canelo did his best to stop the men from walking off the cliff."

"By shooting one of them?" Smith said.

"I shot him to stop him!" Canelo said in a harsh and angry voice.

"The story that's being reported is that you held a gun on them and forced them off the ledge."

Canelo stood up and Siboran came to attention. Smith thought his superior was prepared to restrain Canelo if need be.

"Lies!" Canelo said. "I—"

Arden waved her client to silence. "What you say here is not privileged and can show up as evidence at your trial. Let me tell the story." Canelo subsided, sat down, and put his face in his hands. Siboran slid back in his chair. Arden inhaled and began again.

"It is Mr. Canelo's assertion that the men walked off the cliff on their own and despite his many attempts to stop them."

Smith exchanged a glance with Siboran who looked grim, but not as incredulous as Smith would have expected.

"A suicide pact?" Smith asked.

Arden shook her head. "It's our belief that they were either drugged or brainwashed into doing what they did. I've issued a discovery request to USAMRIID to produce all their past and pending research on any diseases that can cause mass hysteria, mass brainwashing, and any vaccines or drugs in current development to halt such diseases or biological actors. It is my understanding that USAMRIID is in charge of protecting the military from biochemical warfare and that clinical trials are in process regarding several such diseases and their possible cures. It's possible that one of these trials, or USAMRIID's investigation files, can explain what happened on that cliff."

Smith shot another glance at Siboran and again was surprised to see that he wasn't objecting.

"All right. Fair enough, but I don't see how I can help," Smith said.

"Your unit handles biochemical disease and pathogens, does it not?"

Smith nodded. "Currently I'm assigned to the viral side of the unit, not the bacteriological side. For that you'd have to contact another one of our scientists."

Siboran shook his head. "I'd like you to spearhead the review from both sides of the bench. Her access will be limited to research already released to civilian entities."

Arden sat up straighter. "That's not what the court order states. USAMRIID argued that angle in front of a judge and he denied the motion and ended up ordering the documents to be released. He signed a subpoena confirming the request."

Siboran held up a hand. "Let's let Smith look into the matter and draw up a list of projects. It's quite possible that most of the research is not classified, and in that case we'll make it available."

"And if you find classified research?" Arden asked.

"Let's cross that bridge when we come to it," Siboran said.

Arden shook her head. "That's not acceptable. I need whatever research USAMRIID has in this field, not a truncated list of only publicly available information. I can get that on my own through civilian channels."

Smith jumped into the fray before Siboran could continue.

"Most of our research is just that, research, and most of it is conducted under Biosafety Levels Three or Four. I don't see how any of it can have affected a troop of soldiers thousands of miles away."

Arden snorted in disbelief, opened a ringed binder, and flipped a tab.

"Let's see. In 2003 USAMRIID found over one hundred vials of live bacteria buried in the ground under prior administrations. In 2009 over nine thousand vials, almost one-eighth of your entire stock, were unaccounted for in any records. Also in 2009 one of your researchers became sick with her own research bacteria after she failed to follow safety measures. And, of course, in 2001 there were the anthrax attacks that the FBI determined were perpetrated by a researcher here. One of your colleagues, Dr. Smith."

Siboran made a sound of protest and Smith waited to hear his response. What Arden had said was absolutely true. USAMRIID had had its share of safety lapses and outright criminal activity in past years. Smith wasn't going to engage in an argument in which the other side argued in hindsight and he was stuck claiming future perfection. Perfection in any secure setting was only as good as the dedication to the protocol required to achieve it, and USAMRIID researchers were human and had broken protocol many times in the past.

"Since that time we've taken steps to pinpoint researchers at risk for mental health issues and arrange for them to receive proper counseling, testing, and offering them leave should they require it," Siboran said. Smith thought of Taylor and her mad dash from the mental health facility last night.

"Who are these scientists currently under leave and what were they researching?" Arden said.

Siboran stood. "You know that the HIPAA privacy provisions don't allow me to reveal that information. I would hate to reveal the name of researchers grappling with a mental illness and have them possibly stigmatized because of it when we know that many such conditions can be stabilized, by either adjustment of medication, therapy, or both."

Arden shook her head. "The court order included the production of HIPAA documents. And USAMRIID refuses to release the names of those scientists or the research that they were conducting. The upshot is that at any given time this facility is at risk for the accidental release of the very pathogens that it is creating. And now you are aerosolizing these pathogens, which puts the risk even higher."

Siboran glanced at his watch. "I have another appointment so I'll leave you with Colonel Smith." He threw Smith a look that said *Good luck*, nodded at them both, and left.

Smith reached over to a coffee carafe and poured some into a Styrofoam cup. He held the urn up and looked toward Canelo and Arden. Canelo accepted the cup and added some powdered cream.

Arden waved him off. "I only drink green tea. Do you have any?"

Smith shook his head. "You're in an army facility. Strong coffee is the norm." He watched as a ghost of a smile passed across Canelo's features, the first Smith had seen since the meeting began. Smith filled a cup for himself, passing on the chemically laden powdered cream to sip the coffee black.

"The facility is safe and I don't think security can be easily breached from the outside," he said. As he said it he thought of Westcore and his henchman. He'd look further into that situation after his work with Arden was done.

"You've had twelve BSL-4 exposures just last year. That means possible Ebola, anthrax, and God knows what other pathogens are bubbling in this facility."

"That was out of thirty thousand entrances and involved scientists working on their own research when their positive pressure suits failed. I still believe this facility can't easily be breached from the outside."

"It could if there was an insider with malicious intent," Arden said.

"There is nothing now to infer that any such motivation exists in the facility."

Arden threw Smith a cynical look. "It happened once, it can happen again."

"Sure it could, but it's not likely. You're fishing, Ms. Arden, and I don't think that the court will appreciate you trying to hang USAMRIID with a crime that happened thousands of miles away."

"Let's just take a look at the research and then I'll decide."

The last thing Smith wanted to do was take a look at anything Arden wanted, but it was clear that Siboran was foisting her off on him. Once again Smith found himself struggling to control his anger in her presence. He focused on the investigation.

"Were the bodies autopsied?"

Arden nodded. "A few, yes. That's how the bullet was found in one."

"Did they do a toxicology test?"

"They did," Arden said.

"And?" Smith said.

"And all they found was a few traces of marijuana, nothing to indicate recent use. In one there were traces of khat, a local, legal, drug."

"So where is this wild-goose chase coming from?"

Arden bristled.

Canelo spoke up. "From the fact that they just walked into the sea. I kept ordering them to halt and they just kept walking over the edge. I couldn't stop them. I tried to fight with them, then I shot Monroe in the leg to make him stop and he *crawled* over the ledge. What would make a man do that? It had to be drugs." Canelo looked sad and desperate and Smith thought that if he was acting he was doing a fantastic job of it.

"Perhaps, but there's nothing to indicate that those drugs came from USAMRIID," Smith said.

"USAMRIID is the facility charged with protecting the military from chemical or biological warfare the world over, isn't it?" Arden asked.

Smith nodded. "Yes, it is."

"I believe that's exactly what's happened. A biochemical attack. It's possible that the answer to what happened on that cliff can be explained by some of the research being done here. I would think the facility would be interested in investigating this strange occurrence."

"Investigating it, yes. Being blamed for it, no. It's highly doubtful that USAMRIID is involved at all."

"I'd like to confirm that. And I have a court order that allows me to confirm that, so please, Colonel Smith, let's not waste any more time. I'd like to go to USAMRIID now." Arden stood up and Canelo did as well. Smith rose slowly to telegraph his reluctance, a fact that was not lost on Arden, because she looked visibly annoyed. She walked to the door and opened it, where an MP stood ready to return Canelo to his cell. As Canelo walked past Smith he grabbed Smith's arm.

"Find out what happened to my men. Whatever it was could happen again and you should know that if it does there will be no stopping them."

10

Berendt Darkanin stood in a room in Shanghai and watched as a crew of hackers, their eyes glued to their computer screens, pounded away on their keyboards. At forty, Darkanin had risen to one of the highest positions in an international conglomerate of pharmaceutical companies. He'd done it by stealing his competitors' research-and-development trials, and he'd done *that* by hacking.

Darkanin watched as a nearby hacker repeatedly attempted to disrupt an industrial water containment system on the United States' eastern seaboard. He'd successfully paused the system but was having trouble getting through to the main dashboard in order to alter the facility's coded operating instructions. The man, no more than twenty, swore in Chinese as he worked.

Darkanin's silent partner, known only to Darkanin as Yang, stepped up.

"Did you get the password?"

Darkanin shook his head. "Not yet, but soon."

"And the other?"

"Taken as a decoy only. They're both drugged and unconscious. We'll deliver the decoy back none the wiser when our main target talks."

"I have heard that the doctor has fled and is no longer in your control. This I do not like."

Darkanin frowned. Yang's voice was filled with menace, as if he was Darkanin's equal and could scare him into obedience. Never assume that you can threaten me, Darkanin thought.

"That's not your concern, it's mine," Darkanin said.

"I don't agree. We fail in this mission and there are several bad elements that will find us, cut out our tongues and eyes, and feed us to the jackals. You know this."

Darkanin snorted. "Who? The Ukrainian rebels? The al-Qaeda terrorists? Hardly. They can't follow me into America without setting off alarm bells in every intelligence agency in the United States."

"None of those. The Russians, Romanians, and Italians from Naples."

Darkanin waved a dismissive hand. "Mafia amateurs who spend their days threatening their local bakers into protection money will be very unhappy if they attempt to hurt me. You know that."

"The Russians threaten their biggest petrol manufacturers. They poison those who don't cooperate."

The Chinese hacker barked a short laugh and turned to his neighbor, speaking in rapid-fire Chinese.

"What's he saying?"

Yang flicked a glance to the side and then returned his attention to Darkanin. "He says he hacked the water system's dashboard. He still can't alter the coding without more work, but he's one step closer."

"The protection at the facility is tough to crack?"

Yang nodded. "Incredibly so. But he just said that he'd found and exploited a small gap that must have been a coding error."

"How long has he been working on this?"

Yang shrugged. "Two, maybe three days. Not long."

"Once I get the password, how long will it take to hack into the mainframe?"

Yang frowned. "I've told you many times that there is no guarantee. Hacking into a small industrial water system is nothing like hacking into the United States' military drone program. Surely you understand this."

"I understand that I have paid you and them"—Darkanin swept a hand to indicate all the hackers in the room—"a lot of money to be successful. Not to offer excuses."

"And I have offered none. We've already hacked into the hangar inventory list and altered it. That was an easy day's work, but none of the computers on that network fly the drones. Just bring me the password so that we can begin. And if you're worried, come look here." Yang walked over to another hacker's screen and pointed. On it was a grainy movie unfolding from a great height.

"What is that?" Darkanin asked. The image showed a rocky, forbidding mountain landscape that swept by under the fast-moving camera. In the distance Darkanin saw a shepherd wearing a turban and driving a small herd of goats down a narrow, rocky trail.

"It's a live-streaming shot of a Predator drone flight over Afghanistan."

"What do you mean live-streaming?"

"Just what I said. My friend here has been able to hack into the video feed from several of the United States' drones. What you are seeing is a live feed that's being returned to the main command center in Nevada."

"I thought the Pentagon closed that vulnerability in the drone communication systems."

Yang nodded. "They thought they did, but we've been able to restore it. That flight is happening now."

"How long did it take to do that and at what cost?"

Yang asked the hacker a question and he responded in Chinese.

"It took a couple of hours and the purchase of a thirty-dollar software program. But the video isn't the really interesting part. We've been able to infect the drone software system with a key-stroke recording virus. We're one step closer to being able to hack into the main command center. With the password that you obtain for us, we think we can close the loop."

"And then?"

"And then, even if they change the passwords, the keystroke virus will record the change."

"What if they find and destroy the virus?"

Yang shook his head. "It's self-replicating. It will be very, very difficult to annihilate. Once we have control of the drones, we turn them back to destroy their own."

"That's only the first step. You know that, right?" Darkanin said.

Yang nodded. "I know, but it will be a highly satisfying one all the same."

Darkanin's phone began buzzing in his pocket. He waved off Yang and headed to a corner of the room to take the call.

"Where are you?" the caller said without preamble.

"Shanghai. In the collection crew's offices."

"Excellent. Then you can give them the good news. Our friend finally coughed up the first password."

11

Randi Russell stood in a fabulous ballroom in the outskirts of Ankara, Turkey, wearing a red cocktail dress, high heels, and a gun strapped to her thigh. She sipped from a glass of champagne while she smiled at the conversation of the group of people surrounding her. None knew that she was CIA, there to gather any intelligence that she could and to protect the attending U.S. ambassador to Turkey. All thought she was a member of a diplomatic mission bent on enhancing trade between the United States and Turkey. The exclusive guest list for the reception included over one hundred real members of various trade commissions and an additional twenty high-ranking diplomats from a group of surrounding countries, as well as their staff and spouses. Russell estimated that at least thirty of the attendees were spies from their home countries.

They'd been screened on entrance. Russell had taped her weapon to the inside of a metal vase in the back of a cooperating flower vendor's truck. She'd retrieved it from the back kitchen where the vendor had lined up the vases before their final distribution into the main rooms. The vendor himself had suggested the maneuver when she had rendezvoused with him an hour before the event.

"The kitchen staff will be intent on cooking and preparing the meal, waiters will be running in and out, and I and others will be rushing to place our final arrangements. No one will spend a lot of time looking at you, even in that dress," he said with a wry smile.

"Can't you palm the weapon and simply hand it to me outside the ballroom?" Russell had asked, but the man shook his head.

"I can't be seen helping a U.S. spy in such a manner. Should anyone discover the weapon before you retrieve it I will deny any knowledge. You understand?"

Now she stood in the ballroom under the glittering chandelier and cataloged as many of the attendees as she could recognize. The U.S. ambassador to her left was telling a witty, self-deprecating story about his initial posting in Turkey. Near forty, Ambassador Eric Wyler was a clean-cut, pleasant-looking man with an impeccable education and almost eighteen years in diplomatic service. Erudite, well mannered, and divorced, he was considered a good catch by most of the single females in Ankara's expatriate community as well as a few Turkish women bent upon expanding their personal influence and leaving Turkey. At the moment Wyler was expending his considerable charm on Russell.

"You can imagine my chagrin when I discovered that the term actually meant 'to steal' in Turkish," he said as he leaned toward her with a smile.

Russell smiled back. She liked Wyler and he had spent the past month going out of his way to make her feel welcome. He had no idea that she was CIA. This latest field posting was one of the easier of her career, but she still found herself scanning the room for threats. While there had been the usual chatter about an attack, her home office had been unable to pinpoint the source or verify it. Yet during this party something felt off and while she couldn't put her finger on it, she could sense it. Years of listening to her intuition resulted in her heightened attention to everyone and everything that transpired around her.

"Would you care to dance?" Wyler asked her. Russell nodded and Wyler pulled her close as a waltz began to play. His hand holding hers was warm and she caught a slight whiff of his cologne, which smelled like expensive soap with a touch of neroli and citrus. Russell wasn't surprised to find that he was an excellent dancer. She followed along with him as he propelled her across the floor, keeping close enough to move fluidly, but not so close that he would feel the gun's holster at her thigh. He smiled down at her and she smiled back.

"Why do I always feel as though you're never really fully present and always on edge?" he asked. His gaze never left hers.

She lifted an eyebrow. "What do you mean?"

"It's as if you're continually coiled for something to happen."

She broke contact and looked to the side as they circled, unnerved by the depth of his perceptiveness. Russell always prided herself on her ability to focus on a matter, whether it was analyzing a stream of cryptic coded messages in an enemy's transmission or targeting an attacker in a gunfight, but as they danced she was unable to keep her mind on her mission. She searched for a way to break the awareness that had suddenly arisen between them.

"I'm pretty high-energy," she said. "Always was." She hoped that he'd accept the answer and change the subject.

He shook his head. "It's not that. There's something more. To me it seems as though you watch others with an analyst's eye. Almost clinical and definitely intense."

"You're spending a lot of time watching me, then?" she said, keeping her voice light and friendly.

"I notice you in any room that you appear," he said as he stared down at her.

The song finished and he stopped moving. The tension between them rose and they remained in the middle of the dance floor, still wrapped in each other's arms. He kept his eyes on her.

"Are you always so intent on watching others?" Russell asked. His look became guarded and the current running between them shifted and cooled. He took what seemed to Russell to be a reluctant step back, and she was both relieved and disappointed to have to relinquish her place next to him.

"I've been posted in some of the most dangerous areas of the world, so I've learned to be wary." A safe answer, she thought, because it didn't acknowledge what she thought were his true feelings. Russell wanted to tell him that she understood that all too well and wished he would be more specific about the danger.

"Anything here in Ankara that worries you?" she asked. The business-like question broke any last vestiges of the emotion that had run between them just a few minutes before. He took her arm to lead her back into the crowd.

"Absolutely. I've been on edge since I denounced the Syrians for using chemical weapons on the Turkish border. It's never safe to call them out, and their close proximity to Turkey leaves me vulnerable." He waved over a waiter carrying a silver tray holding glasses of champagne. "Drink?" Russell nodded and he handed her one before taking one himself.

"Do you think they'll retaliate?"

He seemed to ponder the question while he sipped. "I hope not. I know of a Russian businessman who was found dead in his car just two months after he refused to sell a second round of arms to Syria. He said they hadn't paid him for the first. I believe that they killed him. Or had him killed."

"But killing a businessman, horrible as that is, isn't in the same category as killing an ambassador of one of the most powerful countries in the world. I can't imagine that they would take such a risk. The blowback would be swift and decisive."

He stared at his champagne glass as he swirled the liquid around. After a few seconds he shook himself and looked up at her.

"I hope you're right. And if you aren't and the Syrians

give it a shot I can only pray that Washington would send its finest to protect me."

They already have, Russell thought.

She put the glass to her lips and took a sip just as the far wall exploded inward.

Shards of glass and jagged pieces of wood flew in all directions. Russell ducked her head before a piece of glass could embed into her cheek, but it hit her scalp behind her ear and pierced the skin to the bone. A second explosion from another part of the estate made the walls shake. Screams filled the air and the partygoers stampeded to the double-door exit opposite the demolished wall.

Wyler clutched her arm and started in the same direction, but Russell shook off his grasp, hauled her gun out from the holder, and grabbed his sleeve.

"Not that way. Toward the explosion." She waved in the direction of the ruined wall.

Wyler glanced at the gun, and a look of comprehension crossed his face.

"You're CIA," he said. A massive, billowing cloud of smoke engulfed them and both he and Russell started coughing. He pulled a handkerchief out of his pocket and handed it to her. "Cover your nose." Russell waved it away and fought against the tide of pushing, panicked people. She and Wyler were the only two heading back toward the explosion's source.

"Why that way? There could be another bomb," Wyler said, close to her ear. The staccato sound of gunshots joined in the cacophony of screaming people.

"That's why. They're waiting outside and picking us off as we leave," Russell said. She pulled Wyler with her to a location against the wall and fifteen feet from the gaping hole. It continued to belch smoke as the night breeze blew through the opening. Flames licked upward, igniting the floor-to-ceiling curtains, and the breeze only fed the fire.

Through the haze Russell saw the envoy to Russia

herding the Russian ambassador and his wife toward them. The envoy also held a gun, and Russell made a note of his face. He looked at her, then the gun in her hand, and one eyebrow crooked up. He came to stand next to her, his back against the wall.

"They're covering the front," he said in English. Another round of gunfire and the stampeding crowd attempted a shift. At least the ones in the front did, because they now understood that there was a gunfight on the other side of the door. But the ones in the back either didn't hear the shots or didn't grasp their significance, because they continued to push outward. The opposing forces ensured that no one would get in or out of the ballroom. The curtain's flames burned higher. Russell strained to see through the blast hole to the outside, but the smoke obscured everything.

"Can you see anything on this end?" the Russian asked her.

"No. We're going to have to give it a shot, because that curtain fire is going to spread and if we don't die from a bullet we'll die from smoke inhalation."

The Russian nodded. "Agreed."

"Help me break some windows." Russell handed her gun to Wyler. "Can you shoot?"

He nodded. "But not well. You keep it. I'll break the windows." He reached over and picked up a chair from a nearby table. The Russian ambassador followed suit, and they both headed to a nearby French window and began hammering at it.

Russell edged closer to the blast hole, keeping her back to the wall. The Russian spy joined her. Her eyes stung from the smoke and her lungs felt thick. She saw that Wyler and the Russian had successfully broken the panes of glass and were smashing the muntin bars that held each small section. At least they could use the new opening as an exit if necessary. Some in the crowd came to the same conclusion and soon Wyler and the Russian disappeared from view as the panicked people surged their way and encircled them. Russell was relieved when she saw Wyler climb through the window and run deep into the yard. A second group of men started pounding on another French window eight feet from the first.

"I haven't heard any more shots, have you?" Russell said.

The Russian shook his head. "None."

"Then I'm going through. You joining me?"

He nodded. "I'm Vladenko."

"I'm Jane. Ready?"

He nodded. Russell positioned herself so that she was opposite the blast hole and prepared to jump over the jagged lower section. She took two steps and leapt, ducking her head and closing her eyes against the flames and heat from the now fully engulfed drapery on her left.

12

Russell sensed rather than saw Vladenko following behind her. She landed on the grass outside and immediately lowered to a crouch. After a quick glance she saw that she was alone, and she rose, kicked off her shoes, and ran across the lawn to the first set of trees fifty feet away. She leaned against one of the trees and inhaled the fresh air. Vladenko joined her a second later.

"You see anything?" he asked.

"No. I don't hear anything, either. Let's make our way around to the front. If we stay far enough away we can keep to the trees."

She darted from trunk to trunk. The crisp night air braced her and the moon illuminated the grassy open pockets between the trees. As she ran she felt the wet dew on her bare feet and the soft, manicured grass underneath. She reached the far corner of the building and moved cautiously around until she had a parallel view of the front entrance.

Light posts illuminated the area. A horseshoe drive passed under a portico where the valet service operated. Several black cars were parallel-parked in the center of the horseshoe and one idled on the drive itself. The idling car's driver's-side door hung open and the overhead light glowed. The chauffeur was slumped onto the passenger seat. All around his car were bodies: some on the asphalt drive, some on the gravel horseshoe section amid the parked cars, and others farther away, as if they had tried to run but had been gunned down. People from inside the ballroom stumbled out the doors. One woman took a look around and covered her eyes. The man next to her made an incoherent sound and held his palm to his head in a stricken gesture.

"You see anyone with a gun still alive?" Russell said.

"No. Let's go take a look."

Russell stood and jogged toward the destruction. As she neared she could see the actual chain of events as they played out, starting with the farthest man and continuing to the one nearest the entrance. Vladenko walked at her side. Russell pointed at the body of a man in a suit slumped near the wheel well of a black car with a sticker on the back indicating it was from the Russian embassy. It appeared as though the man had tried to take cover there. Next to him was another, also slumped against the car.

Vladenko gasped. "Those are two bodyguards for the ambassador." He knelt down and checked the nearer man's pulse before moving to the next. Two more men, both lying on the ground with gaping chest wounds, were in view of each other and both had weapons next to them on the ground. Russell checked those two and then moved around the area checking the rest. In the distance she heard the sound of sirens.

"Took them long enough," she said as she rose from checking the last man.

The flow of fleeing people had slowed. Once they emerged from the house most began to run and kept going until they were out of sight. Two small groups hovered, but far away from the scene of the carnage. Vladenko stepped up next to her and Wyler came at a run from the side yard. He stopped to stare at the bodies around them.

"There's a camera," Vladenko said. He pointed to a security camera in the upper corner. "We need to get to the feed and download a copy before the entire building goes up in flames."

Russell nodded. He was right. They would need the feed to see exactly what had occurred on the rotunda. "The room is just there. On the right of the entrance. The smoke doesn't seem so bad yet. Care to risk it with me?"

"Let's go," Vladenko said.

She turned to Wyler. "I'll take that handkerchief now." He produced it from his pocket. He appeared stunned.

"Are you okay?" she asked.

He swallowed and pointed to a man lying in the middle of the driveway. "That was my driver."

There was nothing to say to that. Russell pressed the cloth against her nose and headed to the entrance. There were two bodies in the hallway. Russell presumed they were security personnel from the office who had witnessed the scene and were gunned down as they ran to assist the others.

Heavy smoke clouds hung in the hall and Russell's eyes stung from it. She turned into the anteroom. It was a small area, about eight feet by eight, and held a long, L-shaped desk and two computers along with an aluminum file cabinet. The computer monitor screen displayed a partitioned grid with various views. The ballroom views were blank and held only a red X where the picture should be, but the hall and front grounds were still transmitting.

She went to the desktop, reversed the program, and clicked through the screens. Vladenko moved up next to her, coughing from the increasingly dense smoke.

"Where are you sending the feed?" he said.

"To the cloud. From there I can forward it on."

She reached the part of the feed that was time-stamped from when the bomb exploded. The images made her gasp and she began choking from the sudden influx of smoke and soot in her lungs. But she ignored the pain and the coughing, because what she saw on the screen astonished her. Seconds after the bomb exploded a second, less deadly one appeared to explode near the parked cars, and the bodyguards and drivers reacted instantly. All pulled their weapons and all moved into battle position.

And then they all shot each other.

The battle raged for a few minutes, until no one was left standing. The last man staggered around, staring at the others with a look of shock. Then he slowly raised his weapon to his temple and shot himself in the head.

13

President Castilla sat in the Oval Office listening to the director of national intelligence deliver his daily briefing. Starting after the attack in 2001, the DNI had created a daily report of collected intelligence from all the major agencies, collated into one document for the president's use. In his mind, Castilla called the DNI's daily brief the "daily dread" because it was full of some of the most dreadful news he could imagine. Chemical gassings from Syria against civilians, terrorist attacks and beheadings in the Kashmir borderlands region between Pakistan and India, and information that a drone mission in Afghanistan had gone terribly wrong and ten civilians had been killed. The brief also cataloged the myriad risks that were arising from various situations at any given time around the world.

"Also, we're still looking into the attack on the embassy reception in Ankara. I've left a message with Carter Warner asking him to head up the probe. I understand from his secretary that he's ill, so his assistant is handling it for the moment. As soon as Warner returns I'll have him take over." DNI head John Perdue finished delivering the overview and paused.

"Strange thing, that Ankara attack," Castilla said. "Anything else?"

"There is something else. Two things, actually. The first is a bit weird and not really something you should be involved with, but Richard Meccean's dog was found half dead on the street with a gunshot wound. I know you two were friends even before you appointed him to HHS, so I thought you would want to know."

Castilla nodded. "He's a good guy and he loves that dog. What did he say about it?"

"That's the weird part. The veterinarian who removed the bullet scanned for a microchip, found one, and tried to contact Meccean first at his home to let him know and then used the office number that was also on the chip. He never reached Meccean but left a message with his secretary. Turns out Meccean had emailed her that he was ill. The secretary panicked when she heard about the gunshot wound. She took the dog to her home to convalesce and tried his cell. When Meccean didn't respond she asked a friend of Meccean's to go to his house. The door was locked and there was no sign of foul play, but the secretary filed a missing person report with the FBI just in case. They're looking into it."

"I don't like the sound of that," Castilla said.

Perdue nodded. "Me either. You know him better than I do; is there anything that would indicate he would take off and not respond to his office?"

"What do you mean?"

Perdue looked uncomfortable. "Well. You know that we've had a couple of cases of government officials just disappearing and then later being found having a fling somewhere without their wife's knowledge. Could this be something like that?"

Castilla shook his head. "Rick's not married and no, he's not as nutty as that, I can assure you. Maybe you keep me posted on the FBI's progress."

"Will do. Like I said, sorry to mention it . . ."

Castilla waved him off. "No, that's fine. I just hope he's okay. And the other thing?"

"A helicopter crew flying a routine mission in Afghanistan crashed their helicopter into the mountains. Everyone on board died. The base collected the remains and listened to the last transmission from the pilots. It seems that nothing was wrong with the chopper, the pilot just forgot how to fly it."

Castilla looked up from a document that he was signing. "What do you mean, forgot?"

Perdue looked perplexed. "That's what I'm told the voice recorder showed. The pilot and another pilot on the transport were overheard panicking as the copter flew. The investigator said they were asking each other what various dials and controls were for and seemingly had no idea how to fly the machine."

Castilla sat back and stared at Perdue. "Were they drunk? Drugged?"

Perdue shook his head. "Toxicology report showed nothing except caffeine. They went back and tested the coffee at the base and it was clean. They have absolutely no explanation for what happened there. The investigation is ongoing, and there's nothing really to be done at this juncture until it's completed, but it was so strange that I thought you should know about it."

Castilla nodded. "Agreed. Keep me in the loop on that story as well, can you?"

Perdue closed his folder and rose. "Will do."

Perdue left and Castilla's phone rang. He punched on the speaker and his assistant said, "Fred Klein's calling from his secure line and needs to speak with you. He says it's urgent. I'm putting him through now."

"Klein, what's happening?"

"Mr. President, I'm not exactly sure, but it appears as though the Chinese have focused on Lieutenant Colonel Jon Smith for reasons that are unclear." Castilla listened while Klein ran down the events of the previous evening, including the fact that a small drone had been involved.

"I don't like that they've targeted Smith. Do you think they're aware of his Covert-One status?"

"I think it's more likely that they were interested in his position as a researcher for USAMRIID. He's the U.S. equivalent of Chang and they've never liked it that we assisted in Chang's escape from China and harbored him here. With all the security around Chang, they may have thought to try to take Smith, hold him, and then negotiate a swap."

"He's safe now?"

"Yes. But I don't like the use of the device. Smith seemed to think it wasn't the most efficient way to attack him, or even kidnap him, when the usual attack would suffice, but I think it shows their willingness to operate illegally within our borders. The FBI has jurisdiction and their counterterrorism unit is on it, but I'd like permission to investigate this deeper."

"Of course. Keep me informed."

Castilla hung up and couldn't shake a sense that something evil was in the works and he was already far behind in the race.

14

An hour after Smith was ordered to assist Arden in her investigation his phone began ringing. He let it roll into voicemail each time without bothering to check the display, and so he jumped when a scientist from another building knocked and entered his office. He couldn't remember the scientist's name, but the excitement on the man's face was unmistakable. Arden looked up from a folder that Smith had shoved at her.

"Sorry to bother you, Colonel Smith, but your phone's on do not disturb and the White House is calling. Something about a press conference."

Arden raised her eyebrows and Smith wanted to throttle the scientist. Arden had been present for his call to Russell of the CIA and now the White House. The lawyer was smart enough to understand that the average scientist at USAMRIID wouldn't receive or make such calls on a usual basis.

Under normal circumstances Smith would never have gotten a call from the White House for either his role as a USAMRIID researcher or as a member of Covert-One. USAMRIID had personnel assigned to handle the press, and the only man who would contact Smith on behalf of Covert-One was Fred Klein. That the call came directly from the White House and with a cover story meant nothing good.

"What kind of press conference?" Smith asked.

"Regarding the new flu shot initiative. They want to see you in ninety minutes and they suggested that you stop at the Anacostia Yacht Club first for some instructions. You'd better hustle."

Arden looked less intrigued and Smith was relieved. The reference to the Anacostia Yacht Club made it clear to Smith that it was Klein calling, not the White House, but Klein's use of the White House gave Smith the opportunity to drop his meeting with Arden immediately. It also ensured that she wouldn't cry foul and claim that USAMRIID was giving her the brush-off. The flu shot initiative gave a valid and mundane cover story for the call.

"It appears as though we'll have to continue this investigation later." Smith tried to sound disappointed but a bit of his satisfaction with the interruption leaked into his voice.

Arden wasn't amused. "Call me the minute you can continue. Here's my cell number." She wrote a number on a Post-it note on his desk and handed it to him.

"Absolutely," Smith said. I'll take my time, he thought.

An hour later Smith was escorted into a situation room at the utilitarian headquarters of Covert-One. The only other occupant was Fred Klein.

Klein was a somewhat rumpled man in his early sixties with an academic air about him. He looked to be a professor and all would be surprised to learn that he spearheaded one of the most effective, and occasionally lethal, groups of covert operatives in the world. Drawn from various professions, all were experts in their respective fields and all were vetted and recruited only after a vigorous background check. Not all were known to each other. Only Klein knew the full list of active operatives. He walked over to shake Smith's hand.

"Thanks for getting here so quickly. We're waiting on one more. Take a seat." Klein waved to the oval conference table. Smith sat down and looked around. The room was deceptively business-like in its appearance, but Smith knew that it had recently been renovated and was wired with state-of-the-art communication and Internet technology.

There came a knock on the door and the same staffer who had shown Smith into the situation room escorted in Mark Brand, the man Smith had spoken to on the phone the night before. His presence there confirmed Smith's view that he was a member of Klein's inner circle, if not Covert-One. Now the tall man with smooth dark skin and Rasta braids tied in a ponytail smiled a broad smile at Smith. He wore a dark suit with a muted tie and strolled over to Smith in a loose, rangy walk that belied his intensity.

"We've spoken to each other more in the last twenty-four hours than we have in two years. Good to see you again," he said.

"I could say the same. How's New York?"

Brand shook his head. "Have no idea. I didn't mention it last night, but I've been promoted since I saw you last. Now I work in the DC branch."

"Mr. Brand has some information that I think you should hear," Klein said.

"About the drone last night?" Smith asked.

Brand shook his head. "We have some specific ideas about that, but I'll let Mr. Klein fill you in. I'm here about something else. This is off the record, you understand. You may hear about this in a more formal manner, but I'm hoping to head off that investigation. The DC office has received a complaint about USAMRIID. More specifically, about you. Seems as though you were less than helpful after being informed about the possibility that an at-risk scientist may have been trying to access pathogens in the lab. You know anything about this?"

Smith sighed. "I suspect you're talking about Dr. Laura Taylor. She's a scientist assigned to the same area that I am. She'd been on medical leave, but I'm told that she appeared in the lab late last night. Two men were after her, and they claimed that she may have entered my office. My keycard was missing and a report left on my desk, but I never saw her, if indeed it was she that took the card."

Brand frowned. "Did you report the missing card?"

Smith nodded. "To USAMRIID security and within minutes of my discovering it. I told the two men who were looking for her that I would and I did."

"The Stanton Reese guys complained that you were highly uncooperative. May I ask why?"

"Intuition, I guess. They seemed pretty sketchy to me."

"Do you know where the keycard is now?"

Smith nodded. "The guard found it on his station desk an hour after I called it in. But the card only allowed access to the lab, not the pathogens. Whoever took it would have needed an additional access method for those. And when I called security they informed me that though she's been on leave her status and access rights have remained the same. I have never heard that she was barred from the labs. No memo or other notice was sent."

Brand looked relieved and Klein's lips quirked. As if he knew the information already.

"Seems to me that those two VA guys are trying to send misinformation around. What's this about?" Smith asked. "I can't imagine that you called me here to have this discussion. We could have done this at either of our offices."

Brand and Klein exchanged glances.

"Continue, Mr. Brand," Klein said. "You can speak freely." He looked at Smith. "Mr. Brand is here to help me brief you on your next mission."

Brand unbuttoned his jacket and sat down opposite Smith.

"From here on out I'm speaking to you not as an FBI agent, but as a fellow operative, you understand?"

Smith nodded.

"The day nurse at the hospital where Taylor was receiving treatment found several vials under her pillow. She turned them over to her supervisor, who gave them to the FBI, which is how we got involved in the first place. Seems as though they were marked as highly toxic and should never have been removed from a secure lab."

"What were they?"

"I'm not exactly sure of the substance. Some chemical she was working on before her mental issues arose. Do you know what she was researching before she went on medical leave?"

Smith rocked his hand back and forth. "A little. She was investigating possible chemical approaches to relieve post-traumatic stress disorder in soldiers. As you can imagine, the military is extremely invested in finding a solution for PTSD. The current suicide rate is the highest that it has been in U.S. history. And last night an envelope was left on my desk containing a report that ran down her tests and results." Smith rattled off the title.

Brand nodded. "I've seen that report. It's logged into the USAMRIID central data storage as well. Did she give you anything else?"

"Whoever was in the office had removed a report of mine regarding aerosolizing pathogens from a sorter on my desk and placed it next to the envelope. It's odd."

"I can fill in some of the blanks for you," Klein said to Brand. "She was testing a possible drug that would wipe out traumatic memories, but leave good memories intact."

Brand's eyebrow flew up. "You can target a memory? How?"

"Apparently the portion of our brain that is involved with storing memory has a fat content that may house the actual memory. Dr. Taylor's vials were preparing to wipe out that fat content. She was using a marker to search out and destroy only the traumatic portions."

"That still doesn't explain why we're having this conversation in your offices," Smith said to Klein.

"Thank you, Mr. Brand. I can take it from here," Klein said.

Brand stood. "I'll let the agency and the VA know

that the card allowed only limited access. In the mean-time, remember when I told you last night to watch your back? Well, I meant it. That someone spun a story to make it appear as though you were helping a mentally ill co-worker obtain dangerous pathogens tells me you've got some powerful enemies somewhere." He nodded at Klein and left.

"Let me show you what we know." Klein picked up a black remote control and pointed it at a flat screen on the wall. The monitor lit up and Klein accessed the Internet and clicked on a link.

"This is the entrance to a ballroom in Ankara, Turkey. The reception was the target of a terrorist attack. You won't see it here, but a bomb exploded in the rear of the building. We had Ms. Russell there in an undercover capacity."

"Is she okay?" Smith asked.

Klein nodded. "Yes, she's fine. What you see next is an on-site feed that she was able to access and shows what occurred within a minute of the explosion."

Smith watched as the various men shot at each other. Within seconds all were dead.

"And now, this."

The screen changed to a side street in a leafy neighborhood where a man walked his dog.

"Where's this?"

"Here in Georgetown. The camera feed comes from a private home a few feet from the action, which is why it's so poor. The man is Richard Meccean."

"The head of HHS?" Smith asked.

"Yes," Klein said.

Smith watched as two men jumped out of a van, shot the dog, hustled their victim into the vehicle, and drove off.

"The homeowner was out of town and only returned today. As soon as he saw the tape he took it to his local police station and they contacted the FBI. In the Ankara case it seems as though the men all shot each other, despite the fact that they were in no way enemies. In fact, the two slumped against the limousine were colleagues. Likewise, we have a case in Afghanistan where two helicopter pilots crashed a copter because while in midair they'd forgotten how to fly it," Klein said.

"How is that possible?"

Klein shook his head. "We don't know. A few hours ago Meccean was located in a small town in Canada. He was fine, if a bit disoriented. He still had his wallet and all his personal belongings on him and was standing in the airport in Toronto arranging a flight home to Washington. When the FBI agent came to debrief him he denied any knowledge of being kidnapped."

"Did they tell him about the dog?"

Klein poured himself a glass of water. "They did, and while he claimed not to remember that, either, it was then that he began to become alarmed."

"And you think these incidents are related?"

Klein pointed the remote at the monitor again. The screen switched to show a series of bubbles connected by lines. To Smith it appeared to be an illustration of a family tree.

"As I think you probably know, the CIA funds various IT companies and tasks them to create software designed to analyze connections. The NSA uses these programs to analyze the billions of bits of metadata that they collect daily from emails, IP addresses, and telephone calls. After that's done they use an enhancement program that adds GPS information drawn from the navigation system in a person's car or cell phone and updates from a target's social media activity that indicate location. The resulting connections map gives a remarkably accurate picture of the social network and activities of just about anyone." He put the pointer on a bubble, one of two, in the center of the diagram. "Take a look at the grayed bubbles here in the center."

"Okay. It just says Actor A and B."

"That's because these two individuals were communicating through a highly complex network of IP addresses and dummy email accounts that the software was unable to crack. Any connection that the software can't identify is flagged and given high priority, because it indicates a determined effort to remain anonymous. We believe Actor A is operating out of China, probably in one of their infamous cyber espionage units. This is trouble for a whole host of reasons, but the second actor is the one we're really concerned about. We have reason to believe that he or she is actually sitting in either Syria or Iran. Now look what happens when we expand this connection map." Klein switched up the view and several more bubbles appeared on screen. On the far edges Smith saw the names Meccean, Rendel, Warner, Wyler, and a list of the helicopter unit in Afghanistan and Canelo's troop in Djibouti. "Interesting, isn't it?"

"It's remarkable that such disparate people have actual connections, but isn't this just the six degrees of separation theory? That all of us are connected once we move six degrees out?" Smith asked.

Klein nodded. "There's that, of course. But watch how the bubbles shift when we add in one factor." Klein hit a button and the bubbles shifted dramatically. Now the group of names became clustered together and jumped several spaces toward the grayed-out Actor A and B bubbles. Only Meccean's name remained on the fringes.

"What factor did you add?" Smith asked.

"Any connection to the United States' drone program."

"That is sobering," Smith said. "But what's the point of attacking such a disparate group of people?"

"We don't know, but we have a list of more possible victims. When we realized what had happened to Meccean we ran a search on the source of the email that was sent to his secretary. It was generated from a remote server that had hacked his computer and had already been logged by the software as high priority, again, through an untraceable series of IP addresses. We found three in total. Meccean's email was first. The others were Carter Warner, undersecretary at the Department of Defense, and Nick Rendel, a computer specialist and contract worker, also at the DOD. Both lived alone and both sent out the exact same email claiming that they were ill. When the FBI went to their homes there was no answer."

"How much lead time did the kidnappers buy?" Smith said.

Klein sighed. "Enough. The metadata analysis took almost thirty-six hours to create an initial connection map, and then it took another few hours to enhance it. When we got the initial analysis, we were only looking for Meccean. It wasn't until we ran the email that the other names popped up on the map through that link. Since the men lived alone it took another day for anyone to become alarmed. During that time the men could have been whisked out of the country."

Smith agreed with Klein's assessment. "You mention that you added in the drone program as a possible connection. Are you aware that I had my own close encounter with a drone just last night?"

"I am. Mr. Brand told me."

Smith pointed at the map. "Maybe you load me into the program and see what connections it produces."

Klein gave him a wry smile. "I don't have to. The only connection that will show is your status as a USAMRIID researcher. Any other connections, such as email and phone usage by you, have been encrypted by us to mask your Covert-One activities. Whatever connection map could be created wouldn't accurately reflect reality."

"Normally I would be relieved to hear it, but right now I would like to know who sent that drone after me. Is there any way to track it?"

Klein shook his head. "Not unless it showed up on someone's closed-circuit camera somewhere or tripped a radar scan. There are already so many drones in private hands that we can't trace every one that may exist. A low-range, low-altitude device such as the one that you saw can be made by any civilian enthusiast. We need to recover those individuals. I have a feeling that whatever is going on here, finding them will go a long way toward explaining these events. We're concerned that someone took a page from the old CIA rendition program and whisked these individuals away to foreign locations to be tortured. We're particularly worried about Warner and Rendel. Both work in the drone program and both had knowledge of the one aspect of passcodes needed to access the drone controllers. I need you to help find them," Klein said. He shoved a file across the table at Smith. "We have reason to believe that both have been taken out of the country, and the latest tip we received suggested Warner is somewhere in Germany. The FBI has some limited international jurisdiction, but generally once a missing person has been removed from U.S. soil we require the assistance of the country in which we think the hostages are being held. You, of course, can go anywhere. Russell is already on it. She'll be in touch once the Ankara thing is finished. Anyone else you'd like to help you?" Klein asked.

Smith nodded. "Andreas Beckmann and Peter Howell. Can you locate them?"

Klein waved at the file. "Known current locations are in there. Howell's in London. Good luck."

"Sounds like I'll need it," Smith said.

15

Carter Warner took the first blow on the soles of his feet twelve hours after his kidnapping. He was lying on a cement floor with his arms still tied behind his back, the hood still over his head, and a cloth gag in his mouth. The blows continued, one after the other in a regular rhythm with just enough space between them to give Warner time to dread the next. He recognized the torture method and it told him that he was in the hands of professionals. He was sweating and biting down on the gag every time the excruciating pain shot through his soles to his legs. He hadn't been allowed a bathroom break and he wet himself from the combination of deprivation and severe pain. Someone hovered at his side.

"We need the drone password." The voice was a sibilant whisper. Warner closed his eyes. They'd made the same statement several times over the last few hours and his response was the same: silence.

He was privy to only one aspect of the drone defense unit. The passwords were spread across several departments and personnel and protected by a highly developed cyber security program. At the time the IT technician in charge of the passwords had argued vociferously against spreading them among several people, pointing out that the more people who knew a secret, the more likely it was to be passed on. Now Warner was thankful for the fact that if he cracked under torture he couldn't jeopardize the entire program.

"No need to speak." The man chuckled. "Just nod your head."

Warner's body shook and he tried to focus away from the pain and instead on the ramifications of giving the man what he wanted. The single password by itself would be useless—a fact that Warner suspected the attacker knew. If so, then he must have a plan to obtain the others. Warner wondered how many the attacker had obtained already. Warner's continued silence worked against him, and the next blow made him scream. He felt his neck muscles clamp in a spasm and he heard only a muffled sound through the gag. He tried to gasp but the gag made it impossible. Sweat poured down his face and the mask pulled against his nose with each inhale, blocking any fresh air from reaching his lungs.

"The password," the man whispered.

Warner stayed silent and began to count the seconds while he waited for the next blow to fall.

16

S mith reached the gated entrance to the clinic and announced his presence on an intercom. The birds sang in the trees and a small breeze made their branches sway. When added to the warmth of the late-July sun the location seemed a world away from the news of trouble that he was bringing to its doorstep. The metal gates swung wide and Smith proceeded up a gravel driveway that curved through the trees. After the second bend a long, two-story building came into view. The modern architecture had clean lines and was built of wood, stone, and glass, giving it the air of a wealthy man's estate rather than a hospital. He reached the end of the driveway, which curved around in a horseshoe shape; to his left a sign bearing the word "Respite" was the only indication that he was in the right place. He parked off to the side and entered through a glass-and-wood door.

Smith's steps were muffled by thick carpeting in the plush and inviting lobby. A massive stone hearth took up the far wall to Smith's left; cold now, but he presumed it would be roaring in the winter. It was surrounded by leather club chairs and a long sofa.

Directly in front of Smith was a reception station behind which stood two men. To the right of the station was a door that Smith presumed led to the clinic's interior. Both men, one young, about twenty-five, and the other in his late forties, looked up from a computer screen. The younger man leaned forward.

"Herr Smith?"

Smith nodded. "Here to visit Andreas Beckmann." The older man leveled an interested gaze on Smith but said nothing. The younger man smiled.

"He's walking in the gardens. He's quite interested in the landscaping."

Smith did his best to hide his surprise. Beckmann was the last person he would expect to be interested in horticulture. The older man shot a sideways glance at his younger colleague and then returned his attention to Smith.

"He's in the garden sneaking a smoke," he said with a lift of one eyebrow.

The younger man frowned. "That's not possible. He doesn't have access to tobacco at Respite."

"Just what exactly does Respite do?" Smith asked.

The younger man's face lit up. "We're an addiction rehabilitation facility. State of the art. Our success rate is over eighty percent. We achieve this rate by running a well-controlled environment for our patients. Herr Beckmann has been exemplary in his behavior, and I doubt that he's breaking the rules." The younger man spoke in earnest tones and sent a pacifying glance at his older colleague. Smith was in the older man's camp. Likely Beckmann was breaking the rules.

"I'll just walk around to the garden," he said.

The older man waved to his right. "Follow the path past the gazebo. He has an unending admiration for the lily pond."

Smith didn't bother to hide his grin at this comment and even the younger man unbent enough to swallow a laugh. Smith nodded at them both and headed out to follow a manicured trail through the trees. After a couple of minutes he reached the gazebo and less than one hundred steps past it he saw a man standing in front of a pond with his back to Smith. Though Smith couldn't see his face, his tall, fit build, close-cropped salt-and-pepper hair, and the cloud of smoke billowing out in front of him matched the Beckmann whom Smith knew. The man turned and a smile creased his face.

"Smith, what the hell are you doing here? All healed from that mustard gas, I see. You look good." Beckmann put a hand-rolled cigarette to his lips, strode across to Smith, and leaned in to shake his hand and slap him on the back. Smith returned the greeting.

"I should ask the same of you. What addiction are you trying to break?"

Beckmann grimaced, retrieved the cigarette, and held it up. "This one. Some young prick was appointed head of risk management at the CIA and decided to reinstitute fitness requirements for certain field personnel."

Smith glanced up and down at Beckmann. "You look incredibly fit. Did you not pass?"

"I passed the cognitive speed, threat assessment, hand-to-hand combat, target shooting, push-up and sit-up tests, but failed the sprint."

"How far did they want you to run?"

"Two miles in a minimum of eighteen minutes, twenty-two seconds." Beckmann took a drag off his cigarette.

Smith nodded. "Sounds like the same standards as the army fitness test that I take every year. So you came here to kick the cigarettes and try again?"

Beckmann shook his head. "No. I came here to spy on one of the patients. There's a Russian lieutenant of the prime minister who has a deep and dirty OxyContin addiction. He's here trying to kick it. Word is that when he's high or coming down off a high he babbles in German, so the CIA saw it as an opportunity to get me clean and pick up some intelligence at the same time."

Smith jutted his chin at the burning cigarette. "I can see that one prong of the strategy is failing, how about the other? You getting any intel out of the Russian?"

Beckmann looked disgusted. "None at all. The guy *does* babble in German, but all he talks about is his young mistress's bedtime antics and how much he needs her. He's desperately afraid she'll leave him for greener pastures. What he doesn't know but the CIA does is that she's already been dancing under the sheets of a Chechnyan rebel twenty years the guy's junior." Beckmann shook his head. "He's looking at sixty, so there's no way he's going to keep up with a guy in his thirties. When he finds out I have little doubt he'll be back to swallowing his painkillers."

Smith put up a hand. "Not true. I'm told that Respite has an eighty percent success rate."

Beckmann inhaled another drag. "The young doctor at the desk tell you that?"

"He did. But the older man is on to you."

Beckmann smiled. "That's Herr Doktor Steiner. Seen it all, that one."

"You feel like getting sprung from here?"

Beckmann gave him a piercing glance. "Absolutely, but what's up? I've been unconnected from the outside world."

Smith told him about the missing personnel. "We're treating it a bit like a reverse rendition. A mass kidnapping, if you want to call it that, but if we're right, they could be torturing information out of them right now."

Beckmann took another drag and nodded. "Sure I'm in, but you'd have to get me clearance to leave. If this guy doesn't cough up some information soon I'll have nothing to show for this mission."

"I might be able to get Russell to lean on someone at headquarters. Get you an extension to meet the fitness standards. It would help if you'd say that you'll continue to try to quit once you're on the outside."

Beckmann sighed. "If Russell gets me out of here tell her I'll give it a shot. Where are we going first?"

"To your old stomping ground. Berlin."

17

Beckmann shoved open a wooden door and entered a rathskeller an hour north of Berlin. Smith walked in behind him. Smoke hung in the air from the fifty or so patrons, mostly men. A heavy wooden bar, worn smooth from years of use, flanked the right, and heavy wooden tables flanked by benches filled the rest of the area. A large stuffed boar's head jutted from the top of a mirror against the wall behind the bar. It had two long, wicked-looking tusks, beady eyes, and dark bristled whiskers. Underneath it a bartender with arms of a stevedore and an elaborate, waxed mustache poured ale from a tap.

Beckmann strolled down the narrow aisle. Smith watched as all the patrons marked their progress. Some openly, some not. They reached the end and Beckmann slid onto a stool. He hooked a second one closer with his foot and indicated to Smith to sit.

"Nice place," Smith said in a low voice. "Looks like the annual meeting of the outlaw biker gang's German chapter."

Beckmann gave a quick, surreptitious look to the side and then back at Smith. "Not an upstanding citizen among them. Fantastic place for information." He shook a cigarette out from a pack and offered it to Smith.

"I don't smoke," Smith said.

"I know that, but you'd better either smoke or drink. You're far too clean-cut for this place and your face screams *American WASP, come and beat the shit out of me*."

Before Smith could reply the bartender tossed two saucer-sized cardboard coasters on the bar in front of them.

"Was willste?"

"Bourbon," Beckmann said. He leaned toward Smith. "What do you want?"

"I'm tempted to order seltzer water just to piss off the clientele."

Beckmann smiled. "Do it. I like a man who spits in the face of danger."

"Whiskey, neat," Smith said to the bartender.

Beckmann turned a bit to face the room, leaned against the bar, and pretended to ignore the others while he spoke to Smith.

"Table at three o'clock is the alpha. Name's Corenger. Dabbles in prostitution, arms, and drugs. Neo-Nazi sympathizer but only because most of his sales are made through that network and he's smart enough to pretend. He couldn't care less about politics. He has an extensive network of spies and informers. If something's going on he'll have heard about it and will be trying to profit from it."

The bartender placed a drink before him and Smith took a sip. In the mirror over the bar he could see the five at Corenger's table eyeing them both as they talked.

"Looks like we're the subject of their conversation."

Beckmann shifted away from the room. "Corenger is no fool. He's checking out that technical black jacket you're wearing and those fancy combat boots and he knows that you've got a lot more money than the average idiot. He's trying to figure out why you're here."

Smith's jacket was a lightweight running model and his boots had a high top, lugged sole, and steel toe. He wore black jeans and an army watch.

"Is he plugged into a national network? Or does he only work Berlin?"

"National, for sure. He's trying to take over the entire market for weapons in Germany. Lots of enthusiasts want German engineering, and I don't mean cars. But he has an impressive network of small-time thieves, pickpockets, and burglars in his pocket, not to mention hit men. If there's something going on in the area they'll tip him to it and he'll demand either a piece of the action or hush money."

Corenger waved at the man next to him, who rose slowly. He was bulky but muscled and had a massive beard that hung to his collarbones. He sauntered toward them.

"Here comes his lieutenant. Rolf something," Beckmann said.

Rolf something stopped in front of Smith.

"Warum biste du hier?"

Smith took a sip from his drink, put it down in a calm motion, and only then looked at the man.

"I don't speak German," he said.

"Sprechen nicht Deutsch," Beckmann translated.

"So I ask in English, yeah? Why are you here? Where are you from?" The man's English was passable. Smith shrugged.

"Not anyplace for very long."

"American? We don't need you here."

Smith took another sip. He leveled a gaze at the man. "And yet, here I am."

"Leave."

"No," Smith said. "I'm here to learn things."

Rolf something's eyes narrowed. "What type of things?"

"Information. About foreigners in the area. I can pay for it, but it has to be solid."

The man looked at Beckmann and rattled off a sentence in German. Beckmann replied and the large man turned back to his table.

"So what was that about?"

"He wanted to know if you were CIA. I told him no. Said you were a hostage negotiator looking to pay off a ransom."

"Nice angle," Smith said.

"Thank you, I try," Beckmann replied.

Rolf something returned and stopped in front of Smith. "Corenger wants to speak to you."

"I don't know who that is," Smith said.

Rolf pointed at the table. "He's over there."

Smith made a show of glancing at the table. "Well, I'm right here. If he wants to speak to me tell him to come over."

Rolf frowned. "He wants you over there."

Smith shook his head. "I don't hold a private conversation in front of strangers. He wants to speak to me he can come over here. Now I'm busy talking to my friend."

Rolf grabbed Smith's left arm, a move that Smith had anticipated. He reached across his body, wrapped his hand over the meat of the other man's palm, broke the grip, twisted the wrist almost ninety degrees, and swept it over his head, bringing it back down as he did. It was one of the easiest and most effective aikido moves that Smith had learned during his combat training in the military. Easy because it took almost no strength to do, but effective because it twisted an attacker's wrist so unnaturally that it created extreme pain.

Rolf howled and his shoulders followed the movement until he was bent forward at the waist, with his wrist bent. Smith turned it even more and took two steps backward, still holding the torque on the wrist and hauling Rolf with him. Smith took two more backward steps and Rolf hit the floor, face-first, with his arm up behind him at an almost ninety-degree angle. Smith levered Rolf's arm up higher and placed his knee on the man's neck. Now the pressure point was on the shoulder joint, which was twisted unnaturally. Smith pushed the arm up so that it was hyperextended, cradled it against his shoulder, and leaned a bit forward to maintain the pressure. Rolf yelled from the floor.

Smith heard the noise of chairs scraping across floors as the entire room rose.

Beckmann hauled a Sig Sauer out from a shoulder holster and pointed it at Corenger. He spoke in German and the men in the room all stayed where they were.

"Don't move," Smith said to Rolf. "At this angle it will only take a small push to pop your arm out of the socket. Once I dislocate it I'll pull right and stretch the tendons. It'll take you three years to heal, minimum." Smith looked up at Beckmann. "What did you say?"

"I asked if they really want to die for this fool," Beckmann said.

"Let's go," Smith said. He rose and stepped back quickly. Rolf put his palms on the floor to rise and stopped when Beckmann shoved the muzzle of his pistol on the back of the man's neck.

"Stay down until we're gone," Beckmann said. Rolf settled back on the wood.

Smith took a slow look around the room, stopping at Corenger. He walked through the crowd and out the door without looking back.

The cool night air smelled fresh after the smoky interior and Smith inhaled it. Beckmann joined him and they headed around the corner to the dirt parking lot, making their way around the motorcycles to their rental car.

"Hey, American."

Smith turned to see Corenger strolling toward them, with two of his men half a step behind. Neither was Rolf something.

Smith waited. Beckmann tensed next to him and reached into his jacket. Corenger put up a hand.

"Just talking. I hear you need information."

Smith nodded. "I do."

Corenger held his hands palms out at Smith. "So let's talk."

Smith shook his head. "Those two stay back." The men behind Corenger looked at their boss. Corenger jerked his head at them and they stayed put while he continued forward. He pointed at Beckmann.

"He stays back too."

Smith shook his head. "He's not a bodyguard, he's a partner. He'll need to hear the information as well."

Corenger narrowed his eyes but said nothing. He came within five feet of them both and stopped. He was a large man with broad shoulders, a paunch, and hair past his shoulders tied in a ponytail. The few threads of gray at his temples told Smith he was in his forties, but his weathered, hard face looked at least a decade older.

"How much will you pay?"

"Depends on the information."

"What if I told you I know where a certain high-ranking American official is being held right now and that you are standing within thirty minutes of his location?"

Smith said, "I'd say that's worth nothing. I need an address."

Corenger shook his head. "No address. You can follow us there. We're going now."

"Now? Why?"

"Because they didn't pay what I asked. I own this area. You want to run an action here you pay me a percentage. How much ransom did they demand?"

Smith pretended to think a moment. "About one hundred thousand euros." Corenger's eyes lit up and Smith waved him off. "But I only have authority to offer twenty thousand."

Corenger gave Smith a speculative look. "You pay me twenty thousand in bitcoins right now and I'll not only take you there but I'll retrieve your hostage for you."

Smith snorted. "Absolutely not. Besides the fact that you're giving me no guarantees, I need him alive. You bring him to me dead and I lose my job and you get nothing."

"We'll bring him to you alive. If you transfer the money to my account now we can get moving."

Smith shook his head. "You promise a lot, but for twenty thousand it's likely they'll hand him over peacefully. Your way is too risky."

"They're not going to settle for twenty. Fifty maybe. But you'll look like a hero if you get him for half."

"We need to watch it go down and we take delivery of him at the location," Beckmann said. "And we'll send the money after."

"Half now, the rest after we get him," Corenger said.

"Twenty-five percent, and only after we verify that he's actually at the location you take us to," Smith said.

Corenger nodded. "Deal." He waved at the others and barked an order in German. "Let's go," he said to Smith. He strode away toward his motorcycle.

"What the hell is a bitcoin?" Beckmann asked when Corenger was out of hearing.

"A form of crypto-currency. Internet-only money. Big in the underground world of arms and drugs. I've dealt with something similar before."

"You think this guy they saw is Warner?"

Smith nodded. "I do. My concern is about what they're going to do when they find out I'm not a hostage negotiator but a lieutenant colonel in the army."

Beckmann opened the rental car's passenger door. "They'll try to kill you, me, and Warner. But hell, that's nothing new for any of us. Let's go."

18

Darkanin stood over Warner wearing a surgical mask and watched as one of his men sprayed an aerosol over the bleeding man's face.

"He's taken one hell of a beating," Darkanin said. The torturer, named Curry, a small man with a glass eye and a bad bowl haircut, nodded.

"He held out longer than a lot of the younger ones I've worked on. His generation is one tough group of assholes."

"I understand that he served in Vietnam."

"Ah, that explains it."

They were in the basement of a tumbledown farmhouse at the Polish border. Warner was tied down on a plank table and unconscious. The table stopped at his ankles and his feet hung over the edge. Below them Curry had placed a bucket to catch the blood and pus oozing from the soles. Darkanin pointed at them.

"I thought there'd only be bruising."

Curry looked nervous. "It wasn't working, so I added a blade as well."

Darkanin felt his anger beginning to boil. "Your instructions were clear. He was to have minimal scarring. What's the point of wiping his memory if he has physical proof?" Curry danced sideways in a nervous, jerky motion.

"Even the bruising would show."

"And would be healed by the time we released him.

This looks septic. I'm not paying you the final installment."

Curry looked outraged. "I did the work! You'd better pay me."

Both men turned at the sound of shoes clattering down the wooden stairs. Brian Gore, Darkanin's lead man on the kidnap project, ducked his head to avoid hitting it on the low-hanging ceiling while he leapt down the last two steps. Gore was a former sniper in the U.S. military who had been arrested after he'd gunned down his commanding officer in Afghanistan. He'd argued that he had post-traumatic stress disorder and didn't recall the incident. He'd escaped from detention before his court-martial could begin and had been hiring out as a mercenary ever since.

"We've got trouble," Gore said. "Corenger's on his way over. Seems he's pissed and wants revenge. I told you we should have paid him."

"If I paid protection for every small-town loser who demanded it I'd be broke and a target for them all. How do you know he's headed this way?"

"I pay one of his guys to tip me when something's up. He just called. Said Corenger's bringing two unknowns with him as well. A German with a gun and an American hostage negotiator."

Darkanin's arm shot out and he grabbed Curry by the throat and squeezed.

"A hostage negotiator? You thought you could cut a side deal and leave me hanging for the crime?"

Curry's eyes bulged and his face slowly turned red. His lips moved and he made a gulping sound.

"Before you kill him let him talk. I know most of the negotiators in Europe and it'll help if we have an idea who we're up against," Gore said. Darkanin let go and Curry stumbled and gasped.

"Who is this guy?" Darkanin asked.

Curry shook his head. "I don't know."

Darkanin punched him in the face. Curry fell back

and landed against a card table filled with various imple-
ments of his trade. The pincers and wrenches fell to the
floor as his weight upended the collection.

"I tell you I don't know! I never cut any type of side
deal. Someone on your end must have tipped him off."
Curry's voice took on a whine of desperation. Darkanin
rubbed the pain from his knuckles while he stared at
the torturer. If what Curry said was true then someone,
somewhere, was funneling information to a network.

Darkanin had spent months and hundreds of thousands of dollars preparing for the operation and he wasn't
about to let a lone hostage negotiator blow up the
scheme.

"How many guys do we have upstairs and what kind
of weapons?" he asked Gore.

"Three, an AK-47 for each, along with three pistols
and an IED with a timer."

"Why an IED?"

"We were going to set it to blow up the house after
we're done here. Best way to destroy any DNA evidence," Gore said. Darkanin hauled Curry toward him by
the shirt.

"Bandage his feet and get him ready to move. Collect
the aerosol and whatever tools you need and get him to
the van." He shoved Curry away and indicated that Gore
should follow him.

"Let's give this hostage negotiator a warm welcome."

19

Beckmann stopped the car on a small dirt road at the edge of an empty meadow. He killed the lights but kept the motor running. Corenger's men rode to a halt around him. Smith estimated that at least five bikers of various ages and sizes had joined the convoy. Corenger got off his motorcycle and sauntered toward them, waving at Beckmann to lower his window.

"He's being held at a farmhouse on the other side of that field. My last information was that he was alive. Whether he still is or not, I can't tell you. We'll go in on foot."

"How many kidnappers are there?" Beckmann asked.

Corenger rocked his hand back and forth. "Four or five. One guy I know for sure. Name of Curry. A twisted son of a bitch who gets his kicks torturing people. He's nothing to be worried about, but the rest?" Corenger shrugged. "I'll be needing those bitcoins now." He handed a scrap of paper through the window. "Here's my address. Wash it through bitlaundry first."

Beckmann raised the window and turned to Smith. "You have any idea what he's talking about? What's a bit-laundry?"

Smith reached to the seat behind him, unzipped a small computer case, and removed a tablet computer from its sleeve.

"Just what it sounds like. It's a money-laundering site. When I transfer the coins online it goes to an encrypted address before depositing in his." Smith tapped on the tablet. The screen's glow lit the small area.

"How many do you have?"

"A few thousand."

"Where'd you get them?"

"Remember Rebecca Nolan from New York?"

Beckmann smiled. "The financier thief. Sure."

"She gave me kilodollars and I exchanged them for bitcoins last year. I'm only transferring two thousand to Corenger. He'll have to provide more assistance if he wants the rest." Smith worked on transferring the funds and Beckmann opened the window again, pulled out a cigarette, and lit it, inhaling deeply. He blew a straight line to the outside.

"We should get backup before we go in there."

"What, you don't like the guys we're with? Now, there's a shock," Smith said.

Beckmann grunted. "They're likely to put a knife in our backs."

Smith shook his head. "Not mine. I figure I'm safe. At least until I transfer the money. You might want to stay alert."

"You're all heart. Where's Russell?"

"Turkey," Smith said without looking up. He'd arranged the transfer and a small sand timer was spinning as the transaction processed.

"Howell?"

"London. I think," Smith replied. "You're too efficient. I didn't expect to get a hit on our first try. Any backup I can arrange will take too long to get here. Why not call the local police? The FBI notified Interpol about the disappearances, so it's not like it's a secret."

"Hmmm. May not be a great idea. I don't know if they'll come at Corenger. He has a lot of contacts in this area."

At that, Smith did look up. "You think they're bought?"

Beckmann shrugged. "Not sure, but I'd feel better if we had time to go to the federal level. Less of a chance there."

A pinging sound from the computer told Smith that the transaction was complete.

"I don't think we can wait. This is an opportunity that won't come back."

Beckmann nodded. "Agreed. You have a gun?" Smith reached once again into the duffel and removed a Sig Sauer.

"I have one magazine. That's it. You?"

"The same."

Corenger had been standing in front of the car watching his phone and after a moment he walked over to the car again.

"I just saw the confirm. Two thousand isn't enough."

Smith leaned toward the window. "It's all for now. I've seen nothing to indicate what you tell me is true. I don't even know if this guy is the one I need. Once I have the hostage you'll get the rest."

Corenger leaned into the car. "You bet I will. Let's go."

"We need ammunition and some weapons. You have any?" Beckmann said.

"It'll cost you another five hundred."

Beckmann looked at Smith. "Pay the man."

"You're pretty free with my money," Smith said.

"It's either that or we stand around like target dummies while the bullets fly."

Smith hit the tablet again and within seconds the ping came.

"It's done. Show us what our options are."

Smith tossed the computer back into the duffel and got out of the car. Corenger waved both him and Beckmann toward a motorcycle with a sidecar storage box attached. He took out a key and opened it.

"Take anything except the G36 combat diver."

"Why the hell do you have a combat diver?" Smith asked.

"We're close to the North Sea. Russian spies dive off the boats and come in underwater all the time. I got that sweet machine off one of them. I know a Swede who wants it."

Beckmann peered inside. "All Heckler and Koch. I should have guessed."

"Only the best and all untraceable," Corenger said. "The assault weapons are HK416s. I've got an order in for some 417s but don't have them yet."

"You have a G28?" Beckmann asked.

Corenger nodded. "You a marksman? Take this one."

"I am," Beckmann said. He took the gun Corenger offered, while Smith removed an assault weapon. Corenger walked to another cycle, opened a soft-sided saddlebag, and removed two canisters. He gave one to Smith, the other to Beckmann.

"Tear gas. Time released. You twist the top and have two minutes to leave the area."

Corenger reached inside and began assembling another assault rifle. He finished two and gave one to a nearby man the size of a mountain.

"This is Karl. He'll stay with you both. When we get the hostage out he'll ride with you until the money is transferred. You understand?" Karl lumbered toward Smith. "Move out," Corenger said.

They began marching across the field toward a stand of trees that Smith estimated were three hundred yards away. Beckmann walked on Smith's left, while Karl stayed on the right. The rest fanned out on either side. The only sound was the crunching of their shoes on the earth and the occasional soft brush of wind through the leaves. From the far right Smith heard the hoot of an owl. They entered the trees and Smith darted from trunk to trunk in a zigzag pattern. Karl marched placidly forward.

"Is he going to just walk on in?" Beckmann whispered to Smith.

"Looks that way. But the tree trunks are too small to hide him anyway. He must weigh almost three hundred."

Smith ran to the next tree with Beckmann right behind him. They both took up a stance behind two side-by-side trunks. They had reached the end of any available cover. In front of them was an open field composed mainly of scrub grass and patchy weeds. A ramshackle farmhouse sat an additional two hundred yards away. They had come in from the rear. A single floodlight on a pole illuminated the yard where a German shepherd was chained to a post in the ground. It stared in their direction, head up and ears pricked.

"The dog knows we're here," Beckmann said.

"Glad he's chained."

"He starts barking and we're done," Beckmann said.

At that exact moment the dog started barking.

20

Smith waited for the barking dog to summon someone from inside. One dim bulb glowed from a window, but otherwise the house was dark. It remained silent. No one came to investigate.

"That's odd. You're hiding a hostage in a house, have a dog outside to warn you when someone approaches, and when the dog barks you don't check it out?" Smith whispered to Beckmann, who nodded.

"Maybe no one's home."

"Maybe Corenger set us up and there is no hostage."

"That feels wrong too. Because unless he produces, there's no way he gets your money."

"He could lure us into that house and hold me hostage until he gets me to transfer the funds."

"If that was the plan why not take us in the clearing? We were outnumbered and there was no neutral bartender as a witness."

Smith had to agree. The only possible explanation for the inactivity was that no one was present to hear the dog.

"So the house is empty," Smith said. "Maybe."

Corenger and his crew stepped into the yard. His men remained with him. They were still spread at ten-foot intervals, but didn't bother to hide or scurry from one safe location to another. While Corenger was close, he was still well beyond the range of a rifle unless it was in the hands of an excellent shot. Most of the men stayed well outside of the danger zone as well.

"Hey! It's Corenger. I'm here to warn you. Trouble's on its way. American trouble," Corenger yelled at the house in English, which gave Smith his first cue that whoever had kidnapped Warner, they weren't German.

"That would be you," Beckmann said to Smith.

There was no response. Corenger stayed in view and then walked ahead toward the shack with his usual saunter. Smith and Beckmann started toward the house as well, but at a much slower pace. Corenger and his men were twenty feet from the back door when the sharp crack of a rifle split the air.

The man farthest to the right went down. Corenger and the rest of his men opened fire, scattering as they did. Smith dropped onto the grass and started crawling backward. Beckmann stayed with him, also doing a military crawl. One of Corenger's men sprinted toward them and was a few feet away when another crack rang out and he spun and grabbed at his arm.

"That's one hell of a shooter. A hit at two hundred yards in the dark," Beckmann said.

"Can you wait for the next muzzle flash and pinpoint him?" Smith asked. Beckmann rolled to his stomach and aimed at the house.

"His next shot I will, but he'll do the same so be ready to move."

"Good. Keep him busy. I'm going around," Smith said.

The next shot landed somewhere to their right. Beckmann fired back and Smith catapulted to his feet and ran. He heard Beckmann behind him and more shots. The remaining men in Corenger's group had made it back to the trees and fired round after round at the house. Their complete lack of strategy had Smith worried that he and Beckmann would be hit by friendly fire.

Smith swerved into the trees and began tacking around in a wide circle. He found Karl walking in their direction in the same placid manner. When he saw Smith he speeded up and fell in step on Smith's right.

Beckmann joined on Smith's left. They made it to the edge of the property and Smith saw the taillights of a vehicle flash to life. From the vague glow he could make out the shape of a dark-gray panel van.

"They're taking the hostage," he said, and he went down on one knee and aimed at the tires. He fired off a volley and was rewarded with the sound of a puncture. Beckmann fired two rounds and managed to place a bullet through the driver's-side window as the van made a turn to the left. He swung the rifle strap over his shoulder and switched to the pistol.

The driver's-side door was flung open and a man emerged, holding a small automatic weapon. He dropped to a crouch and returned fire. Beckmann, Smith, and Karl all fired back, hammering the van's engine area and the surrounding grass. The noise made Smith wince as his ears took a battering and Beckmann's cartridges flew in front of him. For a moment Smith was blinded as the headlights of a second car swung into view. He heard it screech to a halt, and the man from the van kept firing at them as he ran to it.

From the corner of his eye Smith saw Beckmann swing his rifle back into position, aim, and fire. He hit the fleeing man dead center in his back and he went down. The car reversed in a squeal of tires and as it swung to drive away the headlights swept over another man who was racing to the car. That man disappeared into the passenger side as Beckmann fired another shot. Smith thought he saw a hole rip open in the car door's interior. The car drove forward, with its passenger-side door swinging wide with the velocity. The car sped away and Beckmann swore in German when he saw the passenger's hand reach out and close the door.

"I missed him," Beckmann said.

A silence fell over the area. Smith saw no motion near the house, and the van's driver's door remained open. From behind them came the sound of shoes crunching on dirt and Corenger came up to them.

"The one you shot was Curry."

"And the others?"

Corenger shrugged. "Don't know. But I think we drove them off, don't you?"

"Tell your men to stand down. We're going to check out that van and I don't want to get shot by mistake," Smith said. Corenger nodded and spoke into his phone.

"I'll cover you," Beckmann said.

Smith started forward, and Karl came with him.

"Still not leaving me alone?" Smith asked him.

Karl didn't respond, just kept walking in that placid manner that Smith now thought of as his trademark.

Smith was sweating in the cool air as he made his way to the disabled car. When he reached the van without incident he breathed a sigh of relief. Curry's body lay ten feet to the left and he went that way first. He kept his gun out and trained on Curry. Though he thought the man was dead and no longer a threat, Smith was taking no chances. He reached out, rolled the body over, and checked the pulse. There was none. Smith removed the assault weapon from his hand.

"Is this Curry?" he asked Karl.

Karl just shrugged.

Smith moved to the van's back doors and opened them. The van's interior light was on and gave Smith a clear view of the man lying on the metal floor. The man turned his head a bit and looked at Smith through glazed eyes. It was Carter Warner.

"Mr. Warner, are you injured?"

Warner's dazed look turned to one of confusion. "Water," he said.

"I'll look for some in a minute. First I need to know if you're injured," Smith asked.

Warner shook his head. "My feet feel like they're on fire. Why?"

Karl tapped on Smith's shoulder and pointed to Warner's feet. Even in the half-light Smith could see the blood oozing out of the bandages that were wrapped around the insoles in a messy, halfhearted field dressing. Smith nodded his understanding. He stepped into the van and checked for any other signs of injury, but could find nothing.

"Mr. Warner, do you know if any other people are being held in the house?"

Warner shook his head. "What house?"

"Never mind. I'll be right back." He turned to Karl. "I'm going to check out the house. I'd prefer it if you'd stay here and guard him until I get back."

Karl didn't respond.

Smith jumped back out of the van and strode to the side of the house. Karl stayed with him. The dog, still chained in the center of the yard, was huddled as far from the direction where the kidnapper had been shooting as the chain would allow. Smith skirted across the yard, crouching low and keeping to the back wall of the house with Karl walking upright behind him. As they passed the dog Karl veered out and went to the animal. He ran a hand over the dog's back and then unhooked the chain from his collar before standing and catching up to Smith. The dog followed Karl.

Smith opened his phone and got a line to Beckmann.

"I'm going in. Keep an eye out for me."

"Will do. Can you put your phone on speaker and put it in that top zippered pocket? I'll be able to hear you."

Smith did as he asked and entered the house, springing from side to side in the narrow entrance hallway. A few feet ahead and to the left, a door was open. Smith could see a set of wooden stairs leading downward. He moved to the entrance and then began a careful descent, taking care to tread lightly on the wooden steps. He reached the bottom stair and took in the long table set in the middle of the room and the torture instruments strewn on the ground next to another, smaller card table.

A bomb sat on the card table. Smith could clearly see the blinking lights and jumbled wires of an improvised

IED. A cell phone detonator was flashing in a second-by-second sequence.

Smith catapulted back up the stairs, taking two at a time and nearly barreling into Karl, who was at the top.

"There's a bomb," he yelled as he pushed past Karl and sprinted back down the hallway. He heard Karl behind him. His heavy footfalls shook the floor and for the first time he was moving at a pace far faster than a walk.

Smith hit the outside and ran toward the trees. The German shepherd streaked past him on the left and he heard Karl's heavy breathing on his right.

Five seconds later the house blew up.

21

The blast's force knocked Smith off his feet. He hit the ground and covered his head with his arms. Bits of wood and debris rained down on him and he grunted as a large beam landed on his back and pounded him farther into the dirt. He heard a car alarm begin its rhythmic howling and glanced over his arms to see that it was the van. Several pieces of the house had landed on the roof and the alarm blared while its lights flashed. The van itself, though, was intact, and Smith hoped that it had protected Warner. He heard a groan next to him and he saw Karl trying to rise. Smith shook off the debris and sat up.

The bomb had blown a hole in the house's roof and shattered the windows. Smith could see flames shooting upward; black smoke roiled from the structure. He heard footsteps and looked up to see Beckmann.

"There goes the evidence," Beckmann said. He held out a hand to help Smith up. Smith sighed, shook off some more ash that had settled on his shoulders and in his hair, and let Beckmann haul him to his feet. Karl stood as well and Smith watched him as he staggered a bit.

"You okay?" he asked the large man. Karl, true to form, simply nodded. The German shepherd appeared and Karl patted it on the head before turning on his heel and heading back toward the trees.

"You're leaving?" Smith called to him.

Karl didn't look back. The dog trotted next to him and Karl patted it again.

Smith turned to Beckmann. "Where are the others?"

"Gone," Beckmann said. "Remind me not to depend on that crew in the future."

"Let's check on Warner."

They jogged to the van and found Warner safe inside, but unconscious. His heavy breathing was slow and even.

"Drugged?" Beckmann asked.

Smith shrugged. "Maybe." He moved to the driver's side and found a key in the ignition. "Let's get out of here. I'll drive you to the rental."

Beckmann slid into the passenger seat and placed his weapon along the seat at his right leg before closing the door. He lowered the window and maneuvered the weapon so that the muzzle stuck out the side window in a firing position. Once the gun was in place, Smith fired up the engine and drove down the darkened driveway. Behind them he could hear the fire roaring and occasional popping noises as various items created secondary explosions. After a few feet during which the van swayed and lurched down the road, it was clear that the vehicle had taken some damage from the blast.

"Back right tire's blown," Smith said.

Beckmann scanned the area. "Just as well. We should dump it and clean it when we do."

Smith nodded. "Likely it's stolen."

"Keep the lights off if you can. Or use the parking lights if you absolutely need to see. No need to telegraph our location."

They bumped and heaved down the road. The tire must have had some air left in it, because they weren't yet down to the rim, but Smith figured they would lose that very soon. After another fifty feet they did, and Smith kept going on the rim until he saw the rental car come into view.

"Who the hell is that?" Beckmann said.

Smith peered through the windshield, but without the headlights he could only make out the mass of a person standing near the rental. A black shadow, much lower than the first person, came toward them and Smith switched on the lights to avoid hitting it. When he did he saw that it was Karl standing by the car and the dog trotting toward them.

"He doesn't give up, does he?" Smith said.

Beckmann just grunted.

Smith slowed to a halt, relieved to finally stop the grinding noise that was setting his teeth on edge. He swung out of the car and the dog came close to sniff his knee. Smith walked toward Karl and after a couple of steps he saw the mangled motorcycle on the side of the road.

"That yours?" Smith asked.

Karl nodded.

"Need a ride?"

Karl nodded.

Smith waved at the van. "Then help me get Warner out of the back of the van and into the car."

Karl lumbered into motion. Beckmann leaned against the van's front, smoking. He took the cigarette out of his mouth and waved it in Karl's general direction in greeting before returning it to his lips. He took the rental's key fob out of his pocket, pointed it at the car, and beeped open the trunk.

When Smith opened the panel van doors the scent of dried blood, sweat, feces, and urine assailed him. Warner remained unconscious. His eyes were closed and he didn't move. The regular rhythm of his chest indicated that he was still among the living.

"They worked him over pretty good," Smith said. Karl said nothing; Smith hadn't expected him to anyway. Together they maneuvered Warner toward the end of the van's cargo area and Karl lifted the man in his arms with surprisingly little effort. He disappeared around the panel doors and Smith scanned the interior. There was nothing in it that indicated who had owned it. It had been swept clean.

When Smith came back around to the rental he found Beckmann arranging Warner in the backseat, draping his legs over Karl, who sat on one side. When Beckmann was finished he waved the dog into the backseat foot well.

"Let's get out of here," Beckmann said.

Smith got behind the wheel and Beckmann joined him in the front passenger seat. Smith started the car, bumped up from the side of the road to the asphalt, and began a slow acceleration. Within minutes they were on a rural road passing through the forest and half an hour after that were making their way through the small darkened towns between there and Berlin. Smith had stopped at the sole intersection of a small town when he felt Karl tap him on the shoulder. When Smith checked the rearview mirror Karl jerked his chin at the door.

Smith stopped. Karl got out, gave a short whistle to the dog, and it followed, jumping onto the asphalt. Karl slammed the door shut and began a slow lumber toward a tavern a block away. When he reached it he opened a wooden screen door and waited for the dog to go in first before slamming it shut behind him with a gunshot report.

"Do we wait for him?" Beckmann asked.

Smith put the car in gear. "I don't think he's coming back. If he was he'd have left the dog with us." Smith pulled away, once again taking care not to jostle the car too much.

"Where are we headed?" Beckmann asked.

"To an airstrip outside Berlin. I've got the coordinates on my phone. There are two planes waiting there. One to take Warner and one for us."

"And from there?" Beckmann asked.

"To London. I've got a message from Klein. He says that they believe another victim is somewhere nearby and he's contacted Howell to help."

They drove on for another thirty minutes. After two wrong turns Smith was relieved to see a large expanse open up in front of him that contained a tarmac and two Learjets. Smith drove up to the first and killed the engine. A man detached from the shadow of the first plane and began a stroll toward them. It was Peter Howell.

22

Howell approached the car from the side and Smith saw him peer in the backseat and take in the sight of Warner lying there, unconscious. He tapped on the window.

"Smith, good to see you," he said in his clipped British accent. Educated at Cambridge and Sandhurst, Howell was former MI6 and a brilliant linguist and strategist. He claimed that he was "retired" and for part of every year he remained holed up in the Sierras, but Smith suspected that he took missions far more often than anyone knew. Witty and urbane, he was adept at altering his appearance to blend into whatever surroundings he encountered. For the moment, though, he was wearing dark pants, a navy windbreaker jacket, and what looked like black running shoes on his feet. While a wiry man, he was also an excellent fighter and had prevailed against much heavier opponents.

"I wasn't expecting to see you. They told us to hook up with you in London."

Howell shook his head. "I had to fly in over Germany anyway, and decided to meet you here so that I can brief you on the plane." He leaned into the window. "Beckmann! I heard you were hobnobbing with the rich and famous in rehab."

Beckmann grinned. "That I was."

"I also heard that you lowered the facility's success rate considerably."

This time Beckmann laughed. "As well as the quality of their clientele. Good to see you, Howell."

"Who's in the back?"

"The undersecretary of the U.S. Department of Defense," Smith said.

Howell raised an eyebrow. "So you found him. Excellent. There's an official escort here to ferry him home. Three members of the DOD. One is very officious and bureaucratic."

Smith switched off the car. Warner was still unconscious.

"Is he drugged?" Howell asked.

"We don't know."

Howell leaned in closer. "He's been tortured in a unique fashion."

"How can you tell that from here?" Beckmann asked.

Howell pointed at the soles of Warner's feet. "Generally you beat the soles so as to leave the victim without marks. But in this case the soles were slashed as well. Perhaps they were afraid he'd run away?"

"The torturer was a guy named Curry," Smith said.

"Ah, yes. The twisted Emil Curry. Once into a session he's unable to proceed methodically."

"He's dead," Smith said.

Howell raised an eyebrow in surprise. "Did you kill him?"

Smith just nodded.

Howell's expression turned to one of satisfaction. "I doubt anyone will miss the bastard. But the fact that he was involved in Warner's kidnapping bodes nothing good. He's usually seen in the company of some of the worst this world has to offer. You've had a busy night."

Smith nodded again. He wasn't about to dwell on the situation. He'd long ago come to terms with the strange and sometimes surreal nature of his work with Covert-One. Instead he reached into the backseat and began to maneuver Warner out. After ten minutes and with three of them assisting, they had Warner safely stretched out on a couch in the nearest Lear, where a deputy assistant from the DOD was fussing over him. While he did, Beckmann, Howell, and Smith boarded the other jet. They settled in while the plane taxied down the runway.

"What did you want to brief us on?" Beckmann asked.

"The situation in London. We learned that a DOD contractor in charge of the drone program may be held somewhere in the city. Perhaps even in the Mayfair neighborhood."

"Expensive. Not usually the type of place that you'd expect a terrorist cell to be found," Smith said.

Howell reached to a set of decanters secured in a cabinet against the plane's wall and poured himself a shot of what looked to Smith like whiskey. He held the bottle up to both Smith and Beckmann. Smith nodded and Howell poured shots around. He replaced the decanter and held his glass up before him.

"To success in our next mission."

They touched their glasses and Smith took a sip, welcoming the burn that cleared his throat and went a long way to sharpening his mind.

"And what mission is that?" he asked.

"To infiltrate and free Mr. Rendel from one of the most visible and guarded buildings in London without creating an international incident."

Smith didn't like the sound of that. "And what building would that be?"

"The Saudi embassy," Howell said.

23

Russell sat in the main ready room at RAF Croughton, a military base forty miles north of Oxford in Northamptonshire that the Brits allowed the United States to use for a broad swath of covert activities. The U.S. had been using Croughton as a base for its Unmanned Aerial Vehicle program operated out of Djibouti for a few years, but only recently had its role been expanded to include secure communications and spying for the Department of Defense and the National Security Agency. Russell watched a live-feed onboard video from a drone launched from Djibouti traveling to Yemen.

"What's its capacity?" Russell asked. Next to her stood George Scariano, a CIA officer in charge of the DOD forces at Croughton.

"It's an older-model Reaper. Four Hellfire missiles."

"Blast radius?"

He grimaced. "That remains a problem. It can be as large as twenty yards and the shrapnel can go even farther. If you fire four in a pattern you can take out an entire city block, easy. Collateral damage can be extensive. We've been taking heat from the international human rights community for the civilian deaths."

"Are you going to fire?"

"Yes, but we're just watching for the moment because under the administration's new rules the CIA can't target to kill. Only the military can do that, so we're linked to Camp Lemonnier in Djibouti and they'll give any orders required."

Russell watched the grainy video feed. Several people dressed in black, some with guns slung over their shoulders, were walking toward a tented encampment. As the drone grew closer she saw all six of them glance up at the sky.

"Can they hear it?"

"Yes. It makes a buzzing noise. In Pakistan they call them *machar*, which means 'mosquitoes.'"

The men began running toward the encampment. The image moved to home in on them and then she saw the flash of a missile launch. Seconds later all that was left of the encampment was a massive pit of burning fire. Clouds of dark smoke roiled into the air. The drone flew on.

Russell had killed more times than she cared to remember and had never hesitated to tear apart any attacker who threatened her. She had been beaten, shot at, knifed, and had set off plastic explosives that detonated entire warehouses. She was a warrior herself, and so she was surprised at the visceral, sick feeling that she felt at seeing the drone strike. The complete annihilation of an entire encampment, with all the people inside, within seconds, seemed surreal. She stared at the screen and struggled with her emotions. Scariano glanced at her with a sympathetic expression.

"From the look on your face I take it that you've never witnessed a drone strike before?"

Russell shook her head, unwilling to speak in case the shake in her voice would reveal her inner turmoil.

Scariano rubbed his forehead. "I've seen it so many times that I'm afraid its impact has been deadened. Which, frankly, worries me more than a little. Nowadays it's only when I see the strike through the eyes of a newcomer that I realize how sick and twisted it is. I just keep reminding myself that those guys on the ground wouldn't hesitate to kill droves of innocent civilians in their quest for vengeance."

"It's like watching a first-person shooter video game. It doesn't seem real," Russell said.

He nodded. "That's exactly the problem. I've got guys that will pull the trigger without any emotion. I worry that they could be convinced to wipe out entire villages without a thought. When I chide them they tell me that snipers and World War Two bombers did the same thing."

Russell shook her head. There was no real comparison between the two forms of war. "It's not the same. Both the bomber and the sniper are near the field of battle and both have some skin in the game, and I mean that literally. But here? Nothing. They sit in this windowless room in the bucolic English countryside and kill people on live screen while drinking coffee."

Scariano sighed. "I only hope that we don't strike without cause. I presume, though, that you're not here to discuss the ethics of drone warfare, are you?"

"I'm here because MI6 believes that there may be an American citizen being held in the Saudi embassy. We think they're preparing to rendition him to the Middle East for interrogation."

"Rendition him? So they're taking a page from our playbook and kidnapping people to send them elsewhere?"

Russell liked Scariano and his blunt assessment of the situation. No false patriotism or hypocritical bluster. She tried to respond in kind.

"Given all the condemnation we've taken for the program I'm surprised that they'd try it as well. Keeping the targets in an embassy cloaked with diplomatic immunity, though, is an elegant twist."

"I suppose that we've asked them nicely to return him?"

"Yes. We quietly met with them and told them that we'd had some intelligence pointing to a possible missing person being kept at the embassy and requested the right to search the premises. Our request was met with flat denials and faked outrage. I know that the NSA operates out of this air base for the *Stateroom* program and I thought you could help me."

"Our embassy surveillance operation," Scariano said.

"Exactly. I was wondering if we've seen any more information about the supposed hostage. MI6 suspects but can't confirm that someone is actually there."

Scariano waved her over to a second bank of computers staffed by several personnel, all wearing headphones and all typing madly.

"What are they listening to?" Russell asked.

"Transmissions from *Stateroom*-targeted embassies throughout Europe."

Russell raised an eyebrow. "I presume that doesn't include our allies."

Scariano didn't answer, but instead indicated a screen to the far right. "That one is focusing on a Saudi diplomat. We've been unable to bug the embassy, but we've targeted the junior staff and he's one."

"Heard anything that might help me out?"

Scariano tapped the officer on the shoulder and the man removed his headset.

"Tresome, this is Randi Russell, CIA. She's looking into a possible hostage scenario at the Saudi embassy in London. You got anything interesting for her?"

Tresome leaned back in his swivel chair. "Only that this guy, Ali Awahil, has been negotiating a large pharmaceutical purchase and he's arranging to make an announcement to be given at an upcoming conference on international standards for the approval of new drugs."

"Where's the conference?"

"Geneva in two days."

"And the pharmaceutical purchase?"

"Some sort of cognitive enhancement drug. Nothing illegal that we can determine."

"No talk of strange activity inside the embassy?"

Tresome rocked his hand back and forth. "There is one thing. Awahil seems to believe that a member of the diplomatic corps has been poisoned and he's pointing fingers at the CIA and a fake vaccine program. He said that Iran is involved as well."

"They always point their fingers at Iran," Scariano said "Their mutual hatred ensures that whatever happens, one will blame the other."

"Agreed, but the fact that he's also targeting the CIA is new and a measure of their unhappiness with the recent thawing of relations between the U.S. and Iran. And every time he talks about it he claims that they've caught the perpetrator and they've flown in a professional interrogator—you should read that as torturer—to gain a confession and that he was carrying out his questioning somewhere close. The other guy asked if it was at a safe house and he replied that it was the safest there was in London. Said no other country could touch it."

"That certainly describes a building cloaked in diplomatic immunity," Russell said.

"Your guy specialize in poison?" Scariano asked Russell.

"No. He's a mid-level software tech in the drone program stateside."

Scariano frowned. "Does he have access to passwords?"

"I hate to say it, but yes. I understand that they've been changed as a precaution."

Scariano pointed at the screens across the room. "Let's just hope changing them is enough. Can you imagine the destruction if a drone carrying missiles targeted civilian towns?"

After having just witnessed the drone strike, Russell didn't want to consider the possibility.

"It would be devastating. But is this vague information enough to justify a search-and-rescue mission on the Saudi embassy? What if they're truly hammering some terrorist that poisoned their diplomat? Torture is wrong, to be sure, but I'm not sure it justifies us going in guns blasting. And if we find him and claim outrage we'll look like hypocrites after our own rendition activities."

Scariano snorted. "You'd better not ignore it. If there's even a chance that they're holding a drone software guy you can be sure they're working on him to hack the system. Problem is, I don't see how the CIA could run a mission to get him. Going into Pakistan to get bin Laden was one thing; he was in a private home. If a CIA operative was caught infiltrating an embassy building the outcry would be enormous."

At this comment Russell laughed out loud. "You just told me we're bugging the hell out of them! So basically we've already infiltrated them."

Scariano grinned. "I told you that we've *tried* to bug them. We've only been successful at a handful of embassies worldwide, and most of those are located in New York. This particular embassy has eluded our microphones. But running a mission inside an embassy using a government-sanctioned CIA crew? That's not a good idea."

The crew won't be governmentally sanctioned, Russell thought. Instead she changed the focus. "What I can't figure out is to what end? The Saudis don't love us, this I know, but they're not our worst enemy by far. What could they have to gain by angering one of their biggest buyers of oil?"

Tresome looked up from the screen. "I can answer that. They're furious that we've opened a dialogue with Iran. It's the first time in thirty years that we have, and the Saudis want us to stop. What better way to sour the talks than to redirect a U.S. drone to strike at an Iranian town? Problem solved."

And a new, devastating war begun, Russell thought.

24

Darkanin watched Yang on his computer monitor as the other man gave a series of explanations about the upcoming hack of the U.S. drone program. When he was finished, Darkanin took a sip of his cognac.

"So can you do it or not?" Darkanin asked.

Yang frowned. Or at least Darkanin thought he did. Yang's inscrutability when under pressure was a quality that Darkanin would have loved to cultivate for himself.

"You've only given me half of the required passwords. The other half is missing."

Darkanin nodded. "You knew that going in. My partner told us from the beginning that no one person had the complete key to access as an administrator. The full password lies with several people."

"So kidnap the rest."

Darkanin shook his head. "That's impossible. I understood that if you received a portion of the access codes you would be able to hack the rest. Was I wrong? Or was that little show you gave me in Shanghai just that? A show?"

Yang inhaled deeply, which was the only indication Darkanin had that he was angry.

"Not at all. That was surveillance footage and proof that we can hack into the basic video functions. What the passwords will get us, though, is the ability to actually navigate the drones. Take over the dashboard and block the military pilots completely."

"So how long will it take to re-create the entire password?"

Yang pondered a moment. "Each password allows us access to a portion of the dashboard controls. From there we write code that can install a key-stroke reader and replicate virus into that small section of the program. As the virus expands and spreads it obtains more information and breaks through into other protected areas. Of course, getting all the passwords accelerates the hack, but even without them all each one that we do receive gets us deeper into the software and closer to the others. But doing it with only partial passwords takes time. Several more days at least."

"Make it two. That's all I have."

"And then? What will you do with it?"

Darkanin dumped the cognac into a small cup of Turkish coffee and took a sip while he thought about how to respond. His plan was simple and designed to reap the most benefits for his company that he could manage.

"That information is mine alone."

Now Yang looked annoyed, and in a perverse way Darkanin liked the man better. At least when he showed some emotion he seemed more real, less like a shell of a human being.

"I'm doing all the work and you're keeping the final results from me. That hardly seems right."

Darkanin had no intention of taking the conversation down that path. Instead, he changed the subject.

"When you hack the drone dashboard, will you be able to show me how to maneuver them to shoot? Will I see a live feed like you showed me earlier?"

"What I showed you was live footage from a Predator drone on surveillance duty. They fly low and slow, and can be taken out by a missile or even a high-powered rifle. Predators are worthless in a contested environment, and once we launch the hacked drones they will be in an *extremely* contested environment," Yang said.

Darkanin nodded. "I expect the full force and military might of several countries to be involved in stopping it."

"And so we need to think of a plan that would allow the drone to continue flying without interference."

Darkanin took another sip of his spiked coffee. He didn't want to reveal his entire plan to Yang. "I think I have that covered. Just stay on task and call me the minute you gain access to the main drone dashboard."

Darkanin rang off and clicked on the next in his contact list. A swarthy man dressed in the traditional Arab garb of a long white thobe with a red-and-white ghutra on his head came into view.

"Ali Awahil, how are things proceeding?" Darkanin asked.

The man grimaced. "We had to move matters to the embassy to avoid the NSA's eyes, which are everywhere."

Darkanin didn't like the sound of that. "What do you mean? Were they closing in on the first location?"

"Yes. Your Chinese friend intercepted some intelligence that a group is out hunting for the other missing Americans."

Darkanin sat up straighter. "Yang discovered this? I was just on the phone with him and he said nothing. What group?"

"I don't know. Stories are swirling that it is a shadow group of experts accountable to no particular regime."

Darkanin relaxed. This sounded like pure rumor.

"Who told you about this?"

"One of your crew. His name is Denon. He claimed that someone named Smith was able to activate contacts well beyond his usual role. Said the FBI and CIA came swarming out of their holes within minutes of an attempt to collect the man. Are you aware of this Smith?"

"Ahh, now I understand. Smith was one of the first subjects our Chinese friends tried to neutralize with the test drug. He's a microbiologist at USAMRIID. He got away, which has Denon angry, but I don't think Smith is anything special. He just had the good luck to have left a cocktail party that was crawling with various undercover agency types and they were nearby when the kidnap attempt went down."

"Why did you try to abduct Smith?"

Darkanin shrugged. "I didn't. My Chinese partners wanted the drug tested and to obtain some leverage over the United States. They were considering trying to grab Chang, but he was so heavily guarded that night they went for Smith instead. Was a good choice, because as a USAMRIID researcher he has knowledge about the U.S. chemical warfare program that could have been beaten out of him."

"Did it work?"

"The drug or the test drone?"

"Both."

"Yes and no. The drone operated well within its limited capabilities and the drug missed Smith and paralyzed the one it hit and he later died."

"That's a win, yes?"

"No. It was yet another uncontrolled reaction. We need the drug to work consistently so that Bancor's antidote can be tailored to reverse it, but individual reactions vary so widely that we can't be sure what to expect once it's disseminated. Added to that is the problem with efficacy. We spray it in a room or area and some people react and others don't. Most batches become ineffective within minutes of release, while a few others last longer. The only consistent result is that if an active lot is inhaled there will be a reaction."

Darkanin returned to sipping his coffee while Awahil pondered the information.

"I still don't like the rumors about the shadow team. My country can't be implicated in this matter. We need to appear completely innocent when the drug is released against our enemies. We want all suspicion to fall on others while we join them in our outrage at the use of a chemical weapon."

"Then you'd better not let anyone know what you're doing at the embassy. Be sure that the NSA can't reach you."

Awahil nodded. "The embassy is impenetrable. Whoever attempts to enter it without permission will die."

Darkanin certainly hoped so.

25

Smith, Beckmann, and Howell strolled down a street in Mayfair. Beckmann wore a baseball cap but Howell and Smith were hatless. They stopped at a busy intersection and Smith pointed to a large, rotating camera placed on a pole above the streetlamps.

"How many of those in the target area?" Smith asked. The camera swiveled on its base and the lens tracked around in a 360-degree rotation. Howell grimaced.

"There are six million cameras in the UK and thirteen thousand in the London Tube alone."

Beckmann gave a low whistle. "How many is that per person?"

"In the UK? One for every eleven citizens," Howell replied. "So you can be sure that when we go in, someone, somewhere, will be watching us."

"We can't have that," Smith said. "We'll have to disable them all."

"Or at least those around the embassy," Beckmann said.

Howell nodded. "I agree, but it's a dicey proposition. We need someone who can not only access the public network but also access, or at least minimize the impact of, the private cameras. Because, frankly, your friendly neighbor's security camera can be just as dangerous."

"Think Marty can do it?" Beckmann asked.

Martin Zellerbach was Smith's childhood friend and a computer genius. Zellerbach had Asperger's, and he had few friends growing up. Smith had protected him from the worst of the bullies; Zellerbach returned the favor by assisting Smith whenever he called.

"I can certainly ask. I have confidence in his ability to access a known, public network, like a government system, but I don't think he'll have the time or the resources to shut down every private camera."

Their stroll ended on another intersection and they turned left, headed to Hyde Park. On their right they came upon a high wrought-iron fence painted green with insets of gold-leaf palm trees. Beyond the fence a curved driveway intersected a rolling lawn, and beyond that sat a beautiful white two-story building. Two dark sedans, one a Bentley and the other a Maybach, were parked to the side. At the lot's front and at either corner stood two security guards in black cargo pants and polo shirts. Each carried a semiautomatic weapon, a pistol on his belt, and radio equipment strapped to his shoulder. Smith glanced up and saw the two closed-circuit television cameras mounted on each corner.

"CCTVs at every corner," Smith said.

"And probably more that we can't see from here," Howell said.

"Definitely one monitoring the front door," Beckmann said.

"Do you have a schematic of the house?" Smith asked.

Howell shook his head. "When the Saudis bought it they flew in their own construction crew to renovate the building from top to bottom. The renovation was unnecessary, so my sources told me that we can presume they swept the building for listening devices and installed their own state-of-the-art security. They were able to give me the broad outlines of what type of security is likely installed, but not the nuances."

They continued their stroll, walking past the structure and up a gentle incline until they reached the top of the hill. On the other side of a gently curving street was Hyde Park.

"Nice area," Beckmann said.

Howell nodded. "One of the finest in London."

"Are we sure he's in there?" Smith asked.

Howell looked thoughtful. "Our source isn't the best, you understand, but it has been explained to me that the facility contains a newly partitioned basement room where he might be housed."

"Who's the source?" Smith asked.

The light turned green and they walked across and into the park, dodging the bike riders and one lone runner. Howell waved them toward a small building.

"Ice cream is sold there, if anyone's interested." He looked at Smith. "I can't tell you the source, but I've heard that it's a reliable one. Someone who has weekly access to the facility and noticed that the basement room was occupied."

"I don't get it. What do the Saudis have to gain?"

Howell shrugged. "We're not sure. We think he may be a pawn in a larger game, or that they've been coerced into cooperating. Unlike Pakistan, they've generally been helpful to the United States, but they were angry at your president when he flew to Geneva and signed the interim nuclear abatement accord with Iran. They would have liked the U.S. to continue its hard line against that country."

Smith frowned. "The accord was one of the first signs of thawing of relations between Iran and the U.S., but that doesn't explain an attack against U.S. citizens and interests."

"I think they're simply stockpiling information and intelligence for the day that they might need it. They never expected us to learn that Rendel's been kept there," Howell said. "And if we do get him out we're supposed to be sure the world is kept unaware that he was there in the first place. Only the Saudis will know that we've taken him, and we'll hold that marker for the day that we need it."

"So how are we going to do this?" Beckmann said.

"I think our first call is to Marty. See if he can disable the cameras and learn anything more specific about the security system in place," Howell said.

Smith nodded, checked his watch, and pulled out his cell. "No time like the present." He dialed the number and Marty answered on the third ring.

"Jon! Hello! What do you want me to do for you?"

Smith smiled. The one good thing about Marty's Asperger's was that, being unable to understand the etiquette of polite conversation, he usually dispensed with the preliminaries and got right to the point.

"Is this line secure?"

"You mean is the NSA listening? No. I blocked them a long time ago. I don't understand the outrage over the spying thing. It's not like it wasn't apparent."

"Maybe to you, but not to the general population."

"It's safe to speak freely. What do you need?"

"I need to shut down the security system of a government building."

He heard Marty chuckle. "Like the courthouse in DC? Piece of cake." Smith turned off the main path and strolled across the grass to avoid having anyone overhear him.

"Like the Saudi embassy in London."

A long, low whistle came over the line. "That *is* big. And complex."

"Can you do it?"

"Yes, but it will take a while. Maybe as long as a week or two, and you'll need to get me some preliminary information to work with before I can start. Like which company handles their Internet and phone lines."

"Time is not on our side. How much can you do in twenty-four hours?"

The line remained quiet. Smith continued strolling and held his tongue, giving Marty a chance to mull the problem.

"How much information can you give me?"

Smith smiled. "Hold tight. I'll call you right back." He

hit the speed dial for Randi Russell. To his great surprise, she picked up. "I thought you went dark," he said.

"Not anymore, but I'm almost done here. What do you need?"

"All the information that the NSA has from their wiretaps of the Saudi embassy in London."

"No problem, but you don't need me for that since that government contractor dumped it all on the Internet. Just go and plug it in. I think by now the *Guardian* has released everything they've been given."

"I need it sorted, though. I don't have the time to read it all."

He heard Russell snort over the line. "Neither does the NSA, believe me. But I'll make a call and have a tech send what we've been able to catalog to you in a searchable format. And Smith?"

"I'm here."

"Whatever you're planning, I want in."

"Absolutely."

She hung up and Smith called Marty back. "I'll get you preliminary information in a couple of hours."

Two hours later Smith sat on a sofa in his hotel suite and sipped on a shot of whiskey as he stared at a laptop placed on the cocktail table. The screen displayed Google Earth views of the Saudi embassy from every possible angle. He clicked through the various elevations and overhead shots, searching for any wires, cameras, or antennas that would give a clue as to the technology being used inside. He cataloged the locations of any electrical generators, satellite dishes, and ductwork large enough for a man to crawl through. When he heard a knock on his door he stood and rolled his shoulders to release the tension there. After a quick glance through the peephole he opened the door and waved Beckmann in.

"Any luck?" Beckmann asked. He tossed a copy of the *International New York Times* onto the cocktail table. Smith sighed.

"None. The generators on the roof look to be standard electrical backups, the satellite dishes receive only television signals, and Marty told me that their Internet provider was a common company used by half of London."

Beckmann's face lit up. "That's good news, isn't it? Should be a breeze for Marty to hack."

Smith reached down for his glass and took another sip. "That's just it. He was into their system in no time, and what he found was absolutely innocuous. Seems nothing of any real consequence goes over the wireless lines. They must have a second secure system elsewhere."

Beckmann headed to the wet bar and scanned the assorted alcohol on offer. He chose a scotch and cracked the top.

"I took another stroll to the embassy. They change guards completely every four hours, and each set takes alternating fifteen-minute breaks every hour. Honestly, I think they're mostly for show. All it would take is one suicide bomber to toss a grenade over that fancy fence and there would be nothing those guys could do about it."

Smith settled back onto the couch, placing his feet on the cocktail table. The *Times* crackled when he plopped his heels on it, and he reached down and pulled it out from under his foot. The headline gave him pause. It showed a picture of Katherine Arden stepping onto the stairs of a private jet. She held her phone to her ear and a briefcase in her hand. The headline read HUMAN RIGHTS ATTORNEY ARRIVES FOR CONFERENCE. Smith sat up and read the short article that accompanied the headline. Beckmann lowered himself into a nearby chair and took a sip of his drink.

"Don't you find that scotch always tastes better when the agency is buying?" he said.

"Listen to this," Smith said. "'Katherine Arden, the attorney for several human rights watchdog groups and famous for her filing of a human rights case against the

Kingdom of Saudi Arabia, arrived in London today to take part in the second Global Conference for the Advancement of Human Rights. This will mark the first time that she has agreed to attend the conference, which, in an ironic twist, will kick off with a reception at the Saudi embassy. A representative for the embassy confirmed that an invitation was issued to Arden in the hope that "conversation in a setting less adversarial than a courtroom will lead to a clearer understanding of the cultural differences between the Saudis and other countries."'" Smith snorted. "Good luck with that. She'll never agree to go."

"You know her?" Beckmann asked. He slid down in his chair, put his feet on the cocktail table, crossed his ankles, and rested his glass on his stomach.

Smith nodded. "I do. She runs around quoting from the classics while she hits you with subpoenas and threatens legal action if you don't comply."

"Which classics?"

The Art of War," Smith said.

Beckmann tipped his glass in a toast. "My kind of woman. When's the party?"

"Tomorrow evening." Smith settled back against the couch. "I'm surprised the Saudis even bother with her. It's not as though they'll comply with any judgment against them." Smith sipped his drink while he stared at the photo. An idea started forming. He gave a short laugh and pointed a finger at the paper. "That's it."

"That's what?" Beckmann asked.

"That's how we infiltrate the embassy. We attend the reception. Once inside we conduct a reconnaissance operation to find Rendel." Smith stood and began pacing across the small suite.

Beckmann removed his feet from the table and leaned forward to pull the paper toward him. Smith watched him scan it.

"It seems as though the invitations were sent a while ago. How will you crash it?" he asked.

Smith was rapidly texting as he paced. "I'm contacting Howell and Russell. Perhaps between MI6 and the CIA we can come up with something."

"That line secure?" Beckmann asked.

Smith nodded. "All of our phones are secure, and we switch them up on a regular basis."

Smith's phone rang almost instantly and the display told him that it was Howell.

"Can you do it?" Smith asked without preamble.

"Perhaps, but you're forgetting something," Howell said. "MI6 will want to know who will use the invitation and why it's necessary. They're not just going to allow anyone to waltz into an embassy on a last-minute basis without a thorough vetting, and I can't exactly tell them that you're an agent from a highly covert organization that even the CIA is not aware exists." Smith's phone began beeping and he could see that Russell was calling.

"Russell's on the other line, when can you get here?"

"Twenty minutes," Howell said. He hung up.

"Tell me you can do this," Smith said to Russell.

"Three days ago I would have said absolutely, but that was before the attack in Turkey. Now every embassy is on high alert and no one gets in without a thorough check."

"Who's in charge of the guest list? Do you have an operative scheduled to be there? Maybe I can swap identities."

"It just so happens that we do have an operative working the room, but she's female. Your best bet is to go as a guest of an invitee. There are three who were allowed guests. Two have filled their spots, but one hasn't and that's Katherine Arden."

"Has she agreed to go?"

"She hasn't RSVP'd either way. Maybe you can talk her into it and go with her."

Smith was pacing again. "Under what pretense?"

There was a long pause. "How about you say that Fort Detrick deals with the bacteria and viruses that create rampant disease in third-world countries and minimizing the disease risk is a human rights activity."

"Do you know where she's staying?"

"She's at Brown's Hotel. Walking distance from yours."

"All right, I'm headed there right now. In the meantime, Beckmann and Howell are here. If you're anywhere close, join us. We could use your help."

"Be there in a bit." She hung up.

Smith shut down his phone and looked at Beckmann, who was gazing off into the distance with a thoughtful expression on his face.

"I'm headed to Arden's hotel to convince her to go to the function. In the meantime, can you and Howell start brainstorming some ideas on how to get me in there and back out in one piece?"

Beckmann nodded.

"You look grim," Smith said.

Beckmann rose and walked to the bar to splash some water into his scotch. "I don't think you can go in there alone. You'll need backup."

"We don't have the time to get more of us into that reception," Smith replied.

"So let me amend my statement. I just don't see how you can go in there alone and come out alive."

Smith had no reply to that. He shrugged on his suit coat and headed to the door.

"Wish me luck," Smith said.

"Luck. And tell this Arden lawyer, 'The price of inaction is far greater than the cost of making a mistake.'"

Smith paused. "Is that a quote?"

"Yes. Let me know if she recognizes it."

"Did the one who said it follow his own advice and choose action over inaction?"

"He did."

"And is he alive?"

Beckmann shook his head. "Dead as they come."

26

Darkanin sat in a hookah bar in London and inhaled the sweet-scented tobacco. Next to him Brian Gore smoked from his own pipe, and next to Gore sat two Arab computer hackers. Darkanin placed two photographs on the table.

"These men are here in London now and I want every step they take to be recorded."

The first hacker, named Asam, shifted the photos to face him. "Who are they?"

"This"—Darkanin pointed to the first—"is a man named Jon Smith. He's a lieutenant colonel in the U.S. military and a microbiologist. And this one"—he pointed to the next photo—"is named Andreas Beckmann. We're almost certain he's a CIA officer. At the very least he's an independent contractor taking jobs from the CIA. Whatever he is, we need to neutralize him."

"How do you know they're here in London?"

"An informant told us that they flew out of a small airstrip near Berlin after they delivered some precious cargo there."

The Arab took a long pull on the pipe. "You trust your informant?"

Darkanin nodded. "He's a bureaucrat with the U.S. Department of Defense and was there at the airfield when the cargo was delivered. I believe him."

"And when we locate them? Do you want us to take care of the problem?" the second hacker asked.

Darkanin shook his head. "I can't afford questions on

this one, so it has to be a perfect operation. Nothing slap-dash. You just tell me where they are and I'll decide on the next step."

Asam looked disappointed, until Darkanin slid an envelope across the table.

"To start you off," Darkanin said. "How long will it take to get a handle on them?"

Asam pocketed the envelope. "Twelve, maybe four-teen hours. We'll feed the photo into a face recognition program that will match it against recorded images from the twenty main intersections in London."

"That long?" Darkanin said. "I had hoped for some-thing quicker."

Asam shook his head. "Too many cameras and images for us to access before we can even run the program. And when we do we have to be sure that our hacking isn't no-ticed, so we'll accomplish it during routine system back-ups. Those are in the early hours. You'll need to be patient."

Darkanin nodded. "Fine. Do it."

Smith walked into the bar at Brown's Hotel and saw Arden sitting at a banquette in front of a wall of large black-and-white photo images. She had a drink in front of her and her head was lowered over a book. He waved off the host and paused in front of the table. After a mo-ment, Arden looked up and, after another short pause, one eyebrow quirked.

"When I said we should meet to discuss your find-ings, I didn't assume you'd fly thousands of miles to present them," she said.

Smith smiled and pointed at the empty chair across from her. "May I?"

She nodded and closed the book in front of her.

"What are you reading?"

She held it up for him to see.

"*The Conquest of Happiness*, Bertrand Russell," he read. "That's a classic." He pulled out the chair and sat down. Almost immediately a waiter was at his shoulder.

"May I offer you something? We have a complete list of drinks."

"Whiskey, neat," Smith said. The waiter looked disappointed and went off toward the bar. Smith watched him go and slanted a look back at Arden. "Is whiskey neat not on the list?"

Arden leaned forward. "They specialize in concoctions that take at least fifteen minutes to prepare. Whiskey neat is not one of them." She spoke in a low voice.

"Hmm. I'm not a fan of unnecessary complication. Especially when it comes to my alcohol."

Arden smiled. "I'm surprised to see you here. No, shocked. I mean, what are the odds?"

"I saw your picture in the paper."

A look of comprehension spread across her face.

The waiter brought the whiskey and a glass of water on a silver tray. He took time to place them in front of Smith, nodded, and left. Smith held his glass up to Arden before taking a sip.

She watched him, a speculative look in her eye. "The paper said nothing about where I was staying."

Smith put the drink down and decided to go straight to the truth. "I asked my friend to find you for me."

"The CIA friend?"

Smith smiled. "So you remember."

"Isn't that a violation of my right to privacy?"

Smith shrugged. "Not in any meaningful way. You're a human rights watch attorney in a foreign country headed to an embassy party. The recent bombing in Turkey ensured that everyone attending the reception tomorrow will be vetted. It's a precaution that I would think you'd welcome."

"There's not much that the CIA does that I welcome."

"You really should rethink that position. The CIA can be a very helpful organization."

"Really? To whom?"

Smith decided to let that go. He gazed around the room at the myriad framed photographs, many of nudes.

"Interesting work. Whose is it?"

"Terence Donovan."

"Dead?" Smith asked.

Arden nodded.

"How? The photos look as though they're from the sixties or seventies. Old age?"

Arden shook her head. "Suicide. Possibly induced by a drug." She waved her hand at the photographs. "He's been described as *the* photographer of the sixties. A time of upheaval, for sure."

"And decadence," Smith said.

Arden smiled. "Do I detect a hint of disapproval?"

Smith rocked his hand back and forth. "I've never had much use for decadent people. They indulge themselves and sap those around them."

"Perhaps they understand something that the rest of us don't."

"And that would be?"

"That we're going to die anyway, so all this striving and angst is just a waste of time."

Smith rolled his eyes. "That's a teenager's argument and I assume you don't agree with it, because you work very hard to change things. When I hear that rationalization from an adult I think of my friend from high school who became a Montessori teacher. She always said that sometimes people get stuck and don't 'move into the next plane of development.'"

Arden started laughing and her face lit with real amusement. She had a surprisingly joyful sound to her humor and Smith smiled along with her.

"Now, that's a very nice way of calling them immature idiots," Arden said.

Smith nodded. "She always was a nice person."

Arden tilted her head to one side. "What is it you want from me? I presume that it must be important for you to take the trouble to track me down."

"I want you to help me change the world."

Smith watched her face carefully. He'd hoped that he had read her right and his direct approach would work better than any carefully constructed lie, but he had no way of telling if it would overcome her disdain for organized government. He was worried that she would laugh at his sweeping statement, but she instead stared at him with a thoughtful expression. It was all he could do not to babble on, but rather to match her silence. So much was at stake, most of which he couldn't reveal to her, and he wanted her to help him despite her wariness.

"And how can I do that?" she asked.

"I'd like to go with you to the reception tomorrow night."

She shook her head. "I'm not going."

"Why not?"

She frowned. "I don't trust them."

"I can relate to that, believe me, but what concerns you? Despite what happened in Turkey, or actually because of it, I think security will be extremely tight and I doubt that you'll be in any danger."

She shifted uncomfortably in her seat and Smith got the sense that she was holding something back.

"Why do you want to go?" she said. He thought her question was a nice deflection from her real concerns.

"I spend a lot of time working on pandemic viruses and devastating bacteria. Sometimes samples go missing, as you know, and I would like to discuss a missing batch with them." Smith delivered his own deflection with equal aplomb.

"Does this have anything to do with my case and the drugged soldiers?"

"Not directly, though I would change that opinion if you determine that they were, indeed, drugged. Many black-market biological weapons circulate through the Middle East. I would like their assistance in flagging and confiscating them when they're found."

Smith's statement was factually correct, but Arden

seemed unconvinced and the wary expression was back on her face.

"So why not ask your CIA friend to engineer an invite? They'll have several people planted throughout the room, so I should think that inserting another wouldn't be tough."

"There's only one open invitation right now, and that's for your guest."

She stared down at her drink and Smith could almost hear the thoughts ricocheting through her head. She flicked her gaze back to him.

"If I take you will you produce the files of the four scientists at Fort Detrick who have been placed on medical leave?"

Smith paused. He knew that Siboran would likely ask USAMRIID's attorneys to attempt to appeal the court's order before handing the documents over.

"You're asking me to violate their rights without their consent. I'm surprised."

She shook her head. "Not at all. I have a court order, if you recall. HIPAA laws allow files to be released in response to a valid subpoena request. The medical leave files are covered by that subpoena."

"Siboran hasn't decided if USAMRIID will honor that order."

"It's not his decision to make. The subpoena is valid, therefore he must comply."

"He could challenge it on appeal," Smith said.

She nodded. "He could, but I can tell you from long experience that he'll lose. USAMRIID will be ordered to produce. What I'm asking now is for you to sidestep that fruitless waste of time and produce the files."

Smith had little doubt that she was right. She had far more experience in serving subpoenas than USAMRIID had in responding. Even though he knew that he would eventually have to hand over the files, he still wanted to preserve as much documentation as he could.

"If I did such a thing—" She sat straighter, her eyes

brightened, and he put a hand in the air. "Hold on. *If* I showed you those files, you would have to promise to keep them under seal as you've just described and to give USAMRIID notice before you introduce them at any trial."

She sat back again and some of the excitement left her face as she pondered. "I have to keep them protected anyway, and I only have to give the other side notice if I'm going to use them, not USAMRIID. You aren't a party to the court-martial."

"I know that, but if you want them you have to give USAMRIID the heads-up."

"So you can block their use at trial?" Arden said.

"So we can be prepared to show the affected parties the subpoena and explain why we needed to produce them."

"I promise to hold them under seal and to give USAMRIID advance warning before I use them, even though the subpoena allows their use. That's a better offer than even the HIPAA law requires, so you should take it." She watched him over the rim of her glass.

Smith knew he'd take it, but he still paused and drew out the moment before he gave her the answer she wanted.

He nodded. "You're on. When and where do I meet you?" He rose to leave and she stood with him.

"Here at six sharp. I have a car."

He put forty euros down on the table. "I was in Germany just before today and haven't had enough time to change money. Is it enough?"

She plucked them off the table and handed them to him. "I'll buy. Your assistance tonight was priceless."

Her comment left Smith uneasy, but he nodded and walked out, headed back to his hotel. He'd worry about the consequences of his deal after he made it out of the embassy alive.

If he made it out alive.

27

When Smith returned to his hotel room he found Howell, Russell, and Beckmann all staring at the embassy schematic laid out on the cocktail table.

"Did she agree?" Russell said.

"Yes, but she drove a hard bargain." Smith told them about Arden's demand for the medical records. "USAMRIID usually fights subpoenas on the basis of overreaching. While they don't always win, of course, they usually get some concessions. I've just given up the chance to argue against it."

Russell nodded. "For what it's worth, I think that she's right and the subpoena allows her to view those records. Do you trust her to keep them safe under seal?"

Smith sighed. "I don't really have a choice right now." He pointed at the schematic. "How's that going?"

"Not well," Howell said. "We've determined that there are at least ten obvious cameras and figure at least ten more that we can't see. Marty's been able to access seven. He says the others are operating on a separate feed and he can't hack it."

"What about your source?"

"Our source is a weekly cleaning person. She's actually an MI5 agent and she's held the housekeeping position for over a year. She said that there are three cameras that feed a video stream from the door to the lower level, the stairwell downward, and she suspects there is another at the base and in the actual room."

"Has she actually laid eyes on Rendel? Is she sure he's in there?"

Howell shook his head. "No. She only became aware of a possible prisoner after she saw a member of the household staff carrying a tray of food down the access stairs. She's never been able to sneak down there to have a look."

"I don't like the sound of that. It could be one of the Saudi prince's wives and we'll have gone through all of this for nothing." Smith looked at Russell. "What about your CIA officer plant? Does she know anything?"

Russell leaned against the bar counter and tapped on her phone. "I have an internal memo that analyzes the security they expect to have in place at the embassy. There will be a metal detector, of course, video surveillance, a crew of ten additional security personnel in addition to those on staff, and three tasters who will taste the Saudi embassy officials' food."

Beckmann snorted. "No tasters for the guests?"

"I guess they're considered expendable," Russell said.

"How about the kitchen? Can we plant someone there? Catering or wait staff?"

Russell shook her head. "I used the flower service to smuggle in a gun in Turkey, but we don't have any comparable assistance here. The Saudis have hired their own, well-vetted vendors."

Smith walked to stand next to Russell while he prepared a pot of coffee. "I never asked, what happened in Turkey? Were you close to the action?"

Russell nodded. "I was inside the building when the problems started, but never in any real danger."

Howell looked up. "Not in danger? Didn't the entire lobby blow up?"

Russell shrugged. "Well, not in danger the way that everyone in this room defines it."

"Interesting that we've dealt with two timed bombings in as many weeks. First you in Turkey and then Beckmann and me in Germany," Smith said.

Russell looked thoughtful. "You think they're linked?"

"Same strange behavior before the bomb went off," Smith said.

"Not exactly. The men in Turkey behaved oddly before they killed each other. You didn't have that in Germany, did you?"

"No, you're right. But I guess you could call Warner's amnesia odd. And then the bomb."

"Well, it's wise not to rule anything out," Russell said. "But I still don't think I was in as much danger as you were in Germany. The biggest problem we encountered was the smoke from the fires. It made it impossible to see anything."

Smith dumped some cream into his cup and swirled it with a swizzle stick. As he did he watched the beige liquid merge with the darker.

"Wait a minute. That gives me an idea. What if we were to create a distraction with smoke? Almost like a fog? If we could get it to fill the stairwell it might obscure the camera lenses enough to give me a chance to get down to the door below. Once there I could disable any obvious video feed at the source."

A slow smile spread over Howell's face. "There are several companies that have such fog machines as their security systems. They're actually quite common."

Russell pushed off the counter. "Is it actual smoke?"

Howell shook his head. "No. It's a fast-deploying fog system that fills a room in seconds and retains its density before dissipating. It's not toxic and is breathable. Almost like a mist. I know of several art galleries that use it. The theory is that they obscure any potential thief's view of the room while the alarm system dispatches the police."

"Is it installed with the security system then?" Beckmann asked.

Howell nodded. "Usually in a device placed below a window. When the alarm is finished you can open the window to help remove the fog at the source. But I'll bet we could send you in with a canister that you could toss to create the same effect."

"That doesn't really help us, though, because the metal detector will flag any canister he carries," Russell said. "And even if you got past that hurdle there's the internal security to worry about. They see you activate and throw a canister, they'll gun you down for sure."

Smith started pacing. He thought the idea had real merit if they could overcome the problems of the metal detector, the security guards, and the cameras. Quite a list, he thought.

"How long before the fog dissipates?" he asked.

"I'm not sure," Howell admitted. "But if we decide to use it I can find out."

"How will we use it? We need to get the device inside the embassy without triggering the metal detector," Beckmann said. He turned to Howell. "Can your housekeeper spy bring it in on a cleaning cart?"

Howell shook his head. "The crew cleaned the embassy yesterday. Today through tomorrow afternoon is left to set the dining tables and arrange the flowers. No cleaning. Besides, it's likely the security team will sweep the reception room before the guests arrive. If they do they'll discover it. Over the past year our agent tried to plant several small and ingenious listening devices and the Saudis found and disabled them all."

"We need to get it in place just before we use it," Russell said.

Smith kept up his pacing, stopping before the window that looked out onto a quiet London street. Several tiny sparrows flitted past to land on a nearby tree. He heard Beckmann chuckle.

"Got it. We fly it in," he said.

Smith turned to look at him. "Fly?"

Beckmann nodded. "This Rendel is in charge of the drone program, right? How about we get a drone to deliver the payload? Poetic justice. Do you have an idea of how large this canister is? Is it like a tear gas canister?"

Howell poured some hot water into a glass and dropped a tea bag into it before responding.

"I think the size depends on the amount of smoke you need. But I'm sure our engineers can get us one that's small but still quite effective. I must admit, I like the idea, but how will you get the drone inside the room? We still have the same access issue."

"Actually, we don't," Russell said. "I've seen drones as small as hummingbirds. Granted, they're not good for much, but they can stay aloft for ten minutes. If we made a drone that looked like a bird, a larger bird so that it could house the size motor that it would need to carry a heavier payload, we could fly it into the room as the door is opened for the incoming guests."

"And it would hover *above* the metal detector, and so wouldn't set it off," Beckmann said. Smith could hear the excitement in his voice and Smith's own spirits were rising with the suggestion.

"If a drone delivered the payload security would fire on it, not me. A scenario that I find to be infinitely more reassuring," Smith said.

Russell headed to the suite's door. "I'm going to a secure location and contact headquarters. I'm pretty sure we can have a smaller drone prototype here in a few hours. In the meantime, I'll leave the rest of you to work out the details." She strode out of the room, with her phone at her ear.

Smith sat down next to Beckmann. "Okay, let's run through a plan," he said.

28

An hour before the reception, Smith was dressed in a business suit and stood before Beckmann, Howell, and Russell, who had returned a few hours later to report that a drone would be programmed and delivered shortly. Beckmann waved Smith over and handed him a small pen-and-pencil set.

"What's this?" Smith asked.

"Unscrew the pencil."

Smith did and he saw that, instead of an ink cartridge, the pencil housed a small lock pick set.

"I don't know how to pick locks," Smith said.

"Unscrew the pen," Beckmann instructed. Smith did, and found that it housed a small, thin tube with an LED tip and a thicker base. "It's a camera lens. Press the button on the end and it will begin to record images. You use the pick set to move aside any tumblers on an average keyhole and then insert the camera. We'll be watching on this end. If anyone's in the room, we'll see it, record it, and use the feed to raise holy hell with the international community until Rendel is released."

"Will I be wired for sound?"

Russell stepped up. "Initially, yes." She handed him a small device the size of a pencil eraser. "That goes in your ear and acts a bit like a hearing aid. It will both send and receive audio to our computers here." Russell indicated two laptop computers that sat on a folding table. Both had large flat-screen monitors and speakers.

"Who will be manning the computers?"

"Beckmann and I," Russell said. "We debated giving you a video feed device as well, but it's just too risky. Likewise we'll only speak to you when we have to. We have little doubt that they'll be continuously sweeping for bugs during the length of the party, and if you're discovered wearing any type of device there would be no way for you to talk your way out of an accusation of spying."

Smith held up the tiny earpiece. "Then what about this?"

"It's a risk, but a small one. You can legitimately claim that it's a hearing aid. We've devised it to be identical to an actual hearing aid that's on the market now."

"But if you see any type of sophisticated sweeping equipment, you may want to toss it. We have other ways of watching you," Beckmann said.

Smith raised an eyebrow. "How?"

"Marty's tied together a feed from the seven cameras that he was able to access. Take a look." Russell jutted her chin at the computers. Smith walked around and saw that the first computer screen was broken into several quadrants, and each displayed activity occurring at the embassy's entrance. He watched as a guard walked into the frame and then was picked up by the next camera. None of the cameras, though, captured any images from the embassy's interior.

There came a knock on the door and Russell peered through the peephole before opening it. A man dressed in a hotel uniform handed her a large carton.

"Delivery for Mr. Smith," he said. She stepped aside and Smith signed for the box, tipped the man, and closed and relocked the door. Russell placed the box on the cocktail table and they all gathered around while she used a letter opener to slit the tape and move aside protective bubble wrap.

Nestled inside the box was what looked like a radio-controlled device in the shape of a falcon, with a broad wingspan and a curved beak. Russell carefully lifted it from a nest of tissue and held it up for all to see. In its talons it held a small canister the size of the pneumatic canisters Smith sometimes used at his bank's drive-in facility to send his checks to a waiting teller.

"It's gigantic," Smith said.

"Looks like a bald eagle," Beckmann said.

"Someone at your headquarters is a patriot, but should they have announced the identity of the maker in such obvious terms?" Howell asked.

Russell sighed. "I think it was supposed to resemble a raptor. Or a vulture."

"At that size there's a real possibility that security will shoot it down long before it gets through the entrance," Smith said. "If it even makes it through the entrance with that wingspan. What's the usual clearance in a doorway?"

Russell stared at her phone. "According to their email the guys are assuming a single door, not a double, and the usual thirty-two-inch opening. They say that I'll have to figure an inch less to accommodate the door hinges. The bird, whose name is Lawrence by the way, after Lawrence of Arabia"—Howell groaned and Russell ignored him—"has a twenty-inch wingspan, can fire two rounds of nine-millimeter bullets from a belly-mounted magazine, and his beak contains a laser glass etcher and is made from a high-tensile metal that can be used to batter the device through two panes of weakened glass and the average hollow, pressed-wood doors." Russell snorted. "They go on to tell me that they suspect that the embassy doors are likely *not* cheap pressed wood, but the windows do not appear to be triple-paned."

"Are you flying this thing?" Smith asked.

Russell nodded. "Howell will have it in the trunk of the car and get it in position near the embassy." She continued reading her email. "The eyes contain two lenses"—Russell leaned closer to stare at Lawrence's head and Howell, Smith, and Beckmann moved in as well—"that will record and send images and not only supply an accurate view of the area but also display a grid detail to help me pilot it through the opening."

"They're likely to shoot Lawrence down before you have a chance to get him in place," Smith said.

"If so, then abort mission," Howell said. "Finish the reception and come back out alive. We'll find another way in."

Russell handed Smith a small pen.

"Another pen? I'm going to look like an engineer. All I need is a plastic pocket protector and I'll be all set," Smith said.

"It's the detonator," she said. "You press on the cap, just as if you were intending to use it to write, and that will activate the smoke. Once you do, wait ten seconds for the room to fill. From there you have three seconds to open the door to the stairs. The smoke will fill the hall; our engineers think it will take at least another eight seconds for the hall to be filled enough to obscure the video on the stairs."

"How long before it begins to dissipate?"

Russell rocked her hand back and forth. "That's a tough question to answer. A lot depends on how quickly the security team responds, whether or not they fling open a window or adjoining doors. If they do nothing, the smoke will begin to clear about five minutes after deployment and adequate visibility will return after ten."

"That's not very long," Beckmann said. "So you need to be prepared to have your reconnaissance done and your cover story prepared for when the smoke is gone and the cameras find you where you're not supposed to be."

"In the meantime, Howell will be positioned at the top of the hill, across from Hyde Park. He'll pick you up," Russell said.

Smith raised an eyebrow. "How will you manage that without Arden getting suspicious?"

"We've been able to access the car service that Arden is using. I'll be driving you and Ms. Arden. I'd wait closer, but I'd rather not be caught idling on any CCTV cameras. The area I've chosen is a blank zone, at least as far as we can tell."

"Has the CIA operative been briefed on the plan?"

Russell nodded. "To the extent that she can be, she has. She doesn't know who the other operative is in the room and she thinks you're a member of the CIA, not Covert-One. Her orders are to scream and faint during the melee in order to create another distraction. Like you, she has no gun, but she does have a detonator pen as a backup should yours get confiscated."

"Let me repeat the specs to you one more time," Smith said.

Russell nodded. "Go ahead."

"The door to the lower level is on the northwest wall. From there I enter a narrow hallway and take ten steps down. We don't know which door down there houses the prisoner, but there are at least two that I need to check: one left and one right."

"And remember, the plans don't show it, but Marty's been able to pinpoint on a neighbor's CCTV camera the embassy's back exit door. It's possible that you'll be able to access that exit from the lower level as well. There's a two- or three-step riser before the back door, so it's also possible that there will be a window in the room that accesses the outside. Kind of like a basement apartment," Russell said.

"But Marty didn't see a window, right?"

"That's right. Not a window, or bars on a window, so we're speculating as to this last bit."

"Got it," Smith said.

"Ready?" Howell placed a chauffeur's cap on his head to complete his somber private-driver uniform. Smith nodded and they left the hotel and turned a corner. Howell stopped and beeped open a black car parked in a handicapped parking spot.

"Which one of us is handicapped?" Smith asked.

"Me. Old war wound," Howell said and then grinned.

"Does it bother you much?"

"Only when it rains."

"Rains a lot in London," Smith observed.

"Which is why I spend most of my time in the Sierra Nevada," Howell replied.

Smith settled into the car and Howell started it. He stopped a block before Brown's Hotel.

"I'll let you walk from here." Howell consulted his watch. "She's requested the car for six o'clock, so expect me then."

Smith nodded, got out, and headed down the street at a leisurely pace that belied his inner turmoil. The mission bothered him on so many levels that he didn't know which problem to focus on first: the security guards, the massive drone with its payload, or the fact that he'd be watched every step of the way by somebody, whether on the street or in the embassy building.

He stepped into the hotel lobby and saw Arden standing in the center. She wore a dark-blue sheath dress in a material that shimmered with a short jacket over it. She smiled at him with real warmth and for a moment he forgot who she was and what she did and that nothing would make her happier than to hang the deaths in Djibouti on USAMRIID. He shook off his sudden empathy and put back his shoulders. He had important things to do this evening. He handed her a piece of paper.

"The list of USAMRIID employees currently on medical leave," he said.

Arden raised an eyebrow and scanned the list, nodded once, folded the paper, and put it in her evening bag.

"Thank you," she said.

He held his hand out to her. "Shall we go?"

29

Darkanin was putting on his suit jacket when his phone buzzed. The display read "Unknown Caller." He answered.

"Did you find him?" he asked.

"I never discuss business over a phone, and you shouldn't either," the caller said. Darkanin recognized the voice as Asam's.

"My phone's secured by the finest security personnel in Shanghai."

"Nothing that uses the airwaves is secure. Your friends in Shanghai should have told you that. Meet me at my apartment in ten minutes and we'll talk."

Darkanin consulted his watch. "I have a function to attend in thirty."

"I know. But the apartment isn't far. It's above the bar where we met last. Number four."

Asam hung up.

Ten minutes later Darkanin ascended a stairwell lit by weak wall sconces. As he did, the pulsing music from a dance club that shared a common wall receded. He reached the third-floor landing and knocked on the door to his left. After a moment it slowly opened to reveal Asam, in jeans, a white shirt with the top button undone, and bare feet. He stepped aside and Darkanin entered.

The small studio apartment was devoid of furniture except for a narrow table in the attached dining area and a small, low cocktail table in the living area. Cabinets lined the far wall to Darkanin's right and below them was

a counter with a built-in dishwasher and a refrigerator. A large Oriental carpet covered the wood floor, and two rolled sleeping bags along with pillows were shoved to one side under a bank of windows to the left. A hookah pipe sat on the cocktail table and a laptop computer whirred from its location on the kitchen table.

"Not much here," Darkanin said.

Asam shrugged. "It's a safe house, nothing more. The authorities come and I can be gone in an instant. I found your man." Asam walked over to the laptop and pointed at the screen. Darkanin joined him and raised an eyebrow. A frozen frame showed a man, lean and tall with the ramrod posture of a member of the military. The face matched the picture of Smith that Darkanin had given Asam.

"Nice work. Where was this taken?"

"Just over a mile away." Asam bent down and scrolled through a set of still photos, stopping at another. This one showed only Smith's back as he stepped into Brown's Hotel.

"Where is he now?"

Asam clicked on another screen and the action changed from a still photo to a video feed. In it Darkanin saw a line of cars idling in a row.

"What's that?"

"The queue to get into the Saudi embassy."

Darkanin smiled. "That's where I'm going. So Mr. Smith and I will be at the same event tonight? How ironic."

"I presume that now you intend to take him out?" Asam asked.

Darkanin shook his head. "Not just yet. At least not until after the reception. If he's expected there then it would raise alarm bells if he doesn't appear. Afterward he can be taken out quietly."

Asam turned to a nearby kitchen cabinet and opened it. He pulled out a black holster and slid from it a long knife with a wicked-looking, narrow blade. To Darkanin it looked like a knife for gutting fish.

"This is for you," Asam said. "Slip it between his ribs after he leaves the party and leave him to silently bleed out." He slid the knife back into its sheath and held the holster out for Darkanin.

Darkanin shook his head. "Oh, no. Absolutely not. If anyone attacks him it will be you. I hired you to handle this, not to push it off on me."

"Is the big CEO afraid to do his own dirty work?" Asam's voice held a nasty, goading tone.

What an asshole, Darkanin thought. "What about the ten thousand dollars that I gave you didn't you understand? I don't pay that much for a couple of photos. I pay that much for a job completed. You were to find Smith and Beckmann."

Asam indicated the computer monitor. "Beckmann is next, but I found Smith. That's what you wanted, so I've earned half my fee. You'll be at the same party, so it just makes sense that you would follow him out the door and find the right time to take him out while he walks home."

Darkanin felt his anger rising. "I'm the CEO of a well-respected pharmaceutical company! The killing can't in any way be traced to me."

Asam gave Darkanin a wry look. "Fine, then I'll kill him. But as you can see"—Asam indicated the idling car—"he has a driver. I'll need to follow the car and kill both him and the driver. You never paid me for any of this, so the job will cost more." At that moment the limo driver exited the car, walked to the passenger door, and opened it. From what Darkanin could see the driver was older, possibly in his fifties, and lean to the point of being skinny.

"The driver doesn't look like much. He'll be a breeze to knock off," Darkanin said.

"I wouldn't be so sure. Limousine drivers always carry a gun in the car," Asam replied.

"That's in the States, not in London. Here they don't."

"Still, I'll need eight thousand more for the driver."

At that moment Smith emerged from the passenger side of the vehicle and seconds later a woman as well. She kept her head turned from the camera and Darkanin frowned.

"Who the hell is that?"

Asam glanced at the screen. "Presumably his date. She'll need to be killed as well. That's another eight, so now it's sixteen thousand to you."

The woman turned to face the camera and Darkanin stilled. Asam noticed his sudden silence.

"What? You know her?"

Darkanin pulled himself together. Suddenly the additional cost paled in comparison with the result. In one evening Asam could solve several of Darkanin's problems at once. Still, he would continue to act outraged. It might help keep costs in check.

"That's more than double the agreed-upon price! What in the world makes you think that you can simply raise your stated fee?"

Asam looked supremely bored with the conversation, which irritated Darkanin even further. The lying, stinking assassin didn't even care enough to get angry.

"Then you should take the knife and do it yourself. It makes no difference to me if they live or die," Asam said. He strolled to the sleeping bags, reached down, grabbed one of the nearby pillows, and tossed it next to the cocktail table. Then he lowered himself onto it and crossed his legs into a lotus position. He picked up a lighter off the table and used it to light the tobacco in the pan. He put the pipe to his lips in preparation to smoke.

Darkanin wanted to knock the pipe out of his mouth and punch Asam in the face. He was astonished at the man's audacity. Who did he think he was dealing with? At that moment Darkanin knew that as soon as the job was finished, he would arrange for Asam to be finished as well. He'd have a video taken while it occurred so that he could revel in the slaughter. Darkanin smiled in anticipation. *You'll regret the moment you decided to cross* me, he thought as he watched Asam inhale a mouthful of smoke.

"Fine. Sixteen thousand, but only after you prove to me that Smith is dead."

Asam looked at him through slitted eyes. "Pay me now."

Darkanin shook his head. "Half now, half when you bring me proof."

"Pay me now," Asam said.

Darkanin shook his head. On this he would remain firm. He knew, without a doubt, that if he paid it all up front Asam would take the money and never follow through.

Asam shrugged. "Then do it yourself."

Darkanin had had enough. "I'll get someone else to handle it. Clearly you're not as qualified as everyone told me." In one step he was at the door and turning the handle.

"Wait," Asam said.

Darkanin paused, waiting for what he knew he would hear.

"Fine. Half now and half when it's done, but be ready with the money and close by. I don't want to remain in London a second longer than I have to."

Darkanin opened the door. "Don't worry. I'll be at the same reception, remember?" He paused.

"And leave that fish knife somewhere close to the embassy. I'll retrieve it when I leave the reception and have it ready should something go wrong."

Asam blew out the richly scented smoke and leveled a stare at Darkanin. "Don't insult me in this fashion. I've killed many, many times before. Everyone from U.S. Army Rangers to Israeli Mossad. One simple soldier, his driver, and a woman will be easy."

"I still want the knife ready."

Asam shrugged. "As you wish."

Darkanin closed the door behind him and headed down the stairs into the night.

30

Howell pulled up outside the embassy and turned to Smith and Arden.

"It's close. The line of cars is blocking the view. I hope you don't mind walking. It's only half a block but would save me half an hour in gridlock."

"Of course not," Smith said.

Howell got out and opened the passenger door. He handed Arden out first and stepped back to allow Smith to emerge.

"I'll see you after the party?" he said in a low voice.

Smith nodded, put a hand on Howell's arm, and joined Arden on the sidewalk.

"Ready?" he said.

She had been unusually quiet during the short ride to the party. Now she walked next to Smith and kept her right hand in her pocket as they walked to the entrance.

The embassy's elaborate wrought-iron gates were thrown open and flanked by two armed guards, each with a semiautomatic rifle slung over his shoulder and wearing black cargo pants and a matching shirt. A line of partygoers stretched from the portico across the driveway and lawn to the sidewalk. Smith and Arden joined the line and began the slow shuffling progress toward the entrance.

"Can you see what the holdup is?" Arden asked.

Smith stepped out of line to get a better angle into the doors. From there he could see that the guests were lining up in front of reception tables manned by embassy personnel. Guests spoke to the greeter, and then began to fish in their pockets to retrieve wallets. Smith watched as the embassy staff checked the offered identification before allowing the guests to move to the next table, where they were issued name tags. After pinning on the name tags, the guests were allowed to move deeper into the building.

Smith took advantage of the new angle to check out the entrance opening. The first bit of luck was that both doors were thrown open, creating a nice, wide expanse for Russell to pilot the drone through. Smith could see an elaborate chandelier hanging from the ceiling on a chain. The crystal drop pieces sparkled, throwing light rays around the foyer. Smith estimated that once Russell guided the drone through the doors she would have to fly it around the chandelier; it looked somewhat difficult but he presumed the device would be able to navigate around the piece. He stepped back into line to tell Arden what he'd seen.

"It's the usual check-in bottleneck exacerbated by the fact that they're requesting identification before allowing anyone to continue," Smith said. From somewhere deep inside the foyer there was a periodically recurring buzzing noise. Each time this occurred, the line stopped moving briefly before resuming its slow progress.

"What's that noise?" Arden asked.

Smith shook his head slowly. "I'm not sure. I couldn't see that far into the foyer to tell."

They shuffled a few steps closer to the doors. After ten more minutes of the shuffle-and-wait procedure, Smith and Arden had bisected the drive and were within ten feet of the main entrance. Smith watched as the embassy staff worked silently and efficiently, checking identification and waving the guests to the next stage with a smile. The periodic buzzing, the slowing of the line, and then the resumption continued. After a couple of minutes more Smith could see far enough down the queue to discern the cause of the sound. Two black obelisks, about three feet high and eight inches wide, were placed on either side of the open entrance into the main living areas. When certain guests walked past the obelisks they would light up and emit the buzzing sound that he and Arden had been hearing.

"Metal detectors," Arden said in a flat voice after she spotted them.

"Yes," Smith said. "It's the least we should expect."

He watched the detector light up when a man stepped through. Whenever this happened, a guard would use a wand and run it over the guest's clothes. Most of the time it appeared as if the women's jewelry was the culprit.

They shuffled a bit closer. The obelisk went off again.

"I think you should know that I have a gun in my right jacket pocket," Arden said in a voice so low that Smith could barely make out the words, which was why he at first was unsure that he had heard her correctly.

"What did you just say?"

Arden leaned into him and put her mouth to the ear in which he'd placed the listening device and said, "I have a gun in my right jacket pocket."

Beckmann was leaning back in his chair drinking a cup of coffee and watching the line of people snake from the embassy doors when he jumped at Arden's suddenly loud voice as it echoed in the room. Russell sat at the computer next to him concentrating on the small handheld mechanism that would pilot the drone and she looked at Beckmann in surprise.

"Was that Arden?"

Beckmann nodded. "Woman's crazy. She brought a gun."

Russell put the controller down and rolled her chair next to Beckmann. His computer screen showed a close-up of Smith and Arden. Smith wore a furious frown on his face and Arden kept glancing from him to the doorway.

"She's nervous as hell," Russell said.

Beckmann snorted. "She should be. In thirty seconds she's going to pass through those metal detectors and all holy hell is going to rain down on her."

"What does she hope to accomplish?" Russell asked.

At that moment Arden leaned once again into Smith's ear and both Beckmann and Russell bent their heads closer to the speakers to catch what she said.

Smith took a moment to digest Arden's astonishing information, standing still and staring at her while the line moved forward. He felt a slight touch on his arm, which snapped him back to the present. It was Arden, indicating that he should close the gap between them and the guests in front. Smith did, and put his lips to Arden's ear.

"Why in God's name did you bring a gun? You had to know they'd have heightened security."

She nodded. "I want them to discover it. I think they should know that I'm armed and able to take care of myself."

The line shuffled, bringing him and Arden within ten feet of the initial registration table.

"That's insane," he whispered, putting as much emphasis into the word "insane" as he could given the sotto voce way in which they were communicating. "They'll have you arrested. At the very least they'll pull you aside and interrogate you regarding your intentions, perhaps for hours. What can you possibly hope to gain from this?"

They shuffled closer and stood one couple back from the initial security check.

"Oh, I intend to tell them about the gun. I'll explain that I go nowhere without it. I think they should be aware of that fact in all of their future dealings with me."

Smith was scrambling to find a way to salvage what was soon going to be a disaster. "Do you have a permit to carry concealed?"

She gave him an exasperated look. "In the States? Of course. Here? No. But does that really matter? I simply intend to send them a message. They had better not get the idea that they could arrange my 'disappearance' without me putting up one hell of a fight. I told you I didn't trust them," Arden said.

Smith kept his eyes on the couple in front of them while he tried to come up with a way to get rid of the gun without anyone noticing, but there were no bushes nearby, another couple stood directly behind them, and two guards stood sentry on either side of the entrance, never taking their eyes off the line.

"Yes, but you didn't tell me you had a death wish," Smith said. He was hissing the information close to her ear. "They find a gun and you'll be arrested, questioned, and likely charged with spying. How could you have been so shortsighted?" The couple in front moved past the registration table and prepared to step through the metal detector.

"I know how to shoot," Arden said. "And being a human rights attorney means that I have to subvert tyrannical power every day and take actions that make a clear statement that business as usual will not be tolerated. That's what I'm doing now."

"Spoken like a true dissident and arrogant to the core." Smith did his best to smile at the men behind the registration desk while he whispered at Arden.

The couple in front walked through the metal detector without incident. It was Smith and Arden's turn.

31

I'd better get this bird in there fast," Russell said.

Beckmann placed a hand in the air to stop her. "Howell's not in place yet. Let's see if she gets tagged. If so, and they grab him along with her, then there's no call to use the drone."

Russell shook her head. "That's not true. We still have the operative available and she has a detonator pen as well. I'll give her instructions to detonate and head down the stairs. She can take over the main project while the guards interrogate Smith and Arden."

A small quadrant of the computer showed Howell driving away. After a moment he disappeared from the screen entirely.

"I'm in place." Howell's voice echoed in the room.

"So am I," Russell said. "Let me know when you've got the drone out of the trunk and ready to fly."

"It's out. I'm holding it up in the air," he said.

Russell put a headset microphone on her head, her hands on the controller, and activated the drone. A light on the controller turned from red to green.

"The motor just switched on," Howell said. "It's vibrating."

Beckmann rolled his chair next to Russell to watch the proceedings. She carefully flew the bird higher until it was two stories above street level and clear of most of the lower buildings in Mayfair. She switched on the GPS and the bird rose even higher and made a graceful turn to the left. Russell sat back.

"I've plugged in the coordinates for the embassy's side yard. Right now it's on autopilot."

"How does it avoid obstacles?" Beckmann asked.

"It works on a lidar system, which means 'light detection and ranging.' Kind of like an advanced sonar. Once it's there it's programmed to hover until I take over."

"I'll tell Smith," Beckmann said. He rolled back to his console. "The bird is up. Fifteen minutes until the battery gives out. Be ready." He saw Smith nod.

"He got the message."

"Get ready, we're off auto," Russell said.

Beckmann moved to watch her. She began piloting the bird lower. Through the grid display he saw the embassy's wall appear. Trees, power wires, and light poles appeared in fuzzy outlines and each time the bird came within a foot the lines began blinking, slowly at first and then faster as the bird flew even closer. Russell piloted it around the building and stopped it, setting it to hover once again. She lowered the camera lens to focus on the front door. It was closed.

"Shit. They closed the door even though the line continues. What's that all about?" Russell said.

As she spoke the door reopened, and the next couple was escorted inside. The door closed behind them.

"They're opening it for each. I wonder why the sudden change in procedure?" Beckmann said.

"Whatever it is, we can't wait, because we'll run out of battery. I'll need more time than those few seconds that it's open to maneuver through the entrance. I'm going to have to pilot it around the corner and use the laser etcher to weaken the glass on a window. Can you find out from Marty which window has the fewest eyes on it? Human or otherwise?"

Beckmann returned to his desk and began typing a message to Marty, who pinged him back almost immediately.

"He says west wall. The sentries are busy watching the front and rear of the building and the nearest camera that he can see is set up at the lawn's perimeter and far from the action." Beckmann rolled his chair back over to watch Russell maneuver the drone.

Russell flew the bird higher, turned it, and piloted it around the building. She cleared the west end of the structure before starting the descent toward the window. None of the guards on the ground looked up.

"Why not fire the bullets through the pane? Then you can hammer it through the opening."

"Too loud. And there's a risk that the bullets will hit someone."

Russell had the drone in place before the window. She activated the laser etcher and it hit the glass with a tiny, laser-pointed LED. The bird wobbled as it did. Russell found it difficult to move the drone while the laser option was activated. It was as if the bird was pushed backward from the force of the light beam when it hit the glass, and it kept wobbling out of position.

"Lawrence looks drunk," Beckmann said.

Russell didn't respond but kept at it, doing her best to hold the bird in place yet move it in increments to cut a line and weaken the pane.

"You've got ten minutes of battery power left," Beckmann said.

Smith and Arden started up the stairs to the entrance. Smith made a last-ditch attempt to dissuade her from entering.

"You're a weekend warrior and you have no business bringing a gun here. Guns should be kept in the hands of professionals. Military and law enforcement," he said.

"Now who's arrogant? Just because I've armed myself doesn't mean—"

"—Names and identification, please." The first man behind the registration desk spoke to Smith.

"Katherine Arden and guest Jon Smith." Arden stepped up next to Smith and smiled at the man, who bent his head to review a typewritten list. Smith handed his passport to the second guard, who looked at it and then took Arden's for review.

Smith's mind was racing while he thought of and then discarded possible scenarios. Tossing the weapon was out, as was distancing himself from her. As her guest, he would likely be detained for questioning as well.

"I'm going to ring your phone. Pick it up and use it as an excuse to step out of line and buy some time." Smith heard Beckmann's voice in his ear. Seconds later his phone began vibrating in his jacket pocket and he placed a hand on Arden's arm to stop her from moving forward. He pulled her a little to the side.

"Excuse me. This may be important," he said to the men flanking the detector. "Smith here," he said into the phone.

"Abort mission. Leave now. Let the nutcase handle this one alone," Beckmann said.

"I'm not sure that's a worthwhile choice," Smith said in a careful voice. Arden watched him with an intensity that made him nervous.

"They find that gun and you're both detained indefinitely. Abort mission."

"I'll meet you inside," Arden said.

"Wait." Smith shut off the phone and jumped ahead of her. "Allow me." Arden gave him a suspicious look, which he ignored, and he stepped around her and through the metal detectors. They buzzed.

"Sir, place your phone in the bowl," the sentry on the left said. Smith nodded, removed his phone from his pocket, and placed it into a small bowl proffered by the guard. He tried a second time and was through without a beep.

Now it was Arden's turn. Smith retrieved his phone, which was rattling with an unknown caller that Smith was fairly certain was Beckmann, and slid it back in his suit pocket without answering. He moved in closer to the edge of the detector's area and waited.

Arden lifted her chin and her face wore a determined

expression. She stepped through the metal detectors and they shrieked their unmistakable positive warning. Smith moved up next to her and slid his foot against hers in a brushing motion, literally sweeping her foot off the ground.

Arden made a small noise and began to fall and as she did Smith caught her in his arms, wrapping one around her torso and placing his hand on her waist above the right jacket pocket. He slid his hand into the pocket, grabbed the weapon, and then pretended to lurch with Arden's weight. He let his knees collapse and they went down. Smith twisted to take the brunt of the fall onto the hard marble floor. He landed on his side with her facing him and clutched tight. His hand was still on the gun in her pocket and under their bodies pressed against the floor. Smith slid the gun up and between them and continued until it was under his jacket. He placed it in his waistband. When he was done he disentangled from Arden, got to his feet, making sure that his jacket didn't flap open, and held a hand out to her.

"I'm so sorry. Can I help you up? Are you hurt?" he said in a solicitous tone.

Arden frowned at him, shook her head, and grasped his hand. "I'm not usually so clumsy. It was almost as if my feet were swept out from under me by an unknown force," she said pointedly. She gave Smith a sour look before smiling at the guard. "I'm fine."

"I'm glad that you are unhurt," the guard said. "But the alarm went off and you'll need to walk through again. Please place your phone in the bowl."

Arden watched Smith as she reached into her left jacket pocket and dropped her phone into the bowl. Smith kept his expression neutral. The gun's weight at his waist felt both dangerous and comforting.

The sentry stepped aside. "Please go through again," he said.

Arden walked through the detector. It remained silent.

"Enjoy the reception," the sentry said.

32

Smith hauled her away from the door to a bar placed in a far corner of the room.

"What would you like?" Smith asked. "How about some champagne to celebrate our continued existence on this planet without any bullet holes to ruin our evening clothes?"

"You're being just a bit dramatic, aren't you?" Arden said. "I mean, for a *military* man. And give me back my gun."

Smith grabbed two glasses of champagne from a tray set with ten and handed one to Arden.

"To the contrary, I'm a scientist. Drama is not in my nature. And we scientific types don't like surprises, so if you have any others up your sleeve why don't you clue me in now. I hate being the last to know."

Arden took a sip of her drink. "That was a smooth move. Where'd you learn to pick pockets like that?"

"France. During a charitable mission to assist with the Gypsy population there."

"I want my gun back," Arden said.

Smith shook his head. "Not a chance."

"I told you, I don't trust them."

"How about we make a deal? If they come at you I promise to protect you."

Before Arden could answer, a man walked up and tapped her on the arm.

"Ms. Arden, how nice to see you again."

Arden turned and gave the man a brittle smile. "Mr. Darkanin. Hello."

Darkanin gave her an equally brittle smile in return. "So you accepted the challenge. I didn't expect anything less of you." He turned his attention to Smith and held out his hand. "Berendt Darkanin."

Darkanin stood about five-ten and wore a dark suit with a blindingly white shirt and a muted purple silk tie. He wore cologne that wafted toward Smith, and it smelled expensive. His olive-colored skin and dark eyes suggested that he was of Middle Eastern or even African descent, but Smith doubted that he was an Arab. If he had to guess he thought probably Libyan or Lebanese. From his bespoke suit to his clipped hair and English laced with an accent that was melodic rather than strong, Darkanin exuded an air of manufactured refinement. To others he might appear to be a member of the upper crust, but Smith got an overwhelming feeling of menace just standing near the man. Years with Covert-One had honed Smith's personal radar to sense danger; to him it seemed as though Darkanin's real persona was thinly veiled behind the trappings of society.

"Mr. Darkanin is the CEO of Bancor Pharma's Middle Eastern division," Arden said.

Bancor was a pharmaceutical company of recent incorporation. It had appeared out of nowhere five years ago and was pushing a newly developed drug to treat Alzheimer's patients. The drug provided mild cognitive improvement, and though still considered investigational it had been fast-tracked by the United States' FDA for use in assisted living facilities and nursing homes nationwide. The conditional approval was a coup for Bancor, because the usual process could take years. FDA only fast-tracked drugs in cases where nothing else existed and the risk of death from the disease far outweighed the risks from the drug.

"A pleasure to meet you, Mr. Smith," Darkanin said.

Smith nodded and shook Darkanin's proffered hand.

Darkanin watched him with an intensity that Smith found both disconcerting and interesting. He was sure he hadn't met the man before, yet he felt as though Darkanin watched him with particular interest, though he couldn't say why.

"There's Margaret with the World Health Organization. I need to speak to her, would you excuse us?" Arden said. Darkanin raised an eyebrow but nodded. Arden looped her arm through Smith's to steer him away. He strolled with her, but gently moved her in the direction of the door that he knew led downstairs. She shifted with him, keeping pace and walking alongside.

"That was abrupt. I got the definite impression that you didn't like the man," Smith said.

"I don't. His company engages in tactics that I find reprehensible," Arden said. She sipped her champagne and kept her gaze flitting around the room.

"Such as?"

"Such as paying off the guerrilla armies in North Africa to stay away from Bancor holdings. For those that won't be paid off, he hires Stanton Reese to quietly eliminate them."

Smith stopped walking and looked at her. "The contract security company currently under investigation?"

"The Stanton Reese that is suspected of running a rogue army that sacks entire civilian villages, burns them to the ground, and then claims that they were terrorist cells."

"Another case of yours?"

Arden nodded. "I represent three survivors who claim to have seen the carnage. Witnesses under subpoena to testify before Congress. Currently hiding in safe houses afraid for their lives. I think Bancor and Stanton will do anything to keep them from testifying. Including killing their lawyer." Arden took a deep swallow of her champagne. "So you see why I'll need my gun back." Smith did see, but he still wouldn't return it.

"Now I understand why you did it, but getting arrested doesn't help your clients or protect you from a future attack. And it's a bad tactical move to let your attacker know the extent of your defenses. You're taking away the element of surprise. I'll give it back to you eventually, but it's risky to transfer it between us right now." He tipped his glass to indicate a camera high on the wall. "Not when there are cameras at every corner of the room. How about I stay at your side while we mingle? Anything untoward happens and your gun will be close and I promise to use it to protect you."

He placed his glass on a nearby tray, twisting his body slightly so that she wouldn't see him remove the detonator pen from his suit pocket. He held it in his hand with his thumb on the button top and raised his wrist to hit the button on his watch to switch it to chronograph mode. When he returned his attention to her he found that she was watching him with what he now thought of as her contemplative look.

"I'm not quite sure what to make of you, Colonel Smith. Somehow you strike me as much more than a mere microbiologist."

Smith winced. "You make microbiology sound irrelevant. I assure you it's not. One day another pandemic may sweep the earth, like the Black Plague, and you'll be very, very thankful for the microbiologists of the world."

Before Arden could respond, a window at the far end of the room shattered and a large bird hammered through the shards. Smith pressed the top of the pen and the canister in the bird's talons exploded in a billowing black cloud.

33

S mith started the timer on his watch and moved next
to the door to the lower level just as the room turned
thick with smoke. There were people yelling all around
him, but Arden held his arm and he could feel her attempting to pull him away from the door and toward
safety. Sixty attendees, all blinded by smoke and all in a
state of panic, were jostling and stumbling toward the
exit. Smith opened the door to the lower level and stayed
near the wall while the smoke billowed into this new
area.

The smoke was dense but didn't carry an acrid smell
the way real smoke would, and while it filled the room
he still felt as though he could breathe. Visibility, though,
was non-existent. Even the beautiful crystal chandelier
that dominated the center of the ceiling was lost to sight;
he could only make out brighter patches from the bulbs.
He could discern the outline of Arden as she stood beside him, but he couldn't see her features. What he
could feel were her fingers clutching his arm, a problem
because he needed to move. He removed a handkerchief
from his breast pocket, pried her fingers off his arm, and
shoved the cloth into her palm.

"Use this to cover your nose and go ahead, I'll be right
behind you," he said. To his relief she let go of his arm
and he moved a step closer to the lower-level door.

"I think the exit is forty-five degrees to my right. We
need to get out of here," Arden said from somewhere to
his left. She spoke in a remarkably calm voice. He didn't

reply, but instead felt for the open doorway, located it, and started down the stairs.

He put his palms on the walls on either side of him and moved lower, counting the steps. At the bottom he turned right and walked two paces, running his outstretched hands along the wall on his left as a guide. He was rewarded when his fingers hit the brick molding surrounding a door. The smoke was still too thick to allow him to see the handle with any clarity, so he ran his palms around the door until he felt the cold metal of a knob. He located the trim around the knob and was dismayed to find that the plate housed a keypad, not a keyhole. There would be no use for his pick set or his camera. His watch gave an audible beep, indicating that one minute had elapsed. He had three, perhaps three and a half minutes left to complete his search.

He moved along the wall, feeling for anything that resembled a door, and was rewarded when his fingers hit another molding that surrounded one. He found the knob and discovered that this door too was locked. He pulled the small camera on its cord from his pocket and dropped to his knees, using his fingers to feel along the door's base for an opening wide enough to allow him to thread the camera through. There was the usual inch of space and he snaked the line underneath and flicked on the camera. Though dark, the door had successfully kept the smoke from entering the room in large amounts and he was able to make out a desk and chair along a far wall and a set of bookcases on a near one. The rest of the room was empty.

He pulled the camera line back out of the room, rose, and returned to the first door. He dropped again to his knees to fish the camera through, but his fingers hit a metal plate drilled onto the bottom of the door and extending to the floor. By running his fingertips along the plate he was able to discern that it was flush and tight, leaving no space for his camera. He wouldn't be sliding anything under the door. He would have to find another way into the room.

The rapidly diminishing smoke and his clearing vision told him that he was reaching the end of his available cover. He glanced up and for the first time noticed a red blinking LED light on the top right side of the doorjamb. Behind him he heard steps and turned to see Arden emerge from the darkened stairwell into the slightly less dark hall. He scrambled to his feet.

"I've been looking for you. What in hell are you doing down here? Hurry, we need to get out of this building, fast," Arden said. Smith cursed under his breath. Her persistence was maddening. He didn't respond and instead held the small camera a few inches from the door's keypad, doing his best to keep it steady so that Beckmann and Russell would be able to identify what it was they were seeing.

Beckmann and Russell both strained to make out the image that Smith was showing them. Beckmann muted his speaker for a moment.

"No lock," Beckmann said. "The only way to disable that keypad is to shoot it, and even then he would need a crowbar or Wonder Bar or to kick the shit out of the door to open it. And all of those options would be too noisy. Tell him to get out of there." Russell nodded and switched on the audio two-way speakers.

"Beckmann says you'd have to shoot that lock to open it, and even then you'd still need a tool to pry open the door. Abort mission, we'll have to find another way in," Russell said.

She saw a flicker of movement outside the viewing range of the small camera and after a moment the screen went dark.

"I'm going to shoot, step back," she heard Smith say.

Beckmann lurched forward, rolling his chair closer to the microphone, took it off mute, and put his mouth near the device.

"Beckmann here. You shoot that lock and every guard in the building will be pounding down the stairs after you. *Do not do it!*"

Smith heard Beckmann but ignored him as he aimed at the door. Arden had moved behind him but said nothing. He squeezed the trigger. The bullet dented the brass plate and bounced off the buttons, shattering them and sending bits of plastic flying everywhere before it ricocheted upward, embedding itself in the ceiling. The report echoed in the small area. Within seconds Smith heard the thudding sound of running feet as the guards upstairs reacted.

"I can hear that. It's the guards. Move!" Smith heard Russell's voice in his ear.

Before Smith could speak a long, loud, and bloodcurdling scream carried to them from upstairs. The woman stopped long enough to take a breath before shrieking a second time, this one even louder and longer than the first. Smith made a mental note to tell Russell that her operative had a real gift for screaming in terror.

"My God, are you sure that the bullet didn't penetrate the floor and hit that woman upstairs?" Arden said, and this time she sounded rattled.

Smith took two quick steps, raised his foot, and hammered his heel against the spot where the lock met the doorjamb. A space opened between the door and the jamb, but the lock held. He kicked it again and it sprang open. Smith took another shuffle step into the darkened room, felt along the wall, and threw a switch.

In the glare of the overhead light he saw Dr. Laura Taylor huddled against the far wall.

34

S mith crossed the room and stopped next to the bed that Taylor was crouched upon.

"We're leaving. Can you walk?" he asked.

Taylor scrambled across the mattress and stood up. "Get me out of here."

Smith waved both her and Arden to the door. The alarms still pealed and he could hear the klaxon sounds of emergency vehicles overlaying it all, growing louder. The troops were coming. He put a hand on his ear and an arm out to hold both Arden and Taylor in place.

"Tell me what you see up there. Police? Fire?" Smith addressed his question to Arden but it was really meant for Beckmann and Russell and he hoped that they would answer as well.

"I only saw smoke," Arden said.

"Both, but still a block away," Beckmann said in response. "People pouring out of the front door. It's chaos."

"Give me your best guess. Should we just mingle in the crowd?"

"What?" Arden asked.

"Guards at the back. I'd take the front," Russell said.

Smith checked out Taylor's clothes. She wore gray sweatpants and a grimy white T-shirt. Her feet were bare. A piece of clothing was thrown over a chair in the Spartan room.

"What's that?" Smith asked.

"A chador. They make me wear it whenever they

move me from location to location. Do you want me to put it on?" Taylor said.

"No. I want your face plastered on every CCTV camera in London as evidence that you were here, but to do that I need to get you clear of the building and those clothes won't cut it." He turned to Arden. "Can you give her your jacket?"

Arden removed her jacket and Taylor slipped it on. It hung on the woman's painfully slender shoulders.

"Here, put these on. They make everything look better." Arden slipped out of her heels and Taylor stepped into them. Smith had to agree with her, the dressy heels and the satin jacket raised the bar considerably and gave the impression that Taylor belonged at the party. Arden still wore her sheath and flashy diamond earrings and carried an evening clutch bag, so despite being barefoot she looked the part of a partygoer who had kicked off her shoes in order to run.

"Upstairs. I'll go first." He looked at Taylor. "I want you to look scared and head straight for the door. Don't stop for anything. You need to clear the exit for us to get you on a video feed that we can access. Do you understand?"

Taylor nodded.

"Let's go."

Smith hustled up the stairs, slowing only for a moment at the top to peer around the jamb. The room was nearly empty. A flashing warning light near a fire alarm in a high corner gave a strobe light effect. He waved the women across the room, through the door, and into the hallway. Here the last group of attendees was pushing out the door. Two sentries stood outside yelling and waving at them to urge them out of the building.

"Stay close to me. We'll go straight out and get into my car."

"When you leave the front lawn and step onto the sidewalk take a sharp right toward Hyde Park. I'm there at the uppermost corner." Smith heard Howell's voice in his ear. They joined the back of the crowd, but Arden stepped ahead of Smith and pushed her way through. The sea of bodies parted and Smith and Taylor followed, using the crowd as cover. Five more paces and they cleared the doorway.

"We can see you on camera now," Beckmann said into his ear. "You're almost home free."

Smith breathed a bit easier once they were outside the doors. The sentries paid them no more attention than the others and Smith, Taylor, and Arden jogged to the front gates, jostling through the center of the crowd. Smith made it to the gate and three seconds later they were out.

"Right and up the hill toward Hyde Park," Smith said. Arden turned and Taylor followed. Still no one paid any particular attention to them. They were half a block away when Darkanin stepped into the center of the sidewalk. His eyes locked on Taylor and then narrowed.

"Who is that?" Smith heard Beckmann's voice in his ear.

"Why, Mr. Darkanin, I'm glad to see that you made it safely away," Smith said.

"Arden's favorite CEO," Beckmann said. "I don't like the way he just showed up and I don't like the way he looks. Stay close to her. Howell, you there?" Smith tried to concentrate on what Beckmann was saying, but Darkanin was speaking again and drew his attention.

"What did you say?" Smith asked.

"I asked if you require a ride or if you have your own vehicle?"

"We're fine, thank you. We have a car," Arden said.

Darkanin smiled that brittle smile of his. "I'm Berendt Darkanin," he said to Taylor.

"We have to leave. Now," Smith said. He herded Taylor and Arden before him and past Darkanin. "Have a good evening," he said to Darkanin as they passed.

"Get to the top of the hill. Fast. Howell's not checking in," Beckmann said.

35

Howell leaned against the limousine door while he listened to the transmissions from Beckmann, Russell, and Smith. From his left came a couple walking hand in hand down the sidewalk and from his right a lone man approached, striding confidently. The couple Howell noted but ignored; the man, not at all. Something about him set Howell's antenna vibrating. He tilted his head a bit toward the man and swept his gaze over him, taking note of details and waiting for the tell. Dark-skinned, slender, in loose-fitting dark pants and a hoodie covered by an open stadium coat that would easily hide a shoulder holster, the man had all the trappings of trouble.

Howell pushed off the car and settled his weight onto both feet, keeping balanced. One move from the man's right hand toward the coat, or toward a waist holster, and Howell was prepared to react. The man was forty feet away and moving fast. Howell's senses were on full alert and adrenaline was raging through him. He wore no bullet-proof vest and so moved toward the front of the car, preparing to dodge behind it should the man reach for a gun.

The more problematic issue would be if he was a knife fighter. The best were Filipino, and this man didn't appear to be one, but that didn't preclude him being a trained killer. A good knife fighter could travel fourteen feet in a few seconds, and align himself on Howell's left, plunge the knife into the solar plexus or, even better, high on the upper chest, cover the hole with his left hand so that it wouldn't spurt in an obvious show, and continue his stroll while Howell sank to the ground with none the wiser.

Because it was London the odds of gun violence were lower than other cities, and so Howell was betting on a knife as the weapon of choice. The man was now twenty feet away and moving in. And then came the series of tells. His eyes flicked downward and then back up and he tracked Howell's movement to the front of the car. His right hand grasped something that slid into it from the sleeve above. He'd just lowered the knife into position. Once it was there he focused on Howell. His true intent seemed obvious to Howell, though perhaps someone not as attuned to the precursor signals of violence would not have recognized the signs.

Howell reached up and under the back of his suit and removed his own knife from its waistband holster. It was a short one, perfectly balanced with a three-inch blade. He felt the reassuring weight of the hilt in his hand and rotated his balance to the balls of his feet.

At six feet away the man did something that surprised Howell. His wrist flicked and the knife in his hand flew toward him. Howell spun and the knife hit him in the upper shoulder, cutting through the thin suit jacket and shirt into the skin. The injury was minor, but the complete confidence displayed by the man spoke volumes about what kind of fighter Howell was facing. The attacker was on him seconds later, and Howell could see the flash of a second blade in his hand.

Howell twisted to avoid the second stab and slashed with his own knife, slicing into the attacker's clothing, but the layers of jacket, hoodie, and long-sleeved shirt managed to blunt the cut and Howell could tell that whatever damage he had inflicted, it was minor.

The attacker spun on the balls of his feet, and slashed again. Howell jerked back and made his own attempt with a wide, swooping swing. The attacker dodged, pivoted, and attempted another stab, forcing

Howell to retreat again, but this time Howell felt the ground give way under his right foot. He had moved too close to the curb.

Howell stumbled backward, his body lurching and his arms wheeling as he tried to recover and keep his knife hand front and center. His Bluetooth earpiece flew out of his ear and he heard it clatter onto the asphalt. The attacker moved in, feinting and dodging as he tried to find an opening in Howell's defense. Howell stabbed and slashed as well and he managed to back the man off one step. A minor victory, but one that Howell was happy to attain. A small part of Howell's mind noted the other man's complete concentration and commitment to killing him and he knew that he was in the presence of a trained assassin.

The man slashed twice more, cutting a deep gash in Howell's forearm and attempting an underhand cut to his liver, which Howell deflected with his own swipe. The two blades clicked together and the hilt vibrated in Howell's hand.

"Howell!" Howell heard Smith call his name, but he didn't take his eyes off his attacker. The man heard it as well and there was a subtle shift in his attention. His previous all-encompassing concentration on Howell fractured and Howell could tell that he was now preparing to flee. Howell pressed his advantage, slashing back and forth with the knife, opening up a semicircle of air between them. To his left Howell saw Smith hit the top of the rise. At the same moment two men in suits and carrying briefcases came toward him.

"Hey, what's going on there?" one of the men yelled.

The attacker jogged backward a couple of steps, turned, and ran, crossing the street, dodging cars and disappearing at the next intersection.

Howell could feel the sticky blood mingled with sweat as it ran down his arm. One of the suited men moved closer and Howell carefully slid the knife back under his jacket and out of sight.

"Are you all right?" the suited man said. Howell noted that while the man seemed to want to help, he still stayed a careful distance away.

Howell nodded. "Yes. I am. Man wanted my wallet. Thank you for saying something. I would have had to give it up if you hadn't."

The man looked pleased. "Glad to help. Crime getting out of control these days. He didn't get you, did he?"

Howell kept his injured forearm behind him. He could feel the blood soaking into his sleeve.

"No. I'm fine. Thanks again."

The man nodded, rejoined his friend, and they walked away.

Howell leaned against the car, pressed a hand on his forearm to stanch the bleeding, and waited for Smith to reach him.

36

Smith ran up to Howell and noted the other man's pallor and the pain lines in his face.

"You hit?" he said in a low voice.

Howell nodded. "Knife fighter. He was trained and I was targeted. Someone knows we're here and what we're doing. Tell Russell and Beckmann to pack up and go. And we'll need a cleaner in there to wipe the room down. Did you get Rendel?"

"It was Dr. Taylor from USAMRIID."

Howell's face registered surprise. "Was she on the kidnapped list?"

Smith shook his head. "No. So we'll have to revise our thinking on this one. It's bigger than we thought. But right now my problem is Arden. She saw the whole thing go down and any moment both of them are going to appear. Can you sustain your cover until you get us out of here?"

Howell swallowed. "Take these." He shoved the keys into Smith's hand. "I'm gone. Make up a story and use the car, but lose it as fast as you can. They must know about it." Howell turned and walked away. Within seconds he melded into a set of Japanese tourists that crowded the sidewalk. Arden and Taylor made it to the top of the hill and Smith beeped the car open. When they reached him he opened the passenger door.

"Get in. We need to move."

Taylor got into the back and Arden went around to sit shotgun. Smith edged the car into traffic and drove the perimeter of Hyde Park.

"Where's the driver?" Arden asked. Her voice was once again calm and composed.

"Took off. I found the car here with the keys in the ignition."

Arden shot him a glance that made it clear she didn't believe a word of it. He knew enough to stop talking. When making up a story it was best to say as little as possible, especially when in the presence of a lawyer. He glanced in the rearview mirror.

"Dr. Taylor, are you all right?"

Arden gave Smith a sidelong look of surprise before turning to the woman in the backseat.

"Are you Dr. Laura Taylor of USAMRIID? Currently on medical leave?" Arden said.

Smith kept his eyes forward. He should have known that Arden would have already memorized the list that he'd given her. He glanced in the rearview mirror and saw Taylor give a small nod, followed by a weak smile.

"Thank you for getting me out of there," she said. Her voice shook on the words.

Arden reached over the seat. "Give me your hand," she said. Taylor did and Arden twisted to hold it between both of hers. "Don't worry. You're safe."

Taylor nodded again, this time with a bit more vigor, and Arden released her.

"What did they want from you?" Smith asked.

"My memory drug research. They wanted me to aerosolize it. I did, hoping that it would mollify them, but when we used it on mice they acted either erratically or aggressively, or simply died. And the side effects were all over the place. Add to that the fact that most batches remained potent for only a few minutes, but a few lasted longer. They were furious and thought I was deliberately altering the chemical so that it was unusable, but you know that the memory research always was experimental. I couldn't get them to understand that I was several years from a viable product."

"Who were they?"

"Initially they told me they were with the Department of Defense working on a secret protocol in conjunction with the CIA. Later I figured out that they were lying, but by then they had me locked down." She sighed heavily. "I'm exhausted. They wouldn't let me sleep. I think it was part of the interrogation process. But just a few hours ago they gave me some sort of drug that knocked me out. I'm having a hard time keeping my eyes open."

"Go ahead and lie down. We're going to be in this car for a while," Smith said. Taylor nodded and stretched out.

"Are we going to the police?" Arden asked.

Smith shook his head. "No."

"Why not?"

Smith stopped at a light and watched behind him. Nothing and no one seemed to be following him.

"Smith, it's Russell." Russell was speaking softly but Smith could hear her just fine. He hoped that Arden couldn't as well. As if she could read his mind Russell said, "Don't say anything, just listen. We're leaving and you need to get yourself to neutral territory and one without an extradition treaty. Marty intercepted a call from the Saudi embassy and they're scrambling to deflect blame. They have a grainy image of you, Arden, and Taylor in the lower-level hallway. It's too bad an image to match to the photo they have of you at the entrance, but they're trying to sharpen it so that they can use facial recognition software to identify you. I heard what Howell said and I agree that you need to dump the car at your earliest convenience. And keep Taylor and Arden with you. Don't let Arden make any more grandstanding moves, whatever you do. Keep her close until we can figure out the next steps. I'll be in touch, but in the meantime you're on your own and I'm out."

"Did you hear me? I said why not?" Arden said again, this time more forcefully. Smith drove forward at the green and contemplated how much he would reveal. One thing he did know was that whatever he said to Arden next had to be kept in the strictest confidence.

"You're still my attorney, right? From that night in DC?"

She frowned at him. "Why do I sense that a disturbing revelation is on its way?"

"I need to be sure that what I say next will be covered by the attorney-client privilege and can't be repeated by you."

A look of comprehension passed over Arden's face. "Ah, now I understand. Yes, I'm technically still your attorney, but the subpoena to USAMRIID puts our relationship into a slightly different light. While at this point it's not a conflict of interest for me to represent you, because I haven't filed a case against you or USAMRIID, I'm in the process of investigating USAMRIID, so we're skating on the edge a bit."

"But you haven't filed a case yet and if you don't find any evidence then you'll likely never file one. So technically you can still act as my attorney and our conversation is covered by the privilege?"

"Right, I'm still your attorney. Be careful, though. Dr. Taylor is in the backseat and anything you say in front of a third party breaks the attorney-client privilege."

He glanced in the rearview mirror. "She's asleep. I need some legal advice. Where can I go that's neutral territory? One with no extradition treaties with the US. Switzerland is neutral. Will they extradite?"

Arden rocked her hand back and forth. "Switzerland has an extradition treaty with the United States. Even so, they don't generally allow themselves to be sucked into the fray between nation-states. But it's likely that they'd just simply deny you admission and that would be that."

"Anyplace else?"

"Are we looking at just Europe?"

"Yes. Or anything within driving, train, or boat distance. I don't want to deal with airport security."

"Ukraine, Croatia, the Western Sahara, but why any-one would go there is beyond me because prison would be better, and Russia might cut a deal, but the operative term is 'deal.' You'd have to have something that they want. And the leadership is stocked with a bunch of fickle bastards. They'll help you out if the deal is good, but will just as quickly toss you out when you no longer serve their needs."

"So if the United States demanded my extradition, just about every country would send me packing."

Arden paused. "Well, I don't think you're framing the question right. You may have more options than you think."

"That sounds hopeful. How should I frame it?"

"It's not the United States that will be gunning for you, it's the Saudis. It was their embassy that you infil-trated, so they're going to be the ones asking for extra-dition. And they have refused extradition treaties with a whole host of states, so when they come begging for as-sistance it's likely that their lack of cooperation will be thrown back in their face."

"Excellent. Run down the countries that won't agree to extradite if the Saudis request it. Is Switzerland back on that list?"

"Yes it is."

Smith turned a corner and glanced again in the rearview mirror. As far as he could tell they weren't being followed.

"You want to tell me what's going on?" Arden said. "I deserve an explanation, because it's now abundantly clear to me that you used me and pushed for an invita-tion to that party because you knew that your colleague was there."

"Not true. I knew someone was there, but I'm just as surprised as you are that it was Dr. Taylor."

"Who did you expect?"

He shook his head. "I can't tell you that." She looked prepared to argue and he held up a hand.

"I'm not done with my questions. What if we take Dr. Taylor to the police and she files charges?"

"Against the embassy personnel?"

Smith nodded. "Yes. What happens then?"

"Nothing. They've all got diplomatic immunity, which may go a long way to explaining why they were holding her there. Worst-case scenario is the perpetrators get sent home, Saudi Arabia issues an apology, and a new crew takes their place. Case closed."

"What about me? Do I have immunity?"

"Not unless you're a diplomat."

"I'm not."

"Then no."

"So they can get off scot-free for kidnapping Taylor, but I can be arrested for breaking her out?"

Arden sighed. "Look, I know where you're headed with this, and it doesn't seem right, but that's how it is. Without diplomatic immunity countries would play endless games with the representatives of other countries. Arresting them, imprisoning them, you name it."

"You see why I don't think we should go to the police. What good will it do?"

"What is it that you *do* want to happen?"

"I'm going to France. From there I'll drive to Switzerland, and once there I'm going to see that Taylor is put on a flight home."

"Why not just drive to Heathrow and drop her at the entrance? Put her on a plane?"

"Because this country has too many cameras that will trace our every step and provide an easy way to track us and because I think they're trumping up charges against me and"—he gave her a pointed look—"you as we speak."

Arden snorted. "Me? What for? I did nothing."

"Not true. You brought me to the party as your guest and you're on camera in that basement helping me break Taylor out. You provided me with the gun that was used and they might even claim that you had a hand in the explosion. And you have a motive, because you bear a well-known grudge against the Saudis for what you perceive to be their dismal record on human rights."

"I don't perceive anything. It's the truth. Their record speaks for itself and it's dreadful."

Smith took a turn and followed a sign pointing them to Dover and the Channel Tunnel. He merged onto the M20 and accelerated. Arden raised an eyebrow and then groaned, put her head back, and closed her eyes.

"I'll need my clothes and money. They're all back in my hotel," she said.

"And a passport," Smith said.

"I don't go anywhere without that. It's in my purse."

"Will they have flagged them by now?"

Arden cocked her head to the side. "Takes a while for an Interpol notice to go up. We might still be safe."

"I'll cover you."

She slid one eye open and looked at him. "You said that at the reception and look where that got us."

Smith watched the rearview mirror and saw that they had a new problem on their hands.

They were being followed.

37

President Castilla requested Klein's presence at a DC fund-raiser twenty minutes after he'd received the call from the U.S. embassy in London. Ten minutes later, Klein strode into the green room where the president was waiting to be ushered onto a stage for a speech. The president spotted him and his face revealed a mixture of relief and concern.

"Fred, so good to see you again. Ladies and gentlemen, give me a moment here? Mr. Klein and I are old friends and would like a quick catch-up in private." Castilla spoke to the assembled aides, liaisons, and members of the Secret Service.

"You have twenty minutes, sir," an aide said. Castilla acknowledged her with a nod and waited while the people in the room filed out.

"Is this room secure?" Klein asked.

Castilla nodded. "Just swept for bugs no longer than fifteen minutes ago, so probably far safer than most. I saw the news reports about the Saudi embassy. So much for getting this mission accomplished without creating an international incident," Castilla said.

"What are the Saudis saying?" Klein asked.

Castilla waved him to a chair. "The Saudis are furious and crying foul. They claim that a spy managed by us breached their security and attacked their London embassy."

"*They're* crying foul? They're the ones that kidnapped a respected scientist and U.S. citizen. What did they expect?"

"They're claiming that she deliberately used her aerosolized memory drug against a member of the Saudi diplomatic corps and that they were detaining her to question her about it. They said that they intended to hand her over to us when they were finished. Frankly, I think this also has a lot to do with their anger at us for reopening communications with Iran. Add to that their claims that a U.S. military researcher tested her products on an unsuspecting diplomat, the implementation of fake vaccine programs, and the recent revelations that we've been spying on our friends and enemies alike and they're boiling mad."

"Do they know for sure it was us?"

Castilla shook his head. "Not yet. They said that they're still working on the video feed, but they seem certain that it will turn out to be us."

Klein nodded. "That's because they know the game is up and we have her."

Castilla frowned. "But Rendel's still missing. Give me some more information about this Dr. Taylor."

"She's a researcher at USAMRIID working on a treatment for post-traumatic stress disorder and currently on medical leave for mental issues."

"Mental issues? That doesn't bode well for her. Is she the one who may have taken Smith's keycard and raised the FBI's hackles? You think she stole the vials and was attempting to sell them on the black market?"

Klein sat down. "I don't think so. Russell called in and said that Taylor appeared to be a prisoner, not a co-conspirator."

"Where is she now?"

"She, Smith, and Katherine Arden, the human rights attorney, are in a car driving through London."

Castilla frowned. "Why did he bring an attorney and outsider into this? It's bad enough that the Saudis suspect us."

"It seems as though when the mission went south it went badly south. She was present, saw it go down, and now he's keeping her near and trying to contain the damage."

Castilla was up and pacing. "So we're no closer to finding Rendel and we have an international incident on our hands."

Klein sighed. "I'm sorry, but that seems to be the case."

"What about Warner? Has he been able to remember anything that occurred?"

"Nothing at all, but given the extent of his injuries we may have to assume that he cracked under torture. If so, and they're doing the same to Rendel as we speak, then the drone program is well on its way to being compromised. I understand that each password revealed aids a computer hacker tremendously."

Castilla nodded. "I expected as much. All the passwords have been changed and the monitoring personnel put on alert that if one device begins to act strangely it's to be pulled out of service. I've also ordered all of the available equipment scanned and analyzed for any changes or alterations."

There was a tap on the door.

"Come in," Castilla said. The door opened and the aide stood there.

"A call from London, sir. The prime minister wants to speak to you."

"Give me a few minutes more. Let him know that I'm getting ready to give a speech, so that the conversation will have to be a short one until after the fund-raiser." The aide nodded and retreated, closing the door behind her.

"He's an ally at least," Klein said.

Castilla grimaced. "He's furious. Apparently he feels as though we could have picked another location to try to infiltrate the embassy and left his country out of it."

Klein gave a sharp laugh. "Just how does he think we could have done that? They were holding her in London."

"Preliminary investigation shows evidence that she had been moved several times and through various countries. Of course, the evidence is relevant only in light of what we now know. He's Monday-morning quarterbacking and arguing that we should have been able to pinpoint her movements sooner and intercepted before she was moved to the UK. Now he has the Saudis pressuring him to pull out all the stops to investigate the break-in. I'm afraid Smith is on his own. I'm not going to throw him to the dogs right away, but if he's captured I'm going to have to tread very lightly."

"He understands that. Every Covert-One operative does. But I would ask that you delay any official response until I can get a handle on what's going on here. There appears to be a strange mixture of events that I don't like. What do drones and pathogens have in common?"

"One's a killer and the other is a delivery method," Castilla said.

"My thoughts exactly," Klein said. "And it's especially worrisome that Taylor told Smith she was being forced to work on an aerosolized version of her memory wiping drug. Disperse it over an area and subject those below to amnesia. I asked him if it was possible that one drug creates different effects for different people and he said it absolutely could. Just think about the long list of side effects that accompanies most of the drugs you purchase. There can be thirty or forty listed for one pill. Each person reacts differently."

"Collect every bit of information that you can about this Dr. Taylor. Let's look into any possible intersections among her, Rendel, and Warner."

"And Meccean. Don't forget him," Klein said.

"And Meccean. And tell me, what are the odds that Smith will make it out of the UK without detection?"

Klein shook his head. "I can't tell you. The UK authorities have a camera on every corner and all UK citizens can be watched whenever they're outside. He's in a car and they don't have the plates as yet, but if he passes by one camera while driving then his face will be registered."

"It's probably about the worst place he could be right now."

"Agreed," Klein said. "Can you slow down the manhunt?"

"I'll try to hold off Interpol. If they issue an international warrant, then the moment he tries to enter another country he'll be flagged. In the meantime, let's increase our efforts to find Rendel and hope that Smith can elude his pursuers long enough to get some intelligence out of Taylor. We need to hear from her what's going on."

"Agreed. He's been told to go dark, but I know of a way to reach him."

"And how's that?" Castilla asked.

Klein smiled. "That's our secret."

Castilla raised an eyebrow. "That you can't even share with me?"

"Better safe than sorry. Good luck with the prime minister." Klein headed to the door.

38

Arden turned in the seat to gaze out the back window. "Which car is it?"

"Black sedan, two cars back."

"How do you think they found us?"

Smith figured that the crew behind him was involved with the man who had attacked Howell. If they weren't and were actually security forces tracking him from the embassy then they must have decoded the video feed a lot quicker than he had expected. He ran through the other options. His phone was a prepaid one and only Marty knew its tracking signature, so he doubted that it was the culprit. A thought occurred to him.

"Is your phone on?"

Arden nodded.

"Turn it off and remove the battery. They could be tracking it."

Arden dug the phone out of her purse and turned it off. "Why remove the battery? I know they can track it while on, but isn't turning it off enough?"

"No." Smith was annoyed with himself. Forgetting to warn Arden to turn off her cell phone was a piece of sloppy work. The whole mission had spiraled downward so fast that he was making crucial errors. He needed to come up with a plan to lose Howell's attackers and fast.

"We need to shake the tail, ditch this car, and acquire a new one," he said.

Arden was watching the side-view mirror. "That's a lot."

"Smith." Beckmann's voice rang in his ear, causing Smith to jerk the steering wheel in surprise. The car veered a bit off course and Arden stopped monitoring the action in the side-view mirror long enough to shoot him a look.

"What happened? Are you okay?"

"Sorry," Beckmann said.

"Sorry," Smith said to Arden.

"Just want you to know that Marty tracked your phone for us and Russell and I are behind you in a stolen silver Vauxhall Corsa. It's got an engine the size of a sewing machine and I apologize for that. I wanted to steal the brand-new Jaguar F-Type parked next to it, but Russell wouldn't let me. Too flashy. She said everyone seems to have a Corsa in the UK, so you'll blend in better. Can you drive stick?"

"I can drive a stick shift. Can you?" Smith said to Arden.

"That's an odd question. Yes, I can. Are you okay?" she asked.

"Just planning for our next car."

"Got it," Beckmann said. "We're going to take out the black car that's following you. After we do, we'll make the switch. We'll collect Taylor for debriefing, and you and Arden hit it out of here. Stay on course."

Smith maintained his speed, keeping to the left and being sure to keep a steady pace. He couldn't see the Corsa, but that may have been a function of the darkness more than anything.

"Is Taylor still sleeping?" he asked. Arden glanced behind her.

"She's out. I feel sorry for her."

"Can you wake her up? I have something important to tell her."

Arden leaned back and shook Taylor, who moaned and dragged herself into a sitting position.

"What's going on?" she asked.

"We're being chased. By whom, I don't know, but behind them is another car and in that car are two people I do know. When they're done neutralizing the threat they're going to take you to safety," Smith said.

Taylor looked out the rear window. "Which car are they in? The black one?"

Smith shook his head. "Silver. But it may be back a bit farther; I can't see it."

"Who are they?"

"CIA."

Taylor shook her head back and forth. "No, no, no. No CIA. I don't trust them."

Arden smiled. "Smart woman."

Smith rolled his eyes. "Don't encourage her," he said to Arden. She shrugged and returned her attention to the side-view mirror. He caught Taylor's gaze in the rearview. "I know these two. You can trust them. Besides, I don't think that we have any real options right now. You need to get to safety and Arden and I need to go underground until this thing cools off."

"Are they in that silver car that just pulled alongside the black one?" Arden asked.

Smith checked behind them and saw a small car pacing the black one. The black accelerated away and closed the distance between them. The silver car lost ground.

"I think so," Smith said.

"I don't know a whole lot about cars, but can that small one really keep up?" Arden asked.

Smith agreed with Arden, but there was nothing for it but to let it play out. He stomped on the gas and the town car accelerated in a smooth climb. He was thankful for the late hour, because the highway was fairly empty and he was able to cut around the slower vehicles with relative ease.

"You said you can shoot. How well?" he asked Arden.

"Well enough. Why?"

He reached around, pulled her gun out of his waistband, and held it out to her. "Here. Be prepared to shoot through the black car's driver's-side window." She

pressed back against the door and away from the proffered weapon.

"Not on your life. You want me to add murder to
the current list of illegal acts that I've supposedly been a
party to this evening? Well, you can forget it. I don't want
that on my conscience."

"You seemed willing enough earlier tonight when you
thought they'd be after you."

"There's a difference between the threat of violence
to back someone off and actual violence," Arden said.

"Trust me, the actual violence is coming," Smith said.

"I'll do it," Taylor said. "After everything they've put
me through these past few months I'll be happy to blow
them away." Her voice was grim. She reached over the
seat for the gun. As she did, Smith got a look at her gaunt
face and the deep blue circles around her eyes. Those,
and the obvious emotion that she was feeling, made her
a bad choice. She was unpredictable and bound to over-
react.

"Can you shoot?" he asked.

"If you tell me what to do I'm sure I'll be able to figure
it out."

Smith shook his head. "Not good enough. If we had
time I would stop this car and let one of you drive while I
shoot." He glanced in the rearview mirror. "But it's clear
that we don't have that option."

The black car was gaining ground, but so was Beckmann in the silver Corsa. Now all three of them were
only a few lengths apart from each other and Smith
pushed the town car even faster. He was doing ninety,
then ninety-five miles an hour and still dodging through
the traffic. Lines drawn across the highway glowed white
in his headlights and after he drove over them he saw the
flash of a camera.

"What was that?" Arden asked.

"Speed camera," Smith said. The camera flashed
again when his pursuers passed it and a third time when
Beckmann's Corsa sped by.

If he had to go faster Smith would have to put all his concentration into driving. The fact that he was driving in England and oriented on what was for him the wrong side of the road only added to his need to focus. The two lanes in front of him were filled by a truck and a minivan, leaving no room for him to pass. The black car pulled parallel on Arden's side and the driver lowered his window and stuck a gun out.

"They've got a gun!" Arden yelled and bent at the waist and curled lower in her seat. Smith hit the brakes and the attacker's car zipped ahead. Smith's quick deceleration must have caught Beckmann by surprise, because Smith saw the Corsa begin fishtailing as Beckmann slammed on his brakes to avoid rear-ending them.

"And watch the brakes on this tin can," Smith heard Beckmann say. "Good idea, though. Slow it way down and let us get in front." Smith complied by slowing even more and the Corsa shot past him. The black car's taillights glowed red as it too cut speed.

"They're trying to match us," Arden said.

"While you're having an attack of conscience about shooting them, they're going to kill us," Smith said.

"I can see that. The bastards. Give me the gun," Arden replied.

39

Smith handed Arden the gun and slowed even more. He passed another camera, but this time it didn't flash. He held the car at a speed that would keep it behind the Corsa and watched as the black car slowed until it was nearly parallel and to the left of Beckmann. Smith saw the Corsa's window lower and the muzzle of a gun and the slender arm of a woman holding it.

"Looks like your CIA officer is going to handle our problem for us," Arden said.

Smith watched as Russell pulled the trigger. He saw the flash of cartridges ejecting from the weapon and heard the sound of shots. The black car jerked and swerved violently before accelerating ahead. As it did it maneuvered into the far-right lane, the passenger window lowered, and a man leaned out, pointing his own gun.

"Driver doesn't want to be first in the line of fire," Smith said. He, though, stayed in the left lane.

"You'll have to move over as well if you want me to have a clear shot at them," Arden said. "In this lane I'd have to push you aside to shoot out your window."

Smith watched as the Corsa and the black car dodged and weaved across the lanes of traffic and settled into the far right. Beckmann and Russell pulled alongside and the two cars surged and slowed as each attempted to avoid being in the line of fire. Smith stayed steady but moved into the center lane to avoid a passing truck. The black car slowed again, forcing Beckmann, who was directly behind him, to slow with it. Smith passed the Corsa once again and the black car slowed to match him.

Smith didn't see the new danger until it was too late. A red car lined up on his left timed to when the black car had slowed. Now Smith was sandwiched in between the cars, and a man, his face obscured with a scarf that wrapped around his head and neck, leaned out of the black car's passenger side, his arm extended while he took aim with a gun. Smith couldn't slow, because a civilian's car was behind him, and so he increased his speed, but the two cars increased theirs as well, keeping him sandwiched between them. Arden yelled something incomprehensible and fired several times out the open window.

"Taylor, get down," Smith said. From the corner of his eye he saw the holes punch through the red car's window on the driver's side and it dissolved into shards. Smith heard the reports of return fire. Behind him the passenger window of his car shattered as bullets hammered through. He heard Taylor scream and saw a spurt of blood geyser upward.

"Get to Taylor," Smith said. "Give me the gun."

Arden screamed and dropped down onto the center console. More bullets punctured the car and Smith felt one wing past him.

Smith surged ahead, moving around two cars and swerving through traffic, with the two attackers right behind him. Arden shoved the gun at him before crawling over the seat and into the back.

"She's bleeding badly." Arden sounded distraught.

"Put pressure on the wound," Smith said.

Beckmann's Corsa cut across all three lanes and onto the shoulder before it sped ahead. When it was even with the red car Russell fired only twice, but unlike Arden and the men in the red car, two bullets were all she needed to hit her targets. The passenger fell onto the seat and out of Smith's line of vision and the driver slumped forward over the steering wheel. The red car swerved and hit the guardrail, spewing pieces of plastic and glass before spinning away. It drove across three lanes of traffic, onto the shoulder, down into a culvert, and slammed into a stand of trees.

The black car sped up, whizzing away from the Corsa with ease. Another traffic camera flashed as it passed and shortly afterward the car shot off an exit ramp.

"We're not following," Smith heard Beckmann say. "Our first priority is to get you out of that car and Taylor to safety and debriefing. Pull over in the next five hundred yards. Marty told me that we're between speed cameras."

Smith pulled to the shoulder, slowing until it was safe to stop.

"We're making the switch," he said. Arden nodded, and to his relief she seemed unhurt.

Smith threw open his door, got out, and reached for the passenger-door handle as the Corsa pulled up behind. The other car's doors swung open and Beckmann and Russell emerged. Smith was somewhat dismayed to see that they were dressed all in black and wearing full-face balaclavas with two holes for their eyes and one for their mouths. In the darkness and on the deserted road they looked sinister and not exactly like the saviors that he'd been assuring Arden they were.

Russell still held her gun, which she placed in a shoulder holster as she walked toward them. Smith leaned into the back of the car to check on Taylor.

Taylor lay bent from the waist and facedown on the seat. Arden crouched next to her, pressing her hand on Taylor's neck.

"I'm going to roll her over. Try to keep your hand in place."

Arden nodded and Smith gently rolled Taylor over. Blood seeped through Arden's fingers and was pooling on the leather seat. The wound was in Taylor's neck, near the carotid artery. Smith removed his tie and wrapped it once around.

"Slide your fingers out from under the tie and I'll tighten it," he told Arden. He wrapped the wound again, knotting it tight. Taylor's skin was clammy and her pulse so weak that he could barely make it out. He held his hand over the cloth at the wound.

Russell strode up to stand at the open door. "Transfer time," she said. She peered into the backseat. "Oh, no, is she alive?"

"Barely. She needs a hospital, not a safe house," Smith said. Taylor's blood was beginning to seep through the cloth and he could feel it pooling under his palm. In the distance Smith heard the sound of an ambulance siren. "Is that ours?"

Beckmann appeared at Russell's shoulder.

"Not ours," he said. "I presume they've been told about the accident and are coming for the guys in the red car. I called for one of ours about ten minutes ago. The minute I saw the chase car I figured we might need one." He took in the scene in the backseat and said, "I'll find out how far away they are." He pulled out a phone and walked away while he spoke into it.

Russell leaned farther into the car. "Ms. Arden, I apologize for the face masks, but my colleague and I don't want the many CCTV cameras in the UK to record our faces. It's safer if we can work with some anonymity. As it is I've arranged for a third car to be brought here for you and Smith. I'll wait with Dr. Taylor and travel with her to the hospital."

Smith felt the muscles in his jaw unclench at Russell's calm and well-timed words. If anyone could win Arden over it would be Russell, with her pure professionalism and long experience in handling assets and emergencies for the CIA.

Arden looked devastated. Smith could tell that she was trying to pull herself together to respond. She swallowed once. "Are we on camera now?"

Russell shook her head. "We're between speed cameras. This is a dead zone. However, I think you need to assume that you are constantly on camera until you can leave the UK."

"I would like some identification," Arden said. She held out her hand, but pulled it back when she realized that it was covered in Taylor's blood. Smith saw that she was shaking.

Russell nodded. "I understand." She reached into her pocket and removed a small wallet that she flipped open to reveal an official-looking identification card. She held it open for Arden to see. Arden leaned in to look at it.

"It says you're the public liaison for the CIA," she said.

"I am. But I have other duties as well. I'd really like to leave quickly. I don't know when those attackers will return, but I have no doubt that they will." She looked at Smith.

"Be sure to ask...your friend to try to block the feed from those two speed cameras. If he can't, your face will be front and center on every law enforcement computer in Europe. We've called him so many times already that we're hesitant to use our phones again. Yours might be more anonymous."

Beckmann jogged back up to them. "The guys think the ambulance will be here in the next few minutes."

"Where are you taking her?" Arden asked.

"Initially to a fully equipped medical center that they've arranged to open after hours. After that we'd like to get her back to the States. It's easier for us to protect her there."

A white Audi sedan pulled off the road onto the shoulder and stopped behind the Corsa. The driver, a woman in her thirties and dressed in a black cocktail dress and heels, got out. Smith recognized her from the embassy party and it was clear that she recognized him as well, because she nodded once.

"I can't introduce you, but our operative here will drive your car. Smith, Arden, take the sedan." Russell leaned in and placed her hand over Smith's. "I'll take over. Do I just keep pressing down?"

"Yes," Smith said.

Arden pulled out of the other side and closed the door, leaving Smith and Russell alone.

"Will she live?" Russell spoke softly.

"Chances are slim. She'll need immediate surgery to close the wound and a blood transfusion." Smith felt the sadness welling in his chest and he pushed back the emotion. He'd seen worse cases survive and he wouldn't count Taylor out. He slid his hand away and stepped back. Taylor's blood dripped from his fingers onto the gravel.

The operative walked up and handed Smith a small travel packet of tissues and a set of car keys. He wiped the blood from his hands while she watched in silence. When he was done he surrendered his keys.

"Thank you for the distraction that you provided at the embassy. It bought me some crucial time," Smith said to her.

She indicated Taylor. "I only wish I could have bought you some more. How bad is it? Does she need a hospital or can I drive her to the safe house? We have a physician there."

Smith shook his head. "She needs a full-on hospital. Now."

"I've already arranged for emergency dispatch. Once we move her you can drive the car to the safe house," Russell said to her. The woman nodded.

"I'll get it sanitized and retagged," she said. She handed Smith an envelope and a small black plastic device with two leads. "There's a new passport with a fake name in the envelope as well as a few thousand dollars. The license plate on the car is clean but I didn't have time to burn the tires. You might want to do that as soon as you can."

Smith nodded.

"You and Arden need to go," Russell said to Smith. "Now, before the ambulance gets here."

Smith strode to the white car, which was a two-door coupe.

"You drive, I'll keep the gun," he said to Arden. Her face was set and she didn't respond. He tossed her the keys across the car's roof and Arden caught them in one hand. Once inside, she put the transmission in drive, waited for an opening, and punched the gas to merge into the lane. Unlike the earlier car, this one accelerated like a rocket.

"Keep it within the speed limit. We've been photographed enough this evening," Smith said.

Arden settled the car back into a steady pace. She was unusually quiet and Smith wondered just what she was thinking.

"Will she make it?" Arden asked.

"It's bad," Smith said. "I don't know."

"You're with the CIA, aren't you?" Arden shot him a glance before returning to watch the road.

"I am not."

She looked irritated. "I really wish you would tell me the truth."

Smith sighed. This conversation was the last thing he needed. What he needed was to get Marty busy erasing their images from the speed cameras.

"I *am* telling the truth. I'm not with the CIA."

"You're awfully cozy with them."

He nodded. "USAMRIID has all kinds of connections to the CIA. We used to devise chemical weapons for warfare, so it makes sense that the CIA would consult with us."

"Consult, yes. Run a search-and-rescue mission? Not so much."

Smith's phone rang and he was relieved to have an excuse to cut short her line of questioning. The phone number was unknown, so once again he assumed it was either Russell or Beckmann.

"Smith, here. What's up?"

"You have two hours to deliver Dr. Taylor back into

our hands." The male voice was inflected with an accent that Smith couldn't place.

"Who is this?" Smith asked. Arden glanced at him in concern when she heard his sharp tone.

"This is the man who is going to kill you."

40

Smith's line went silent. The man had hung up. He shut off the device and began disassembling it.

"What's going on?" Arden asked.

"Someone, I don't know who, just threatened to kill me if I don't deliver Taylor back to him."

The color drained from Arden's face. "He knows you have her and he has your phone number."

Smith nodded. "Yes. And while both facts alarm me, it's the phone number that really concerns me, because this is a brand-new model that I picked up when I landed in London. He's been able to track a prepaid phone purchased with cash only two days ago and registered in a phony name."

"Who can do that? Can the CIA?"

"Not that quickly. It would require a whole series of steps that would take time to implement."

"Like what? Run down the steps for me."

Smith sat back and tried to settle his racing mind long enough to consider her question. "Well, he'd have to know who I am, for one, and that I am the person who helped her escape from the embassy. Then he'd have to identify my phone's signature."

"How is that done? You say you used cash and the phone is not registered in your name. There must be thousands of phones sold every day in the UK."

Smith thought back to the few minutes that he was in the embassy building. Beckmann had called him right at the entrance, before Smith had stepped inside.

"I was told that the embassy has a grainy image of us outside that locked room. It's possible that they've finally been able to identify me and put it together that I have Taylor. From there it's a short step back to the moment that I used the phone at the entrance. If they've reversed to that moment in time they may have been able to access all the incoming signatures and pinpoint which was mine."

Arden shook her head. "There's no way they are able to do that this quickly. I may not know much about the latest stealth technology, but I know the most common methods that law enforcement uses to track individuals. When you're a defense attorney it comes with the job. It's my understanding that most phones only provide triangulating tracking, not pinpoint tracking, and in a city as large as London there could be thousands of phones in use within a triangulated area. They would have to sift through them all. You're thinking too technically. Think simpler."

"Then they have a CIA insider with access to the CIA's network."

"Okay. Statistically rare, but possible. Those two we just met. You told Taylor that you trusted them, but could one of them be ratting you out?"

"Absolutely not," Smith said.

"Then who else has access to you? USAMRIID, right?"

"Yes, but they have no way of tracking a phone and I never informed them of the prepaid." And they have no idea I'm running this mission, he thought.

"What about the woman that brought this car. You know her?"

"I don't."

"So there's one unknown link. She knows that you have Taylor, but possibly not your phone number, so it's not a complete hit. Any others?"

Her line of questioning was efficient and designed to get at the core of the matter. The logical way she took apart the facts was impressive and went a long way toward explaining why she had risen as high as she had in her field. Smith shifted in his seat, because his next statement might blow her logical and unemotional approach out of the water.

"I hate to say this, but that would be you."

To Smith's surprise she didn't seem offended. He watched her ponder his statement.

"That's absolutely correct. While I can assure you that I haven't told anyone of your phone number, because I don't know it and have no way of obtaining it, right now you can't verify my statement. But like the woman, I know you have Taylor. Okay, using me as the starting point spreads the circle wider. Where have our lives intersected?"

"USAMRIID and your client Canelo. But we've already dismissed USAMRIID as an option, so that leaves Canelo."

"Who's currently sitting in the brig and that puts him at a very low probability."

Smith thought some more about the people he had met through Arden. "There was the head of Bancor that you introduced me to at the reception."

"Darkanin, yes, that's right. I really dislike him. But even if I didn't we have to put him on the list as an unknown. Just like the woman who brought the car."

Smith nodded. "And he met Taylor in my company, so he's aware that she's with me."

"Which elevates him on the list."

"Which makes him equal to the woman. Your bias is showing," Smith said.

Arden grimaced. "I can't help it. I'll try to be more neutral."

Smith watched the road fly by while he thought about the threatening call. A sign came into view.

"Take that exit. It says there's a rest stop and gas station. Maybe we can pick up a new phone."

Arden took the ramp and pulled into a large complex

that boasted a coffee shop, McDonald's, clothing shop, and small packaged food area. Next to the complex was a chain hotel popular in the United States. While most of the stores were closed, the coffee and packaged food shops were not.

"We should stock up. There's no telling when we'll be able to eat."

"And I have bits of blood all over me. I'm going to hit the restroom and wash up."

Arden got out of the car and when she came around to walk next to Smith he noticed that she was barefoot.

"You didn't take back your shoes," he said to her.

She looked down. "I walked all the way from the embassy to the car and then after the shooting it didn't seem right to take them off her feet. Almost like stealing from the fallen. I hope they don't kick me out of the building."

Smith held the door for her and checked the area as they entered. Although it was just edging toward ten o'clock, the complex only had a few scattered patrons and a CCTV camera at the end of the hall. Arden headed to the restroom and Smith scanned the area and then stood near the door to watch the parking lot. None of the arriving cars seemed out of place. He counted four more cameras mounted on light poles scattered throughout the lot. Arden returned to his side.

"See anything strange?"

"No. But I still would like to keep moving."

They headed toward the packaged goods store where a lone employee had his back to them while he wiped down a rear counter. The pastry items in the glass display cabinet had already been removed and placed on several baking trays; half were wrapped in cling wrap. By the time the clerk noticed them both he and Arden were flush with the counter. From that angle the clerk couldn't see Arden's feet.

"Are you open?" Arden asked.

The clerk nodded. "We close in ten minutes. I've covered up the trays, but if you want something from them just let me know and I'll get it for you. Our coffee is still up and running."

Arden kept close to the counter while she pointed at several items on the remaining free trays. True to his word, the clerk nodded and grabbed several items. Arden finished by ordering two large cups of coffee.

"Add two extra shots of espresso, please," she asked the clerk.

While Arden stocked up, Smith did a quick reconnaissance of the remaining stores. To his dismay, none of the open places carried prepaid phones.

"No phones," he told Arden when he returned to her side and stepped up to pay for her items. "Without one I can't access my contacts to find a place to sleep for the night." He saw Arden glance at the hotel through the pane glass window with a look of longing.

"Tired?" he asked.

She nodded. "Beyond tired. Even though it's not that late I feel as though I've been run through a wringer."

"It's the adrenaline. While it's ricocheting around in your system you can go forever. It's a deep, dark tumble once it's gone."

She took a sip of her coffee. "Consider me tumbling. Hopefully this will help. And if you care to hear my opinion, I think we should keep pressing through to stay ahead of whoever is after us. If we slow we just give them time to regroup."

"Normally I would agree, but rest is going to be difficult to come by and if we have any safe places to crash now we need to take advantage of them. Once we become seriously sleep-deprived we'll start to make mistakes that we can't afford." He grabbed the paper bag with their food items and waved her toward the car.

When he was settled into the passenger seat he opened his own cup of coffee and sipped it while he weighed their options. Arden took the ramp to the highway and soon they merged into the lanes and kept to a steady pace. Smith had an almost overwhelming desire to reassemble his phone to see if the caller had tried again, but he restrained himself. Instead he watched the traffic behind them and analyzed the cars, looking for any suspicious patterns.

"If you're sure you want to stop and sleep, I have someone that might help," Arden said.

Smith stopped watching the traffic to look at her. "I'm sure. Tell me."

"It's a client. And if we do this you'll have to be very careful with what you say."

"That sounds ominous. Why?"

"He's an anarchist. Well, that's what he likes to call himself, but basically he's an environmentalist and animal rights activist. He's been arrested more times than I can count, and his most recent brush with the law was at sea when he tried to harpoon the sailors on a Japanese whale fishing boat."

Despite their current dire circumstances, Smith found himself smiling.

"He wanted to give them a little taste of their own medicine? What happened?"

"He missed, luckily for him. And for the sailors in question, of course. The Japanese had him arrested and I flew in and arranged his release."

"How did you manage that? Sounds like he was guilty as hell."

"Oh, he was, but I was able to prove that the trawler had killed more than its allowed quota and the Japanese quietly dropped the charges and threw him out of the country on his ear. He's on probation and right now lives in a cottage overlooking the ocean about fifty miles from the Channel Tunnel, where he's plotting his next adventure at sea, I'm sure."

"Will he take us in?"

"Me? Absolutely. You? Only if you don't breathe a word about your role in the military."

"Another one who hates the industrial governmental complex?" Smith asked.

Arden glanced at him and nodded. "He makes me look like an amateur."

Smith rubbed his eyes. "This is going to be fun."

"If it's sleep you want..."

Smith put up a hand. "I want to sleep, but not with the enemy, if you know what I mean. But still, let's go on. We can always reverse direction if necessary."

Smith returned to watching the road behind them and brooding about the phone call.

41

After half an hour, Arden exited the highway and proceeded on a small roadway that wound through a wooded area. She switched on the high beams to navigate. The trees loomed around them and normally the scene would have been tranquil, but when they were alone on the road and in the dark the shadowed trunks appeared ominous. After another ten minutes of driving through the woods, Arden pulled onto a small, dirt road. Half a mile down the car's headlights illuminated a red "No Trespassing" sign hammered onto a trunk. Arden drove past it without slowing. Finally she turned onto a slender, pothole-filled dirt drive and stopped some distance away from a small cottage with a pointed roof painted white. A man, about thirty-five years old, stood in front of the house holding a shotgun.

"A nice warm welcome," Smith said.

"I told you, he's a bit jumpy. Remember, no military or CIA references. And hide the gun."

"He gets a gun and I don't?"

Arden shot him a quelling glance. Smith toasted her with his coffee cup and shoved her gun into his waistband. He swung open the door, got out, and waited for her to come around to the front of the car. She stopped next to Smith, but still about forty feet from the man and his gun.

"Hey, Winter, don't shoot. It's your attorney," Arden called to the man.

"Winter? Really?" Smith said to Arden under his breath. He took a sip of his coffee.

"Shh," Arden said. "And did you have to bring the coffee?"

"Yes. It's a prop. No one assumes that a guy holding a cup of coffee is going to kill them. It makes me look less threatening."

"It makes you look like you don't care."

"I care very deeply about not getting shot."

"Who's that with you?" Winter called back to them.

"A friend. I was hoping you could let us in. I'm in a bit of trouble and need your help."

Arden walked forward and Smith kept pace with her, still holding his coffee cup. When only ten feet separated them, Arden stopped. Winter stood about five-ten, with a rangy body and an earnest look. His hair was cut short and a small, silver peace sign earring hung from his left ear.

"What's your name?" Winter asked Smith.

"Jon Smith."

Winter snorted. "Sure it is."

Smith started to respond, but Arden nudged him with her elbow. Smith took another sip of coffee instead.

Winter turned his attention to Arden, taking in her bare feet and elegant dress.

"You look like Cinderella after she ran away from the ball."

Arden smiled. "That's actually pretty close to the truth."

Winter stepped to the side. "This I gotta hear. Come in."

The cottage's interior was homey and far more inviting than Smith would have expected, given their initial cold meeting. A main room flowed into a small galley kitchen. A sofa, hooked rug, rocking chair, and cocktail table, the last two with elegant curves and made from gleaming wood, flanked a fireplace where a fire crackled. The lights were low and Smith was surprised to see a kerosene lantern on a wooden kitchen table in the attached dining area.

"Can I make you some tea?" Winter said.

Arden nodded. "I'd love that."

Smith just held up his cup and shook his head. After Winter finished making the tea he sat down with them.

"So what the hell happened?"

"I went to the Saudi embassy party," Arden said.

Winter gave a low whistle. "You were there? It's all over the news."

"I was. And I ran out. Without my shoes, as you can see."

Winter flicked a glance at Smith. "You were there as well?"

Smith nodded. "I was."

"So what do you need?"

"A safe place to sleep for the night. I presume that the police, Europol, and every other law enforcement group is attempting to locate and interrogate the guests. I'm afraid to use my phone or credit cards to book a room for fear that they'll locate us."

"So why don't you want to be questioned?"

Arden sighed. "My relationship with the Saudis is less than friendly. I want to have an attorney by my side before they try to hang anything on me."

Winter's suspicious manner eased a bit as he seemed to accept this explanation.

"You use a credit card and they will track you. But going off the grid ain't easy, I can tell you."

"Are you?" Smith said.

Winter nodded. "As much as anyone can be. You can't tell from the front of the cottage, but I have a solar panel system out back that provides a limited amount of electricity for the house. I try to use the kerosene lanterns as often as possible to conserve it. There's also a propane tank. I've managed to have the land records sealed and I pay my taxes through a nominee."

Smith was intrigued. "How did you get the records sealed?"

Winter smiled. "I have a hacker friend who flagged the file. But if you truly want to remain off the grid you have to live in a way most people can't. No phones, no utilities through any services, no credit cards, grocery cards, or even online shopping. No Internet at all if you can help it. Sometimes you can't, and then I'm careful to go to public cafés or areas where I can use free Wi-Fi. Once there I purchase items using bitcoins in a swap system and with yet another pseudonym."

"What about the cameras?"

Winter walked over to the front door and reached down into a basket next to it. He lifted out a helmet.

"When I'm outdoors I ride a motorcycle and keep the helmet on at all times. When I'm not on the bike I wear glasses and a hat, and I wrap a scarf around my face in the cold months."

"Sounds like a lot of work," Arden said.

"Worth it, though. I can't imagine how people walk through the world so unaware."

"Perhaps they have nothing to hide," Smith said.

Winter raised an eyebrow. "I presume that's not you or you wouldn't be here."

"You presume right," Smith said.

"We need to get across to Calais. Is using the Channel Tunnel out?" Arden asked.

"Absolutely. Even if you bought your ticket with cash the cameras are everywhere." His face took on a slightly sly look. "I have a way to get you over there, but it will cost you a donation to the cause."

"How?"

"Remember the *Arctic Waters*?"

"Your ship? Sure."

"Well, it's docked not far from here. I would be willing to use it to get you across the channel."

"You can sail it solo?"

Winter laughed. "No. It requires a crew, but we've

smuggled people in and out of England using the boat without anyone being the wiser."

Arden looked at Smith. "You didn't hear that."

Smith shrugged. "Sorry? I was distracted and didn't hear what was said."

"Exactly," Arden said. "Can we stay the night here? Leave in the morning?"

"You can stay, but we should leave before dawn. It's best to get away from the shoreline before the sun comes up."

"Then let's crash."

"There are only two bedrooms, and the one down here is mine, so you both will have to share the attic room," Winter said.

"An attic room sounds perfect. I'm so exhausted that I'll be asleep in minutes," Arden said.

"And how about I lend you some clothes? That dress isn't going to be warm enough once we're at sea," Winter said. "I have some left here from the transient guests that should fit you."

Winter led them up a set of wooden stairs to an attic room that stretched the length of the cottage. The ceilings slanted on either side, but at the far end was a bench built into a window alcove. Pillows filled the area, and a teetering stack of books and a reading lamp made it clear that it was a favorite nook for someone. Bunk beds lined the room, leaving a small aisle between them. An armoire sat against one wall and next to it was a small occasional table with a lamp that Winter switched on.

"No kerosene up here. You're too close to the roof. The reading lamp takes the smallest amount of energy, but don't worry too much. With our string of sunny days the panels have stored a lot of electricity." He looked at Arden. "Come on downstairs with me and I'll give you towels and clothes."

Smith followed them down to the main floor. Arden announced that she was taking a shower and disappeared into the cottage's one bathroom. Winter settled into a chair near the kitchen table and Smith sat down opposite. The table and chair were also in a flowing and stunning design that was at odds with the small cottage.

"This furniture is beautiful," Smith said.

Winter's face flushed a bit. "Thank you. I made it."

"You're very talented."

Winter shrugged, but Smith could tell he was flattered.

"Would you like me to lend you some clothes as well? You're a bit taller than I am, but I might have something you can wear," Winter said.

"Thanks for the offer, but I won't be here long enough for it to matter."

Winter gave him a considering look. "What does that mean?"

"It means I won't be going with you and Arden to Calais. I'm going to strike out on my own. It's safer for her if we do it this way."

Winter raised an eyebrow. "Does she know this?"

Smith shook his head. "And I really wish you wouldn't tell her until after she's slept."

Winter took a sip of his tea. "Why don't you tell her yourself?"

"She's been seen with me at key points this evening. If you don't make it across, the authorities will focus on her, not you. The less she knows the better."

"Will she be angry that you left her? Are you lovers?"

Smith thought about how to answer that question. He never discussed his personal affairs with strangers.

"No. She may be a bit angry, but not with the fury of a jilted lover."

Winter kept his gaze steady, and Smith couldn't tell if he believed him or not.

"Who are you really? One of Arden's clients?"

Smith smiled at that. "In a manner of speaking, yes. Right now I need to understand what I'm facing. You're dedicated to living off the grid. What things should I worry about in the trip to Calais? Assuming that I want to take the Channel Tunnel and not a boat."

"As I said before, I'm not sure it's even possible to do that with any anonymity. Why not the boat?"

"The tunnel is faster."

"Okay, that's certainly true. First off, you need to understand that no one really 'lives off the grid,' they just think they do. You'd have to bury yourself high in the Alps and grow your own food even to have a shot at it."

Smith thought of Howell and his lair in the Sierra Nevada. The decision to live so far from others was suddenly making more sense.

"Okay. But you've done it."

"Not really. Every time I head into town, even with the helmet, I'm captured on a camera. Which means that *someone* sees me. Whether they choose to investigate further is the deciding factor. I depend on the fact that the average government worker is not that interested in analyzing the thousands of images and people they monitor daily, and this disinterest is the only thing that keeps me somewhat protected."

Smith downed the last bit of his coffee and stood. "Is it safe to be outside here? No cameras?"

Winter nodded. "No cameras, and the satellite won't pass over again for another twenty hours or so. Even if it does, the trees block the front of the house. They'll have a shot of the panels, though. Nothing I can do about that, they need to be open to the sky to soak up the sun."

Smith went back outside to the white car and knelt next to the rear left tire. He pulled out the device that the operative had given him. He heard the crunching of Winter's shoes on the ground behind him, but didn't look up. Smith switched on the device and ran it around the tire's rim. It beeped once at the three-quarter mark. Smith took the probe, held it close to the rim, and pressed a button. The small probe turned red and the device gave an answering two-beep signal. Smith rose and went to the next tire.

"What are you doing?" Winter asked.

"Burning out the RFID chips," Smith said.

"They're in tires? That never occurred to me. Why?"

Smith finished with the second and headed to the third. "Easier if there's a recall."

"I usually use a disposable camera's charge to burn RFIDs. That's a nice little device you've got there."

When Smith was done with the last one he waved at Winter's cycle.

"Want me to check yours?"

Winter nodded. "Hell yes."

Smith ran the leads over the motorcycle's tires and deactivated two more chips. When he was done he switched off the device.

"I think you should assume that you've been pinged every time you've ridden that cycle."

Winter grimaced. "Like I said, I knew that I was watched, but it's worse than I thought."

"Do you really think it's possible to get Arden out of England without the authorities knowing?"

"I'm pretty sure. I've done it a lot of times."

"Why?" Smith asked.

Winter raised an eyebrow. "What do you mean?"

Smith shrugged. "Why live a life constantly at odds with your fellow man?"

"Because my fellow humans are a bunch of murderous bastards out to defile every inch of this planet to ensure their own pleasure."

Smith shook his head. "You don't really believe that."

"What makes you think I don't?"

"Because it's not true. Statistically and objectively. There are billions of people on this planet and the majority of them try to do what's right every day."

"You're an optimist."

"I'm a scientist. I'm just stating a fact."

"Scientists are some of the people who got us here in the first place. They invent the technology that creates the problem and then they try to sell the rest of us the solution."

Smith wanted to argue that the majority of scientific advances had benefited humankind, not harmed it, but he sensed that it would be a futile discussion. He suspected that Winter would trot out the one example that leveled the argument: the nuclear bomb. It was an invention of the darkest variety.

Smith shoved the device in his pocket and headed back into the cottage. The bathroom door hung open and the smell of shampoo and soap wafted in the air. Smith took the stairs to the attic and found Arden on a top bunk, sound asleep. He crawled into another top bunk closest to the exit, placed his jacket at the foot of the bed, set his watch to wake him in three hours, and tried to get some rest.

42

Russell stood near the door of a safe house only ten miles from where they had first intercepted Smith and Arden. Taylor's condition had deteriorated too rapidly for them to reach the hospital and they'd opted for the closer location. Now Taylor lay on a bed while a physician connected to the agency attempted to address her injuries. Russell watched him from across the room. His head was bowed over Taylor as he worked and Russell's operative, still in her cocktail dress, held a desk lamp next to the doctor's shoulder to provide more light. From the bed came a rattling sound—a sound that Russell had heard many times before. The physician's head bowed lower.

"Is she dead?" Russell asked. The physician straightened.

"Yes," he said. "I'm sorry. The damage to her artery was too extensive."

Russell turned and walked through the house and out the front door, where Beckmann leaned against the physician's car while he smoked a cigarette.

"Taylor didn't make it," Russell said.

Beckmann tipped his head to the sky and closed his eyes a moment before looking at Russell. "This whole mission has taken a wretched turn. I feel like we're reacting to someone else's game instead of playing our own."

Russell knew what he meant. "We're reacting because we don't have the time to really analyze the facts.

We still don't know why these disparate people were kidnapped all in one night."

"Taylor wasn't kidnapped at the same time. At least I don't think she was."

Russell began to reply, but stopped when she heard the cracking of a twig. Trees surrounded the house, which was in the center of a stand of them that stretched across five acres. Beckmann stared steadily at Russell, but it was clear that he had heard the noise as well.

"We have visitors," Russell said in a soft voice.

"Yes, it appears as though we do." He offered her the cigarette. "Hold this a moment?"

Russell took it. Beckmann slowly reached across his body and slid his hand under the lightweight jacket he wore, where Russell knew he had a gun in a holster near his left shoulder.

"I left my gun in the house."

"Then I suggest you take cover at the count of three. One, two, three."

Russell dropped below the car window and pressed her shoulder against the door. Beckmann dropped with her. The only sound was the creaking of the tree branches as the wind blew through them. Russell reached to her ankle, where a knife in a holder hugged the outside of her leg. She removed it, held it at the ready, and wished it were a gun. Beckmann shuffled forward to the front of the car and peered around the headlights.

"See anything?" Russell whispered.

"Nothing. We'd better get back into the house. Whoever's out there could be making their way around," Beckmann replied.

From the back of the house came the crash of breaking glass. Russell was up and sprinting toward the front door, with Beckmann right behind her. She ran through the hallway and dodged right to pick up her own gun, which she had left on a credenza. When she reached the bedroom entrance she pressed against the wall next to the doorway. Beckmann joined her and stayed close while Russell inched toward the opening, holding her gun high. When she hit the door panel edge she peered into the bedroom.

The doctor was sprawled over Taylor's body with a gaping wound at the base of his skull. The operative sat on the floor to the right of a shattered window and pressed her back against the far wall. She saw Russell and held up two fingers.

"Detmar says there are two, so we should expect a pincer movement," Russell whispered to Beckmann. She slid her knife back into its holder at her ankle and checked her gun. She watched as Detmar crabbed across the floor, bent low. She came through the door and pressed against the opposite wall.

"I'm pretty sure I saw two before I dropped down," Detmar said.

"Do we have any other backup close?" Russell asked.

Detmar shook her head. "Nothing. This safe house was just added to our list this week. It's so new that it hasn't even been staffed yet. I wonder how they found us. I'm positive we weren't followed from the highway."

Russell wondered as well. "We need to get to the car and get out of here," she said.

"Agreed. With Taylor gone there's no reason to stay."

"I've got the car keys. I'll count it down and then we'll head to the car. Don't stop," Beckmann said.

On Beckmann's count Russell and Detmar burst from the door, guns high, and sprinted the short few feet to the car. Russell heard the compressed air noise of a silenced shot and Detmar grunted once and stumbled into Russell, almost knocking her down.

"Right, thirty degrees," Russell said.

Beckmann laid down fire and Russell wrapped her arm around Detmar to hold her up. She dragged the woman the last few feet to the car and opened the back door. Detmar fell into the backseat while Russell slammed the door closed and opened the front passenger door. She stayed behind it, using it for whatever cover it could provide while she joined Beckmann and fired into the trees. As she fired, Beckmann continued working his way around the vehicle to the driver's side. Russell was relieved when she heard the engine start up. She scrambled into the seat and Beckmann shot down the driveway. A bullet punched through the back window and exited the windshield without doing any further damage, but it was the last close call Russell wanted to have that evening.

Beckmann barreled down the snaking drive and turned on a hard left, bumping up over a large boulder painted to glow in the dark that marked the driveway's end. The car's shocks squeaked as the car hammered back down. The sedan swerved a bit but Beckmann managed to keep it on the road as he straightened. Russell watched the side-view mirror as they accelerated down the road. When she was certain that they'd outrun the attackers, she put her gun in the holster and leaned over the seat.

"Where are you hit?" she asked Detmar.

Detmar grimaced in obvious pain. "In my side. I think it went clear through."

"I'm driving to the hospital we were supposed to take Taylor to," Beckmann said.

"Don't go there," Russell said.

"What are you talking about? She needs medical attention."

"Someone is feeding information to these guys and I don't think we can afford to use any of our usual haunts until we know who," Russell said.

"The woman still needs a doctor," Beckmann replied.

Detmar's gaze switched from one to the other as Beckmann and Russell debated the issue.

"Do you know anyone outside the agency who could handle this for us?" Russell asked Detmar.

She shook her head. "No one. A bullet wound would have to be reported."

"Beckmann?" Russell asked.

"I'm thinking," he said. "But no. I don't." They drove a few miles in silence.

"I wish Smith were here. He's great at field dressings," Russell said. "I don't have any ideas either. We'll use the agency medical center, but I won't call ahead and this time we'll guard the perimeter." She looked at Detmar. "Hang in there."

Detmar nodded and closed her eyes.

Beckmann turned off the motorway and headed to the medical center, which was on a quiet cul-de-sac. It was a squat, nondescript two-story brick building with white window frames and double glass doors. Light glowed from the interior, but the four available parking spots were empty. Beckmann pulled into one marked with a sign that said "Visitors" and killed the engine.

"I'll reconnoiter," he said. Russell opened her door and stepped out, keeping low and tracking to the right. Beckmann was at the door in four long strides, also keeping low and to the door's edge. He peered into the building through the glass door, his gun in his hand. Russell saw him go still.

"*Scheisse*," he said under his breath.

"What is it?" Russell asked.

"You'd better come see this," Beckmann said. Russell jogged up to him and he pointed to the door.

Through the glass Russell could see the center's reception area. A woman was draped over a counter, her arm hanging limp next to a plaque that said "Reception." Blood dripped down from her fingers and onto the carpeting below, where a pool was forming. Two feet and to the left of her, on the other side of the counter, a man lay, also facedown. His hand disappeared under his body. Three feet from that man another woman was sprawled against a couch, and her sightless eyes stared forward. Blood covered her clothes from a gaping wound in her neck.

"What do you think?" Beckmann asked.

"I think we've got a mole," Russell said.

43

Darkanin stood outside the shattered window where Taylor lay dead. Asam stood next to him.

"I pay you to kill Smith and you don't. I pay you to kill the lawyer and you don't. I pay you to kill the chauffeur and you don't, and I pay you *extra* to recover Taylor alive and she's the one you kill? Give me my money back," Darkanin said.

Asam shook his head. "Maybe if you had told me the truth I could have done the job right, but you lied to me every step of the way."

"What are you talking about?"

Asam turned to stand in front of Darkanin. His dark eyes glittered with anger as he pushed his face into Darkanin's.

"I'm talking about the chauffeur. I know a trained fighter when I meet one, and he was trained. And whoever he was, he was a professional, not some local gym rat who knows a few martial arts moves."

It took all Darkanin had in him to stand his ground as Asam crowded him.

"What makes you say that? Trying to assuage your ego?"

Asam stabbed a finger at Darkanin. "In the past five years I've handled any number of jobs and all of them, *all* of them, have been successful. I am the best. That this man managed to evade me and stay alive is testament to his training and the training of the entire crew." Asam spun and pointed at the doctor's body.

"And after Smith shot at me and another set of killers in a silver car wiped out two of my best lieutenants, I was nearly killed by two more that were guarding this guy. You're into something big and you've underplayed the risk every step of the way."

Darkanin stayed glued to the ground while Asam raged.

"I need more money," Asam said.

Darkanin's own anger began to bubble. He should have expected extortion. "Not. Another. Dime," he said. "I needed that woman alive to finish the work that she began. She's a microbiologist from one of the finest research institutes in the world. She's brilliant and innovative and now she's dead."

Asam spit on the ground. "Then maybe you should have told me the truth about what I was up against." He shrugged. "She's dead and she's not coming back, so you'd better find another one." Asam bent down and picked up one of the two gas cans at his feet. "Let's get to work," he said.

Darkanin shook his head. "No. I'm not going inside. I'm not stupid. Even if you burn the house to a crisp there still can be evidence left behind. You go inside and burn it."

To Darkanin's surprise Asam headed toward the house without further argument. As he did Darkanin looked again through the window at the two dead people. What Asam said had struck a chord in him. Perhaps he could salvage the situation after all. What he needed was someone to finish the work that Taylor had started. He removed his gun, checked the magazine, and waited.

From within the house came the whooshing sound of fire igniting. The sound repeated two more times and Darkanin watched Asam back into the bedroom, his body bent as he trailed gasoline. He tossed the remaining gasoline on the dead physician, threw the empty can on the bed, and turned to climb out the shattered window. Darkanin shot him in the chest.

Asam's body jerked back from the hit and a look of surprise spread across his features. After a moment he dropped to the floor, landing in a puddle of the gasoline that he had just spilled. Darkanin reached into his pocket, pulled out a book of matches, lit one, and leaned back through the frame to toss it onto the trail of gas. Flames licked upward.

Darkanin went around the house to where his car was parked. More flames shot out of the windows and bits of ash and clouds of smoke floated in the air. Darkanin started his rented Mercedes and drove down the drive at a steady pace. When he reached the main highway he dialed a number.

"Do you have her?" a voice said.

"She's dead."

"You used Asam, right?" The voice sounded incredulous.

"That's right," Darkanin said. "You told me he was the best."

"He is."

"He was. He's dead."

"Dead? How?"

"Smith killed him."

"I'm surprised. Asam should have been able to take him out from a distance. I funneled him the tracking information every step of the way."

"Who was helping Smith?"

"The same guy that my contact said had found and delivered Warner back into the hands of the DOD. Smith and another man named Beckmann. But you knew about them."

"Asam said there was more than just him."

"There were. A CIA cell working London. They'd received a call for assistance from him and I intercepted the call and patched it through to Asam. What happened?"

"Smith must have been aware that someone was tracking him, because he was surrounded by guards. More guards than just this Beckmann. Guards that Asam claims were professional fighters. You know of a group within the CIA that can field a team better than one of yours?"

"No one is better than us. Not the CIA, not the FBI. None of them. If such a group exists I can assure you it's not from an authorized governmental organization, because I have access to every one of the sanctioned teams."

"Then it's another contract security agency. Like yours."

"No one is like Stanton Reese. No one."

"Then it's a privately managed set of mercenaries."

"Not a chance. The truly good fighters are all taken by everyone that you just mentioned. Any mercenaries left are the dregs who weren't good enough to make it anywhere and certainly not better than Asam and his team. I don't like it. And what do we do now that Taylor's dead? It's three days to breakdown, and we don't have the final product. We need someone to finish what she started. Who can do that? Think."

Darkanin accelerated onto the highway while he pondered the question.

"How about Chang Ying Peng?" Darkanin said. "The microbiologist from China?"

"We should be so lucky."

"Why not? We can have him picked up in DC," Darkanin said.

"No, we can't. At least not now. The FBI has him under watch twenty-four hours a day."

Darkanin watched the road signs and kept a steady pace to avoid any speed camera flashes.

"Then what about Smith?"

Darkanin heard the other man snort in disbelief. "Forget it. He'll never agree."

"Who said he has to agree? We'll do to him what we did to Taylor."

"She started out thinking it was a sanctioned mission. He knows better."

"You put a gun to his head and he'll do it," Darkanin said.

"What if we use the product now? In its current state? What will happen?"

"How the hell would I know?" Darkanin said. "Probably fail. Won't reverse a thing and we'll have legions of dead bodies. And you forget the key here. Without the reversal there's nothing to sell, and without a salable product there's no money. Who do you have left to get Smith?"

"Gore's in Europe. He's unstoppable. You should have used him first. Westcore and Denon are back in DC."

"Send Gore after Smith and the other two here. We capture Smith, force him to finish the research, and then kill him."

"And if he doesn't?"

"Then we still have Plan B. We sell the weapon to the highest bidder. It's not as good as having the antidote, which can be sold over and over again for a thousand times the profit, but at least we get a payday for all our efforts."

"Fine. I'll send them. Just remember to warn me before you launch the weapon so that I can arrange to be back in the States when the people start dying."

"Of course," Darkanin said. No need to tell him that the weapon would be used in the States, Darkanin thought.

44

Smith drove through the predawn hour while sipping a cup of a strong brew that Winter had pressed upon him. He'd left quietly while Arden slept on. The few hours of sleep had helped, but he would be happy when the sun rose. When it did he would stop and take a short walk in the sunshine to clear his head even further.

Winter had given him a new prepaid cell phone from a stash that he had from the various transient guests who had made their way through the small cottage.

"They're all registered in false names," Winter had said. "This one is Becky Rose." Now Smith turned it on and dialed Russell. After several rings an automated message announced that the phone had been disconnected.

That's not good, Smith thought. He dialed Beckmann. Same result. He dialed Marty.

"Hello?" Smith was relieved to hear Marty's voice.

"Marty, it's Smith."

"Who's Becky Rose?" Marty asked.

"She's a fake. Doesn't exist. The other phone was hacked and I needed a new untraceable one." He told Marty about the threatening call. "I have no idea how they got the number, because that phone was a prepaid burner. And now both Russell and Beckmann's phones have been disconnected. Do you have any idea what's going on?"

"Sorry, I don't. No one's called me."

"I need to get across the channel without detection. Any idea how to do that?"

"Not from the UK side. Too many cameras. Perhaps a disguise?"

Smith had already considered a disguise, but to obtain the things he needed he would have to head into a store, purchase the items, and then find a confidential place to put them on. At the very least the store purchase would be recorded on a camera.

"If you hear from Russell or Beckmann can you give them this number?"

"Will do," Marty said. Smith rang off and contemplated his next move. He could call Klein, and was fairly certain that Klein's phone system was impenetrable to hacks, but he would also have said that about Russell's and so was loath to take the risk. Besides, what he really needed was someone to assist him with a disguise. After a few moments, he dialed a number he hadn't dialed in over a year.

"Yeah, what do you want?" a rough voice said.

"I'm looking for Ruby," Smith replied.

"At five in the morning?"

"I know she's awake. She works the morning rush hour near Bordeaux."

"She's not in France anymore."

"Where is she, then?"

"Who are you?"

"A friend. Have her call this number and tell her Smith is looking for her."

"Smith? You a Traveler?"

"No. Not a Roma, either."

"*Gadjo*, what do you want with Ruby?"

"Just let her know I called. Thanks."

Smith hung up and contemplated his next move. He wasn't prepared to attempt a tunnel crossing until he knew he could make it through undetected. Once in the tunnel he'd be trapped for the entire duration. His phone rang and the words "Private Caller" showed on the display.

"Hello," Smith said, being careful not to identify himself.

"I knew you would call me one day." Ruby's voice

held the same low timbre and dark tones that he remembered.

He smiled into the darkness. "Your crystal ball tell
you that?" Smith asked.

"The cards did."

"What did they say?"

"That Jon Smith would return, marry me, and take
me away from all of this." She laughed her soft laugh.
Smith's smile broadened. Ruby hadn't changed.

"You're already married." Like many Roma, Ruby had
been married at fourteen. When Smith met her last
year she was twenty-seven and the mother of four. He'd
volunteered in the Roma camp near Bordeaux, France,
treating the children for various childhood ailments, en-
couraging the parents to get them immunized, and trying
to convince them that the children needed to go to
school. The immunizations and treatment were successful, the push for education was not. The literacy rate
for the Roma in France was dismal and infant mortality
high. "I need your help."

"Anything for you," Ruby said.

"I need you to find out from your friends there how
they move between England and France."

"Ah, well, things have changed. You've heard about
the purge? Last year we were rounded up like cattle and
many forced out of France. Most were sent back to Romania or Bulgaria. The rest of us scattered."

"Where are you now?"

"England. They opened their borders last year."

"That's right. The waiting period for Romanians to
travel throughout the EU has ended, hasn't it? Life is
better in the UK?"

"A bit. I've filed for the dole. Me and my fourteen
children."

Smith snorted. "You only have four."

"Four that eat as if they were fourteen."

Yes, Ruby hadn't changed.

"It just so happens that I'm in England. Where are you?"

"Margate. On the sea. So you want to go to France, not toward England?"

"Yes. Is Margate near the tunnel?"

"It's close. A bit north is all. Why don't you come here and we can talk." She gave Smith directions to Margate and he rang off and hit the gas.

An hour later he pulled into a parking lot next to a boardwalk by the sea. Tents and caravans filled every inch of space and the rest of the population slept rough under the lightening sky. Smith had visited Gypsy and Traveler camps before and was familiar with the poverty and homelessness that often accompanied the population. Gypsies were a maligned and ostracized people that faced discrimination every day. He picked his way around the small barbecue grills and propane-driven stoves already in use by the few who were awake. As he walked an older man stepped up to him.

"Look. I found a gold ring! Is it yours?" The man tried to shove a heavy gold ring into Smith's palm. Smith waved it off. The man persisted and jostled his way closer.

"Back off, I know the drill," Smith said. The man paused, then grinned, shrugged, and walked away. Smith checked his pocket to ensure that his wallet was still there, walked a few steps farther, and Ruby stepped out of a small camper.

She was thinner than he remembered, which made her angular features even more pronounced, and her dark hair was longer and messy from sleep. She wore tight-fitting black yoga pants and a sweatshirt with a wide neckline that had slid down to reveal one shoulder. She gave the impression that she had just slipped out of bed, in what may or may not have been a carefully staged presentation. She stepped down, walked to him, and stopped only when her body was pressed full against him. She twined her arms around his neck and rose up on tiptoe to be able to kiss him. He moved his head back a bit and wrapped his fingers around her forearms to hold her in place while he smiled down at her.

"Where's your husband?" he asked.

She shrugged and the sweatshirt slid lower. "Romania, I think. When the French offered free flights back and three hundred euros apiece he took it and ran. You look very handsome in that suit." She tried again to kiss him. He forestalled her by giving her a quick peck on the cheek and gently put her from him. She released her arms and stepped back, putting her hands on her hips. "Still the *gadjo* gentleman, I see."

"Actually, I'm concerned that someone will think you're running the Sexy Young Woman scam on me. I already dodged a gold ring."

This time she smiled. "Whoever tried that one on you doesn't know you, eh? And I'm truly hurt that you think I would ever run a scam on you. Especially that one. You're barely older than I am."

Smith knew that the scam was a favorite of Ruby's, used on aging men who were eager to win her favors. It never involved sex—the Gypsy women that he knew never prostituted themselves—but instead just companionship. The men paid some bills and in return obtained the fawning interest of a pretty young woman for a while. Once they realized that no sex would be forthcoming the men often lost interest and the Gypsy woman would move on.

He waved at the caravan. "Can we go in? Or are the children sleeping?"

She nodded and stepped aside to let him enter. "They sleep in the tents. It's just me in here."

Smith had to bend his head a bit to avoid hitting it on the low-hanging doorway. Inside the tiny caravan was spotlessly clean and decorated with gaily colored curtains and bright pillows and blankets. Her bed had been lowered from its location in the far wall and was still strewn with sheets and a crocheted blanket. She quickly collected them to raise it.

"Let me help," Smith said. He locked the piece in place and she folded the linens, placed them in a storage unit below. When that was closed she lowered a panel that locked into place to create a small table for eating. Within a minute the room was transformed from a sleeping area to a kitchen.

"Sit. I'll make us some tea." She started a burner, filled a teapot, and set it in place. Smith was glad to see that she had running water and propane. Back in Bordeaux she'd had none.

"How are the children? Are they enrolled in school here?"

He saw her face harden a bit. "They are, but they're being bullied. It's the same everywhere for us. George will stop soon."

"George is only twelve. He should continue." Smith kept his voice neutral. It was an old battle between him and Ruby and he knew that she struggled with the change that traditional schooling would make in her children's lives. In the usual Gypsy tradition, she had stopped attending school at ten to help care for her younger siblings. Education beyond primary school was rare for her family. None went to high school and only 1 percent of the entire Gypsy population in France attended tertiary school, making a university education nearly unheard of among the families. She remained quiet until the teapot began to steam. She poured him a mug, added a tea bag, and placed it in front of him. She poured another for herself and slid into the booth.

"You didn't come here to talk about that, I think. Tell me what you need." Ruby proceeded to dip her tea bag up and down in her cup as she watched him.

"I need to get into France undetected."

She raised an eyebrow. "I can't believe that a man like you is in trouble with the law." She put up her palm. "Not that it would stop me from helping you."

He shook his head. "I'm not, really. But I need some anonymity and I can't get it in a country with six million cameras."

"I know a Traveler who regularly smuggles off the

coast. He can take you by boat. He leaves once a week. More often if there's a need and someone willing to pay. Right now, though, he's in France."

"I had hoped for a quick tunnel ride."

"They'll flag you when you present your passport at the border."

"I've got that covered."

She stared at her cup of tea in thought. Smith watched her bob the bag up and down.

"I'd say you could go with a group of us, but when the police see us they watch even closer. You need a disguise."

"That's what I thought. Can you help me?"

She nodded. "I'll get Maje. She works the carnivals; dresses as a clown, a woman from the eighteenth century for the medieval fairs, those kinds of things. She can give you a beard, some glasses, and even a wig."

"Can you wake her? Tell her I'll make it worth her while."

Ruby stood. "Stay here. I'll go get her."

Twenty minutes later Ruby returned, dragging a large woman in her late fifties whom Smith presumed was Maje. She had a jovial face and wore a long, peasant-style dress that Smith thought of as classic Gypsy attire. She placed a large, square brown luggage case on the table in front of him.

"So you're Ruby's friend?" she asked.

"I am."

Maje cocked her head to one side as she contemplated him. "You're too handsome and that suit reeks of money. Women will notice your face and men will notice the suit. Both are not good."

"I might be able to find more casual clothes for him," Ruby suggested. Maje shook her head.

"We don't really have the time. First train leaves soon. Do you have children?"

Smith was surprised at the sudden change of subject. "No."

"Well, you do now." Maje opened the luggage case and removed a piece of what looked like short hair and a jar of theater glue. She glanced at Ruby. "Can he take George? They won't expect him to be traveling with a child." She removed the glue's lid and used the attached brush to coat a piece of beard.

Smith was impressed with Maje's insight. A child would be the perfect foil. Anyone searching for him would have his description and would expect him to be traveling with Arden, not a child. Yet he shook his head.

"I won't take George. How will he get back from Calais? And he needs to be in school."

Maje stopped applying the glue. "You'll buy him a round-trip ticket. He's old enough to get himself home. School? We're talking one day at the most. And you'll pay George to go with you, won't you?"

"He has a thing about school." Ruby's voice was apologetic.

Maje rolled her eyes. "Most *gadje* do. But George is old enough now to begin to apprentice. School isn't our way." She bent toward Smith to apply the beard.

He put his hand on her wrist to stop her. "No pulling George out of school."

Maje searched his face, then sighed. "Okay. I have a granddaughter. She's sixteen. Married. No school. She can go with you."

Smith shook his head again. "No children. It's an excellent idea, but I'd prefer to go it alone."

"Hold still," Maje said. She leaned into him and carefully placed the beard. The glue felt cold on his skin.

"How about I go with him and carry Sylvie's baby? We can be a family," Ruby said. She looked at Smith. "And the baby's not even a year old. Even you can't argue that she should be in school."

"Sylvie's baby screams bloody murder if anyone but Sylvie carries her. She'd only make a scene. You need an older child that understands the game," Maje said.

"No children," Smith said.

"Your friend here is stubborn," Maje said to Ruby. She began placing adhesive on another strip of beard. She focused back on Smith. "Let me teach you how to run a game. The key to getting past people is to either blend or distract. Preferably both. You have a car?"

"I do," Smith said.

"The first step would be to try to blend. I'm going to give you a briefcase, hat, and once you park the car you should stare at your phone all the time. Pretend to be texting and returning emails. Most people never raise their heads from their phone." She prepped a tiny strip of hair and placed it from his eyebrow to the center of the bridge of his nose. She did the same with the other eyebrow.

"You're giving him a unibrow?" Ruby said.

Maje nodded. "I learned the trick from an Irish Traveler I met in Sheffield. He said it helps to block those software programs that the police use to match your face from the CCTV photos."

"Facial recognition programs," Smith said.

"Exactly. My friend said they search here." Maje waved her finger in a circle at the center of her face. "And they measure the distance between eyebrows. Usually I would put a lock of hair there, but yours is too short." She sat back and handed Smith a mirror. A bearded, dark-haired man with heavy eyebrows and blazing-blue eyes stared back at him.

"My eyes jump out."

"It's the contrast of dark and light. You would need brown contact lenses to change them and my little bag of tricks doesn't go that far," Maje said.

"What about some sunglasses?"

Maje shook her head. "Not indoors. They'll only make you look like you have something to hide. Now, here's what you do. You drive into the station and onto the shuttle. When you leave the car you keep your hat on and your head bowed over your phone. Keep those eyes lowered. I know a family that works the tunnel. I'll call

ahead and give them your description. If they see anything that looks dicey at the entrance they'll wave you
off."

"And in Calais?"

"The same only in reverse."

Maje stood. "I'll be going now."

Smith stood with her, reached into his pocket, removed his wallet, and handed her one hundred pounds.
"Thank you," he said.

Maje seemed pleased with the amount. "Be safe on
your travels." She patted Ruby on the arm and left. Ruby
watched him with a somber look on her face.

"Are you sure that you aren't in trouble with the law?"

"I'm sure."

"I'll walk you to the car."

"Not a good idea. We might be picked up on camera."

"Don't worry. The first thing we did when we came
here was break them. There are no cameras. Let's go."

Smith followed her out of the camper and they
strolled side by side to his car. When they reached it he
took out four hundred pounds, picked up her hand, and
placed it in her palm. She looked down at the money
then up at him and a flash of humor lit her eyes.

"Aren't you worried that someone will see this and
think I'm running the Sexy Young Woman scam?"

He smiled back. "I don't care. It's for you and the
kids. Keep them in school."

Her smile fled. She reached up, grabbed his lapel,
pulled him down, and kissed him full on the mouth,
snaking her tongue between his lips in a slow caress.
Despite all the danger around him he felt himself responding and he kissed her back. After a moment she
stepped away and said something in her language.

"What did you say?" he asked.

"May you remain with God," she said.

"And you as well," he replied. She nodded and he
climbed into the car. The sun was rising as he drove
away.

45

Smith was through the passport checkpoint and headed to the long, low-slung building that housed the car transport shuttle when a crowd of teenagers surrounded his car. The oldest of them, a boy of about eighteen, rapped on the driver's-side window.

"You Smith?" he said when Smith had lowered the window.

"I am."

"Maje sent us. Don't go in there. She said..."

"—Let's not have this conversation here. You climb in and send the others away."

The boy waved off the crowd and joined Smith in the car. Smith turned out of the line and idled in a far corner.

"What's your name?"

"Pilar."

"Okay, what did you see?"

"There's a man walking around holding a picture of you and some woman and shoving it in the face of everyone he meets asking if they've seen you. He's wearing a BTP uniform but I know them all and he ain't one."

"What's a BTP?"

"British Transport Police."

"Maybe he's a part-timer?"

Pilar gave an emphatic shake of his head. "No way. He's a fake. And the guy has the weirdest, deadest eyes I've ever seen."

Smith gave Pilar forty pounds. "Get the others and

leave here. Now. And don't come back for a couple of days. You understand?"

Pilar pocketed the money and nodded. "That's no problem. I want to stay as far away from him as possible." He was out of the car and gone.

Smith turned the car and began a slow drive out of the transport area. In his rearview mirror he saw a man in uniform step out into the morning sun. In his hand he held a piece of paper. Smith didn't stay to see any more, but instead reversed his commute and drove back onto the motorway toward Margate.

His phone rang twenty minutes later. He let it go to voicemail. When he listened, he heard it was Russell. He called her back.

"What happened?"

"We've got trouble." Smith listened while she laid out the facts that pointed toward a mole.

"Who do you think you can trust?"

"That's just it. I don't know. And Detmar is here and injured. Can you get back to us and prepare a field dressing for her?"

"On my way," Smith said. "Is it safe for you to retrieve some items from the center without detection? Would make the dressing easier."

"Yes. What do you need?" Smith listed the supplies for her and hit the motorway at the fastest speed he could without triggering a camera.

After an hour of driving into the English countryside, he pulled to the side of the road and found Beckmann leaning against a black sedan, smoking. Russell stood next to him. Smith saw no sign of Detmar. Russell pushed off the car and came to greet him. He watched her face as she took in his newly acquired beard and unibrow.

"That's an interesting look. I hope the costume shop didn't have a camera."

"It came courtesy of an actor's makeup kit. Where's Detmar?"

"In the backseat."

"Is she stable?"

Russell nodded. "I think so. She thinks the bullet went right through her side. We were waiting for you. Half a mile from here is a second CIA safe house. Empty. No staff and a lockbox that will provide the keys."

"I thought you were concerned about a mole."

"I am, so I won't call it in until the last minute. Whoever the mole is he'll have no lead time to get someone there. At least, not right away. With any luck we'll be able to use it as an operating theater for you for an hour at least before we have to leave."

"Not ideal, but let's go. I'll follow."

The road ended at the entrance of a modest, two-story house with a pitched roof and the air of a second home closed for the season. Russell punched in a code at the gate and the lock buzzed and sprang open. She walked the fence wide to allow Beckmann and Smith to drive through. Russell headed to the front door while Beckmann came around to the sedan's passenger side. Detmar emerged, leaning heavily on him with her arm flung over his neck. She wore loose-fitting men's sweatpants and a men's white undershirt that hiked up on the side where she clung to Beckmann. The cotton flapped in the slight breeze, revealing a large piece of gauze wrapped around her waist. Without her cocktail attire and makeup and in the baggy, oversized clothes she looked less sophisticated and more vulnerable. Her skin was pale and her face set in pain. She spotted him and gave a wan smile.

"We meet again. Did you burn the tires?"

"Yes sir," he said. She rewarded him with a slightly wider smile and he walked to her free side and held her up while they ascended a short two steps into the house. The interior was a standard split with a living and dining area on one side, a small home office on the other, a stairwell in front to the right that led upstairs, and a hall down the center that presumably led to the back of the house.

"No stairs. It'll hurt too much," Detmar said.

They kept moving down the hall. It opened into a large room with a kitchen on one side, a breakfast nook in a bay window overlooking the backyard, and a family seating area opposite with a couch, a chair, and a cocktail table facing a television and media center.

"Let's go to the couch," Smith said. "Russell, can you look in the bathroom for some towels? We'll put them underneath her to protect it from blood." Russell jogged back through the hall and he heard her feet on the carpeted stairs. A minute or two later she returned and placed a large white bath towel on the couch. They lowered Detmar onto it and Smith heard her sigh in relief.

Smith unwound the gauze, which was sticky with blood. When he reached the end it clung to the wound and he heard Detmar's sharp intake of breath.

"Sorry, but this has to come off." She nodded and he worked the gauze free.

An examination showed that the bullet had not entered her torso at the front and exited the back as she thought, but instead had nicked the fleshy part of her waist. There was a lot of blood, but if they kept the wound clean he expected her to make a full recovery. While Smith worked to clean the wound with antiseptic he thought of Arden's comment that Detmar was a point of connection between the two of them. He watched the time as he worked, ever aware that they were racing against the clock. He covered the wound with a breathable bandage and rewrapped it lightly with another long strip of gauze.

"You're going to be okay," he said. She nodded. "And I'm sorry, but I'm going to have to ask you some questions." Out of the corner of his eye he saw Beckmann turn from his post at a back window to look at them.

Detmar's attention focused. "Okay. Can you help me sit up? This sounds serious and I'd rather answer from an upright position."

Smith assisted her to a sitting position and Russell walked over and handed her a glass of water.

"Who assigned you the embassy party detail?"

"My supervisor at the CIA."

"Here in England?"

"Yes."

"Where?"

"I'm a member of the joint CIA-NSA project at Croughton."

"I was just there," Russell said. "Do you work for Scariano on the drone program?"

She shook her head. "No, I'm with the SCS."

"What's that?" Smith asked.

"The Special Collection Services. We manage the covert surveillance and collect information for the *Stateroom* program. I was in charge of the Saudi embassy."

"Who else knows about *Stateroom*?"

Detmar took a sip of water.

"Well, the NSA heads, of course, and the CIA. Probably the director of national intelligence, since they do the president's daily briefing."

"Was your attendance at the cocktail party a routine procedure?"

"No. We were there in case Katherine Arden changed her mind and decided to attend."

Smith exchanged a glance with Russell. "What's so interesting about Arden? I mean, beyond her crusade for human rights."

"I'm actually not sure. I just got the word that she was to be watched at all times. The directive came from NSA central headquarters in Fort Meade, which was unusual because we generally operate with a fair amount of independence."

"Who sent the directive?"

"I don't know."

Beckmann stepped closer. "Have you heard of any intel that would give us assistance in finding Nick Rendel?"

"I don't know that name."

"How can you not? He's one of the kidnapped Department of Defense officials that the Department of

Homeland Security, FBI, and CIA are all racing to find. I would think Croughton would have been put on notice at the very least, because he's intimately involved with the drone program."

"Out of Croughton?"

"No. Out of Nevada."

She shook her head. "You presume too much. We have our small pocket of the intelligence world and we focus on that exclusively. We spy on embassies, tap phones, and implement drone strikes out of Djibouti. We don't run search-and-rescue missions."

Smith watched Detmar closely. Officers were trained in how to give safe answers to probing interrogations, but he thought that she was actually telling the truth. She was assigned to a party to watch a certain person and so she went. In the distance he heard a buzzing noise. Russell pulled out her weapon and went to the bay window to watch the yard.

"What's that?" he asked.

"A drone," Russell said. "Looks like our mole found us already."

46

Beckmann joined Russell at the window.

"You sure it's a drone? Could be a kid flying a radio-controlled plane."

"Could be, but I doubt it. We're only a few miles from Croughton and they run a drone program."

"No, they don't," Detmar said from the couch. "At least not here. As I said, they operate in conjunction with our base in Djibouti."

"Agreed, but what's to stop them from flying drones here? Do they have any?"

Detmar tried to rise and Smith helped her up. "They have several, of all sizes. But they're not supposed to fly them, just repair them." She leaned on Smith.

"Maybe they're testing a repair," Beckmann said.

"Not this far from base. Airspace rules don't allow it."

The buzzing noise grew louder. Smith felt his anxiety rising as the sound increased. He had an overwhelming feeling of dread.

"Is anybody else concerned that we're holed up in a safe house that could be targeted by a mole and we hear the unprecedented sound of an incoming drone?"

"Let's get away from the window," Russell said. She and Beckmann joined Smith and Detmar in the center of the room. Beckmann removed his gun from its holster. Russell looked at her watch. "We've been here thirty-two minutes. Fast work."

"There's no way it's a drone from Croughton," Detmar said. "New CIA rules since the whistleblower leaks don't allow the agency to use drones in civilian airspace or in targeted assassinations."

"Well, someone didn't get the memo," Smith said. "Let's go. Back to the car."

Before they could move, an object the shape and size of a sewer cover came into view over the tops of the trees at the end of the yard. Smith could see the guns mounted at the base. Russell dove over the couch as it fired and the back window shattered. The drone shot upward out of the line of sight. Beckmann hustled down the hallway.

"I'll shoot while you guys head to the car. When you get there drive the hell out of here," he said.

Smith pulled Detmar's hand over his neck, yanked the bloody towel off the couch, and hauled her toward the front door with Russell right behind them, walking backward and watching for another glimpse of the drone. He heard the buzzing noise from somewhere overhead and stopped in the hall entrance. Beckmann waved them backward and began a slow walk to the door. The buzzing increased and he dodged into the living area. Gunshots cracked and the sidelight windows around the front door broke as bullets flew through them.

"Back into the family room," Russell said. Detmar removed her arm from around Smith's neck.

"I'm okay to run. Just stay close in case we have to climb." They reassembled in the family room.

"Hide behind the side of that couch," Russell said and Detmar did as she was told. Beckmann backed into the room.

"How many bullets did Lawrence have in his belly-mounted magazine? Do you remember?" he asked Russell.

"Four. But his motor was small and he ran on batteries, so he had limited capacity both to hover and fire. This drone seems to be larger."

Beckmann stood at the bay window's edge watching the sky above him.

"Detmar, do you have any idea of the flight time of the drones at Croughton? The small ones?"

"Forty-five minutes at the outside before they needed a recharge. And none of them were equipped with more than twelve rounds. More and they became too heavy."

Russell consulted her watch. "I don't hear it anymore and it's been circling us for almost twelve minutes. I presume that it took ten to fly here and requires at least ten to fly back. We should try to make a run for the cars again."

"It's a risk," Beckmann said. "But I agree. Let's not wait here for the next one to arrive."

Detmar wrapped her hands around the arm of the couch and pulled herself upright. Smith stepped up next to her and held out his hand, but she waved him off. She limped toward the front door, where Beckmann was waiting. Smith grabbed Russell's arm as she walked past, holding her in place.

"Wait a moment," he said in a low voice.

Russell nodded.

"I think you need to isolate Detmar. Keep her out of the loop."

Russell flicked a glance at Detmar's back before responding. "You think she's funneling information to the mole?"

"I'm not sure, but Arden identified her as the point of intersection between Arden and me."

"Okay, that's interesting. Any others?"

"Darkanin. The CEO of Bancor Pharma."

"Big difference between the relative power of those two players. Bancor retains massive military government contracts. They provide most of the medicines and personnel at our bases worldwide. Taking out a relatively minor CIA officer in an obscure position seems to be far too minor a play for them. And to what end? She's a nonentity."

"I agree. Detmar is expendable, but she also has a direct link to the CIA and potentially all of our movements.

We need to split up and someone needs to keep an eye on her. Misdirect her."

"Are you coming?" Beckmann's voice held a note of impatience.

"We split up and whoever goes with her draws the short straw. Either she finds a way to call them for help or she never was the informer, but now the mole knows that she's with us and has seen too much. Either way, the one minding her is at greater risk."

Smith saw the logic in Russell's thinking. "Then we keep her close and watch her. No access to phones or any other devices." Russell nodded and jogged up to Beckmann.

"Where are we going?"

"I've got that covered," Smith said. "Follow me. And put Detmar in my car. I have more questions to ask her."

They made it to the vehicles without incident, but Smith was jumpy and nervous, straining his ears to hear the dreaded sound. He tossed the bloody towel into the trunk for disposal later. They pulled onto a main road and within twenty minutes merged onto the highway. He set the cruise control and shifted into a more comfortable position.

"I need to ask you some more questions," Smith said.

Detmar had her head on the head rest and her eyes closed. She opened them and nodded. "Okay."

"You said Croughton was the location for covert surveillance by the Special Collection Services. Did the base run any other covert operations?"

"Like what?"

"Like wiretapping lawyers and their clients. Companies and their private research projects."

Detmar frowned. "I'm pretty sure that lawyers' communications have been inadvertently swept up in the net." Smith thought of Arden and his warning to her to keep his communication privileged.

"Aren't those communications supposed to be private?"

"The NSA decided that if a lawyer was communicating with an overseas client, those communications were subject to tapping. And so we did. We retained them, though, at the base. We weren't supposed to use them in any way if they revealed things that weren't relevant to a valid security interest."

"So if the lawyer and the overseas client were discussing, oh I don't know, say payment of fees, the NSA would listen but not use them?"

Detmar nodded. "Well, that was the theory."

Smith glanced at her. "Was? What actually happened?"

She shifted in her seat and had the grace to look ashamed. "I don't work that area, as you know, but I've heard that the communications are reviewed right along with everything else and there have been instances when information beneficial to a U.S. corporation has been leaked to that corporation."

Smith drove ahead, digesting this information.

"And Arden? How often has she been wiretapped?"

"Hers is continuous," Detmar said. "She represents all sorts of fringe elements and she's under a microscope. The NSA wants to take her down."

"Seems like a petty smear campaign for such a large organization."

"I agree it's odd. The directives about Arden seemed very personal. But I guess to lots of people at the NSA she's considered the devil. Where are we going?"

"To someone who I know will help us."

"Who's that?"

"Katherine Arden."

47

Smith drove up to an overlook at the edge of a winding road that followed the coastline near Margate. Fifty feet below them a small dinghy located in a craggy, rock-filled area bobbed on the water. The waves rolled against the platform's weathered boards. Seabirds circled and called overhead and the air was sharp and cool. A rickety, slick-looking set of wooden stairs led from the overlook to the boat.

Detmar had slept most of the way there and Smith suggested she stay in the warm car until he reconnoitered the area. Beckmann and Russell pulled alongside and cut their engine. They joined Smith to look down onto the boat below.

"There is no way that dinghy will make it to Calais," Russell said.

"He must have a boat elsewhere," Smith said.

"How far was his cottage from here?"

"Not far. But when I called him he suggested that we meet him here."

"Then let's go."

Smith turned to leave and stopped when he saw a motorcycle carrying two people headed their way. As it drew closer Smith could see that it was Winter's. He parked between the two cars, kicked the stand down, and both he and Arden dismounted. Arden pulled off her helmet and he was glad to see that she looked rested. She had changed into dark-blue skinny pants in a sweatshirt material, a gray T-shirt, and a jean jacket with the sleeves rolled. She still wore the oversized watch on her wrist. She acknowledged Smith with a small nod.

"I assume that's you, Smith, under all that hair?" Her glance at Russell and Beckmann was wary.

"I thought you were long gone," Winter said.

"I could say the same for you. What happened?"

"I overslept and Winter let me," Arden said.

"A lucky break for us. These are my friends Russell and Beckmann."

"It's good to see you, Ms. Arden," Russell said.

Arden raised an eyebrow. "I recognize your voice. You're the CIA publicity liaison."

Winter took a step back. "CIA? You've got to be joking."

"Public liaison only," Russell said.

"You don't really expect me to believe that," Winter said.

Russell sighed. "I guess not. But whatever you believe is irrelevant, because right now we're all in danger."

"Why? Because you're here? Maybe you should leave then," Winter said.

"What's going on?" Arden directed her question to Smith.

"We think there's a mole in the CIA sending drones after us to kill us."

Beckmann's eyebrows flew up in surprise and Russell shot Smith a concerned look.

"I'm not sure you should..." Beckmann began, but Russell waved him to silence. Smith took heart at her show of confidence and plowed on. He pointed to his vehicle.

"In that car is a CIA officer who's been working on a covert surveillance operation at the Royal Air Force's Croughton base. She's also the woman from the embassy party."

Arden glanced at the car. "The point of intersection between us."

"Exactly," Smith said. "And there's more."

"Stop. Don't tell me in front of witnesses. You know it voids the attorney-client privilege."

Smith shook his head. "It doesn't matter. Every conversation that you've had with any client overseas, and probably stateside as well, has been recorded."

Arden paled.

"And I suspect that your client Canelo is somehow involved. He's an army officer at the Djibouti base that the joint CIA-NSA program run out of Croughton uses to implement their drone strikes. Whatever happened there is linked. I can't figure out how or why, but the points of intersection are just too numerous to ignore."

"What else?" Arden asked.

"Dr. Taylor is an outlier in this scenario, as is the Bancor CEO. But whatever their connection is I think that we're into something deep, dirty, and very, very illegal. A violation of civil rights at the most basic level. And you're right in the center of it all."

Arden stared at him in open amazement. "Why are you telling me this?"

"Because I need you to think about all the angles and all the clients that you're currently working on. The answer is somewhere in there. And because I need you, once again, to help me."

"Why not ask your CIA buddies here to help you?" Winter asked. His voice held an aggressive edge. Smith kept his eyes on Arden while he answered.

"We can't access CIA resources until we identify the mole." He turned to Winter. "I'm asking you to take us as far as Calais on your boat. From there we'll be gone and I hope not to have to impose upon you again."

"What if she's the mole?" Arden said with a glance at the car.

Smith nodded. "I've considered that angle as well. We're watching her and keeping her away from cell phones or any other devices that she might use to broadcast her position."

"What about Taylor? Is she on her way to the States?"

"Taylor didn't make it," Russell said. "She died while the doctor was trying to save her."

Arden put a hand to her head and began pacing. The wind ruffled her short hair and a flock of birds swooped overhead. She stopped and turned to Winter.

"Where do you stand on this?"

"Your CIA buddies here are asking me to use my boat to get them to Calais while a drone tracks us down to blow us out of the water. Where do you think I stand?"

She nodded. "It's probably how I'd feel as well. But may we use the boat? Before we go I'll transfer enough money to your account for it as a precaution."

Winter's mouth dropped open. "You can't seriously be considering helping these guys. They're CIA agents. They'll lie, cheat, steal, and set you up for a fall, all before breakfast." Winter stabbed a finger in Smith's direction as he ranted.

Smith's anger surged and he took a couple of steps toward Winter as he struggled to control it through his stress and exhaustion. "I'm not a CIA officer and I don't intend to cheat Arden. Nor do I intend to set her up."

Beckmann moved between them, holding his palms out to keep them separated. Smith gave a curt nod and took a step back, but Winter held his ground. Beckmann eyed the other man for a moment and then removed a cigarette from a pack, put it to his lips, fished a lighter out of his pocket, flicked it on, and cupped his hand over the flame while he lit it. He inhaled deeply, blew a long stream of smoke into the air, and offered Winter the pack.

"Have a smoke. It'll calm you down."

Winter glanced at the pack in disdain and then back up at Beckmann. "I would never take a smoke from a CIA agent."

Beckmann took another puff. "At six fifty a pack U.S. I would think you'd take a free one whenever you could get it. And we're not called agents, we're called officers, and no one here is looking to get Arden in trouble, she's already there. What we are here to do is find out what seriously skewed son of a bitch has infiltrated the organization. If you don't give us your boat we'll find another, but if you walk away right now don't leave here thinking you've scored one for freedom. What you will actually have done is turned your back on a friend."

Smith thought it was one of the best speeches he'd ever heard Beckmann deliver. He also thought it nailed the situation exactly. He watched as a series of emotions crossed Winter's face. He was relieved to see Winter walk toward the steps. Beckmann and Russell exchanged glances and he saw Arden exhale in relief.

"That boat doesn't look big enough to hold us and it sure won't get us to Calais," Russell said.

Winter looked back at her. "The boat we'll use is docked at Margate. It's too shallow here to dock anything bigger than a dinghy. That's not mine, anyway."

"I'll get Detmar," Smith said. "We should dump the Audi."

When he reached the car it was clear that Detmar had been trying to overhear the conversation, because she was upright in her seat and her window had been lowered. The breeze whipped around him and the seagulls screeched and that, coupled with the distance the car was from their gathering, made it doubtful that the conversation had carried far.

"What's going on? For a minute there it looked as if you were going to punch that other guy," she said.

Smith opened the door and offered his hand to help her out. When she was standing he raised the window and beeped the car closed.

"He's not a fan of the CIA," Smith said.

"You told him you were CIA? Isn't that a breach of protocol?"

"Well, if I was CIA and undercover I would presume that it would be a breach."

Detmar raised an eyebrow. "Wait a minute. All this time I thought that you were CIA."

Smith shook his head. "I'm a microbiologist for USAMRIID at Fort Detrick. Dr. Taylor was my colleague. We have a boat that will get us to Calais."

Detmar shook her head. "I'm not going to Calais, I'm going home."

"And if that drone returns to take you out?"

"I think that drone is after you and the rest, not me."

Smith considered his options. He could force her to go with them at gunpoint, but he wasn't sure he wanted her on the boat at all. What he wanted was enough time for them to get away before she had a chance to notify anyone of their position.

"Wait here," he said. He went back to the cliff's edge where Beckmann was waiting.

"Do you know how to disable a car?" he asked.

Beckmann nodded. "I do."

"Detmar wants to take her chances here. She thinks she's not the intended target."

"All right. Guess that's her choice."

"Exactly. But I still think we can't risk her notifying anyone about our location. So I'm going to suggest we disable the car."

"Got it."

The others had already boarded when Beckmann and Smith returned to the Audi. Detmar stood outside the car by the hood.

"Can I have the keys?" she said. Beckmann went down on his belly and looked underneath the car. After a moment he emerged with a small, black disk in his hand. He held it up for Smith and her to see.

"It's a GPS tracker," Beckmann said. "Looks like the CIA already knows our position."

Detmar groaned. "Oh, no," she said.

"You told me it was clean. That all it needed was for the tires to be burned," Smith said.

She nodded. "I know, I'm sorry. Between getting shot and being chased I forgot all about it."

"It's a little late now," Beckmann said.

Smith opened the passenger door and popped the hood. Beckmann shoved his cigarette between his lips while he opened it. He disappeared under the hood a second and then stepped back, slapping his hands together.

"Hey, wait," Detmar said. "What are you doing? And I need the keys."

"You should be able to fix it easily," Beckmann said.

Smith waited until Beckmann reached his car and Russell, Winter, and Arden had also climbed inside. When he heard the engine start, he turned and threw the keys across the road and up a way on the opposite hill. He jogged to the car and climbed in.

"Hit it," he said to Beckmann.

As they roared away Smith looked behind him and saw Detmar hobbling toward the keys.

"Do you think she's in on it?" Beckmann asked.

"Hard to say," Smith said.

Twenty minutes later they were on a small cabin cruiser headed out to sea. Smith braced himself by grabbing at the back of the bench seats while he made his way to Winter and tapped him on the shoulder. "There's been a change in plans. Can you land us farther from Calais?"

Winter raised an eyebrow. "We never were going to Calais, that's just what I wanted you to believe."

"Okay, so where are we going?" Russell asked.

"A free dock near Dieppe."

"Do you have any binoculars on this boat?" Smith asked.

Winter nodded. "In the cabinet above the sink."

"I'll take first drone watch," Smith said. He retrieved the binoculars and sat down near the transom to watch for attackers and brood.

48

President Castilla eased into his morning with a cup of coffee and a meeting with a friend. He shook Rick Meccean's hand.

"Good to see that you're fully recovered from the attack. Take a seat. I have about five minutes before the director of national intelligence arrives to deliver the daily briefing. Tell me what's going on."

Meccean sat opposite the president's desk and crossed one leg over the other. Castilla thought he looked thinner and perhaps a bit drawn since his kidnapping ordeal, but he did not appear to have any lingering injuries. At least not physical ones.

"I'm sorry to say that I still don't remember a thing about the kidnapping. Various doctors have been poking and prodding me, and that includes a whole team of psychologists, but I keep coming up empty."

"Any diagnosis at all?"

"Just that it could be a form of selective amnesia. That my brain has closed off access to that particular piece of memory. It doesn't seem to have affected other aspects of my processing, I'm pleased to say, which is important because I'm headed out to Geneva for a meeting on international standards for approval of new drugs."

"Anything there that I need to know about?"

Meccean shrugged. "Nothing you need to do. We're closing in on a penalty against Bancor Pharmaceuticals for their inappropriate marketing of a cognitive enhancement drug and they'll attend the meeting to try to talk us out of it. The rest of the items on the agenda involve the marketing of supplements and alternative medicine. Both are bigger issues in Europe than in the U.S., so we're going to let the EU take the lead on that one."

Castilla stood and Meccean rose with him. "I'm glad to see you're okay. If there's anything you need give Belinda Carrington a call and she'll get a message to me."

Meccean opened the door to leave and Castilla saw John Perdue waiting in the outer office. Meccean looked back at Castilla and smiled. "The director of national intelligence is waiting for you. Looks like your morning is starting with a bang. Have a great day."

Perdue nodded a greeting to Meccean as he entered Castilla's inner sanctum. When the door closed Castilla waved him to the seat that Meccean had just vacated.

"Tell me what's going on."

"I have some troubling news from the UK."

Castilla nodded. "Ah, yes, the Saudi embassy incident. I spoke with the prime minister yesterday. I thought we had reached an understanding and he seemed somewhat mollified. Did I misread him?"

Perdue shook his head. "I don't mean that. There's some new trouble. About three hours ago a drone from the RAF Croughton air base in Northamptonshire targeted a CIA safe house. Multiple shots were fired into the house from the drone's nine-millimeter gun mount before it reversed and tracked back to the base. I know that you wanted to hear about any unusual behavior from the drone program and this one was *very* unusual."

"Was anyone hurt?"

"A CIA officer had just requested and received permission to access the house. A fairly high-level operative named Randi Russell."

Castilla did his best to retain his neutral demeanor at the mention of Russell's name. "What does Russell say happened?"

"By the time our crew came to investigate she was

gone. We didn't find any blood or signs of a struggle, but we've been unable to establish contact with her either, so we're not exactly sure what's going on."

"Who was piloting the drone?"

"That's the real problem. Somebody accessed the drone's dashboard. They piloted it remotely."

"We've been hacked," Castilla said. He did his best to keep his voice even, but the idea of the drone program in the hands of a bad actor was enough to make his mouth go dry in alarm.

Perdue sighed. "So I thought, but our IT guys insist that it's impossible. They say drones go haywire all the time and crashes are frequent."

"Are they aware of the fact that two of the parties with partial drone passwords have been kidnapped? That one has been recovered but the other is still missing?"

Perdue nodded. "They are aware, sir, but they still believe that the recent password change and firewall bolster make the drones resistant to a cyber attack. They think that this situation is a case like the one in Arizona."

Castilla frowned. "What case in Arizona?"

"An apprentice military pilot decided to take a drone out for a spin despite the fact that he wasn't yet certified to fly one. He crashed it, of course."

"Is there any evidence that this drone was piloted by someone within the program?"

Perdue rocked his hand back and forth. "Not yet, but the investigation is just beginning. I suggested that they also review the clearance of everyone in the program as a precaution. If someone on the inside piloted the drone, it may raise the specter of a double agent in the system."

"Which is worse than a pilot taking a drone on a joyride."

"We've changed all the passwords on every existing drone once again and took several offline until we can figure out where it's coming from."

"Ideas?"

"If it's been hacked? Iran or China."

Castilla groaned. "Not Iran. We've just opened up communications with them and they do this?"

"Perhaps it's payback. They claim to have finally reverse-engineered the Sentinel drone they captured inside their airspace a few years ago."

"Their ability to do that was always in question," Castilla said.

"Could be China. They're expert hackers."

"Sure, but to what end? The Chinese hack to steal corporate trade secrets to allow them to reverse-engineer our products and advance their own technological push. We haven't seen any incidents where they've taken an aggressive, militaristic stance against the U.S. Why now?"

"I have no idea, but we have a team in Croughton working on it and hope to have some clearer answers soon. In the meantime we're keeping the information flow contained. We're just lucky it shot at a CIA house and no civilians were involved. It was recorded on radar by entities outside of Croughton, of course, and we received a call about it. We told them that we had a glitchy drone without mentioning the fact that shots were fired. So far they seem to have accepted our explanation."

"Tell the CIA to halt all drone movement out of Djibouti as well until they can figure out how this one went rogue."

"They're not going to like that. Especially since the drone in question has been taken offline and was nowhere near Djibouti. They have several missions nearing fruition and a halt would mean tracking the target to a new location. It takes thousands of man-hours to isolate some of these terrorist ringleaders enough so that a drone strike is possible and a delay would mean starting all over again. Their budget is approved by the appropriations committee and they've been warned not to incur any cost overruns."

Castilla slammed his hand on the desk and Perdue jerked in his seat.

"I don't care. Offline isn't good enough. The CIA reports to *me* on the implementation of the drone program. The last thing I need is a drone carrying Hellfire missiles being manipulated by an outside source. If something like that occurs there won't be enough money in the world to make it right. Tell them I said to halt it." Castilla's voice was sharp and Perdue sat up a bit straighter.

"Of course, Mr. President. I'll contact them immediately."

"And as soon as you know something funnel it to me. I'll try to keep away from any conversation on the UK side until I hear from you."

"Will do," Perdue said. He strode to the door and as soon as he closed it Castilla punched a number on his phone. When he heard Fred Klein's voice he didn't bother with niceties.

"I've just had a conference with Perdue over the drone in the UK. I understand Russell was involved."

"I had a call in to you. I suppose you've just heard the gist of what I was going to tell you."

Castilla stood and started pacing. "Any news from Russell?"

"I'm afraid not. She's gone dark. The last bit of information I received was that Dr. Taylor died from wounds she sustained during the car chase. Before she died Taylor claimed that her kidnappers wanted her to aerosolize her memory drug. She claimed to have done it, but it resulted in wildly unpredictable effects. Shortly after our conversation it appears as though Russell tossed her phone so I've been unable to reach her, Smith, or Beckmann."

"What about Howell?"

"Recovering. I've asked him to head to Croughton to poke around and ask some questions. He retains excellent contacts with MI5 and will go in that capacity. Nothing will be said about Covert-One."

"Other than the news of Dr. Taylor, did Russell say anything else?"

"She wanted all the information we could obtain on Katherine Arden. It turns out we have quite a bit of it, because the NSA has been collecting her conversations for almost two years."

Castilla sat back down. "Attorney-client privileged information?"

"NSA hasn't bothered to parse it out."

"I thought Congress made it clear since the leaks that attorney-client conversations are to be off limits."

"Those with U.S. citizens under indictment were always supposed to remain privileged. The situation with foreign clients is not as clearly defined and the American Bar Association is pushing hard to extend the protection."

Klein's voice was mild, but Castilla could hear an underlying thread of anger. While Fred Klein ran a covert group of operatives, he tried to never employ them to spy on American citizens and had been a vocal objector to the several CIA-sponsored domestic surveillance operations over the past few years.

"You're angry about it," Castilla said.

Klein's sigh was audible over the phone. "I am. No one knows better than I that we live in a very dangerous time, but I just can't help but think that the day we begin to turn on our own is the day that we're finished as a democracy. We're beginning to swallow our own tail."

"Tell me about the drone. Any ideas?"

"None. I'm hoping Howell can find out more. But you may recall that we've changed the passwords once already and this drone still took flight. Whoever these hackers are they're quite good."

"If they're hackers. Perdue reported that the source isn't confirmed as of yet. I've already ordered all of the drones taken out of commission until we figure out what's going on here."

"That's the second piece of bad news I have for you today. When reports of this got out Djibouti began to inventory their drones and they found that six are missing."

Castilla stood and resumed his pacing. "Why didn't Perdue mention this?"

"He doesn't know yet. I got this information just a few minutes ago from a source of mine."

"Stolen?"

"They're not sure. The manifest lists them, but a physical check run today couldn't locate them. You may recall that the entire drone program moved nearly overnight from Camp Lemonnier to Chabelley Airfield after a series of crashes, the final one into a neighborhood. They're thinking that these fell through the cracks somehow."

"And how likely is that? It sounds like they've been stolen. Size and reach?"

"Various. One the size of a hummingbird with under an hour flight time, one much larger that can fire multiple NATO rounds in automatic or semiautomatic mode, and a third that carries two small rocket-propelled grenades. The last three are unarmed video surveillance drones. All three can fly for eighteen hours without refueling, are equipped with radar refracting paint, and have an anti-radar array in their belly."

"We have got to find Rendel. He's the last kidnap victim still missing and linked to the drone program. There has to be a connection here. Has the Department of Homeland Security or the FBI gotten any closer to finding him?"

"No. And with Smith trying to stay below the radar in the embassy action and Russell gone dark we have to assume that their investigation is stalled until we can get them some more intelligence."

A sharp rap at the door echoed in the room. "Come in," Castilla said. Perdue burst into the office. His face held a frantic expression and he began to speak, stopping when he saw the receiver in Castilla's hand. Castilla held up a palm to still him.

"Please keep me informed," he said to Klein and hung up. "You look terrified. What is it?"

"The other shoe just dropped. The Iranian ambassador is calling. He says that he has information that a drone was used to disperse a chemical weapon that just killed almost thirty people and left two in a severely disoriented state in a small village at the border with Iraq. He said that the preliminary information he has shows that the drone came from the U.S. base in Djibouti. They're decrying our use of chemical weapons."

Castilla stilled. It was at times like these that his much-admired ability to keep focused during a crisis came to his aid. He took a deep breath and kept his voice level.

"What does Djibouti say?"

"They're flatly denying any involvement. They say that they've disabled every drone in their control."

"Which leaves six drones outside of their control. Their inventory revealed that some drones are unaccounted for."

Perdue groaned.

"I'll need everyone in the situation room, now. Where's the secretary?"

"Nearby. She's in Israel but perhaps she can meet with Iranian diplomats to settle things down while we investigate."

"I need Rendel found, now."

"I agree. I was told that all available personnel are on the search, but they're coming up empty. And Djibouti asked if we have any information on the chemical that may have been used. They say the preliminary reports are that the people went crazy, but in different ways. Some screamed and dropped dead, others laughed as they stabbed their neighbors and then they stabbed themselves. They continued to laugh as they bled out. The Iranians provided grainy satellite footage." Perdue put a shaking hand to his head. Castilla felt a wave of sympathy for him. "Should I alert USAMRIID? Chemical weapons are within their purview, aren't they?"

"I'll handle that. You gather everyone to the sit room,"

Castilla said. "I'll meet you in a few minutes." Perdue strode out and Castilla redialed Klein. "More bad news," he said when Klein answered.

"I've heard. It sounds suspiciously like the troops in Djibouti."

"Agreed. We need someone in USAMRIID to review Taylor's research. The minute you hear from Smith put him on it as well. I'm calling Rick Meccean. He's headed to a conference in Geneva that will be attended by some of the top pharmaceutical companies in the world. Perhaps someone there will have a researcher who can give us ideas for an antidote for this drug."

"The Saudis have identified Smith in the video feed. We'll need to deal with them very soon. They're pushing for an Interpol red notice to go out on him and possibly Taylor and Arden. They haven't realized yet that Taylor was killed."

"And I'll tell the Saudis what I think about them holding a U.S. citizen hostage. They'd better not issue that notice. This is shaping up to be a cataclysmic international catastrophe. I guess I don't have to tell you what will happen if another one of our lost drones takes to the sky with a chemical weapon on board. Let's stop it now."

Castilla hung up, took a deep breath, and headed to the situation room.

49

Smith, Russell, Beckmann, and Arden all watched as the French coastline came into view. Winter maintained a stony silence as he piloted the vessel, but Smith noticed that he was smoking a cigarette, presumably one of Beckmann's. While Smith deplored smoking he had to admit that in this case it had worked as a peace offering and he wasn't going to argue against it. His relief at leaving behind the UK and its myriad cameras was profound.

"Is it safe to pass by so close to Calais? Won't they see us and wonder where we're going?" Russell asked.

"The border patrol is overworked and in disarray. Their biggest concern is immigration toward the UK, not in the French direction, because to be an illegal on the Brit side is infinitely more appealing than on the French side." The boat rose and fell on the waves and Smith steadied himself by holding on to the back of the copilot's seat. He handed the binoculars to Arden.

"Hear any drones?" she asked. Russell scanned the sky.

"Impossible to hear anything over the roar of the engine," Smith said. "But I didn't see anything. I'll be relieved to get to Dieppe and head inland just the same."

They landed at a tiny harbor an hour later as the evening sky was darkening. Winter pulled into a small dock that appeared to be attached to a private home. He'd taken the last few miles slowly, explaining that the water was shallow, shoals prevalent, and the dock illegal but generally ignored by the authorities. Smith breathed

a sigh of relief when he stepped off the boat back onto
dry land.

"There's a jeep and a motorcycle at the back of the
house. I'll take the cycle, I suggest you all take the jeep.
Keys are in a magnetized metal keyholder attached under
the chassis at the left front corner. Leave it somewhere
safe and get me a message about where to find it," Winter said. He stepped up to Arden and gave her a hug. "Be
careful with this crew."

"You know I will," she said. Winter put his hand out
to Beckmann. "Thanks for the smoke."

Beckmann returned the gesture.

"Let's go," Russell said.

"I'll stay behind and close up the boat. I don't need to
know which direction you decide to go," Winter said.

Smith jogged down the dock and up a small rise
toward the back of the house. To the right he saw a
carport, and underneath it the jeep and motorcycle.
He retrieved the keys from the holder and started the
car. He drove around to pick up Arden, Beckmann,
and Russell. Ten minutes later he was on a main road
headed in the direction of what he hoped was Paris.
No one spoke. Arden sat up front with him and stared
out the side window. Smith switched on his phone
and waited until it obtained a signal. When it did he
dialed Klein. The call rolled into voicemail, as it usually did.

"I'm checking in. We're near Dieppe and headed toward Paris," he said.

Less than a minute later the phone rang.

"So glad to hear from you," Klein said. "I was concerned when I heard about the drone."

"So you know. Any information on what's going on?"

"Only that it did, indeed, launch from Croughton,
but that they are claiming that someone else controlled
it. And it wasn't Djibouti."

"Russell thinks we have a mole."

"Perhaps. But it's just as possible that a hacker has

accessed the drone program passwords. It's still impera-
tive that we locate Rendel," Klein said.

"Agreed. Any further intelligence on his possible
whereabouts?"

"None, but I have some bad news."

"Hold on a minute." He drove a bit farther and pulled
over at a wider section of the two-lane road. "I'm ready."

"Interpol has issued a red notice for you. The Saudis
put pressure on them. It's clear that the Saudis think
they'll have a stronger bargaining position if you're in custody. We'll work on getting it rescinded."

"I have a false passport. I'll use it until you can get
the matter cleared up."

"I'll have another one waiting for you at a house outside Geneva. You need to get there sooner rather than
later." Klein ran down the drone strike and the theory that Taylor's drug had been used. "We've put two
scientists at USAMRIID on the project to review her research, but there's a piece missing."

"What piece?"

"A report that she claims to have written. We have an
email where she refers to it and claims that she encoded
a portion, but we couldn't find anything on her hard drive
or in print."

Smith stared into the inky blackness around him.
Something niggled at the outer edges of his memory, but
he was so tired that he was having a hard time retrieving
the thought. After a moment more it came to him.

"Before she disappeared she gave me a manila envelope that contained a report. Brand is aware of it,
because he said he'd accessed it on USAMRIID's main
database. She scrawled my name in blue crayon on the
front cover. There are a series of numbers below my
name. It looks like a date, so that I never thought about
it, but perhaps it's the encoded location of a second report?"

"Where is this envelope?"

"Desk side drawer."

Klein gave him the coordinates for the safe house outside Geneva.

"There's a conference beginning tomorrow afternoon. Some of the biggest pharmaceutical players in the world will be there, as will Richard Meccean. I'm going to have the researchers at USAMRIID put their findings on the secure network for you to access. Any insight about this drug that you can bring to the table will be appreciated. There is also a large weapons stash at the house as well as secure communication devices."

"Got it." Smith hung up and pulled back onto the road.

"Where are we headed?" Beckmann asked.

"Safe house outside Geneva. We need to be there before tomorrow afternoon. But we need to split up long before the Swiss border."

"Why?"

"Interpol issued a red notice for my arrest."

Arden groaned. "So I assume that they've decoded the video feed?"

"Yes. The U.S. ambassador is trying to convince the Saudis to drop the matter and get it quashed."

"It never seems to work." Arden sounded disgusted. "Interpol issues red notices far too quickly. They allow oppressive regimes to manipulate them into issuing notices against political dissidents. There's basically no oversight."

"The Saudis are relying on diplomatic immunity to shield them from the consequences of their actions while hammering me for the rescue mission," Smith said.

"The joys of international law in the modern age," Russell said.

"Switzerland is a part of the Schengen area. Which means that the crossings are lightly staffed, nearly a passthrough. Even so, deserved or not, every border patrol in over one hundred and fifty countries will be looking for us. You two should cross on your own just to be safe," Smith replied.

"Then we'll need another car and we all should get some sleep somehow. We can't keep going without it. Russell and I will head out separately," Beckmann said.

"I'm all for obtaining another car. Where and when?"

"Head toward the U.S. embassy in Paris. I have an idea how we can get our hands on some vehicles with diplomatic immunity. Two can play the Saudis' game," Russell said.

"And how do you intend to do that?" Beckmann asked.

"I have friends in high places. Or in this case, in a red-notice-free zone. Ambassador Eric Wyler is in Paris while the situation in Turkey settles down. I'm fairly certain he'll help me."

"This one would have to be off the books. Would he be willing to do that?" Smith asked.

"I think so," Russell replied.

"What about the CCTV cameras?"

"Fewer cameras in Paris than London. Lots of areas aren't monitored."

"But the residence of the U.S. ambassador to France won't be one of them."

"He's not staying there. He's at a private home rented for his use while he waits out the situation in Turkey. I have the address."

"How will you call him? Likely his phone is bugged," Smith said. "And yours."

"The old-fashioned way. Stop halfway down the street from his house. I'll go over and toss a rock at his back window."

Arden gave a short laugh. "Watch for cameras."

"I'll do my best."

"All right. I'll let you know when we get closer."

An hour later Smith pulled onto a narrow street in a nicer section of Paris. Russell got out and headed to the door of an impeccable town house. A camera attached to the front corner captured a view of the front door and so she circled around and disappeared between the houses.

"I hope the stones at the window don't set off the house alarm," Arden said. Ten minutes later Russell returned and Smith rolled down the window.

"Wyler's offered me a place to sleep tonight and the use of one of his cars with diplomatic plates. I think both offers are a good idea. I'm exhausted and I'm not prepared to face the border and the cameras in this condition. You and Arden should take the car. No one will bother you once they see the diplomatic plates. Beckmann and I will stop here for the night, get some sleep, and meet you in Geneva."

"Not necessary," Beckmann said from the backseat. "I'm going to walk a bit and then find a cab."

"To where?" Smith asked.

"My ex-wife's house."

"She lives in Paris?"

"She does," Beckmann replied.

"And she'll let you in?" Russell asked with a smile.

"I'm pretty sure she will. We've remained on good terms. She's one of the best people I know. She just couldn't handle my covert lifestyle and I couldn't handle any other type of job."

He swung out of the car. "I'll be at the safe house in time for any briefing." He walked away, crossed the street, and turned a corner.

"Beckmann never fails to surprise me," Russell said.

"Agreed," Smith said.

"Want to take the official vehicle?"

Smith shook his head. "I'd rather just keep rolling. You use it tomorrow."

She tapped the jeep's door. "See you in Geneva."

Smith and Arden continued through the night.

50

Russell sat in an armchair while Wyler poured a drink from a crystal decanter. He wore a white dress shirt with the sleeves rolled and the tail out over a pair of thin sweatpants. His feet were bare. He handed the glass to her.

"What is it?"

"Armagnac," he said. He poured himself a shot, placed the decanter back on the wet bar counter, and walked over to tap his glass on hers.

"To your health," he said.

She sipped the liquid. The cognac was smooth and she welcomed its warmth. Wyler settled onto a couch opposite her.

"I was surprised to see you tonight. I wasn't sure that you'd gotten my texts about the move." He paused a beat. "Or the suggestion to have dinner."

"I had, but before I could reply I had to go dark."

"How much can you tell me?"

She sighed. "Not a lot, I'm sorry."

He waved her off. "Don't be. I know how things work. Can I assume that this house won't explode with a well-placed device?"

She smiled. "I would hope not. Thanks for letting me stay. I'm beat and have to be up and out tomorrow very early."

"Where are you headed?"

"Out," she said.

He lifted an eyebrow. "Wow, you really can't tell me much, can you?"

She shook her head. "Does the car have a GPS tracker on it? If it does I'll have to disable it."

He nodded. "It's armored, has a tracker, a listening device, a high-powered antenna that can obtain a satellite signal for calls, a secret compartment in the side panel that houses a gun, money in six currencies, and three fake passports."

"Impressive. How does an ambassador get assigned a car with all of those toys? They're generally reserved for cabinet-level officials."

He took a sip of his drink. "Since Turkey I'm considered a target. Well, at least that's what I argued when I asked for twenty-four-hour bodyguards. My request for the manpower was declined, but they threw me a bone and delivered the car."

"And moved you here."

"And moved me here."

"Is it safer in Paris?"

He nodded. "I think so. Turkey is a real conduit. Its borders are porous and lots of contraband crosses from there into the EU proper. I miss Ankara, though. It's a great city. Although it got significantly less interesting after you left."

She smiled and finished her drink. For a moment she stared at the empty glass and the small U of amber-colored liquid left at the bottom.

"You look pensive," he said.

She nodded. "I always am the night before a mission. I can never be sure if it will be my last, so I guess some concern is natural."

"You say that so casually," he said.

"I'm used to the danger."

"It's hard for me to be that blasé. The idea of this night being your last is disturbing, to say the least. Is there anything you can tell me about the mission?"

Russell inhaled while she thought about what to say. She couldn't tell him about any of her activities for the CIA and tomorrow's trip to Geneva for a Covert-One mission was even more secret. For a moment the isolation of her existence hit home.

"I'm sorry, but I can't." Wyler raised an eyebrow but said nothing. He seemed to have expected her response.

"Why do you do it?"

"I can't imagine doing anything else. Sitting at a desk all day would drive me crazy. And it's good to know that I'm making a difference in the world." She could see that her comments had disturbed him and she mentally shook herself. "Sorry, I didn't mean to upset you."

He watched her for a moment and then came to her chair and gently took the glass out of her hands. He put it on a side table and bent his head down to kiss her.

Russell kissed him back, tasting the liquor on his tongue. She reached up and put her hand on the side of his face, pulling him closer and deepening the kiss. Russell knew she should care that the world was receding and the only thing that mattered was kissing this man, but the heat between them rose so quickly that she didn't want to stop it or analyze it. When he responded by running his hand up from her neck and sliding his fingers into her hair, pulling her even closer, she stayed with him. After a moment he shifted a scant distance away and looked at her with a serious expression. She smiled into his eyes.

"Come upstairs?" he asked.

She searched his face, not surprised by the request, but more surprised by her own response to it. He'd been telegraphing his interest for the entire time she was in Turkey and he'd gotten her to drop her usual defenses on more than a few occasions. The nature of her work required her to keep her distance from others, but he'd chipped away at her bit by bit. Even though he hadn't realized she was CIA until he saw her react at the bombing, that knowledge hadn't cooled his interest. In fact, the revelation seemed to free both her and him. She no longer had to hide her true reason for being in Turkey, and he'd taken the change of perspective in stride. Now she wanted nothing more than to go upstairs with him. She nodded.

He reached out and switched off the lamp, straightened, and held his hand out to her. She walked with him across the Persian carpet in the sudden gloom, through the living room and up the stairwell. He guided her into a back bedroom that held a king-sized bed covered in a gray duvet. A bench with a navy throw blanket ran the length of the footboard. He unbuttoned his shirt halfway down and then yanked it over his head before tossing it in the direction of the bench, where it slid off and landed on the carpet. She did the same, reaching to the edges of her button-front cotton shirt and lifting it off.

She saw him pause as he took in the shoulder holster and gun. He glanced up at her and raised an eyebrow. She held his gaze while she unfastened it and placed it gently on the bench. She kept undressing, stepping out of her dark jeans and dropping them on the carpet. His gaze traveled down her bare legs before pausing again, this time at the knife in the holster at her ankle. Both his eyebrows flew up and he shook his head with a bemused expression on his face. She rested her foot on the bench while she unbuckled the holster and placed it next to the gun. She continued removing each of her remaining pieces of clothing in a slow sequence. He watched her in silence, and when she was naked he followed suit and removed the thin sweatpants. His body was lean and lightly muscled.

He reached for her and they resumed their kiss while he walked her toward the bed. He gave a soft laugh as she lay across it, naked, and he joined her, gathering her in his arms. She pressed against him, rolling him onto his back and stretching out to lie fully on top of him. She used her arms to rise up and see his face one more time before she lowered again.

Russell woke some time later. The room remained dark and Wyler was on his side with one hand, palm down, lying on her naked shoulder. His even breathing told her that he still slept. She cast her attention wider, trying to hear what it was that had woken her. In the distance she heard the klaxon call of a police siren and the whirring noise of car tires on the street below. After a moment the sound returned: a creak in a floorboard from the hardwood floor below.

She slipped out of bed and went to the bench to unclip her gun from the holster. She grabbed the navy throw to try to cover her nakedness, but quickly rejected it in favor of Wyler's shirt on the carpet at her feet. She lowered it over her head and put one arm through, transferring the gun to the other hand to put it on completely. It gaped open and she buttoned it one more button while she moved back to the headboard. She placed a hand on Wyler's shoulder and shook him gently awake, putting a finger to her lips when he opened his eyes. She held the gun at the ready and soft-stepped toward the door, detouring back to the bench to pick up her knife kit. From the bench she could see that the house alarm keypad next to the bedroom door displayed "Off." She was sure that Wyler had set it when she first entered the house.

She took a position to the right of the door, with her back against the wall. Wyler slipped out of bed, swiped his sweatpants off the floor, and put them on before crossing the room to stand shoulder-to-shoulder with her. She handed him the knife.

The complete silence told Russell that the intruder had reached the heavily carpeted landing. She strained to hear anything that would reveal how many attackers there were, but the carpeting made an estimate impossible. For both her and Wyler's sake she hoped there was only one.

Her heart pounded as she watched the doorknob rotate in a slow turn and she felt the familiar surge of adrenaline fizz in her veins. The door opened equally slowly and a man, dressed all in black and wearing a ski mask, stepped into the room. He aimed a gun complete with a silencer at the bed, but raised it back up when he saw that it was empty. Russell took two steps and placed her gun against the back of his head.

"Lower it. Slowly," she said.

The man lowered his arm. Russell nodded at Wyler and he stepped forward and reached for the weapon. The man jerked sideways, spun, and aimed a fist at Russell's face. She fired and he staggered back, bringing his own weapon up to shoot. Wyler dove at the man's legs and Russell catapulted sideways to get out of the line of fire. She heard the compressed sound of the silenced weapon. The shot went wide, the glass on a picture frame on the opposite wall shattering. Russell staggered a bit from her sudden shift in direction and grunted when what felt like a pile driver slammed into her from behind. She landed on the carpeting face-first under the weight of another attacker who seemed to appear out of nowhere and her gun hand was trapped under her body. His was as well, and she could feel the cold form of his weapon pressing under her rib cage. She twisted to put even more weight in that direction to hold his hand in place and he fired.

The heat of the bullet seared her skin as it passed and she heard a man cry out. She pushed upward and managed to successfully upend the weight from her back and he rolled to the side, but not far enough to give her clearance to shoot him. Wyler loomed over them both and she saw his hand holding the knife. He hammered it into the upper part of the attacker's shoulder and she transferred her gun to her left hand and fired. The man collapsed onto the carpet. Both she and Wyler gasped in the sudden stillness. From below she heard a door slam.

"There are more," Russell said. She scrambled to her feet, lurched to the door, slammed it, threw the lock, and hit the panic button on the alarm keypad. A screeching filled the room and a mechanical voice repeated "intruder" over and over again. Wyler held the dripping knife in his hand; his own blood pumped from a wound

in his forearm. He looked a bit dazed by the sudden violence.

"Window," she said, and took three long steps to the
glass, which faced into an area enclosed by other buildings
and bisected by a narrow gangway. She discarded the idea.
The configuration gave them limited options to escape
and it was likely both ends of the gangway were being
watched. "Too risky. Bathroom."

She headed to the master bathroom, which had the
advantage of a different exposure. Something big threw
itself against the bedroom door with a thud and she
turned and pumped four bullets into the panel, sending
bits of wood flying in all directions before continuing into
the bathroom.

"Lock the door," she told Wyler. He did and grabbed
a hand towel from a rack to press against his wound.

The master bath had a glass-block window in the
shower area off to the side and a skylight overhead. No
other windows or possible exits. Russell cursed under
her breath. They'd gone from bad to worse when it came
to escape paths, and glass-block windows were extraor-
dinarily difficult to break. They'd have to go up. She put
her gun on the vanity and used her arms to hike herself
onto the marble to stand between the two sinks. Wyler
aimed a small remote at the skylight and it whirred open
forty-five degrees to allow fresh air inside. Russell rose
on her toes to try to reach the light, but even though she
was tall for a woman she could only touch the edges with
her fingertips.

"Hand me the garbage can," she said.

Wyler handed up a small, round metal garbage can
and Russell used it as a step stool. With the vented
skylight open she could hear the sound of police sirens
converging on the house. From inside the bedroom a
loud cracking noise followed by a splintering sound told
her they had breached the bedroom door. Wyler leapt up
to join her on the marble vanity and helped her push
against the skylight. The screws holding the crank mech-

anism pulled free from their housings and the glass panel fell backward, clattering as it fell down the slanted roof.

"I need my gun," Russell said. Wyler picked it off the vanity and handed it to her.

"They're going to come through that door any minute," he said.

"They're going to shoot through that door, just like I did. They're not stupid enough to walk in first."

As if they'd heard her, a shower of bullets punched through the bathroom door, but the vanity was in a recessed area and they flew by, embedding themselves in the far wall. Russell used her arms and pulled up until her shoulders were through the skylight. She felt Wyler's arms wrap around her legs to help her go higher. She was out and sat down, holding on to the skylight's edge as she swung her legs free. Wyler came next, first stepping onto the can and then levering himself upward. He performed the same maneuver. The police sirens came to a halt below. The cool night air flowed around them, but Russell was sweating despite it. The pistol grip was slick and wet, and she clutched it tight so as not to lose it.

"Keep moving in case they shoot through the roof," Russell said. She began a slow shuffle toward the back of the town house where she originally had hoped to escape. The slanted roof ended only a few feet from the flat roof of the house next to it. One section of the other house's roof had a finished deck surrounded by a three-foot-high fence. She skittered over until she was opposite. Wyler joined her.

"You're not thinking of jumping?" Wyler asked. He'd wrapped the towel around his forearm and tucked the edges in. A large red stain bloomed through the fabric.

Russell nodded. "It's not that far and from this angle it should be fairly easy to land on that deck."

"It's not necessary. The police are here and they never came through that bathroom door. They must have heard the sirens and taken off. It's safer to wait here until the police give the all-clear."

"Not if they left another timed bomb at the door, just like in Turkey."

"Ah shit," Wyler said. "You're right."

Russell swallowed once, rose up, took two steps downward, and jumped. Her trailing foot hit the deck's railing but the rest of her had cleared it easily and she landed on the deck with a thud. Wyler performed the leap and cleared the railing with far more free room than Russell, but he landed heavily and staggered as the forward momentum took him.

Russell took two steps toward him before the roof behind them blew up.

51

Russell stood next to Wyler and watched as flames leapt out of the town house roof. She heard a clicking behind her and the sliding glass door that accessed the deck slid open. Beckmann and a wide-eyed woman in a bathrobe stepped out. Russell held the gun behind her back and tried to look like a homeowner who had just fled a burning house rather than a CIA officer who had just thwarted an attack on a high-ranking ambassador. Wyler stepped toward the woman.

"Madame Clochard, thank you for helping me. My friend and I smelled gas and were just able to leave the house before it exploded." He put his hand out to the woman but she bypassed it and wrapped her arms around his waist.

"Monsieur Wyler, I am so happy to see that you are not hurt." She glanced at the bloody towel wrapped around his forearm. "Oh, no, you are hurt."

Wyler shook his head. "Only a scratch. Nothing to worry about."

Beckmann remained where he was and Russell saw him take in first her state of undress and then Wyler's before turning his attention to the burning town house next door.

"Looks like you've had a busy night," he said.

Russell exhaled and headed to the door, taking care to keep her gun out of sight as she passed Wyler, who was attempting to disengage from a determined Madame Clochard. She passed Beckmann the gun and he slid it into his waistband and dropped his lightweight wind-breaker over it. Russell waited for Wyler, who managed to charm his way out of the clutches of his neighbor and join her. They took an interior stairwell to the ground level and Wyler again managed to talk his way out of leaving by the front door, instead using the back gangway. They emerged at the side of the house and out of sight of the assembled squad cars.

"This is a friend of mine," Russell said, indicating Beckmann. "I don't think it's advisable that either of us meet with the police."

Wyler nodded. "Let me handle this. Go ahead and take the car. It's in that garage." Wyler indicated a low-ly-ing garage building a block away. "Give me a minute and I'll retrieve the keys." He strode away and Russell sighed. The adrenaline that had propped her up through the or-deal was already dissipating.

"How did you get here so quickly?" she asked Beck-mann.

"Marty reached me. He'd managed to code a stand-ing intercept that pings him whenever one of us is mentioned on an NSA site. Seems as though they had bugged Wyler's house. They saw you go in and then several hours later picked up an image of guys in ski masks."

"Now the NSA is bugging our own ambassadors? And here I thought his house would be a safe zone."

"We need to find Rendel and this mole and fast. Any idea where they came from?"

Russell shook her head. "Could have been the same group that attacked the reception in Turkey."

"That seems likely. It was another bomb, right? I'm starting to think of the bombs as their signature," Beck-mann said.

"Wyler was concerned that he had been targeted, and had requested but been denied a bodyguard."

"He's lucky you were there. He couldn't have asked for a better bodyguard."

"Thanks for the compliment, but I'm genuinely concerned that the next time he won't survive it."

"Do you want to bring him with us? It's his car after all. I'm sure he can give a plausible excuse for a couple of days off. From what I saw back there on the deck he's a quick thinker, cool under pressure, and a diplomat to the core. We could use someone with authority and such an easy manner at the border. After that we can split and go our separate ways."

Russell was tempted to agree, mostly because she wanted to keep Wyler close, but she thought that this time his request for additional bodyguards would be granted and he'd actually be better off away from her. Especially if the mole gave killing her another shot.

"I don't think it's a good idea. We're somewhat of a lightning rod for danger. Let's get to Geneva and assist Smith. I'm done playing their game."

Wyler reappeared, wearing gym shoes and a black T-shirt, carrying a set of keys and a messenger bag. He handed them both to Russell.

"Here are the keys and some clothes for you to wear. I'm sorry, I wasn't able to recover yours. They were incinerated in the blast. These are from a workout bag I keep in the front hall closet." Russell took the items and opened the messenger bag to look inside. "It's a pair of sweats. Mine, so not your size and for that I apologize, and a sweatshirt."

Russell reached in and removed a flask. "What's in here?"

"Scotch."

"Excellent," Beckmann said. "Why don't you give me the keys and I'll go get the car." Russell tossed him the keys and he put his hand out to Wyler. "Glad to know that you're okay." Wyler shook his hand.

"Thanks. You take care tomorrow. I hope that whatever your mission is, it's successful and you both skate through without injury."

Beckmann walked away and once he was out of sight

in the garage Wyler reached to Russell and pulled her into an embrace. She wrapped her arms around him and held him against her, pressing her cheek against his chest and listening to the slow beat of his heart through the shirt. After a moment he shifted and bent down to kiss her. A band of light swept across them as Beckmann pulled up.

"I'll be in touch as soon as it's safe. This time insist on bodyguards and don't back down until you get them," Russell said.

"I'm saving the Armagnac for us to share when you return," Wyler said.

Russell didn't trust herself to speak. Instead she nodded and got in the car, and Beckmann drove away. Through the side-view mirror she could see that Wyler watched them until they turned the corner and she could see him no more.

52

How are you holding up? Do you want me to drive?" Arden asked.

Smith shook his head. "So far I'm doing okay."

"Tell me about the drone program."

"The one in the UK?"

"Yes."

"It's a joint CIA-NSA program. Croughton gathers the intel and sends it to Camp Lemonnier in Djibouti. The CIA can't launch assassination strikes anymore, so they contract them out to comply with the new law."

Arden nodded. "And if it's a U.S. citizen that's the target, then the strike can't continue without first seeking Department of Justice approval. Can you find out if the DOJ was notified?"

"Of the strike on me? Are you thinking that this was a sanctioned strike? That never occurred to me. I'm actually shocked that you would even consider it."

"It could be an attack on you or the others with you. Croughton could have sent a request to Djibouti."

"They deny any knowledge of the attack before it began."

"There must be several drones parked at Croughton. It's conceivable that the actual operator was sitting in Djibouti when he launched them, but I can't believe that a drone strike within an allied country, and Britain to boot, can be managed out of Djibouti. Someone, somewhere in Croughton would have seen the thing take off and raised the alarm."

"They claim to have only learned of the problem when the drone was picked up on radar and questions called in."

"Do you believe that?" Arden asked.

"I'm not sure what to believe."

"I'll tell you one thing. Follow the money or track the power and you'll find the culprit."

Smith smiled into the darkness. "A certain financier I know always insisted that money was the driving force behind most of the crime in the world. She didn't believe that power was ever a driving force except when it was a drive to accumulate more money from that power."

"People are strange and those with money are often the strangest. There's a study out that found that most CEOs of major companies are psychopaths."

"Really?" Smith was intrigued. "I hadn't heard that. Have you read it?"

"I didn't have to. I deal with so many psychopathic CEOs that it was old news to me."

"Well, I hate to tell you, but by tomorrow afternoon we're headed into a pharmaceutical conference that will be loaded with them."

"Why is that?"

"We need their help."

"For what?"

Smith paused, trying to decide how much more to tell her.

She waved him off. "Never mind, I can see that you won't tell me why. But they won't help you unless you pay for it."

"I intend to appeal to their better instincts."

"They don't have any," Arden said.

Smith thought the assessment a little harsh, but he kept the thought to himself while he drove.

They reached the border almost six hours after they'd left Dieppe. Smith slowed about a mile before the checkpoint and pulled off the road.

"So tell me about red notices. What can I expect?"

"Not much unless we get some very ambitious border guard who decides to actually check a passport. But if he does, and his system is up to date, he'll get a ping and you'll be taken into custody. Most of the time the border guard station is closed this late at night. Budget cuts."

"But there will be cameras. How about you lower the seat and look like you're sleeping. Keep your face below the dash and turned toward the door."

"What about you?"

"I'm hoping the beard will help."

Smith started forward again and Arden lowered her seat into the full recline position and turned her head to the door. As they neared the border the lanes narrowed and Smith could see a large bridge-type structure ahead. A spotlight illuminated a Swiss flag that flapped in the night breeze on the top of the bridge. They slowed behind three other cars and each was waved through by a guard on his telephone. Smith pulled up next and the guard hung up and leaned out.

"You'll need to buy a vignette," he said. Smith nodded and handed him some euros. After a moment the guard gave him back a sticker for his windshield and waved the next car forward. Smith drove through.

"That was remarkably easy," Smith said.

"At least something is going our way." Arden moved her seat back into a sitting position.

Thirty minutes later Smith pulled onto a private road. The only illumination came from reflectors placed on sticks at regular intervals on either side. After half a mile they came to a rustic-looking ranch house with a horseshoe drive. Smith killed the engine and soaked in the sudden silence.

"Looks deserted," Arden said.

"There should be a lockbox and key around the doorknob."

Smith got out, stretched, and reached in the back passenger seat where he'd thrown his suit jacket. He was looking forward to getting out of the suit, which he'd been wearing for almost thirty-six hours straight. Klein had promised to have new clothes in the house.

Smith freed the keys from the holder and opened the door. The house's interior was clean and the furniture minimal. A front foyer area opened into a great room with an open design. A stone fireplace separated the front area from the kitchen and dining room. A hall to the left led to three bedrooms, with a bathroom door on one side and a master bedroom and bath in the back. Smith threw his coat on the master bed before returning to the kitchen, where he found Arden filling a pitcher with water. She handed him a glass.

"From the tap. There's a computer set up in the corner of the great room."

Smith passed through the kitchen to the far corner, where he found the desktop. While he waited for it to boot up he opened a door that led through a short hallway to a back mudroom. It had the usual pegs on the walls to hang coats over a built-in bench that had nooks in it to hold boots, but the opposite wall had a large built-in cabinet. Smith opened the doors and whistled. It was a gun cabinet. Every manner of weapon was lined up there: AK-47 automatic assault weapons, high-caliber sniper rifles with telescopic sights, pistols, ammunition belts, and boxes of bullets. At the end were several bulletproof vests and two helmets. A box at the base appeared to hold hand grenades and another had six cell phones still in their original packaging.

He headed back to the computer and accessed the secure USAMRIID network. He sipped some water, sat down, and proceeded to read the various clinical trial reports and test results that the researchers had sent him. A separate email from Klein attached the report that Taylor had given him that evening at the lab.

After an hour his head was swimming and his eyes blurring from sleep deprivation. One thing, though, was abundantly clear: Taylor had known that the drug she had created had the potential to derange or kill those who were exposed to it. At four thirty in the morning he felt a tap on his shoulder.

"Why don't you get some sleep?" Arden said. She leaned over his shoulder and read the screen. Smith had it open to a particularly interesting aspect of the research in which Taylor had attempted to halt memory consolidation by blocking protein synthesis. A few drugs had blocking capability, but the most common was a staple on the dance club circuit: MDMA, or Ecstasy.

"Ecstasy blocks memory?"

Smith nodded. "It seems that there are a few drugs that can do it. Taylor was trying to create a cocktail that would inhibit the reconsolidation of traumatic memory only."

"Reconsolidation? What's that?"

"Our memories of an incident aren't static, we just think they are. Each time we access a memory our brain actually has to reconsolidate it from various locations. Do this often enough and the memory deforms."

"Like eyewitness accounts in a trial. They're notoriously inaccurate and change as time goes on."

He nodded. "Exactly like that. And we don't know it's happening to us. We actually believe it's not. We're wrong, of course. Taylor proved that many of our most cherished or reviled memories can not only be altered, but may not even be accurate after the third or fourth time that we access them."

"Was she trying to change them in a certain direction?"

"She was. She could manage it in rats, but there were enough problems with the research that she was unable to obtain clearance to test it on humans. Her cocktail either made rats forget a recent bad memory, a good thing, or made them behave in a crazy manner, a bad thing. On the extreme end it was killing them by short-circuiting all of their brain function. A very bad thing. Aerosolizing it led to unpredictable results across the board and she wrote that in her opinion it should never be altered in that manner."

"Is there an antidote?"

He shook his head. "But there is one fascinating aspect of it. The drug only worked when administered close to the actual memory. Wait too long and the brain found a way to circumvent the block."

"So if you're in the area you'd better hope that you came late to the dance? Then the drug is ineffective?"

"Except for the death aspect. If your brain was the one that was predisposed to shut down then that would happen no matter when you were exposed."

"How long after exposure comes death?"

"About sixty seconds."

"There's got to be a way to block the blocker."

He sighed. "I agree. And given more time I probably could get close to creating it. But time isn't on our side on this one and right now I'm too tired to think." He exited the program and stood. "And I'm done with this beard. Time to remove it."

"Oh, I almost forgot," Arden said. She went down the hall and returned a minute later holding a bottle that she handed to him.

"Baby oil?" he said.

"I found it in the near bathroom. You can use it to remove the adhesive that holds the beard. While you do that, I'm going to make some food. I found some spaghetti and bottled sauce in the cabinets."

Smith managed get the beard off and take a short shower before he heard Arden calling down the hall. He joined her at the kitchen table, where a steaming bowl of spaghetti and a glass of wine waited. They ate a few minutes in silence.

"I was ravenous," he said. He pointed at the oversized watch on her wrist. "That watch is interesting."

She smiled. "It was my father's. He died several years ago and I've worn it ever since."

"What did he die of?"

"Heart attack. My father was an attorney. He worked around the clock. My mother used to try to get him to relax, but he never was able to take a break. It was as if he was trying to outrun death."

"That never works," Smith said. He saw that she was finished eating and took her plate and his to the dishwasher. After a few minutes the kitchen was clean and he felt the crushing exhaustion finally settle on his shoulders. "I'm about done."

Arden nodded. "Me too."

Smith went to the mudroom, chose a pistol and a matching magazine, and returned to the kitchen to place them on the table in front of Arden.

"Let me show you how this works." He showed her how to load a magazine, drop it out, and set the safety switch. "This one has a laser sight." He pointed the muzzle at a far wall and the red dot hit a point near the doorjamb. "Put the dot on the area you want to shoot and pull the trigger." He handed her the gun. She placed it on the table in front of her and stared at it in silence. "What are you thinking?" he asked.

"That it all boils down to this." She indicated the gun.

He shook his head. "Not all of it."

She glanced up and he could read the disbelief in her eyes. "Tell me what part of it doesn't, because I've spent most of my career battling violence and now I'm the one holding the gun. And this time it's not for show."

Smith placed his hands on the table and leaned across it. "You've spent your career defending those who have been victimized by violence. And that is a good thing. I'm handing you this gun so that you won't be victimized in turn."

"I'll become the perpetrator."

"No. The one trying to kill you for your work in defending those less fortunate is the perpetrator. He always was. Now you're just using the tools of a different trade to stop him."

"Tools of whose trade?"

"Mine," Smith said.

She searched his face. "That is the closest you've ever come to telling me what you're really about. Will you ever tell me it all?"

"No."

"Kind of keeps a distance between us," she said.

"I don't want to stay removed, but some things you have to take on faith. In this case, faith in me."

"I'm an attorney. I believe in facts. Faith doesn't play in a courtroom."

"We're not in a courtroom."

"Sometimes you scare me." That surprised Smith. He would have said that nothing scared her. "Want to know what I think you are?"

Smith wasn't sure he did want to know, but he nodded anyway.

"I think you're some sort of covert operator. At first I thought you were a part of a government black ops team and I made a silent vow to bring you down. But now I think that whatever game you're playing or master you're playing it for, you mean to peel away the grime and get down to the core. I think that core is on the side of good and not evil."

"Why does that scare you?"

"Because I've never had blind faith in anyone. But I do now. In you."

He smiled. "Thank you. I'd never hurt you."

She nodded. "I know. But if it came down to the wire and what you are doing is illegal I won't defend you. I have faith but not facts. If the facts fall the wrong way you'll have to find someone else to defend you."

"I thought attorneys stayed neutral under the theory that everyone deserves a defense."

She nodded. "That's true, but if I ever discovered that you were actually a bad actor I would be too upset to be unbiased."

He leaned over and kissed her. After a moment he

broke away. His head was spinning and he pulled himself together. "I promise not to cause you pain."

A bit of humor lit her eyes. "I'll hold you to that." She rose and picked up the gun. She reached the hall and leaned against the corner of the wall.

"Good night."

"Same to you."

She went to the near bedroom and he heard the door quietly close. Just as quietly he returned to the mud-room, picked a pistol off the rack, loaded a magazine, and headed to the master bedroom to sleep.

53

Darkanin sat in front of a breakfast tray in the private villa on a golf course outside Geneva. The country club boasted a restaurant, eighteen holes, and a small hotel and conference compound where the pharmaceutical meeting was to be held. It also touted its private, forested setting near enough to Geneva to make a commute to the city easy, yet far enough to retain a rural beauty. The gated compound emphasized privacy and exclusivity.

He had taken care to rent the villa farthest from the conference compound and close to an access driveway for the various workmen and gardeners that the club employed. The club had been closed to all visitors and club members during the conference, and the weather was brisk. Gore sat opposite him.

"Tell me what happened in Paris."

"Wyler had a bodyguard."

"I thought none were assigned."

"He must have hired private."

"One rent-a-cop takes out four trained mercenaries? How is this possible?"

Gore's face darkened. "It wasn't four at first. I remained with the vehicle and so didn't get there until the situation had already deteriorated. Wyler was holed up in the bathroom and Westcore and Ralston were dead."

"And Denon?"

"He remains in England and never came near the arena."

"And again I ask, how did one poorly trained private cop take out three highly trained Stanton Reese contractors?"

Gore shook his head. "Whoever it was he wasn't a poorly trained private cop."

Darkanin sipped his coffee. He was happy to take his frustration with the situation out on Gore and wouldn't tell him that he knew exactly who had been in the room that evening. Let him believe that his crew had been outdone by a common security guard. Darkanin would use the assumption to short Gore on his fee.

Darkanin's only regret was that he had vastly underestimated Ms. Russell and had blithely assumed that one woman was no match for four Stanton Reese operatives. He wouldn't make that mistake again. When he found her next he'd kill her after feeding her to another torturer equal to the late, great Curry. He flicked a hand at the door.

"Get the rest of your crew ready for the action this afternoon. I'll not have any more slip-ups, is that understood?" Gore shoved away from the table and stomped out of the villa. Darkanin dialed his phone and placed it on speaker to leave his hands free to finish eating.

"What's Gore's excuse?" Yang said when he answered the phone.

"So the news traveled to Shanghai already?" Darkanin replied.

"Bad news travels faster than most. This is the second try against Wyler that's failed and both times this Russell operative has been the one to derail the action."

"Honestly I don't know why you hate Wyler so much. He's the smallest player in our plan."

"He's the smallest player in *your* plan, but not in my backers' plans. He's been pushing back at them, shining a light where there should be darkness."

Darkanin snorted. "The Mafia bakery mob? What does the U.S. ambassador to Turkey have to do with them?"

"Idiot. It's not the Comorra. It's Syria. Wyler has proof that the rebels used chemical weapons on the villages that line the border between Syria and Turkey and that despite their assurances to the world that they've destroyed those weapons, they've actually stockpiled them."

Darkanin sat back and stared at the phone. "You've been lying to me all this time. You told me that you were only interested in helping me to steal Taylor's research and selling it to the highest bidder after we disseminate it with the hacked drones. Now you tell me that you've been backed by the Syrians?"

Darkanin rose and began to pace. The whole plan—its shape, size, and possible payoff—had been misrepresented to him from the beginning. He'd assumed that Yang wanted what most of the Chinese state-sponsored hackers wanted: to steal U.S. trade secrets in order to engineer the products quicker and cheaper, then sell them on the world market. Even when the hacker was busy attempting to manipulate the U.S. drone force, Darkanin had been assured that once the hack was accomplished a Chinese company would ride to the rescue and offer a programming patch to the U.S. military. For a price, of course. And he'd assumed that the Arabs wanted to use the drug to snap back against the Iranians, their most hated enemies. Now he realized that both had used him and his money to further their own agendas.

"Why are you so shocked? You're the one planning to wipe out half of Europe's pharmaceutical regulators in one afternoon," Yang said.

"Not wipe them out, force them to see that Bancor's cognitive enhancement drug is essential to ward off this new and imminent danger."

"Semantics. There's no way you'll be able to control who lives and who dies when you unleash the drug and you know it. They could all die."

"The computer module predicts only forty percent.

It's an unfortunate but necessary loss," Darkanin countered.

"And your drug doesn't even work. You needed Taylor's expertise to tweak it and now she's dead."

"You let me worry about that," Darkanin said. "The Syrians must want a different outcome. Tell me what their angle is."

"The same as yours. Once the drug's devastating effect is shown they want to use it on Washington."

Darkanin's mind raced. He sensed that Yang still wasn't telling him everything. "We need to bring my backer into this conversation. He is not aware that you've been negotiating with the Syrian rebels."

"Yes he is. He's always been aware. In fact, it was his idea. You're the only one out of the loop on this one."

Darkanin contemplated then discarded several scenarios in which he utilized the information that Yang had just given him to his advantage. He realized that the plan's essentials remained the same, but the arena had widened from a plan that included governmental officials from several countries to one that put the highest governmental official and the largest concentration of powerful men and women in the world in its crosshairs. The drug that would circumvent an attack on the president of the United States and Congress would be worth very much indeed. Bancor would be seen as a savior and Darkanin a hero.

"You need to tell the Syrians to give me a bit more time to research altering Bancor's drug before they unleash the weapon on Washington. Without Taylor it will take me a little longer to work out the science."

"That's not going to happen. The Syrians don't give a rat's ass if the drug kills everyone in DC. In fact, that would suit them just fine."

"Tell the Syrians that I don't care if they release their drug in the States, just not in DC. Dead politicians don't authorize multibillion-dollar military contracts. They have to be alive to do that."

"The Syrians don't care."

"But I do."

"Like I said, what you want and what the Syrians want are not necessarily the same. But I can tell you one thing that may make them a bit more willing to negotiate with you."

Now it comes, Darkanin thought.

"And what is that?"

"Wyler dead, Russell dead, and Smith dead."

Darkanin breathed a sigh of relief. The task would be easy.

"I don't care about the others, but Smith? Why? I may need his expertise now that Taylor's gone."

"That's just it. Smith is the researcher at USAMRIID who's been working on aerosols similar to Taylor's. They're concerned he'll find a way to stop the drug's effectiveness."

Darkanin wanted to throw the phone across the room. Stopping the drug's effectiveness was exactly what he'd hoped to do with the Bancor drug. He and the Syrians were working at cross-purposes. He wanted to sell the antidote and the Syrians wanted to ensure that no antidote was ever created. He took a deep breath to calm himself. Fighting the Syrians wasn't advisable. They'd find a way to assassinate him. He'd have to come up with a solution before they attacked the United States.

"Tell them it will be done."

54

FBI agent Mark Brand stepped into the plush hotel suite in Geneva reserved for Ambassador Wyler. The FBI had gotten and received permission to investigate the possible connection between the recent attack on Wyler and the Washington kidnappings. Fred Klein had called Brand and asked him to push to be the FBI point man so that he could manage the investigation in a way that would keep Covert-One's participation in the kidnapping search quiet. Klein's request was clear.

"Wyler's neighbor stated that a woman was with Wyler the night of the attack. The FBI initially was unable to verify her identity, but last night an anonymous video feed was sent to the Washington branch that showed a woman walking into Wyler's town house earlier that evening. The sender claimed that the woman was Randi Russell," Klein had said.

"Where did the feed come from?"

"The NSA office in Croughton. But when contacted they insisted that they are not conducting any type of surveillance on Wyler and they don't know who from inside their office sent the video. Can you get in front of this?"

Brand pushed, received the assignment, and flew to Geneva, where the ambassador was preparing to attend a pharmaceutical conference. It would be a delicate balance to keep the investigation thorough while also keeping Russell's multiple affiliations secret, but Brand was confident that whatever Russell had done at the town house to protect Wyler had been necessary.

Wyler stepped into the suite flanked by two members of the Secret Service. Brand had read a dossier on Wyler in preparation for the interview and so he knew that Wyler had been educated at Georgetown University, began his career as an intern, and worked his way through the diplomatic ranks as a junior consular by accepting postings that were considered low-value. One of those postings had turned to gold when he'd been in the right place during the initial overthrow of Saddam Hussein in Iraq, and from that moment his star had begun a steep climb. The dossier revealed that he kept an apartment for his own use in Washington, was divorced, had no children, and paid his taxes. He never seemed to want for female companionship, but since the divorce had kept most women at a safe distance and had had a series of short-term relationships only. The latter issue may have been a function of his constant movement. He'd held three different posts in three years.

An FBI dossier wasn't complete unless it dug for dirt, and Wyler's name had been run through the usual files for escort service invoices, strip club credit card receipts, improper expense report items, or deviant or other sexual behavior that would make a government official vulnerable to a possible blackmail or extortion attempt by spies of a foreign government. In compiling the dossier they'd also searched for any signs of addiction, including gambling, alcohol, and prescription drugs. Wyler had come up clean. Clean, that is, until the video leak. Then a second sweep revealed that he had exhibited an unusual interest in a CIA officer assigned to Turkey and that the same officer had been in his home on the night of the recent attack. Fraternization between a CIA officer and an ambassador did not violate any policies on either side of the equation, but it was unusual enough behavior for both parties that it was flagged for further investigation.

Wyler acknowledged Brand with a handshake and waited for the Secret Service guards to leave. He closed and locked the suite's door behind them.

"I see you have security," Brand said.

Wyler nodded. "Temporarily, yes. I'm told they'll be pulled once the investigation into the bombing has been completed. Please, sit down." Brand took a chair near the window and Wyler sat on a nearby couch. "How can I help you?"

"I'm here to talk about a rash of kidnappings in Washington and the recent attack against you."

Wyler looked surprised. "Does the FBI believe that they were intent on kidnapping me?"

"We don't know, but we can't rule out the possibility. What do you think they were after?"

Wyler ran a hand through his hair. "I'm sure you've read my report on the bombing in Turkey. I thought it had something to do with my activities there in pressing back against the Syrians. Why does the FBI think this was a kidnap attempt?"

"One of the men found dead in the town house was the same man who, while posing as a member of the Department of Veterans Affairs, confronted a USAMRIID researcher about a missing colleague. It wasn't until later that it was discovered the colleague had also been kidnapped. We now think that perhaps he was attempting to kidnap you."

"Posing? How did he manage that?"

"He actually had some clearance in security. He was a non-governmental official assigned to the Department of Veterans Affairs."

"Through what organization?"

"The Stanton Reese contract security company."

Wyler's face turned grim. "This is not the first time Stanton Reese has employed some bad actors, is it?"

"True. But it employs over sixteen thousand people worldwide, so some problem employees are to be expected. My real concern is with Officer Randi Russell, who I understand may have been present during the attack."

Wyler nodded. "She was."

Brand was surprised at Wyler's quick affirmation. In all prior interviews with the local police Wyler had invoked his diplomatic immunity and carefully avoided mentioning that a woman was involved that night. It was only after the net had been thrown wider and the neighbor interviewed that the fact that he was not alone had been revealed. Even then, though, he had refused to give her name in order to protect her privacy and kept assuring the local police that whatever had happened that evening, it had little to do with the woman. When pressed he invoked diplomatic immunity once again.

"In what capacity was she there?"

Wyler's pause was nearly imperceptible, but Brand had long experience conducting such interviews and to him the pause was obvious.

"She's a friend."

"And I understand that you are aware she's also a CIA officer?"

Wyler nodded. "I am."

"So was she present at your home in her capacity as a CIA officer or as a friend only?"

"As a friend only."

"Where were you when the attack began?"

"I was asleep."

"And Officer Russell?"

"Also asleep."

"Down the hall?"

"No."

"Nearby?"

"She was asleep next to me."

Beyond friendly fraternization, then, Brand thought. Still, since both were adults and consenting, he didn't see any real problem with the connection.

"How long have you and Officer Russell been... friends?"

"We met when she was posted in Turkey. We became...closer very recently. I'm very thankful that she was there. To put it frankly, she saved my life. I have no doubt that I'd be dead right now if she hadn't taken the heroic steps she did. She was the one who alerted me to the intruders and she was the one who fought them off and guided me to safety."

"Did she tell you anything about her current assignment?"

Wyler shook his head. "Nothing at all. She wouldn't breach any confidentiality, nor would I press her for such information."

"Do you intend to see her again?"

"I certainly hope so."

Brand stood and Wyler did as well. "Thank you for your time. I've a scheduled meeting with the police in Paris. I'll emphasize to them your cooperation with the investigation and will assure them that the woman was not involved with the attackers."

Wyler shook his hand. "Thank you."

Brand opened the door.

"Agent Brand?"

Brand looked back.

"Do you know Ms. Russell?"

"I've met her, yes."

"Will you be speaking to her?"

"I can't say. Perhaps." Brand watched as a bit of hope entered Wyler's eyes.

"If you do, please tell her that I did my best to keep her involvement a secret, but that I couldn't lie to an FBI agent. I wouldn't like her to think that I don't keep my promises."

Brand nodded. "I'm sure she'll understand."

Brand closed the door and wondered whether Russell had any idea of the impact she had made on Wyler.

55

Howell stood in the conference room at RAF Croughton and listened while Scariano lied to him about the recent drone flights and video leaks emanating from the base. Howell couldn't fault the man entirely, because Scariano thought that he was talking to an MI5 investigator, not a freelance covert operator in the employ of his own government, but Howell was becoming annoyed at the lack of urgency he sensed in Scariano.

"Something has gone terribly wrong within your organization and you need to get a handle on it now," Howell said.

Scariano gave Howell a pacifying smile. "Please inform your superiors that we are doing all we can to discover the source of these leaks and put an end to them."

Howell had had enough condescension for one day. "That's not good enough. Your program has lost several drones, one that has fired upon individuals not thirty miles from here, and another that may have been implicated in the deaths of an entire troop of U.S. military men in Djibouti. I expect you to open your network to me so that I can track the mole."

Scariano stood up. "What in the world are you talking about? What military troop? The one that walked off the cliff after their commanding officer fired on them?"

"Canelo never fired on his troop. It's clear to us that someone out of this office is manipulating the drones to test a chemical weapon."

Howell was fishing, but he was pleased to see Scariano's mouth drop open. Most covert operatives were excellent actors, but Howell thought that perhaps Scariano was truly shocked at the accusation. "Tell me if *Stateroom* has turned up any more suspected hostage situations. There's still an American official missing who was heavily involved in the drone program."

Scariano pursed his lips. "Then why are you here and not a representative of the U.S. government?"

"I'm here because we don't need another hostage situation on UK soil, that's why. Don't forget that we allow you to use this base for your surveillance program, but that permission can be withdrawn at any time." Howell put some steel into his voice. The explanation seemed to satisfy Scariano, because he waved Howell over to another man who was wearing a headset and staring at a computer screen.

"Tresome, you got anything happening out of any embassies?"

Tresome shook his head. "Just that one I mentioned when the woman was here."

"What woman?" Howell asked, though he knew that it had been Russell.

"She represented American interests," Scariano said in an offhand manner. "I promise to let UK authorities know if we find anything."

"Tell security that I'll be doing a sweep of the base, taking photos and generally examining it. I don't want to be disturbed while I do it," Howell said. He strode out of the office and the building.

The air was cool but the sun shone and the base was set in a beautiful part of rural England. Howell walked the perimeter, around the massive, looming satellite dishes and several humming electric generators. At the far end of the fenced area, in what looked like a little-used parking lot, he saw a small aluminum shed next to a cluster of thirty-foot-high poles with several smaller satellite dishes arrayed at the top and facing in all directions. A single electric wire ran to it that Howell supposed provided electricity.

Throughout his stroll Howell had been taking videos on his phone and sending them to Marty to review. He spent a few extra moments recording the shed and the attached pole and was not surprised when Marty called him a few seconds later.

"Can you take another pass around the shed and send it to me? This time from the other side of the pole?"

"I thought that shed was interesting," Howell said.

"Actually, it's not the shed. I'm particularly interested in that line of white boxes under the cluster of small satellites. I would like to know if there are some on the other side."

Howell returned to the pole but this time took a video from the back of it. There was one box on that side, also white, but alone and in the middle of the pole and Howell zoomed in on it. Seconds after he'd sent it Marty called him back.

"Do you need more?" Howell asked.

"No. That's it. That's a splitter," Marty said.

"Splitter? Explain."

"It's taking the signal and splitting it off. Turn on your Wi-Fi and give me the names or signatures of everything you see displayed."

Howell did as Marty asked and read off a list of six networks, all password-protected.

"Yeah, it's not there. They've hidden the SSID."

"Hidden the signature? Is that hard to do?"

He heard Marty snort. "It's a simple click on a router. Anyone can do it and it's essentially meaningless because a good Wi-Fi scanner can pick up the signal. You can hide visibility, but you can't hide the signal itself. It continues to broadcast."

"Can you track where this one is going?"

"I'm already trying, but right now all I can tell you is that it's being split off, not what's traveling over it. I'll need some time to work on cracking the password. Has anyone there bothered to walk the perimeter and do a simple Wi-Fi scan? Do they even know that their signal is being split?"

"They said they've checked them all. They gave me a list of the networks and cleared each one."

"Read the list to me."

Howell retrieved the document that he'd folded and put in his pocket and scanned the list. He read them all to Marty.

"So there are ten active signals listed?"

"Yes," Howell said.

"But that unidentified signal is eleven. They haven't cleared it."

"All right. I'll handle this from here. You've been exceedingly helpful, Marty, thank you."

"What are you going to do?"

"Put a gun to someone's head and force them to do their job."

He heard Marty chuckle over the phone. "Wish I was there to see that. Good luck."

Howell headed back to the base at a brisk walk. When he reached the office it reeked of the heavy smell of fried oil and salt and he found Scariano eating a hamburger with a bag of French fries at his desk. Howell dropped the network list next to the open paper that had wrapped the hamburger.

"This list is incomplete," Howell said.

Scariano shot him an annoyed look, put down the burger, wiped his hands on a napkin, and picked up the paper.

"This list is complete. Ten networks, all cleared." He tossed the paper aside. "Tell MI5 we've got this covered."

Howell removed a gun from his shoulder holster and pointed it at Scariano's head. He watched as all the blood drained from the man's face.

"Now, I'm only going to ask this once," Howell said. "And if you give me an answer that later proves to be wrong I am going to return here and you will never give another answer again, do you understand?"

Scariano nodded.

"Who compiled this list and ran the check? Tresome?"

Scariano shook his head. "An officer named Natalie Detmar. She's from the Berlin office and was assigned here temporarily."

"Where is she now?"

"Down the hall. Third office on the left."

Howell jerked the gun. "Let's go."

Scariano began to slide his hand under the desk and Howell moved in closer and pressed the gun's muzzle against the other man's skull.

"Press the panic button and you'll be the first casualty of the covert wars."

"This is outrageous! You can't come in here waving guns around and threatening people. I'll have you arrested."

"No, you won't. Whole swaths of your program aren't supposed to exist. You complain and I'll be sure that your activities at this cyber nest will be plastered on the cover of the *Guardian* the next day. NSA leaks round two."

Scariano removed his hand and stood. He turned and headed out the door. Howell grabbed a jacket that was slung over the back of a chair and threw it over the gun to hide it. Scariano raised a hand to knock at Detmar's door, but Howell reached around him and opened it, swinging it wide and pushing Scariano through.

The office was small and utilitarian. A metal desk held a computer, a letter sorter, and a plastic filing system. The stacked system was labeled; In, Out and Pending. Detmar sat behind the desk facing them. She was a young woman with dirty-blond hair and pale skin and eyes. Howell guessed she was from the north of Germany. She was typing furiously at a keyboard, but stopped when she saw Howell and Scariano.

"What's happening?" she asked.

Howell circled Scariano, keeping the gun under the coat aimed in his direction, and tossed the paper in front of her.

"Did you compile this list?" Howell asked.

"Who are you?" she asked Howell.

"He's MI5. Answer him, please," Scariano said.

Detmar glanced between them again. "I did."

"When?"

"Yesterday."

"Alone?" Howell asked.

She shook her head. "With the help of Blaine Trigard."

"Who's that?"

"Temporary posting out of Washington."

"Did you do a scan on the wireless networks?"

She nodded. "Of course."

"And this was the result?"

"Yes," she said.

"Did you walk the entire compound?"

"Trigard did. He was in charge of the perimeter sweep."

"Where is he now?"

"He's gone. Been reposted to Geneva."

"Can you prove that he actually swept as he said he did?"

Detmar nodded. "Yes. It would be on video. The entire base is monitored."

Howell jerked his chin at her computer. "Show me the portion when he scans the poles by the shed at the far end of the field."

Detmar hesitated and glanced at Scariano. He nodded his agreement and she turned her attention to the computer.

"Here it is." She turned the monitor to face them. Howell saw a distance shot of a man walking along the fence line holding a device. He reached the pole and stopped to type.

"Zoom in as deep as you can. I want to see what it is he's typing," Howell said.

Detmar hit some buttons and the screen zoomed.

"Freeze it there," Howell said. He stared at the screen, not quite believing what he was seeing.

"Well?" Scariano said.

Howell tossed the coat on a nearby chair, put the safety back on his gun, and returned it to the holster under his jacket. Detmar raised her eyebrows at the sight of the gun, but remained quiet. Scariano sighed in relief.

"Now do you believe me?" he asked. "We've got this under control."

"You supercilious bastard, you've got nothing under control," Howell said.

"What do you mean?"

Howell pointed at the screen. "That man's name isn't Blaine Trigard. His name is Nicholas Rendel."

56

President Castilla sat in a chair in his private chambers watching the sun rise and marshaling his thoughts and strength for the coming day. The phone rang and he saw the name of the Anacostia Yacht Club scroll across the caller ID screen.

"Klein, you're up early," Castilla said. "Please tell me this is good news."

"We found Rendel. Or at least we think we know where he is," Klein said.

"Our last victim. Where is he?"

"He's not a victim but a perpetrator, and he's somewhere in Geneva, Switzerland." Castilla listened while Klein explained Howell's findings.

"I want to know how Rendel was able to hide in plain sight," Castilla said.

"They claim that he'd kept to himself and holed up in a spare office that they keep for visiting contract personnel. He'd changed his hair and added a beard and Scariano said that they had no reason to doubt his credentials. Also, while they received a memo about Rendel's alleged kidnapping, they hadn't received a photo of him along with it. Turns out they had, but Rendel managed to delete it before it hit anyone's desk. We have to assume this is a deliberate piece of sabotage on Rendel's part."

Castilla tried to tamp down his anger and think logically, but he was having a difficult time of it. His fury at the thought of the damage this man had caused was making his heart race and the blood rise to his head. And the fact that the saboteur was still out there was horrendous.

"He's a Stanton Reese contractor, isn't he?" Castilla was surprised at how normal he sounded as he asked the question.

"Yes. Assigned to the drone program out of Nevada, but he's also had access to the Croughton facility for some time now. I think it's safe to say that he's accumulated quite a bit of inside knowledge of how our drone program functions, both here and abroad, not to mention the coding aspect of the software. He has an extensive computer background. I won't be surprised if we find that he arranged for the drones to go missing in Djibouti. He was assigned there before being transferred to Washington."

First Snowden and now Rendel, Castilla thought. That yet another private contractor working within classified government programs had compromised those departments also stoked Castilla's fury. But even Snowden hadn't deliberately manipulated a high-level drone attack fleet to his own ends, as it appeared that Rendel had.

"Tell me where the Covert-One team is right now," Castilla said.

"In Geneva. Smith's there to avoid extradition under the Interpol notice and Russell's with him. Rendel told his colleagues at Croughton that he was headed to Geneva. I don't like it. Half the pharmaceutical industry is converging on that city and it's too odd that he was headed there. That's not a coincidence."

"I agree. We need to be prepared for something. How tight is security?"

"Tight. It always was because there are high-level governmental officials of several countries headed to the meeting."

"Let's get Smith, Russell, and anyone else we have available into that conference. In the meantime I'm going to find out who among the attendees has a shot at figuring out if the chemical used against the village was

Taylor's. I've asked for tissue samples to be taken and transported to the WHO for analysis, but I already told Perdue to get as many chemists, biologists, and whoever else might solve this puzzle actively working on it. I don't care if they're governmental scientists or pharmaceutical employees in the private sector, I just want some answers. Fast."

Twenty minutes later, a tired-looking Perdue joined Castilla in his office.

"I've put every available agent in Europe on the search for Rendel," he said. "Our real problem is that he could be anywhere in the world and still manipulating the drones. We fly them in Afghanistan while the pilot sits on a base in Nevada, for God's sake."

"What about radar? If one takes off it should ping something. Correct?"

Perdue shook his head. "They're designed to avoid all radar until they reach very low levels."

"And the pharmaceutical angle?"

"At the Department of Defense's request there was a call placed to Berendt Darkanin, CEO of Bancor Pharmaceuticals. Bancor is the company that maintains various contracts to provide drugs and devices required by the military. Vaccines, diabetes sharps, things like that. Darkanin is attending the conference and the word is that his company has been pushing an off-label use for a cognitive enhancement drug they've been developing. The DOD thought the parallels between his drug and Taylor's were so striking that Bancor might have research already completed that might help."

"I've heard that name before, but I can't place it," Castilla said.

"It's been in the news because the Justice Department has been gunning for them on a matter. They were preparing to charge them with illegal marketing of the cognitive drug."

"And now we're suggesting that they use it? Why?"

"When they were told about Taylor's research Bancor insisted that it will have a positive effect on cognitive impairments. It's all we've got right now."

"All right. And the missing drones?"

Perdue rubbed a hand over his face and sighed. "Still not located. We think they've been dismantled for transport and taken somewhere to be reconstructed. That way the parts can be placed in freight trucks. They could be anywhere. I'm leaning toward Iran being the culprit. Two of the missing drones are the same type as the one they brought down in their airspace. Maybe by now they've been able to successfully reverse-engineer the software. They could be setting us up to take the fall while they attack their adversary with impunity and then pretend outrage."

"Keep at it. I want those drones found. And if it's Iran behind this thing I want to know about it. Someone's funding Rendel. I don't believe he's acting on his own."

"It's not entirely out of the realm of possibility. Snowden seems to have operated alone."

Castilla shook his head. "This is too organized. Too complex on every level. Keep at it."

"Understood," Perdue said.

When he left Castilla stood at his window and pondered what he would say to Iran's representative when he called and whether he could keep his head during the conversation.

57

Darkanin dialed his partner and Nicholas Rendel answered on the first ring.

"You traitor," Darkanin said.

Rendel smirked. "Why, Berendt, I don't know what you mean."

"I thought we were partners in this deal. Now I learn from Yang that you've been double-crossing me every step of the way."

Rendel leaned back in his chair and Darkanin got a glimpse of the room behind him. Elaborate curtains flanked a tall, French window. From what Darkanin could see through the glass, Rendel was in a beautiful, bucolic setting.

"You're getting what you want, aren't you? The U.S. has conveniently come to you for the antidote, the drones are set to fly, and the chemical is loaded on each."

"You need to stop the Syrians from using the chemical in DC. I need the key players alive to sign off on the purchase orders to stockpile the drug. And who authorized the Iranian release? You had to know that the United States would gear up for battle once they were put in the crosshairs like that. Up until then they were aware of the drone theft, but were proceeding with the investigation at the usual bureaucrat's pace. Attacking the village has sent them into emergency mode."

Rendel put up a hand. "Nothing I could do there. The Syrians wanted to stick it to Iran and it was a perfect setting to test the drug. They asked me to program the flight and I did."

"You mean they paid you to program the flight. You'd better hope nothing goes wrong today."

Rendel shook his head. "It won't. But if I were you I'd bring a bodyguard to the conference. You never know who might be after you."

Darkanin felt his mouth go dry. "Are you threatening me?"

Rendel shrugged. "Not at all. Let's just say that the Syrians are not in agreement with any antidote development or sale. I've been able to convince them that your drug doesn't work and so they're safe to assume that after the main pharmaceutical players are annihilated today there won't be any way for the next attack in DC to be stopped. But you know how suspicious they are..." Rendel let his voice trail off.

Darkanin swallowed. "You tell them that I'll kill Smith, Russell, and Wyler for them and in return they need to hold off until the military contracts are signed and the funds are in Bancor's account."

"I'll do my best to hold them off, but they can be mean bastards when they want to be. Good luck today."

Darkanin rose. "I don't need luck. What I need is people I can trust. People unlike you and the Syrians."

Rendel snorted. "It's about business. People don't really come into the equation, do they?" He reached out to his computer mouse and Darkanin's screen went dark.

58

Russell drove Smith through the gates and onto the golf course grounds where the pharmaceutical conference was to be held. As they had expected, the sedan's diplomatic plates worked their magic. The guard at the initial checkpoint took Smith's name before waving them through and the guards at the top of the hotel's circular drive nodded them on as well. They were in a line of cars inching their way forward.

"I'll call you if anything seems unusual," he said. Russell nodded.

"You know what Rendel looks like, right?"

Smith nodded. "I'll recognize him. If I see anyone that looks even remotely like him I'll snap a photo and shoot it to you."

"Beckmann and I will be just outside. Howell's on his way. He caught a plane ride from the Royal Air Force at Croughton and should be here shortly."

Smith looked around him. "Looks like they've beefed up security."

Russell nodded. "A bit, but they always had security planned for this. It's the UN that is concerning them now, and the bulk of the extra security is assigned to that building."

"Makes sense," Smith said.

"Good luck at the Bancor meeting."

He got out, closed the door, and headed inside while Russell executed a three-point turn and drove back out the way she had come.

Smith's new directive came from USAMRIID. He was to attend a meeting between Meccean as head of the HHS and Bancor Pharma to discuss stockpiling Bancor's cognitive enhancement drug against a possible air strike involving Taylor's drug. He made his way into the circular building that housed the conference center. A large rotunda in the middle created the main focal point of the building, with a massive overhead glass dome ceiling that filtered the sun, sending sprays of light across a marble floor. Several halls ran like spokes from a wheel and fed into a wide corridor that circled the perimeter of the building, with a bank of windows on one side that faced the outside and various interior conference rooms on the other. He felt a tap on his shoulder.

"Jon Smith? Rick Meccean, HHS. Ready for the meeting?"

Smith nodded. "I understand that Bancor will try to negotiate a deal to downgrade the charges that they improperly marketed the cognitive enhancement drug."

Meccean grimaced. "We had them dead to center and the Justice Department was closing in on a record-breaking fine."

"How much?"

"Over two point five billion dollars. A figure that constitutes the entire profit for the sales of the drug during the time that they marketed it in violation of labeling."

Smith whistled. "That's remarkable. And now?"

"Now I'm going to have to eat crow and not only negotiate that away, but turn around and buy the drug and stockpile it."

"Are we sure it will function as an antidote to Taylor's?" Smith asked.

"Not at all, but Bancor claims that they'll be able to prove its effectiveness and I'm told by your colleagues at USAMRIID that it will take them quite some time to fashion their own. We're going to set up a test there. A controlled test, of course."

"Of course," Smith said.

"And you seem to have the inside track on the research. Do you think you can deliver an antidote quicker than Bancor?"

"I'll do my best, but it's prudent to have a fallback. From what I've seen of the effects of Taylor's it would be devastating if the drug was released on an unsuspecting public."

They'd reached the double doors of a small conference room at the far side of the building. From behind them Smith heard a cacophony of voices and around the corner came Ambassador Wyler and a small entourage. He nodded at Meccean and strode past.

"What's his role here?" Smith asked.

"He's going to present findings about a possible chemical attack on a village close to the Turkish border. He's hoping to use the event as a springboard for new regulation of certain ingredients that can be mixed to create chemical weapons."

Smith entered their conference room behind Meccean and saw that the only people in the room were Darkanin and another man who appeared to be a bodyguard. Darkanin's eyes lit up at the sight of Smith and once again Smith had the impression that the man's interest in him was acute, though he didn't know why.

"I would like to get right to business," Meccean said. He turned to the additional man with Darkanin. "May I ask in what capacity you are here?" he asked.

"Mr. Gore is my assistant and personal bodyguard," Darkanin said.

Meccean shook his head. "I'm sorry, but he can't be here. I thought it was understood that this meeting was to be kept in the strictest confidence."

"Mr. Gore is a trained professional and has security clearance."

"Oh? I didn't know that. May I ask through what organization is your clearance?"

"Stanton Reese," Gore said.

Meccean seemed to ponder a moment, and then shook his head again.

"I'm sorry. I still don't think that we can proceed."

Darkanin waved a hand at Smith. "How high is Mr. Smith's clearance? I understand he's a scientist with USAMRIID but that doesn't necessarily translate into a high security clearance either."

"Colonel Smith is here at my request."

"Still, I don't think his security clearance is such..."

"Perhaps we can arrange for a confidentiality agreement to be drafted and brought here before we begin," Smith said. "If we all sign it we can then move on."

Meccean frowned. "I'd have to call in-house counsel in Washington for that and it's too early in the morning there. I'm afraid it will delay the meeting. And the matter is too serious to delay."

"And I insist that my bodyguard stay. Security around this conference is tight for a reason, and Mr. Gore can't do his job as a bodyguard properly from several rooms away, can he? Let's try to move on." Darkanin gave Meccean what Smith now thought of as his signature fake smile.

Smith was surprised by Darkanin's insistence on the guard, but the man seemed jumpy and Smith saw him rub his palms together, as if they were sweaty.

"I can have an agreement here in less than thirty minutes," Smith said.

Meccean brightened. "Excellent. Do you have a USAMRIID attorney attending the conference?"

Smith nodded. "My attorney is nearby. I'll just give her a call." Smith excused himself and left the conference room to stand by the windows and dial Arden. She answered on the first ring.

"Everything all right?" she asked. Smith thought she sounded worried.

"Yes. But we've hit a bit of a snag." He told her about the additional man and Meccean's requirement for confidentiality. "I don't like bringing you into this, but the man's insistent."

"I've never seen him without a bodyguard. Given the

way that he does business, it just may be required. As for a confidentiality agreement, Meccean's smart to demand it. I have a standard form I use. I'll print it out and have Russell squire me over in the diplomatic car, get the agreement signed, and get out of there, fast."

Less than half an hour later there was a soft knock and Arden walked into the conference room. She wore a handwritten name tag and carried a manila envelope. Smith was impressed with her professionalism as she walked them through the terms of the agreement and handed it to each of them to sign.

"Normally we'd have a court reporter or notary verify signatures, but I'm simply going to record the signing on my phone and we can agree to notarize them later."

"No," Gore said. "No videos."

Arden frowned. "I suppose we can locate a notary, but it will only delay matters and it's my understanding that time is crucial with regard to your meeting."

"No videos. I'll sign the paper but I refuse to be videotaped doing it," Gore said.

Darkanin's face darkened. "Mr. Gore, please allow Ms. Arden to do her job. I don't expect a video to be a problem."

Gore looked at Darkanin and then at his watch. "We have eight minutes."

"What are you talking about?" Meccean asked.

"He means we have the time to wait for a local notary." Darkanin's voice was smooth as silk and Smith felt a prickling sensation across his scalp. The man was lying. Smith could practically smell the falsehood on him. "But that won't be necessary. Mr. Gore, please allow the video."

Gore gave a short jerk of his head and Arden switched on her phone. They all signed the confidentiality agreement.

"I had my secretary email you the DOD's contract offer with the terms. Did you receive it?" Meccean asked.

Darkanin nodded. "I did. And I'll sign it now."

Smith did his best to avoid showing his surprise. He'd

been told that Darkanin generally drove a hard bargain in his negotiations. That the man accepted the DOD's first offer was unusual. Darkanin turned to Arden.

"Please record the signatures."

Arden started her phone once again and both he and Meccean signed multiple copies of the contract. Darkanin shoved a copy into his briefcase.

"I'd like to discuss the future marketing plans for the pill with you both," Darkanin said. "I have another document being prepared, in draft, of course, that I'd like you to read. It will only take a few minutes and would avoid many future problems. But first, please excuse me. I'd like to discuss something with Mr. Gore for a moment." The two men stepped out of the conference room.

"Call me biased, but I still dislike that man," Arden said.

Meccean did his best to hide a smile. "I am aware of your lawsuit against his company," he said.

Smith marked the time. Something about Gore's "eight minutes" comment didn't sit well with him. When five minutes had passed he rose.

"Let me go see what the holdup is," Smith said. He stepped out of the conference room and looked around. The hall was empty. Neither Gore nor Darkanin was anywhere in sight. Smith hauled the conference room door open.

"Both of you, get out of here. Now." He held the door while a startled Arden grabbed her manila folder and stood. "Leave that. They're gone and I don't like it." Arden dropped the folder back onto the table and hurried out the door past Smith. Meccean trailed behind her.

"What's the matter?" Meccean asked.

"Get out of here. Now. Both of you. Before those eight minutes are up," Smith said. He pointed to an emergency exit.

"What's going on?" Arden asked.

Before Smith could answer he heard a scream from somewhere in the bowels of the conference center.

59

Smith herded Arden and Meccean toward the emergency exit. Someone triggered an alarm and the screeching set Smith's teeth on edge. He dragged Arden with him to the exit. When they stepped outside, Smith heard the now familiar and frightening buzzing noise of an incoming drone. He looked up to see one flying toward the conference center.

"Back inside," he said.

To his great relief neither Arden nor Meccean questioned his authority, but instead both turned and bolted back to the center. Smith pulled the door closed as the drone began to close the final fifty feet. Smith saw the shadow of the aircraft, which had a wingspan of six feet. It looked like a white glider plane with a dark tube attached to its belly. At ten feet from the conference center building it released a cloud of some sort of fine particulate from the belly-mounted canister.

"It just released some kind of drug," Meccean said.

"Get as far from the windows as you can," Smith said. "Head to the center of the building." Smith ran behind them, removing his gun from the holster as he did and pulling out the phone he'd taken from the stash in the house. He dialed Russell, and she answered on the first ring.

"The drones are here and spraying something."

"I'm aware," she said. "Three security guards called in a sighting right before they cleared the perimeter."

"Tell them that Darkanin of Bancor is involved, as is his security guard. A man named Gore."

"I can't tell them anything. They're all dead," Russell said. "Beckmann and I are on the north side. Were they headed this way?"

"No. West."

"I'm on it. Keep everyone inside, and close every window and door."

Smith ran down the curving hall. The attendees poured out of the individual conference rooms, responding to the blaring alarm by attempting to flee. They ran past him, all running toward the flashing neon "Exit" sign above the doors.

"No! Not outside. Everyone stay indoors," Smith yelled.

A wild-eyed man in a business suit ran past Smith. "It's a fire alarm! No way am I staying indoors, and you shouldn't either." He headed to the emergency exit.

"Do *not* open that door!" Smith yelled. "The air's been poisoned..." Before Smith could finish his statement the man had flung open the door and ran outside. Several more people followed him, jostling in their attempt to clear the entrance.

Smith could see the cloud of dust and particulate gust into the building through the open door. The cloud began to eddy, spreading outward and downward.

Smith watched in horror as, one by one, those who had run outside began to stagger. One woman began shrieking and holding her head, another man ripped off his jacket and flapped it in the air. "Get them away!" the man screamed. He took two more steps and dropped to the grass, writhing and batting at his face and eyes. Two more people fell dead next to him and he screamed at them. He rose to his knees and tried to stand, but his legs kept collapsing under him and he clawed at the ground.

"Grab my hand and stretch out," Arden said. "We'll make a human chain and block them." She stood in the center of the hallway and held Meccean's hand. Smith took two steps to join her before he realized that the cloud had shifted and was blowing their way. He shook his head.

"It's behind you and the next time someone opens that door the breeze will disseminate it further. Get out of this hallway," he said. "And start herding people into the rotunda."

Meccean jogged down the hall to the main rotunda. Arden kept at it, yelling and running in front of those headed to the exit. Smith joined her, telling them over and over again that the outdoor air had been poisoned and they needed to take shelter in the rotunda area. Many listened and Smith and Arden successfully turned them back, but four more didn't.

"We need to go farther inside before they reach that door and we're all dead," Smith said.

Arden nodded and ran to him as the four opened the emergency door. One man dropped three feet from the opening and died so suddenly that another man right behind stumbled on the body and pitched forward.

Smith heard a louder buzzing noise and the lawn darkened as the shadow of a much larger drone passed overhead. It dropped another cloud over the building, like a massive crop duster spraying crops. From somewhere outside Smith heard several gunshots and he hoped it was Russell and Beckmann and not security guards losing their minds. He and Arden ran toward the rotunda, yelling at those who still thought the building was on fire and were intent on leaving. From around a corner came Wyler followed by twenty people but no Secret Service guards.

"Ambassador Wyler, where is your Secret Service detail?" Smith asked. Wyler waved Smith in the direction that he'd just left.

"Go back. They're behind me and they've lost their minds. They gunned down two people and they're hunting me."

"We can't go that way either," Smith said. "The emergency door was opened. I think whatever chemical the drones are dropping on the building has wafted inside." Smith pointed to a third hallway that branched off the rotunda. "What about that direction?"

"Let's try it," Wyler said.

Arden, Wyler, Smith, and Meccean began herding the remaining attendees into the hallway. Arden hung back, grabbing a couple of women running past and warning them not to go in that direction. This passageway didn't empty into the circular hall like all the others but instead to an exit door with a glass window in the upper section. Arden, Smith, Wyler, and another woman attendee stopped. The other fifteen or so people filled the hall.

"We're trapped," Wyler said.

60

Russell and Beckmann parked the car on a frontage road near the conference center. Both wore bullet-proof vests and both carried weapons. Beckmann's was a high-powered sniper rifle with a telescopic sight and Russell carried an AK-47 and extra ammunition. They also were equipped with two hand grenades each. What they didn't have were face masks. The small safe house hadn't any.

They worked their way to a location at a forty-five-degree angle from the conference building. Close enough to see what was happening but far enough to avoid being drenched by the drones' payloads. Beckmann looked at his watch.

"Been ten minutes since they dropped the chemical. Didn't Taylor claim that the drug didn't last long?" he asked.

"And she also said that a few batches did, so we're taking a risk here," Russell said.

"Move ahead carefully," Beckmann said. Russell nodded and they walked together, six feet apart and in lock-step. Halfway to the conference center's back door they saw the first body. It was a woman. Her face was turned toward them and her eyes were open and staring. Ten paces later they found another, but she was sitting back on her heels and gazing into space.

"Hello? Are you okay?" The woman didn't acknowledge either Russell or Beckmann. "You should come away from the building. If you go half a mile in that direction you'll see a group of local police and firemen. They can help you." Russell pointed in the proper direction. The woman didn't move. Beckmann glanced at Russell and shook his head. They walked past her, stopping at the line where the trees met the perfectly manicured grass.

Twenty more steps closer and they saw a man with a gun stalking around the building. He wore an earpiece but was dressed in plainclothes.

"Someone's private security," Beckmann said.

Russell nodded. "But he doesn't look normal."

"Agreed. He's definitely been drugged."

From above Russell heard the buzzing sound of another incoming drone and tried to tamp down the immediate anxiety she felt.

"I hate that noise," she said to Beckmann, who just scanned the sky in silence. From behind she heard the crunching of boots on the ground and they both turned to see the local police commander wearing a gas mask.

"Another incoming," he said. "Get back. And take these. They're temporary and only good for seven minutes, but the long-term ones are all in use." He handed them both masks made of a clear plastic hood with an attached nozzle.

The wandering security guard spotted them and sprinted toward them.

"Watch out for this one," Beckmann said. "Don't turn your back on him. And be prepared to shoot if he raises his weapon." He, Russell, and the commander waited until the security guard was about twenty feet away. Beckmann glanced at the gun in the man's hand and raised his own.

"Don't come any closer," Beckmann said. The man stopped.

"Can't you hear it?" The man screamed the sentence so loud that the veins on either side of his neck stood out and spittle formed in the corners of his mouth.

"Take it easy. I can hear it," Beckmann said.

"Then take that fancy rifle of yours and shoot it down!" the man screamed.

The droning noise grew louder.

"We've got to get out of here." The commander's voice held a warning note. "Now."

"Put down your gun and come with us," Beckmann said to the security guard. "We need to leave the area."

"Shoot it!" the man screamed.

"I can't—"

Before Beckmann could finish his sentence the drone was overhead. Russell wanted to clap her hands over her ears to muffle the awful buzzing sound.

"Go away!" the man screamed at the drone. He raised his gun.

"Don't shoot!" Beckmann yelled. "You'll rupture the tank."

Please let him miss, Russell thought.

The man fired, and he didn't miss. The drone jerked as the bullet hit it and it tilted sideways. The man fired six more shots in rapid succession and every one hit its target. Three hit the drone's body and three more pierced the tank holding the payload. The drone tilted downward and smoke began pouring from the exhaust pipes along with a cloudy material from the ruptured tank. The drone angled its nose downward and headed for the conference center.

"It's going to crash," Russell said and she took off running back into the trees. The commander and Beckmann ran along with her. The man stood on the grass, screaming, but Russell couldn't make out the words. She slowed and looked back just as the drone slammed into the conference center's floor-to-ceiling windows. They collapsed inward in a shower of glass and aluminum. The drone's payload exploded outward in a massive white cloud. The man on the grass screamed one more anguished scream, aimed his weapon, and fired it into his own thigh.

Russell ran as fast as she had ever run in her life. She held her gun before her in both hands and sprinted.

The Swiss commander stayed with her, but Beckmann dropped behind. At first she could hear his harsh breathing in her ear and the next minute it was gone. She glanced back.

Beckmann had slowed to a jog and was gasping for each breath. Russell spun on her heel, doubled back, and ripped the gun from his hands, trying to reduce the weight that he had to carry so that he could focus solely on running. She spun back around and picked up speed once again. She kept going for another quarter mile and only slowed when she reached the outer line of police cars and hazardous incident vehicles that had been summoned by the sirens. A fireman wearing a gas mask and holding a small, one-liter oxygen tank ran up to her, shoved her temporary hood aside, and clapped the mask on her face.

"Breathe," he said in French. "It'll dilute whatever the hood didn't block."

She inhaled, and startled him by shoving Beckmann's gun into his free hand. He released his grip on the mask to clutch at it. She took the tank from him, then turned and ran back into the trees. She could hear the fireman yelling for her to return but she dodged the trunks and leapt over a log as she headed back to Beckmann. She had slung her own weapon over her shoulder by the strap and it banged against her back with each step. She found him holding his side and gasping, but still moving at a fast walk. She inhaled one more time and held her breath while she shoved his hood aside and put the mask on his face.

He nodded and put his hand over hers, holding the mask in place while he continued to stumble ahead. She saw him take a deep breath and then he removed the mask and placed it over her nose. They continued taking turns until they reached the emergency vehicles once again.

Russell stood next to the fire truck and listened. In the distance she heard the sound of another drone.

61

The only door left leads to the outside," Wyler said.

Before Smith could respond the building shook and with the vibration came the sound of exploding glass and creaking metal. The collected people screamed at this new threat and several tried to run past Smith. He blocked their way and pointed at a side door with a sign that indicated it led to a stairwell.

"Up the stairs," he yelled. A man in the lead pulled open the door and the crowd surged ahead, pushing their way up the stairwell. Both Wyler and Arden hung back to wait for Smith.

"Go. I'll bring up the rear."

Wyler nodded and started up. Smith shifted to a crouch behind the metal door and waited for the Secret Service detail to appear. The first man came charging down the hall, with his gun held high and a crazed look in his eyes. Smith aimed at his foot. He wanted to disable the man, not kill him. His shot missed and he heard the man scream and grab his ankle. Smith heard a banging noise and saw the second Secret Service agent standing outside. He pounded on the exit door glass before taking aim at him. Smith dove into the stairwell and the agent's shot smashed through the glass and hammered into the closing metal door.

Smith ran up the stairs, taking them two at a time. Emergency lighting bathed the area in a white glow punctuated with a flash of red from a warning light. The strobe light effect was disorienting and Smith did his best to focus on the stairs. The building was only three stories high, so his options to hide were limited. He reached the second-floor landing and found Wyler and Arden waiting for him. Arden had her gun in her hand.

"Where are the rest?" Smith asked.

"Headed to the third floor," Wyler said.

"I shot one of your guards but there's another still out there." From below Smith heard the sound of a man pounding up the stairs. "That one. Get to the third floor with the others." Smith took up a position near the railing of the final set of stairs. From that angle he would see the man once he emerged from the last landing. They'd be ten feet apart and the only thing separating them would be a metal railing. The footsteps slowed and stopped. Smith stood by the railing and did his best to see down the stairs, but the restricted view only showed him the cement steps. He heard a soft creak, like that of a shoe when the leather was new.

"Don't come any closer," Smith shouted. "I don't want to hurt you. You've been drugged. It's affecting your judgment." Smith heard the scrape of a shoe on cement, which told him that the man was still there. From above came a hollow, banging noise.

"Get up here," Arden called.

Smith spun and took the stairs two at a time. From behind him he heard the man resume climbing the stairs as well. Smith reached the last landing and saw Arden standing in the doorway frantically waving him forward. He leapt over the last step and through the doorway. Arden slammed the metal door closed behind him and Wyler helped her thread the wooden handle of a fire ax through the lever to block it from being opened. Smith heard a booming noise as the man on the other side kicked the metal panel. The door opened a fraction as he pulled on the handle from the inside, but the ax successfully blocked it from opening.

"Where are they?" Smith asked.

"In a far room that has a drop-down ladder access to the roof," Arden said.

"They can't go out. The drones may still have some payload left."

She nodded. "We realize that. Wyler's on the phone trying to get a helicopter rescue patrol here. His idea is to airlift everyone off the roof. But first he's trying to figure out where the drones are and if the air is still poisoned."

The Secret Service agent unloaded what sounded like an entire clip into the metal door. Smith yanked Arden out of the direct line of fire and watched as the metal deformed with each shot. He thought he counted sixteen shots and that, coupled with the earlier shots, might mean that the magazine was empty. Smith only wished that he could be sure the man didn't carry a spare.

He headed in the direction Arden had waved. He found Wyler in the second-to-last section with a phone to his ear as he listened. His eyes lit up when he saw Smith.

"Hold on a minute," he said into the phone. He lowered the receiver. "Are you Smith from USAMRIID?"

"I am."

"Meccean told me that you may have some idea of how long the drug remains toxic."

Smith rocked his hand back and forth. "It can be anywhere from two minutes to an hour depending on concentration."

Wyler looked at his watch. "It's been at least that since the first onslaught. So that round should be almost dissipated."

"But the second was more dense and delivered only ten or so minutes ago. You should tell whoever you're talking to that he's taking a risk. Waiting would be prudent."

Wyler returned to his conversation and Smith edged to the window on the side facing the rear yard. One of Wyler's Secret Service guards staggered down the lawn holding his leg, which was gushing blood. Smith was almost certain a major vessel had been hit and the man wandered, wide-eyed, in an aimless circle. After a moment he dropped to his knees, then fell to the ground and lay still. Smith dialed Russell.

"Russell, you there?" he said into the phone. Wyler jerked around to look at Smith at the mention of her name.

"I am," Russell said. Smith exhaled in relief.

"Thank God. What's the status out there?"

"The forward guards are all dead. Those who didn't drop from the dust turned on each other. Several attendees are dead and those that survived are wandering around behaving bizarrely."

"Where are the drones?" Smith asked. But he didn't need to, because at that moment he heard the buzzing in the distance.

"The drones flew up and out, but I can still hear them," Russell said. "We've called the local police and also warned the security detail at the UN building, because we're concerned that they're heading that way. Fighter jets are taking off to shoot them down, but the CDC is in contact warning them not to fire until they're sure that they've got an empty payload. The concern is they'll shoot them down and they'll crash, rupturing the tanks and disseminating the drug. I can attest to the risk, because that's what just happened."

"The entire building just shook. Was it a bomb?"

"No. The man on the lawn shot at the drone and it crashed into the building."

"He was a member of the Secret Service."

"Oh, no," Russell's voice sounded anguished.

"I see the problem with shooting down the drones, but what other choices do they have?"

"They're going to flank them and wait. Technicians in Djibouti are trying to hack into the dashboard and retake flight control."

"And until then?"

"Until then we need to come up with a plan, because

I'm told that their flight path is set to come back here. The authorities have set up even farther away."

"They can't stay aloft forever," Smith said.

"Forever doesn't worry me; it's the next forty-five minutes that does."

"What are the Swiss authorities doing in the meantime?"

"Trying to figure out how to safely evacuate everyone left standing."

"Ambassador Wyler is here. I understand that he's trying to arrange a helicopter airlift from the roof. What do you think?" Smith waited, but Russell didn't respond. "Russell, did you hear me?"

"Sorry, yes, I was distracted a moment. I think it's a good plan as long as we can hold off the drones. They seemed to be preprogrammed to fly in circles around the perimeter." Smith's phone beeped, indicating an incoming call. "Let me know what the local authorities decide."

Smith switched to the next call and was relieved to hear Howell's voice.

"I heard that you were flying in, but stay the hell away. We've got a lot of trouble here," Smith said.

"I'm already at the perimeter. I'm flying with an RAF helicopter pilot and we've locked onto the nearest drone."

"He knows not to shoot, right?"

"He does. Hold tight. We'll get you out of there."

"I'll wait to hear the plan," Smith said. He hung up.

Arden stood near the window and watched the circling drones. After a moment she glanced at Smith and he could see a level of rage in her eyes that startled him. She pointed out the window.

Smith walked up to her.

"What?"

"They're marching in to kill us?"

Smith looked where she was pointing and saw a troop of soldiers fanning out through the trees. They appeared to be military, though they wore no insignia.

"Swiss army?" Smith said.

Wyler came to stand next to them. "No insignia, but they look official."

"Don't you think it's a bit unusual that they're coming in from the side that has no driveway or road access and opposite the official rescuers?" Smith said. "Every other division is over there." He pointed to a cluster of police at the opposite end of the course near the front gatehouse.

"A quiet governmental action to clean up without having to reveal that they've been engaging in illegal wiretapping and while doing so one of their employees went rogue?" Arden suggested.

"You can't really believe they intend to kill us. Who?" Wyler asked.

"I have no idea, but they don't look official—and wouldn't the authorities have told you that they were coming in?" Arden asked.

Wyler nodded. "They would. In fact, they just said that they were preparing to create a sort of temporary tunnel for us to evacuate through and their forces were donning containment suits before they approach."

"These guys have masks but no suits," Smith said.

"If they're not sent by the Swiss, then who are they?" Arden asked. She returned to stare out of the window. In the next instant her face changed.

"Oh, no," she said.

"What?" Smith asked.

"I think I know who they are. They're an army run by Stanton Reese."

62

S mith called Russell. "There's an additional problem."
    Russell didn't like the sound of that. "What type of problem?"

"There's a guerrilla force of about eight men spreading out around the conference center and moving forward in formation."

"Swiss army coming to the rescue?" Russell asked.

"No. They're not wearing any insignia. Arden thinks they're a rogue army run by Stanton Reese. She's heard of the same type of action in Africa."

Russell shook her head in disbelief although she knew Smith couldn't see her. Beckmann, though, could, and he lowered his oxygen mask and came to stand next to her. She switched her phone to speaker so that he could listen.

"They would have been stopped by the local police. They've cordoned off the area," she said.

"Not the villas. I think they've been hiding in there, within the perimeter, all this time. They're equipped with gas masks."

Russell felt the air punch out of her at that. She tried to collect her scattered thoughts.

"So I'll tell the fighter jets to shoot them down. Or tell the army to get over here and pick them off."

"Forget it. They're wearing flat, disk-like canisters on their torsos. Both sides. I'll bet they're filled with the same chemical that the drones are carrying. Shoot them and they'll release the drug. Besides, they're almost to the center already and the whole golf course has been declared a toxic zone and off limits, so I don't think that the foot troops will come."

"But I will," Beckmann said.

"Hold on a minute," Russell told Smith. She put the phone on mute. "Tell me what you're thinking," she said to Beckmann.

He checked his gun. "I'm thinking we come in behind them and take them out, one by one. They won't be expecting it. They think their circling drones have the regular army pinned down and their chemical payload will force the jets to hold off, and they're right. What they didn't consider was targeted assassination. They'll never know what hit them and they won't have time to release their payload."

Russell hesitated. She thought the idea had merit but there were so many things that could go wrong she was hesitant to green-light it.

"Come on, Russell, you know that if we do nothing they're all dead anyhow. This way at least some may make it out alive," Beckmann said.

"Let's get the Swiss to help," she said.

Beckmann shrugged. "The more the merrier. Tell Smith to have Wyler make the request. But I think you and I move now."

Russell nodded. "I'm in."

She told Smith their plan and slung the two straps attached to her oxygen tank over her shoulders, allowing her to carry it like a backpack. She put her mask back on as she slung her rifle strap over her shoulder.

They walked away from the collected emergency vehicles and started a slow jog along the far boundary of the property. When they were at a forty-five-degree angle from the destroyed portion of the center Russell cut in, jogging from tree to tree. She spotted the first group of soldiers about fifty feet in. They advanced in a controlled manner. Some moved from tree to tree but others kept a brisk walk in a straight line.

They don't expect to meet with any resistance, Russell thought. That expectation wasn't entirely wrong, because with the possible exception of Smith and Arden, Russell doubted anyone else carried any weapons whatsoever. The attendees would have been depending on the perimeter guards and additional security to keep them safe. Beckmann waved her to a place behind a small building that housed restrooms. He crouched at the corner.

"You have any type of silencer on you?" Beckmann asked. "I know the AK doesn't have one, but are you carrying a handgun as well?"

Russell nodded. "And a silencer. You?" He pulled a slender tube from inside his bulletproof vest and screwed it on the muzzle of his rifle.

"I'm good to go."

He raised the gun to his shoulder, targeted a man lagging at the very end of the group, and fired. Russell saw the man pitch forward and land on the grass. None of the others looked back.

"They can't hear the shot over the drone noise," Beckmann said with satisfaction.

He targeted another and shot. The man appeared to cry out and clutched his shoulder. Another next to him turned his head and Beckmann brought him down as well. The rest of the troops were busy crawling over the broken glass and remaining jagged edges of the window where the drone had crashed and none bothered to look behind them. Russell put a hand on his arm.

"Hold off. Let them get inside and then we'll sprint to the other side of the terrace wall."

A large terrace with a stone wall extended from the conference center outward. Russell thought that it likely was an outdoor eating area, but the weather was still too cool and the terrace was empty. Russell watched as the last man crawled over the drone wreckage.

"Ready?" she asked Beckmann. He nodded and she took off running toward the next available cover.

63

Smith watched the troop moving toward them. At Russell's suggestion he'd given Wyler the task of attempting to talk the Swiss military into sending in a sniper team to take out the cell. Smith could only hope that they would agree to try to infiltrate and kill the intruders.

He'd taken stock of their weapons. They had only two pistols: his and Arden's. None of the other remaining survivors had any weapons. Wyler returned and from the grim look on his face Smith doubted the man had good news.

"They have a sniper team here already. They were called in from the moment it became clear that the center was under attack. I gave them the plan."

"And?" Smith asked. Arden stepped up next to him.

"I'm not sure. The biggest problem is the lack of containment suits should the troops release their chemicals. They don't have enough and we have none. They're deciding whether it's safest to allow the troops to take us hostage and then negotiate terms. They're pondering."

"There's no time to ponder," Smith said. "We need to collect every available fire extinguisher that we can."

"You think they're intending to burn the center?"

"Maybe. But if we shoot one and he releases the drug I want you to spray him with the foam. My hope is that it will smother the drug enough to contain it."

"I'll get those that are in the stairwell," Arden said.

"I'm going to the first floor," Smith said. "The Secret Service agent who chased us is still in the hall. We need his weapon." He handed Wyler his.

Wyler shook his head. "Keep it. You're going to need it in case you run into them down there."

"If I do I'll have the agent's to use. He's in the stairwell. If I don't make it to him then you'll need it."

He joined Arden at the stairwell door. The ax handle was still in place.

"You think he's behind that door waiting for us?" Arden said.

"I don't know, but we need to try," Smith said.

She nodded. "On three."

She counted it down and on the third count he slid the ax handle out of the door and Arden opened it slowly. She peered around the door's edge a moment, and then swung it wide.

"He's dead," she said. Her voice broke on the sentence.

Smith followed her through and knelt down next to the man. In fact he wasn't dead, he was simply flat on his back on the carpeted landing and staring upward. Smith reached down and gently removed the gun from his grasp. Wyler knelt down next to him.

"Should we carry him out of the stairwell?" he asked.

Smith shook his head. "Weapons first. Help Arden collect the fire extinguishers. I'm going down to guard the entrance at the bottom." Smith sprinted down the steps. The cement enclosure lent any noise an echo and the thick walls successfully blocked most sounds from outside. Smith felt his heart begin to race as he headed lower. He hated the idea that the troop could at that moment be preparing to open the stairwell door. He made it to the bottom without incident and swallowed once. The lower stairwell door was ajar.

Now he could hear the relentless buzzing of the circling drones and the sound of the killers making their way down the hall. He took a careful step to the side and held his gun aloft while he waited for the first man to step through the door. He heard Wyler breaking the glass on the extinguisher one flight above.

When they came through the door they came in a group of four. They looked neither right nor left but jogged upward. Smith fired twice in rapid succession and killed the first two, shooting each one high on the shoulder to avoid piercing the canister. The shots echoed in the enclosed space and he heard a man yell. The two others swung around and opened fire on him. He gave his own yell as he dove beneath the stairs, scuttling lower in the small area available to him.

From above he heard two more gunshots followed by the whooshing sound of a fire extinguisher. Shoes pounded down the steps above his head and he crawled out from his hiding place in time to see one of the soldiers fleeing. Smith shot at him and missed.

"Smith, you down there?" Wyler's voice echoed in the stairwell.

"I'm coming back up. Don't shoot," Smith said.

He dodged the two dead bodies and when he got to the next he found the third man facedown and covered with foam. Arden held the extinguisher and Wyler the gun.

"I've got the gun. Back upstairs," Smith said. He followed Wyler and Arden back to the second-story landing and the still-living Secret Service agent. "Now we move him," Smith said. He picked up the man's legs and Wyler slid his hands under his arms and they maneuvered him out of the stairwell into the second-story hall. Arden replaced the ax handle.

"Did the canister explode?" Smith asked.

Arden shook her head. "Not exactly. But I could see that the bullet had pierced it and I thought it would be best to lay down some foam. It seemed to work to contain any spray."

"How many entrances to this floor?" Smith asked. "Because you can be sure that once they discover the bodies they'll have figured out that we're up here and armed. They won't make the mistake of charging into the stairwell unprepared again."

"Two elevator banks and a third freight elevator," Wyler said.

At that moment they heard the ping of an arriving elevator car.

64

Smith yanked the ax handle away and hauled the stairwell door open. Arden ran through and Wyler followed. Smith hid in the entrance and peered around the jamb, waiting for whoever was on the elevator to appear. He saw a soldier slowly edge his way out. Smith fired and the man jerked back inside. Smith backed into the stairwell.

From below he heard a team coming up the stairs. From inside the hall he heard the soldier laying down fire, the shots getting louder as the man approached. Below him the sound of footfalls increased and he hurdled up the stairs. Gunshots echoed around him. A bullet pinged off the metal banister. He reached the third floor and Arden was there, holding the stairwell door open.

As Smith tumbled onto the third floor Arden slammed the door closed and Wyler, Arden, and two other men began pushing a heavy desk across to block it. Bullet-sized dents formed in the metal panel when the soldiers on the other side began firing.

"There's an access to the roof on the far end of the hall," Wyler said.

Smith followed him around the curved hallway. Through the windows he saw a large drone fly by.

Behind him he heard the ping of another elevator arriving.

Accessing the roof would leave them exposed to the chemical if the drones chose to release their payload, but staying on the third floor was no longer an option. The two men ran into a small utility room and Smith could see a narrow set of drop-down stairs leading upward.

Arden waited her turn and Wyler after her. Before he took a step up he glanced behind him and Smith saw his eyes widen. Smith turned to see Russell and Beckmann in the hallway. Both wore oxygen masks and both carried weapons. Russell nodded at Smith and he saw her pause a moment, looking at Wyler, and it seemed to Smith that she was relieved to see him there and still alive. Wyler moved out of the line. He took the fire extinguisher from Arden's hands and put a second next to Smith.

"I'll work the extinguisher," Wyler said. Beckmann stepped up and offered a hand grenade. Russell stayed several feet closer and kept her weapon aimed at the stairwell door, where the men from the other side were attempting to shift the desk from its place against it.

"Hold your fire. Let them shift the desk enough to open a small space. When they do, I'll pull the pin, toss the grenade in and then we need to push the desk back, fast," Smith said.

The desk slid farther out and Smith moved it to position it at an angle that kept him safely behind the door but nearer to the action. It was clear, though, that unless he could throw a curve the grenade would not land far enough inside the stairwell. He would have to step into the line of fire in order to have a clear shot to toss the bomb.

The desk shifted again, opening a small gap between the door and the jamb. The pushing stopped. Smith pulled the pin on the grenade, moved forward and to the side, stretching his arm out. From his new location he saw the backs of two soldiers as they pressed themselves against the door. He flicked the grenade into the small opening and threw himself sideways. Russell, Wyler, and Beckmann joined him in pushing the desk back. It moved with surprising ease and Smith realized that the men had scattered at the sight of the grenade.

"Let's move," Russell said. She, Beckmann, and Wyler began sprinting toward the utility closet. Smith ran halfway, but stopped there, knelt down against the wall farthest from the glass with his back to the desk and his face to the wall.

The resulting explosion blew the door open and sent the desk tumbling. The draft from the opening hit Smith in the back and he pitched forward, but managed to rise. He directed the extinguisher nozzle and sprayed the foam, hoping to force any accumulated clouds of chemicals back into the stairwell.

Russell came up next to him and placed her oxygen mask over his nose. He took a deep breath and nodded, and she put it back over her own face. She waved him toward the access stairs. From the left he saw Beckmann aiming a gun downward, through a hole in the glass that the grenade had blasted open. He jerked his head in that direction and Russell moved with him to line up next to Beckmann.

On the grass below Smith saw Gore, in army fatigues and wearing a gas mask, aiming a rifle at the third floor, targeting Beckmann. The men fired and Gore went down. Beckmann's body jerked back and he landed hard on the carpet. Smith watched Gore, who wasn't dead but was rolling around in the grass holding his arm.

A man stood at the tree line and Smith squinted to try to make out who it was. He dropped the extinguisher and went to Beckmann.

"Where is he hit?" Smith asked.

"In the chest. The vest absorbed it," Russell said.

"I think it may have broken a bone in my shoulder," Beckmann said.

"Let me have your gun," Smith said. He dropped the extinguisher, took the rifle, and went back to the window bank. The man at the trees was no longer there, but he saw another standing over the prone Gore. It was Darkanin. He raised a gun and shot Gore once. Gore jerked and lay still. Darkanin took two more steps closer to Gore. Smith stepped up to the window. From that height and from that angle the shot was a difficult one. Smith aimed, but before he could pull the trigger he saw Gore raise his own gun. He shot Darkanin square in the chest.

The hall went quiet except for the buzzing sound of the drone as it flew by.

65

Howell watched while the pilot, a young officer in the Royal Air Force, maneuvered the chopper until it was flying parallel to the nearest drone, a larger plane with a twelve-foot wingspan and a payload canister attached to its underside. The Swiss authorities were issuing frantic requests to Howell and his pilot to remove themselves from the area, and a fighter jet flew alongside and repeated the demand. It rose up a bit and rumbled somewhere above their heads.

"Ignore it," Howell told the RAF pilot.

He shot Howell a concerned look. "It *is* their airspace," he said.

"And if I were Swiss I'd also be angry as hell, but I'm not." Howell ran through his mind the names of his friends in the Swiss army who might be able to back off the jet long enough for Howell to assess the situation.

"They're the ones in charge here," the pilot said.

"And you are a member of Her Majesty's Royal Air Force flying a high-ranking official to the scene of a disaster that may have its origins in the UK."

The pilot inhaled and shot Howell another look from the corner of his eye. "Whatever we do, it would be my suggestion that we do it fast. The Swiss won't put up with this much longer," he said. Howell heard a beep through his headphones. "We have a call coming in from Fort Meade in America." The pilot punched a button and patched it through to Howell.

"Is this Peter Howell?" the caller asked.

"It is."

"I'm Kimball Canelo, an officer in the U.S. Army based in Djibouti, and until recently I was in charge of the piloting and implementation of the joint CIA-NSA Unmanned Aerial Vehicle program. Mr. Scariano asked me to contact you. I understand that you're having a problem with a drone that may have originated out of Djibouti."

"Shouldn't you be at Djibouti managing this crisis? Why are you calling me from Fort Meade?"

"Because I'm in the brig."

Howell exchanged a look with the RAF pilot.

"Who do you recommend I talk to in Djibouti? If this is being piloted out of that base then I want the best there is tracking down the hacker and I want to talk to him now."

"As we speak the technicians in Djibouti are in communication with the Swiss authorities. But I wouldn't recommend you speak to them anyway. There isn't anyone left in Djibouti senior enough or with the experience that you need. They all walked off a cliff when the chemical that I think these drones are releasing was sprayed on the troop."

"Ah, now I understand. You're Katherine Arden's client."

"I am."

"All right, Commander, tell me what I'm dealing with here. It's circling the area and clearly capable of delivering some sort of chemical payload as it does. We're afraid to shoot it down and risk having its canister rupture. How long can this thing fly?"

"That depends on its size and fuel. From what Scariano told me it sounds as though it will remain aloft for at least another forty-five minutes to an hour. Maybe longer."

"Can you tell me where the man is who's operating this thing? How can I reach him and put my hands around his throat?"

"You can't. They're usually run out of a command center, but if this one has been hacked you'll have to follow the signature back to the base. I've already asked the technicians in Djibouti to do that and they found no signature to follow."

"Okay, what does that mean?"

"That means it's very likely that it's preprogrammed and flying driverless. Completely autonomous and pilotless UAVs are experimental, but the ones that I have seen use a basic laser-light-beam technology to map the environment. It will also have multiple mounted sensors that will detect obstacles. You'll be able to determine that quite easily. I understand you're in a helicopter within line-of-sight distance of the UAV?"

"I am."

"Then have the pilot fly an intercept route. If the drone automatically adjusts its flight pattern downward you can assume that it's self-correcting."

"Why?"

"Because a technician-piloted UAV in that situation would take greater evasive action, perhaps even line up to fire. It's the contrast between a vindictive pilot who wants to play with you, perhaps fire upon you and kill you, and an indifferent robotic device that simply wants to get out of your way."

Howell looked at his own pilot, who raised an eyebrow and then nodded.

"Officer Canelo, you've got an excellent grasp of human psychology," Howell said.

"Thank you."

"Hold tight." Howell nodded at the pilot.

"I'm going to get ahead of it and then turn hard into its path. Be prepared," the pilot said.

Howell braced himself as the helicopter sped up. When it had opened a gap between it and the drone the pilot yanked on the collective and the copter swung around, cutting across the drone's path. A light on top of the drone flashed once and the drone dropped lower. It passed under the helicopter and continued on at the new level, neither speeding up nor slowing down.

"I believe it's driverless," Howell said to Canelo.

"That's very good news."

"Is there a way to reprogram it?"

"Probably not. But it operates off a GPS signal. If you can spoof or block the signal, or alter it in such a way that it begins to receive improper input, then there is a chance you can move it off its current path."

"Is it difficult to spoof a GPS signal?"

"Not at all. The local military can likely do it and fairly quickly. Then my suggestion would be to have jets surround the drone. Cluster them so that it senses all of the obstacles, but leave the direction that you want it to fly free of obstruction. In this way it will continue to find the open flight pattern. You can use the spoofed signal to guide it out to sea and it will land there."

"We're on it. Please stand by in case we need you again."

"Of course."

Howell nodded at the pilot. "Okay, this time when the Swiss demand you leave the area ask to speak to the one in charge of the fighter jets," he said. "We have a plan."

Within ten minutes Howell and the RAF pilot were surrounded by Swiss military helicopters. The drone kept its circular flight path, trailing fighters in its wake.

Howell's RAF pilot turned to him. "They're concerned that it's programmed to release its payload if it deviates too much. Any chance of figuring that out before they get into formation?"

"Get Canelo back," Howell said. When Canelo answered, he asked the question.

"We've programmed drones to self-destruct their dashboard software if they deviate, so it's definitely possible that a release code on deviation was programmed," Canelo said. "But here's the better news, our programming didn't work."

The RAF pilot groaned.

"What do you mean?" Howell asked.

"Just that. The drone that the Iranians captured a few years ago was programmed that way, but as far as we could tell when it began to deviate it didn't activate any of the self-destruct programs in place. Once they head off on their own it's impossible to predict what they'll do. I still think the cluster and redirect plan is the best."

"And let it drop its payload as it flies? Not a good idea and I don't know how we're going to sell that plan to the Swiss," Howell said.

"It's the only play you've got, because eventually that bird's going to run out of gas and crash and it will definitely release its payload then. Tell them to roll the dice. It's what I would do."

Spoken like a man sitting in the brig, Howell thought. Still, he had to agree with Canelo. Their options were few. Five minutes later the Swiss began to close in on the drone.

"They got the green light," Howell's pilot said.

As the helicopters flanked the drone they began tightening the flight pattern. Howell and the RAF pilot joined and Howell watched as the drone made an adjustment. It turned away and instead of flying in a circular pattern adopted a straight-line path.

"The first aspect is done. Let's hope it doesn't release the payload," the RAF pilot said.

They flew on, keeping the drone between them as they steered it over land toward the sea. Every minute that the drone didn't release its payload Howell counted as a win. They continued on and sixty-five minutes later Howell watched the drone as it flew over Genoa, Italy, and began a slow descent over the Ligurian Sea. He smiled when it plunged into the water.

66

Smith waited as the Swiss police guided the remaining attendees out of the conference center. Each person had been given an oxygen mask. Wyler left last, and he nodded at Smith as he stepped outside.

After it was clear that the grenade had scattered the troops, the Swiss sniper team, clothed in containment suits, had caught the rest as they fled the center. Wyler had received the all-clear notice in a call from the authorities.

"We don't need to be here when they arrive," Russell had said.

She, Smith, and Wyler had helped Beckmann get to his feet, and Smith had helped Beckmann make his way to a far exit while Wyler had returned to the roof to manage the evacuation. Once Beckmann and Russell had made their way to the property border Smith returned to assist Wyler and Arden on the roof.

Now Smith watched as Wyler was surrounded by several envoys from the American embassy the moment he was free of the contained area and hustled into a consular car. Smith and Arden walked with the remaining crowd, which was being corralled into a separate containment area where two military transports stood by to take them to a secure military hospital outside Switzerland. Smith could have told them that anyone still standing and sentient was not in need of a hospital, but it was clear that the area had been earmarked for containment with those within it subject to quarantine for a number of days until any chance of infection was passed.

An official waved Smith forward. "Please keep moving to the transports," he said.

Smith hung back and Arden stayed at his side. Smith had retrieved his suit jacket, which had survived unscathed and was still hanging from the back of his chair in the conference room, and he hoped the formal clothing would go a long way toward cloaking him with an air of authority.

"I'm not going," Arden said to him in a quiet voice. "And you shouldn't either. Once they find out that there's a red notice for your arrest they'll take you straight from the hospital to jail."

"Stay with me. I've texted Russell and I expect her to appear any minute and ferry us out of here."

True to his word, Smith watched as another consular car worked its way toward the staging area. Russell stepped out and approached the crowd. A Swiss official stepped in front of her and after a short conversation, in which Russell held a name badge on a lanyard around her neck aloft for him to see and twice pointed out the consular plates on the car, he nodded and she continued toward Smith.

"Let's go before the next official tries to stop us," Russell said.

Smith and Arden stepped to the car. Before they could get in a Swiss officer approached, nodded at the two officers with him, and they surrounded Smith.

"Monsieur Jon Smith?" the first man asked.

"I am," Smith replied.

"You are under arrest. Please place your hands on the vehicle."

"There must be some mistake," Russell said.

The officer shook his head. "There is no mistake. Mr. Smith is the subject of an arrest warrant issued through Interpol."

"That *is* a mistake. Mr. Smith is a lieutenant colonel in the U.S. Army as well as a microbiologist, and is here on official business," Russell said.

The two assisting officers patted Smith down. One reached inside Smith's jacket and removed Smith's gun. He held it up for the other officer to see.

"As I mentioned, Mr. Smith is a lieutenant colonel in the military and authorized to carry a gun," Russell said.

"One can only hope so, for Mr. Smith's sake," the arresting officer said. The man who had found the gun pulled first one, then the other of Smith's wrists off the car to handcuff him behind his back.

"I really wish you'd call your superior and check this out before you take Mr. Smith away. It will save all of the parties a lot of time," Arden said.

"I'm sorry. Mr. Smith can address this matter with the judge at the appropriate tribunal. I am obligated to execute the warrant. The rest"—he gave a classic Gallic shrug—"is up to the judge."

Smith blew out a breath and looked at Arden. "Represent me?"

She nodded. "We'll follow you to the jail. I'll make a few calls from the car."

Arden got into the back of the sedan as Russell put it in gear. Smith watched from the backseat of the police car as they navigated out of the crowd, down the long drive, and through the hastily erected fencing that created a thirty-foot-buffer zone between the actual gatehouse and the incoming drivers. They waited there and pulled out behind the patrol car when it passed.

An hour later Smith was sitting in a straight-backed wooden chair in an interrogation room. He had once again removed his jacket while he waited for whatever would happen next. The door buzzed and his nerves jumped at the sound. He looked up to see Arden step into the room, and he smiled at her in relief.

"You bailed me out," he said.

She shook her head. "I didn't have to. The red notice was strangely, miraculously, withdrawn less than an hour ago."

"Good news for me."

"In fact," she continued, "not only was it withdrawn, but I received an email from the head of Interpol begging my forgiveness and asking me to convey his deepest apologies to you."

Smith smiled even wider.

"You, sir, have backers with some amazing mojo behind you. Care to divulge who they are?"

"Nope," Smith said.

"And there's more good news. Your colleague called. Before she was kidnapped a second time, Dr. Taylor left a note on a remote server at USAMRIID. She must have seen this coming, because she deliberately engineered the drug she was forced to make with a diminishing half-life. All existing batches will be rendered inert after a few days. They seem to think that whatever is left out there will be useless."

"That *is* good news. Is this over? Can we just walk out of here?"

Arden nodded. "You sure you don't want to tell me who moved heaven and earth to get this red notice quashed? A contact like that would be infinitely useful in my line of business."

He shook his head. "Can't." He gave her a sidelong look as he put his jacket back on.

"I don't know how you maintain a relationship with a woman when you insist on such secrecy," she said.

He cocked his head to one side. "I don't have many relationships, but if I did I can think of nothing better than having one with an attorney who is required to keep every word I say confidential. Would such a woman be interested in me, do you think?"

Arden smiled a broad smile. "I think she would. Where to?"

"I know a private house on the outskirts of Geneva

that boasts an excellent wine bar, a fully stocked kitchen, and a well-appointed gun case. Care to join me there for some dinner?"

She nodded. "Let's go."

Russell sat in a hotel restaurant and stared at her drink. Beckmann walked up and sat down in the seat across from her.

"You've been quiet since the whole thing went down. You okay?"

Russell smiled and tried to shake off the melancholy that had enveloped her after the mission was completed.

"Just coming down from the stress, I suppose. How's the shoulder?"

"Not broken, just badly bruised. It looks like I was kicked by a mule. I got some good news from Howell. He says that Rendel fled Switzerland but was picked up outside a strip club in Berlin. The Swiss found him. They're hoping to add their own charges to the long list that the United States will slap him with."

"Nice. He deserves everything he gets."

"And Arden wanted you to know that the charges were dropped against Canelo. Scariano said he's being reinstated and possibly promoted."

She nodded again. "Also nice."

"And I want to thank you for getting me a waiver on the smoking thing."

"I still would like you to try to shake it."

He nodded. "I know. But at least now I can do it in my own time." He rose. "I'm headed back to Paris. Where are you going?"

She gave a vague wave. "I checked in here. I'll need some rest before I return to Washington and this hotel is as quiet as they come."

He snorted. "At these prices it should be. But you deserve every bit of it."

"Thanks. For everything," she said. He smiled at her and strolled away.

She returned to staring at her drink. The waiter walked over with a bottle on a silver tray.

"Excuse me, Ms. Russell. A gentleman at the bar sent this to you. We wanted to bring you a fresh bottle, but the gentleman insisted that it be only half full."

The waiter placed a bottle of Armagnac on the table in front of her.

Russell's melancholy fled. Her boring days off had just taken a turn for the better.

She picked up the bottle and headed to the bar to find him.

ACKNOWLEDGMENTS

I was thrilled when the estate of Robert Ludlum asked me to write another in his Covert-One series. I love the characters and relish the opportunity to write about covert operatives functioning in a world that is increasingly complex and technological. While this is a book of fiction, some matters mentioned in the novel are taken from documents released by Edward Snowden detailing the National Security Agency's surveillance activities. The *Stateroom* embassy surveillance project is mentioned there, as is the use of the United Kingdom's Croughton facility in conjunction with the drone program out of Djibouti. A few facts regarding the drone program are real as well. They do crash with some frequency, have been captured and possibly reverse engineered by Iran, and come in an array of shapes and sizes.

I'd like to thank Ting Ting Branit for her assistance with the Chinese names in the book and the entire Branit family for trooping through the London tube with me and pointing out every CCTV camera that they could find.

Thank you to my editors, the excellent Mitch Hoffman and Lindsey Rose for their insightful changes, production editors Kallie Shimek and Jeff Holt, copyeditor Laura Jorstad, and everyone at Grand Central Publishing for their assistance. Thank you also to Henry Morrison, to the estate of Robert Ludlum, and to my agent, Barbara Poelle, to whom this book is dedicated. And of course, thanks always to Klaus, Alex, and Claudia for their love and support.

Jamie Freveletti
September 3, 2014

ABOUT THE AUTHORS

ROBERT LUDLUM was the author of twenty-seven novels, each one a *New York Times* bestseller. There are more than 225 million of his books in print, and they have been translated into thirty-two languages. He is the author of *The Scarlatti Inheritance*, *The Chancellor Manuscript*, and the Jason Bourne series—*The Bourne Identity*, *The Bourne Supremacy*, and *The Bourne Ultimatum*—among others. Mr. Ludlum passed away in March 2001. To learn more, visit www.Robert-Ludlum.com.

JAMIE FREVELETTI is the internationally bestselling and ITW and Barry Award–winning author of thrillers *Running from the Devil*, *Running Dark*, *The Ninth Day*, and *Dead Asleep*. A trial attorney with a diploma in international studies, she is an avid distance runner and holds a black belt in aikido, a Japanese martial art. She lives in Chicago with her family.

Top Covert-One operative Colonel Jon Smith is sent on a mission to recover mysterious material from wreckage of the Fukushima nuclear reactor—and it may be evidence of a dangerous new weapon that could spell the end of civilization...

Robert Ludlum's™

THE PATRIOT ATTACK

Written by Kyle Mills

Please turn this page for a preview.

Prologue

Fukushima Daiichi Nuclear Power Plant
Northeastern Japan
March 11, 2011

Dr. Hideki Ito felt the floor shift and braced himself against the elaborate control console in front of him. He waited for the earthquake to subside, reminding himself that the structure had weathered a number of powerful tremors two days before with no issues.

Still, he could feel the tension creeping into his stomach the way it always did when the earth decided to move. There was no reason for it, he told himself again. The general had chosen to shut down Reactor Four and use it as a research facility, ostensibly because of its ability to contain a radiation leak in the face of just these kinds of shocks. It wasn't radiation they were asking it to hold in check, though. The work Ito had dedicated his life to was far more dangerous and difficult to control.

The vibrations seemed reluctant to subside as they had in the past, and he glanced nervously behind him. The room itself was unremarkable—a nine-meter cube of treated concrete lined with insulated pipes of every imaginable diameter. The only access was through a small titanium hatch centered between tables covered in computer equipment. His two research assistants had pulled back from their keyboards and sat holding the edges of their chairs, feet spread wide to keep from toppling to the rubber-coated floor.

The young man had the same stoic expression he'd been wearing since Ito had recruited him two years ago.

The woman, a brilliant postdoc recently coaxed from the University of Tokyo, was searching the stark bunker with quick, birdlike movements of her head. Looking for cracks, Ito mused sympathetically. He felt compelled to do the same thing a thousand times a day.

The elderly physicist faced forward again, squinting through ten-centimeter-thick glass at the tiny room beyond. At its center was a secondary glass enclosure containing samples of concrete, plastic, and steel. Interspersed were organic materials—various dirt and stone specimens, as well as a few carefully chosen plants. And hovering above it all was a disinterested white rat stretching lazily on one of the robotic arms that serviced the enclosure.

The electron microscope reacted to the joystick in Ito's hand as he tried to compensate for the continuing tremors and maneuver it over a patch of moss. Its deep-green color suggested that it, like the rat, had been unharmed by his experiments. Of course, that hypothesis would have to be confirmed at the atomic level. To the naked eye, none of the human-made materials in the enclosure had suffered any damage either. The deeper truth, though, was very different.

With the scope finally over its subject, Ito was able to examine its fundamental structure on a monitor set into the wall. It looked precisely as it always had. A thriving biological specimen unaffected by the war being silently fought around it.

After so many years of failure, Ito was having a difficult time adjusting to his recent string of triumphs. Were they real or was there a fatal error hidden somewhere in the thousands of calculations he'd made? Were his carefully designed safety protocols as foolproof as they seemed? Was his sense of control just an illusion?

The euphoria he'd experienced when he first realized that he was influencing the fundamental forces of nature had slowly turned to a sense of dread. Had Einstein felt this way when his equations were used to create the bombs that had been dropped on Ito's own country so many years ago? Had Einstein understood that, while intoxicating to explore, nature would never allow itself to be mastered by something so trivial as the human mind?

As if reacting to his thoughts, the intensity of the earthquake began to grow. This time, though, something was different. Within a few seconds, Ito was struggling to stay upright, even with both hands gripping the console in front of him. The roar of the tremors filled his ears, making it impossible to understand the high-pitched shouts of his new assistant.

A pipe snaking across the ceiling burst, showering him in a stream of frigid seawater powerful enough to finally knock him off his feet. He crawled across the heaving floor toward a cutoff valve, eyes burning from the salty spray and a wave of panic beginning to take hold. By the time he made it to the wall, he could no longer keep his eyes open. He was forced to feel along the wet concrete until he found the metal wheel he'd been searching for.

It didn't move with his first effort, but his adrenaline-fueled muscles *finally* managed to break it free. He spun it right and when it stopped, so did everything else—the tremors, the water, the light. Chaos had suddenly turned to silence.

Ito pressed his back against the wall, struggling to fight off the disorientation brought about by the unex-pected collapse of sensory input. He focused on the sound of dripping water, eyes open wide but seeing only blackness.

Power had been lost. That was why the lights were out. No electricity.

That simple bit of analysis was enough to build on, and he clung to it as he evaluated his situation. Beyond the sound of falling water, he could make out the erratic breathing of his two assistants. The room was stable, so the earthquake was over. Aftershocks were possible—

even likely—but when and how powerful could only be guessed at.

In the rest of the plant emergency protocols would be under way. Active reactors would go into automatic shut-down, and backup generators would be brought online to keep the cooling systems running. None of this was of any importance, though. The only thing that mattered was his own lab's security.

"Isami!" Ito called into the darkness. "The emergency lights! Can you reach them?"

A grunted affirmative was followed by the splash of lurching footsteps. They'd trained for this situation and after only a few seconds, the room was bathed in a dull-red glow. Isami was predictably at the switch, but Mikiko was huddled beneath a table, her eyes locked on the thick glass wall that ran the length of the room's north side.

The dust and water vapor hanging in the air created a kaleidoscopic effect, but not enough to hide what she was fixated on from Ito's aging eyes: a jagged, lightning-shaped crack that ran from floor to ceiling.

Mikiko suddenly bolted for the door, slamming into it and clawing for the handle. Ito moved more quickly than he would have thought possible, leaping to his feet and shoving her out of the way before sliding back the cover from a keypad. He managed to enter only two digits of his personal lockdown code before she grabbed him from behind. His air was cut off as she snaked an arm around his throat but he kept one hand wrapped around the door's handle and refused to be torn away. Her terrified shouts filled the room as he fought to get the remaining sequence into the pad.

Isami managed to get to them and pulled the woman off, dragging her back as the metal-against-metal grind-ing of the lockdown bolts filled the room. The sound prompted the woman to fight even harder and Isami fi-nally threw her to the floor, grabbing a fallen stapler and slamming it twice into the side of her head.

Ito stared down in horror at the blood flowing from her temple but then turned away. There had been no choice. Their lives were meaningless when weighed against the devastation that would ensue if his creation escaped into the world.

Once again silence descended, broken only by the gentle drip of water and the rhythm of their breathing.

Ito walked hesitantly to a hatch in the cracked glass wall, opening it as his heart pounded painfully in his chest. He slid through, having already forgotten about the unconscious woman on the floor and the emotionless man standing over her.

The glass cube containing his experiment was supported by hydraulic shock absorbers and thick rubber pads—additional insurance against eventualities exactly like this one. They were all intact, as was the glass upon first inspection. He went around it slowly, running a bare hand carefully along its sides. His heart rate began to regulate as he moved, but then his finger hit something. It was nearly imperceptible—nothing more than a slight roughness in the meticulously ground surface. He held his breath, moving his head back and forth in the red light, praying to the Christian God he'd adopted so many years before that the imperfection was just a trick of perception.

But like so many times before, his prayers weren't answered. The crack was only a few centimeters long, and there was no way to determine with any certainty if it had fully penetrated. Not that it mattered. No chance of a loss of containment, no matter how remote, could be tolerated.

"We have a possible breach," Ito said, his voice shaking audibly as he passed back through the hatch.

It took the combined efforts of both him and his assistant to open the bent locker that held their radiation gear. They put it on without speaking. There was nothing to be said.

Ito secured his face mask and connected it to an oxygen supply as Isami went to the unconscious girl and began trying to get her limp body into a bright yellow hazmat suit similar to the ones they were wearing. The safety gear would be sufficient to keep them from being killed outright by the radiation-driven sterilization process, but that was all. They would trade a relatively quick death for a drawn-out, painful one.

Ito used the key around his neck to unlock a cage protecting a fluorescent orange lever. He put his gloved hand on it and closed his eyes. In that place, in that moment, it was impossible not to look backward and question his entire adult life. To wonder if he had spent the last forty-five years shining a light into a place that God intended to remain dark.

1

Northwestern Japan
Present Day

Lieutenant Colonel Jon Smith had parked his rental car in the trees about a mile back, negotiating the remaining descent on foot. The dirt road was steep as hell and turned slick near the bottom, but there was no other way into the remote fishing village without a boat.

Behind him the mountains had swallowed the stars, but ahead the clear sky above the Sea of Japan was dotted with tiny pricks of light. Combined with a few salt-encrusted bulbs still burning below, there was just enough illumination to make out the sloped roofs of buildings hugging the shore and the long skiffs beached in front of them. The haphazard paths among the tightly packed homes, boathouses, and processing buildings, thankfully, were inky black.

He skirted the hazy glow of a porch light and eased along the edge of a shed that smelled of fresh diesel and rotten fish. The simple rhythm of his surroundings remained unchanged: the quiet lapping of waves, a southern wind just strong enough to get hold of the occasional loose board, the nearly imperceptible hum of power lines. Beyond that, nothing.

Smith followed the dim arrow on his GPS watch toward a narrow passageway between buildings, still wondering why he'd been chosen for this job. While his complexion and military-cut hair were relatively dark, a six-foot-tall, blue-eyed American slinking around rural

Japan at 2:00 AM had the potential to attract more attention than would be desirable under the circumstances. And then there was the matter of his Japanese-language skills, which consisted of a few phrases incorrectly remembered from reading *Shogun* in high school.

There was just no way Covert-One didn't have access to Japanese operatives. Hell, even Randi would have been a vast improvement. A little makeup and hair dye would be good enough to make her 90 percent invisible, and while most of her operational experience had been China-based, Japan was at least somewhere in the general vicinity of her area of expertise.

No doubt Klein had his reasons—he always did. And the job itself didn't seem all that difficult. Meet a man, get a standard-sized briefcase weighing in at a manageable twelve pounds, and bring it back to Maryland on a military transport out of Okinawa.

Piece of cake, right? Hell, he'd probably have time to grab a little sushi and have his spine walked on.

The darkness deepened as he entered the narrow space between the buildings, forcing him to slow his pace to a crawl. The GPS said he was only twenty yards from the rendezvous point, and he slid a silenced Glock from beneath his sweatshirt. Not that he thought he'd be needing it, but you never knew.

The passage came to a T and Smith poked his head around the side of a warehouse to quickly scan both directions. Nothing but darkness. He was starting to regret not bringing light amplification equipment, but as hard as it was for a six-foot, blue-eyed American to remain anonymous in this part of the world, cover those blue eyes with an elaborate set of night-vision goggles and he might as well be juggling chain saws in a top hat.

He turned right, inching along for a few seconds, unable to completely silence the sound of his boots crunching on something he swore were fish bones.

"I'm here!"

The whisper was heavily accented and barely audible. Smith froze, squinting into the darkness as a vague human outline appeared from behind a stack of wooden pallets. He resisted the urge to speed up, keeping his steps careful as he approached with his gun held loosely by his side. Even in what little starlight could filter between the buildings, he could see from the man's body language that he was scared. No point in making things worse by leading with a suppressor-tipped semiautomatic.

Unfortunately, his attempt to project as much casual calm as circumstances would allow seemed to be failing. By the time he eased alongside the man, it sounded like he was starting to hyperventilate. On the bright side, no discussion was necessary and the briefcase exchanged hands without problems—other than the fact that it was probably twice as heavy as Smith had been told. A rare error in detail by Fred Klein.

"Are you all right to get out of here on your own?" Smith said quietly.

The man nodded as a gust of wind kicked up. The old buildings around them protested, but there was something about the sound that didn't seem to follow the pattern it had before. Something out of place.

Smith grabbed the man by the front of the shirt and tried to jerk him back behind the pallets, but he panicked and resisted. A moment later there was a dull thunk followed by the man's legs collapsing.

He followed his injured contact to the ground and dragged him behind cover. The man was still breathing, but there was a wet sucking sound to it that Smith had heard too many times in his years as a combat doctor. A crude examination—while trying to watch both directions for people moving in on their position—turned up a crossbow bolt sunk to the fletching between two ribs. The man started to choke on his own blood, and Smith felt a rare moment of hesitation. The physician in him was finding it impossible to just abandon the man despite the fact that there was nothing he or anyone else could do to save him. The covert operative in him was screaming that he was being boxed in and if he didn't get out soon, he wasn't going to fare any better than the man fighting for breath on the ground in front of him.

Knowing in excruciating detail what the remaining minutes of the man's life would be like, Smith pressed his suppressor against his chest and fired a single round into his heart. The muffled crack of the round was followed by a now familiar thunk from the opposite direction of the first. Smith threw himself backward and slammed into the weathered boards behind him as a crossbow bolt hissed past his face.

That confirmed his fear that whoever these sons of bitches were, they were coming in from both directions. And they were good. He still hadn't heard either one, and that shot had been threaded through a gap in the pallets.

Smith grabbed the briefcase and held it behind him as he broke cover and darted toward the unseen man who had just shot at him. Crossbows were accurate, quiet, and hit like a runaway train, but they weren't fast to reload.

A rickety staircase that ran up the side of the warehouse to his right was only a few yards away and he adjusted his trajectory toward it. Not that he had a chance in hell of getting up it, but he'd seen the outline of a single window beneath it on his way in and filed its location away in the event of a situation just like this.

The heavy briefcase hung over his shoulder was slowing him down as he tried to run, but the trade-off proved a good one when he heard a bolt slam into it from behind. With his right hand, he grabbed the support for the stairs and swung beneath them, throwing the briefcase through the window and leaping through after it.

The remaining glass in the frame raked across his torso and the landing was a pile of wooden crates, but he was still breathing and a few scrapes and bruises weren't anything that would hinder him.

Smith stayed low, tripping awkwardly across the

warehouse interior toward a door warped badly enough to let the starlight bleed around it. Instead of bursting through, though, he ran his hand desperately along the wall next to it. When he found what he was looking for, he went completely motionless, trying to blend into the rough-hewn boards and watching the shattered window he'd entered through. While he'd elected to leave his night-vision gear at home, he was willing to bet that the men coming after him hadn't.

When a dim human outline slipped cautiously into the empty window frame, Smith hit the lights. As expected, the man grabbed for his goggles, and at that moment Smith squeezed off a single round. Even for him it was a low-percentage shot—the sudden glare of the overhead lights, a partially obscured moving target, a heart rate running in the 160s. So he was surprised when the man's head jerked back and he sank from view. Like his dad used to be fond of saying: better to be lucky than good.

Smith shoved through the door and, as suspected, someone was waiting for him out front. Also as expected, the man had lost a good second pulling off his night-vision goggles and now had to hit a backlit opponent with a medieval weapon. Advantage lost.

Smith fired a round into his chest as he sprinted away from the warehouse and toward the water. The man went down hard but immediately started to get back to his feet. The body armor that was obviously beneath his black sweater wasn't as effective at stopping the close-range round that Smith pumped into his face when he ran past.

Another bolt released behind him and he instinctively went into a crouch, hearing it hiss by just to his right. Too close. It was another fifteen yards to the edge of the water and the chance of him making it alive was starting to look remote.

He abruptly cut left and sprinted toward an open fishing boat pulled halfway onto the sand, diving head-first into it. The brief illusion of safety, though, exploded in the crack of shattering wood and a powerful impact to his right shoulder blade. There was a stainless steel cooler in front of him and he crawled behind it, aware of the strength draining from his limbs. As he rolled painfully onto his side, he heard the crossbow bolt jutting from his back scrape against the bottom of the boat.

A few lights had snapped on in the buildings around the shore, and the shadows were dissipating at about the same rate as the adrenaline that was keeping him going. He could hear cautious footsteps moving toward him in the sand and he unscrewed the suppressor from his gun, firing a few blind rounds in the general direction of his attackers.

The unsilenced Glock would be enough to wake the rest of the town, but probably not in time to scare off the men who were about to kill him. The water was clearly his best chance at survival.

The briefcase was too heavy to swim with so he pressed his thumb against a hidden screen behind the handle and was surprised when the locks actually popped open. Klein had redeemed himself.

Smith wasn't sure what he was going to find, but a ziplock bag full of what looked like garbage wasn't high on his list. An odd thing to die for, he mused as he stuffed the bag into a pocket in his cargo pants and fired a few more noisy rounds over the cooler.

The pain in his back was becoming debilitating and it took him more than five seconds to slither to the back of the boat. Gritting his teeth, he grabbed hold of the outboard motor and used the leverage to throw himself over the stern.

The water was deeper than he anticipated—good for cover, bad for drowning—but the pain was so intense that he wasn't sure he'd be able to swim. Finally, he forced himself to start kicking and managed to pull with the arm that would still move. The gun dropped from his hand in the black water as he tried to parallel the surface, not sure how deep he was but hearing impacts in the water. Crossbow bolts at least, but probably also bullets now. Stealth had been lost and there was no reason for the men hunting him to be bashful.

He went deeper. Or at least he thought he did. His sense of direction was being swallowed by blood loss, pain, and lack of oxygen. When his head started to spin, he followed the bubbles up, breaking the surface only with his mouth as he gulped desperately at the sea air. When his mind started to clear, he brought his head far enough above the surface to look back in the direction of the beach. Three men. All wading in after him.

Smith dove again, swimming awkwardly and trying to ignore the drag from the bolt in his back as it carved into muscle and bone. He came up only when he began to feel consciousness slipping away and to make sure that he was still heading in the right direction. Unfortunately, that direction was out to sea.

He had no idea how long he'd been in the water when he finally had to admit that he couldn't go any farther. Surfacing, he rolled onto his back and bobbed helplessly in the swells. Based on the lights that were still coming to life on shore, he'd only made it about four hundred yards. The silhouettes of people coming out of their homes were easily discernible, but all he could hear was the hypnotic whisper of the water.

A quiet grunt brought Smith back to alertness and he swam away from it, using a modified sidestroke with his right arm floating uselessly below the surface. He was barely moving, though, and it was only a few seconds before a hand closed around his ankle.

Smith flipped onto his back in time to see an arm burst from the water, knife in hand. He kicked at his attacker's head, connecting solidly enough to make the man miss but not enough to do any damage. With no other option, Smith took a deep breath and grabbed the man's knife hand. Then he dragged him under.

The man started to fight, but Smith was too weak to

do anything but try to control the knife. He wrapped his legs around the man's waist, their proximity and the density of the water taking the sting out of the blows he was absorbing.

The advantage Smith was counting on was that he had been floating motionless for some time while his opponent had been swimming as hard as he could in pursuit. The hope was that he'd already been in oxygen debt when they'd gone under.

His lungs started to burn, melding with the rest of the pain racking his body, and he looked in the direction he thought was up to see only blackness. Eventually, the pain started to fade and he felt an unfamiliar sense of peace taking hold of him.

The air was bubbling slowly from his mouth when he became aware that the man had stopped fighting. What did that mean again? What was he supposed to do?

Primal instinct more than anything prompted him to push the limp body away and kick. He felt himself floating gently upward toward...what?

The air flooding back into his lungs was accompanied by the return of the unbearable pain in his back and the reality of the hopelessness of his situation. The silhouetted crowd on the bank had grown, but there were still two men in the water coming toward him. Neither seemed to be as good a swimmer as their friend whom he'd sent to the bottom, though.

Smith rolled onto his side again and began moving away from shore and into the darkness.

When he couldn't go on anymore, the lights from shore were gone—either turned off or lost in the swells. He floated on his back, feeling the crossbow bolt being tugged at by the current. The pain had faded. Like everything else. Blood loss, most likely. His head felt like it was full of gauze, and he was having a hard time remembering where he was. In the ocean, but which one? Or was it a sea? What was the difference between the two again?

A sudden burst of light appeared in front of hi[m] he squinted into it. Not particularly bright, but st[a] in the complete darkness. Voices. The lapping of [ ] against a wooden hull.

A final, weak burst of adrenaline brought hin[ ] mentarily back to the present. The contents of the [ ] case were still in his pocket and he had no idea wha[t] were or of their importance. No idea what kind of [ ] they could pose in the wrong hands. But the fac[t] he'd been sent, that Klein was involved, suggeste[d] capture wasn't an alternative.

He had no strength left to escape the boat or t[o] the men in it. And that left him very few alternativ[e]

Smith exhaled, reducing his buoyancy and f[ ] the water close in on top of him.

One mission too many.